M000046232

Becoming NORA

A NOVEL

Book Design & Production:
Columbus Publishing Lab
www.ColumbusPublishingLab.com

Copyright © 2021 by
Margaret Farrell Kirby
LCCN: 2021912895

All rights reserved.
This book, or parts thereof, may not be
reproduced in any form without permission.

Paperback ISBN: 978-1-63337-526-0
E-Book ISBN: 978-1-63337-527-7

This book was based on a short story, previously
published as "Untethered," in *The Boardwalk*
(Cat & Mouse Press, 2014).

Printed in the United States of America
1 3 5 7 9 10 8 6 4 2

Becoming NORA

A NOVEL

Margaret Farrell Kirby

proving
press

PART ONE

Love never dies a natural death. It dies because we don't know how to replenish its source. It dies of blindness and errors and betrayals. It dies of illness and wounds; it dies of weariness, of witherings, of tarnishings.

—*Anaïs Nin*

CHAPTER 1

The day began innocently and full of promise. Nora stood at the door of the beach cottage and called, "Love you! I'll be back." The sun slanted on her husband Brad, back from his morning run as he sat on the couch reading the *Washington Post*. Six-year-old Clare and ten-year-old Jack ate their bags of Cheerios on the floor by the TV, too engrossed to respond. Brad nodded and waved. Nora gathered her thick, curly hair into a ponytail, blew them a kiss, and left.

After she got her bike from under the porch, Nora glanced at the cottage they'd rented every summer for the past ten years: aqua-blue clapboard siding, the yard dotted with seagrass and flowering perennials, and window boxes full of pink petunias. Unlike their home in Maryland, a staid colonial with a manicured lawn and shrubs lining the maroon door, this house evoked a sense of freedom. Small and compact—one floor, three bedrooms, and a screened porch where Nora sat in the morning with her coffee—expansive in its simplicity. Here she was untethered from her ordinary life. She stood for a minute and watched a rabbit dart from under one of the scrub pines that lined the yard.

She smiled and hopped on her bike. As she did each morning after Brad finished his run, Nora rode three miles to the boardwalk and found a bench, today in front of a pizza carry-out and an arcade, and watched the action: bikers, walkers, and joggers; parades of beachgoers laden with chairs, coolers, and umbrellas. She loved to study faces and listen to conversations, curious to capture a glimpse of other lives. Today, she glanced sideways at a couple on the next bench who were arguing—she couldn't hear the words, only the raised voices—a contrast to the prevailing mood, a contagious lightness of spirit. When the woman glanced at her, Nora pulled her gaze away, embarrassed to be staring, as if she were seeing something of them exposed.

Later, she would think it ludicrous, her judging the couple on the bench as she sat in her own fragile bubble filled with complacent contentment. She would remember feeling sorry for them; she and Brad seldom argued, or if they did, never in public. In those last moments, Nora planned the picnic they would have on the beach. An Italian sub for her and Brad to share. Peanut butter and jelly sandwiches for the kids. And ice cream from the snack stand. Pizza for dinner tonight. Always pizza on their last night of vacation.

Her sister Becky once said, "Don't you ever get tired of going to the same place?" No. Nora wanted a vacation with no purpose other than this. Every year, the same routine. The puzzle table in a corner of the living room, tote bags of books from the library, movies on rainy days, miniature golf, the beach at twilight. She loved watching Jack and Clare jump off the lifeguard stand at the end of the day, dig for sand crabs, and wait for the first star to wish upon. Maybe someday she would tire of it and want to travel to an exotic place.

Occasionally, she glanced at the angry couple, silent now, staring ahead at the ocean. They looked to be near her age, around forty she guessed. Just a bad day? Or were they unhappy? Nora raised her face to the warmth of the sun, to the deep-blue sky dotted with colorful kites taut against their twine. She closed her eyes and listened to gentle waves breaking and seagulls squawking.

"Hi, Nora."

She jumped when she heard Brad's voice. He stood in front of the bench with two carry-out coffees. She checked her watch. Ten o'clock. An hour before she was due back. "Where are Jack and Clare?"

"I asked Marci to come."

After a brief twinge of annoyance—*this was her time*—and surprise that he'd gone to the trouble to ask the fifteen-year-old girl who lived in the house next door to babysit, Nora smiled. "You must have missed me," she said, when he sat and handed her a coffee.

His sunglasses obscured his eyes, but not his tight smile, the one he used when distracted or deep in thought. She looked at his face, tanned and handsome, his thick brown hair curly and graying at the temples. For a minute, he didn't look at her and, in that interlude, a distinct feeling of foreboding crept in.

When he turned to face her and said, "I need to talk to you," the first real stab of fear hit. Had something happened at work? With one of the children? Had her mother called?

She grabbed his arm. "What's wrong?"

Brad stared at his cup, then recited a string of sentences, his voice so low, his words so rapid, she needed to move closer. He'd been confused, unhappy, not himself, boxed in, needed time to sort things. She stared at him as he talked, still looking down and shaking his head as if he didn't quite grasp his own words. She struggled as her mind zigzagged from one foreign word to the next.

He took off his sunglasses and faced her after he finished his litany—a peculiar sharing of his feelings, like he had learned a new vocabulary. Refusing to allow the words to take hold, to become real, she searched his face for a clue, for his eyes to crinkle with secret amusement, for it to be a joke of sorts. She tried to recall what he had said. Confused and unhappy?

"Why are you unhappy?" she asked. "What happened?"

He shrugged. "I don't know."

Defensive, detached. Familiar and yet foreign. His words were so out of place. So not him. Sure, precise, quick to state his opinions, Brad rarely admitted uncertainty. Her tendency to analyze her thoughts and emotions before she answered caused him to fidget. What had happened to him? How had she missed it? They'd been together for so long and knew each other so well. College sweethearts—he from Boston and she from a small town in Pennsylvania—they'd dated from age twenty and married the day after graduation. She became a kindergarten teacher and he an accountant. They had everything: careers, house, family—two children, the first one born when they were twenty-eight, spaced four years apart, just as planned. Everything perfect.

Something unimaginable crossed her mind. "There's someone else."

4

"No. No." He shook his head. "I'm mixed up. I've been see-ing a therapist."

"A therapist?" He had shared his unhappiness with a stranger. It was as if in that he had been unfaithful.

She fought back tears. "Why didn't you talk to *me?*"

"I couldn't," he said in a gentle tone. "I can't until I can get a grip on it. It's about me."

"About you?" She slid a few inches away. "No. It's about *us*. Me. The kids." She wanted to shake him. Make him return to his normal self and let her return to her peaceful morning.

How odd that he picked the last day of their vacation here on the boardwalk to spill his secret. "Why are you telling me now?"

"I didn't want to talk in front of the kids." He faced her. "I wouldn't ask to do this if I thought there was another way."

"Ask to do what?" Although the sun was higher—no lon-ger gentle, now glaring and harsh—she shivered, afraid, as if an unforeseen threat headed toward her at high speed.

He spoke in a low voice. "I'd like to move into an apart-ment nearby."

"An apartment?" The word brought a sickening realization of his intent. A word more concrete than a dubious emotion. A cold and sterile word. She wiped her eyes on her shirt. Worried she might throw up, she slid farther from him until she reached the edge of the bench.

"For a while. Until I can figure things out." He took his handkerchief from his pocket and handed it to her. "I've planned how we can arrange things."

Like he had already left her. Just this morning he ran, read the paper, ate his granola bar. Just last night they had dinner, sipped wine. As if everything were normal. She threw his handkerchief on the boardwalk. "How long have you been making your plans?" Now the throngs of people annoyed and taunted her with their smiles and laughter. The backs of her thighs stuck to the seat.

"I don't know. I tried—"

"You tried?" The couple she'd pitied in her naïve smugness looked at her. "How in the hell did you try?" Heat rose in her face. "Did your therapist tell you to leave me?"

"Nora, please," he said as people stared.

"You never said a word." Her head throbbed. "How long have you been planning this? We've been here for two weeks. Now you tell me. Here on the fucking boardwalk?"

Inhabited by an unfamiliar fury, Nora stood, took the lid off her coffee, poured it on the bench, watched as it ran and pooled on the glossy white paint, as it seeped toward his khaki shorts.

Brad jumped. "Jesus, Nora." He bent, picked up his handkerchief, and mopped himself. The brown stain was visible on the seat of his pants.

Dazed, she hurried from the boardwalk toward a path to the ocean and walked to an area past the umbrellas, past the "normal, happy" people lounging in their chairs. On the sand at the edge of the water, she sat and let the waves lap over her feet as her tears released. She couldn't remember the last time she had wept. As she sobbed, her anger ebbed, and a panicky fear filled her. She remembered such fear as a child when she was four or five and had gotten separated from her mother at an amusement park. Her terror had mixed with guilt, as if she'd done something wrong. She'd cried for what seemed like a long time, but was probably only a few minutes, before her mother's arms wrapped around her.

Today, there was no one to rescue her. She could call Ann, her best friend, but what would she say? To Ann, or to her mother, her sister, her colleagues at work, their neighbors? Humiliation, even shame filled her, and, like the day at the amusement park, she was sure she had caused it. Numb, she stayed until her skin burned under the hot noon sun and a wave washed over her, soaking her shorts.

CHAPTER 2

Seawater dripped down her legs as she headed to her bike. By the time she arrived at the cottage, her shorts had dried and were stiff from the saltwater. She caught her reflection in the hall mirror. Her T-shirt, soaked with perspiration, clung to her chest; thick strands of her hair were loose and frizzed around her head. The foul smell of her sweat nauseated her.

In the kitchen, Brad stood at the counter spreading peanut butter on bread. She wasn't sure what to expect. Anger at the coffee she threw on the bench? An apology? He glanced at her. "Are you okay?"

"What do you think?" She pulled off a paper towel, soaked it with cold water, and pressed it to her face. "How in the hell would I be okay?"

"I'm sorry, Nora."

She leaned against the sink and stared at him. "You're sorry. Really."

"Can we talk more at home? I don't want the kids to hear."

He pointed to the sandwiches. "They're putting their suits on. I'm getting lunch. I have our subs in the cooler."

"Now you want to wait and talk at home? And have lunch on the beach as if nothing happened?" Again, her anger rose. As if it were a normal beach day and she would sit next to him under the umbrella and eat without gagging. "We need to go home. You take them to the beach. I'm going to pack."

Brad put the knife back into the jar of peanut butter and looked at her. "We have one more day. They'll be disappointed."

"Are you crazy?" She wondered at his mental state, his logic. It was like being in a weird dream with a stranger. "Tell them. Make an excuse."

Silently, he put peanut butter and jelly sandwiches into a ziplock bag and took cans of sodas from the refrigerator and stuck them in the cooler. Like a robot.

Clare ran in and hugged Nora. "Mom, are you ready? We're having a picnic." She laughed. "Your hair is sticking out all over."

"I need a shower. Dad's taking you. Let's find Jack and put on sunscreen."

As Brad left with Jack and Clare, he told them they'd be going home later that day. Nora couldn't hear their response. As she surveyed the house, she made a mental list of what she needed to do. First, she emptied her dresser drawers and threw everything into her suitcase, and then she packed Jack and Clare's clothes. In the kitchen, she put the cereal, peanut butter, and granola bars in a bag, and tossed the leftover food from the refrigerator into the trash.

After she finished, she poured a glass of wine from the half-empty bottle of Chardonnay, the wine they had sipped last night—when he knew, when she was still innocent and happy.

She took the glass with her to the front porch. She sank into one of the Adirondack chairs. She ached. Her head, her heart, her stomach. The sky had lost its sharp clarity as the afternoon turned hazy. The breeze was gone. This house she had loved was now inhabited by something malevolent. She wanted to escape. From the house, from him. It would be easier to be a widow, done with having to see him again. Then she experienced a wave of guilt for wishing him dead.

If someone had asked her yesterday if she had a good marriage, she would have said, yes, a great marriage, imagining nothing that might interfere with the pattern of their lives. What had happened? The longer she sat, the hotter she got. Her mind veered from one thing to another as she tried to reconstruct the morning. Reality and denial crept in and out. It hadn't happened…he loved her…it happened…she had failed him.

"Hi, Mrs. Stanton," Marci said from the yard next door. By then Nora had finished a second glass of wine.

At the sight of Marci, she shivered. She forced a smile and said, "Thanks for babysitting today." *Please don't come over*, she thought. In her mind, Marci had become an accomplice in Brad's betrayal. An unwitting one, but still. As soon as Marci went into her house, Nora realized she wasn't thinking straight—the heat and the wine had made her dizzy—and she brought the bottle inside and poured the rest of the wine into the sink. She took the jar of peanut butter out of the bag she had packed and ate a thick spoonful.

After stripping off her damp clothes, she got in the shower and stood under the cold water until her body cooled and her mind cleared enough for her to plan to confront him. How could he dismantle their family for something he couldn't even express? There had to be more. Had he lied about another woman?

CHAPTER 3

Nora was in the kitchen with a cup of coffee when they returned. After she helped Jack and Clare decide who would go first in the outdoor shower, she went into the bedroom where Brad was packing and she closed the door. His empty suitcase sat on the bed. In his methodical way, he took each shirt from the closet and folded it into a neat package.

When he looked up, she said, "I need to know. What made you unhappy?"

"Nothing happened."

"There must be something." Nora paced the room. "Or someone." She watched his expression for a hint of guilt or shame. "Are you lying?"

"No. I told you." He sat on the side of the bed and took his coffee-stained handkerchief and wiped his eyes. "I told you how painful this is for me."

The last time she'd seen him cry was in college after the sudden death of his parents. She fought a ridiculous urge to comfort him.

"You're causing the pain. Doing this to us."

"I still love you—"

"If you did, you wouldn't do this to me, to the kids." She walked to the window and stared at the row of pines. Her hands were cold and yet she was sweating. "When do you plan to move?"

"I have to find a place." He gathered his books and magazines off the nightstand. "I'll sleep in the guest room."

She stood at the window, her back to him. "No. You need to leave when we get back."

Clare barged in with a towel wrapped around her and her hair dripping. "Jack and I don't want to leave," she said with a pleading look on her face. "Why do we have to?"

Nora got another towel and wrapped it around Clare's hair. "Honey, we just do."

"I can't find my clothes."

"I'll get them in a minute. Go back to your room." She closed the bedroom door and faced him. "You need to rent a hotel room."

"What if I sleep in the basement? For a few days?"

Nora's head throbbed. "Jesus. You honestly thought we'd stay here until tomorrow? And you'd be in the house until you found a place? What the hell is wrong with you?" Her shred of sympathy had vanished, and she fought an urge to grab his clothes and stuff them in his suitcase.

By the time they loaded the car and emptied the house, it was past four. Nora looked back at the house. The day had become cloudy. In the milky light, the aqua-blue siding appeared dull, no longer bright and crisp. The petunias in the window boxes were wilting. She'd meant to water them.

Clare and Jack, still angry about leaving early, were quiet. Soon Clare fell asleep leaning against the large stuffed panda she'd won at the arcades, while Jack played a handheld video game. Brad switched on a classical music station. At times, he glanced toward her as if about to speak. Nora listened to Clare's steady breathing and the clicking of Jack's video game as they passed the busy retail stretch that led to two-lane roads, farms, and the small Delaware towns. Odors from the bags of dirty laundry permeated the air. Because she couldn't sit still, she held onto her knees to stop her legs from jiggling. As she replayed the scene on the boardwalk, the meaning of his words grew sharper and more devastating. She strained to grasp a single emotion, to halt the torrent washing over her. Fear, shock, betrayal, woven with...anger? Yes. Dread at what loomed? Yes. And hurt, such deep hurt. A twinge of guilt? Should she let him stay and find a motel tomorrow? No. She couldn't bear to see him, to feel his presence.

The trip to the beach, only two weeks before, seemed an eternity ago. Although Nora remembered her relief at getting away and the excitement of Jack and Clare, she had no recollection of Brad's mood. Had he talked? Chimed in on the word games she played with the children? Not only had she missed any signs on the way there, but the weeks seemed no different to her from past years. His patterns hadn't changed. He ran every day, helped plan picnics on the beach, spread a new jigsaw puzzle across a card table to do with Jack and Clare. Nothing erratic to give her cause for alarm. Nothing amiss. And yet there was. Had she missed an altered tone in his voice or a look of sadness? A tightened face? He must have been torn, wrestling with the decision.

But something *was* different this time. They didn't have sex. As if by unspoken agreement, so she had thought. As the kids got older, they went to bed later; Jack was often awake reading after she and Brad had fallen asleep. The bedrooms were close together, the house not well insulated. But now she wondered.

CHAPTER 4

As Brad drove, Nora remembered how easy it had been to fall in love with him. Often, she'd replayed the evening she met him when her roommates dragged her to a party in an off-campus apartment at the University of Maryland.

Nora had sworn off dating after a relationship that had ended badly earlier that year. She had painful memories of parties during high school where she would stand at the edge of clusters of classmates—who seemed to possess an easy self-assurance—unable to think of quick and clever remarks to hold their attention. She envied them their confidence and poise, their secret laughter, an elusive standard that was out of her reach. Nora had a few friends she made in high school—ones on the fringe like her—and they spent their weekend nights watching movies and having sleepovers. Although a boy as equally unpopular asked her to the senior prom, saving her from the humiliation of sitting at home, it was an excruciating night with clumsy dancing and a sloppy kiss at the end. It was no different in college. In the beginning, she tried; she dated a few people and even had awkward sex, unpleasant enough that she was sure there was something wrong with her.

The party was in April of their junior year. Nora pictured herself back then—in jeans and a sweatshirt, her mass of hair twisted into a thick braid as she stood in the crowded living room and sipped a beer. Observing the cliques of animated girls, it was as if she were in high school, on the edge, without the skill to enter the circle. She moved to an open window to get away from the odor of cigarette smoke.

From across the room, a guy with intense brown eyes stared in her direction with a focused gaze. She glanced to either side of herself to see who had caught his attention. It was her; no one was near her. He stood next to the keg of beer like he was in charge and smiled at her. Tall, broad-shouldered, shaggy dark-brown hair, a few days' growth of beard, and he had a wide smile that transformed his face. Emboldened by her beer, she stepped out of character, walked to him, and held out her red plastic cup.

He filled her cup and smiled at her. "I'm Brad. I live here."

"I'm Nora. Nora Tobin."

Just then, a bubbly blond girl ran over and threw her arms around him.

"Hi, Kim." He hugged her. "This is Nora."

Kim regarded her for a second and turned her attention back to Brad.

Nora took her cup and walked outside. She sat on the porch stoop in the cool breeze and sipped her beer as the sky turned purple and orange.

The screen door opened. "Here you are." Brad sat next to her and handed her another beer. "I was afraid you'd left."

Now, as she sat in the car, she rubbed her fingers over her wedding ring, remembering the way he'd looked at her, his smile, her surprise at his intense love and desire for her. Her surprise at the awakening of her own desire. Impossible that he'd want to leave her, leave *them*.

For much of the drive, Nora stared out her window. She loved to study the windows of houses, fascinated by ones with blinds and curtains closed. What was hidden inside those rooms? How dark it must be! She had a fantasy of knocking on the door and saying, "Let me show you what it would look like if you opened the blinds." She remembered the suffocating atmosphere in her childhood home—the shuttered windows making rooms dim and the glare from harsh fluorescent lights exposing her father's anger and her mother's unhappiness—and now she thought it didn't matter that she'd kept her own house airy and light. Unhappiness had entered regardless.

As they drew closer, the knot in her stomach grew. What would she tell Ann? She imagined Ann saying, "Brad did what?" As if steady and reliable Brad didn't have the imagination to leave her.

At six thirty, they pulled into their driveway. The maroon door waited. The humid haze hung like a blanket over the deserted street. Sprinklers watered parched laws. Air conditioners hummed.

As they unloaded the car, after Jack and Clare ran inside with their duffel bags, Nora said to Brad, "You can pack your things. I'll wait downstairs." Then she added, "You have to tell the kids."

He shook his head. "I'd rather tell them tomorrow. Let them get settled today."

"No, you need to do it today," she said and moved past him into the house.

While he was upstairs, she walked through the first floor, through the rooms that, two weeks ago, felt warm and cozy. Now, cold and foreign. Musty and stagnant. Full of objects that once had meaning. An Edward Hopper print of a painting he knew she loved, an aquamarine pottery vase he used to keep filled with her favorite yellow roses (*when did it last hold flowers?*), a mahogany box she gave him inscribed with the date of their tenth anniversary, a silver wine cooler.

In the kitchen, she unpacked the half-used peanut butter, mayonnaise, and mustard. She gazed into the refrigerator at the empty shelves. A lone apple withered in the vegetable drawer. Often on Saturdays they planned dinner—pizza and a movie—and made the grocery list for the week. Unsteady, she leaned against the counter. She had trouble catching her breath.

When Brad came into the kitchen, he looked annoyed, as if he should be able to take his time to move, as if sharing his unhappiness should have evoked her understanding and sympathy. "I've got my things."

"You can get the rest tomorrow," she said. "Now you need to tell Jack and Clare."

"I want to do this by myself." He called upstairs and asked the kids to come to the family room with him. Jack and Clare sat on the couch and elbowed and teased each other, innocent of what awaited them. Nora stood in the doorway, hesitant to leave them. Brad, in a chair across from them, looked at her and waited. She stared back at him. He glanced at his watch and cleared his throat.

Clare said, "Mom, what's wrong?"

"Nothing, sweetie. I'll be upstairs." She went to the bedroom and flung her clothes into her dresser drawers and the laundry into the hamper. The sight of the king-sized bed brought another realization. Except for the handful of nights when Brad had traveled for work, she'd sleep alone for the first time since they married. She grabbed his pillow and flung it into the closet. When Brad climbed the steps, she picked up a book from her nightstand and sat on the edge of the bed.

He tapped twice on the open door of the bedroom. "I talked to the kids. They're okay. I'll call tomorrow."

With the book hiding her face, she waited. Waited for him to come and hug her, apologize, and tell her he'd made a mistake. When she didn't answer, he sighed and moved away. "I'll go next door and pick up the mail. I'll pay Adrian." She was a fifteen-year-old neighbor they hired to get their mail while they were on vacation.

Nora didn't reply and listened for him to go and come back. He called upstairs to say he was leaving, the mail was on the table, he'd get the bills tomorrow. When the front door closed and the house had quieted, she went downstairs and followed the sound of the basketball thumping in the driveway. The sun had almost set and the spotlight over the garage was on. Red-faced with spots of perspiration on their T-shirts, Jack and Clare played and laughed like nothing had happened. Jack, at ten, resembled his father—square-jawed, determined, lithe and athletic, with thick brown hair, and like Brad, dark eyelashes framing his large eyes. Clare, long-legged like Nora, had a thin and small-boned frame, and at age six, couldn't keep up with Jack. Her mass of curly auburn hair flew around her head as she reached to dribble the ball away from him. The sun poked through the haze and Nora squinted at their blank faces.

"Hey, Dad said he talked to you."

Jack nodded and grabbed the ball from Clare.

"What did he tell you?"

"He said he has a lot to do and has to work all night at the office." Jack pitched the ball into the net.

Clare turned to her. "He'll be home in the morning. Poor Dad."

Poor Dad. He didn't tell them. *The coward. The jerk. The asshole.* But he gave them another day before they'd have to face it, another day for her to get her bearings. Another day before it would become real.

CHAPTER 5

Nora wandered around the house foggy, unfocused, forgetting and remembering. She gave Jack and Clare some granola bars to tide them over until she could figure out dinner. No one had mentioned stopping for food on the way home. She took two Tylenol for her headache and sat at the island with the mail. Ads, bills, magazines, and an Amazon box with school supplies she had ordered for her classroom. As she slid a knife across the edge of one of the flaps, it missed the box and hit her on the palm of her other hand. She got a paper towel, pressed it to the wound. As the blood soaked through, she was surprised at the release she experienced. The pain distracted her and gave her a measure of relief.

She had finished washing and bandaging the wound when the doorbell rang. Ann stood on the porch with Eddie and Maddie. "You're back! We're on our way home from the pool. Eddie and Maddie saw the bikes and begged me to stop."

They hugged, and then Ann stepped back and looked at Nora's face and then her hand. "Are you okay? What happened?"

"Just a cut. You know how clumsy I am."

Eddie and Maddie ran to the backyard, and Nora led Ann into the kitchen. She moved the toilet paper rolls off the counter-top of the island and slid the boxes of cereal to clear a space. "Tea? Water? Wine?" she asked.

"No. I'm fine." Ann studied her. "What's wrong? You look exhausted."

"Brad and I had an argument."

Ann said, "Is that why you came home early?"

"No. It's supposed to rain tomorrow, and I have to get my classroom ready next week and then we go to Pennsylvania to visit my family. Too much going on." All true.

"What happened with you and Brad?"

"I'll tell you later." She forced a smile. "I've missed you." They usually got together a few times a week—dinner out one night, and an early morning walk in nice weather.

"I've missed you too. It's been boring without you." Ann smiled. "Can you come over? We're having a late dinner. Nick's grilling hamburgers."

"I'm so tired. I need to unpack."

"Let the kids come and spend the night."

Nora jumped at the chance to be by herself. "That would be great. They'd love it." The children were like brothers and sisters; Ann and Nora had grown together as they navigated the stages of motherhood. Jack and Eddie, four years later, Clare and Maddie. First days of school, birthday parties, broken bones and trips to the hospital.

Ann looked outside at the children playing. "Where is he?"

"Brad? At the store." She didn't remember ever lying to Ann before. *Not too big a lie*, she thought; too tired, too numb to explain. Ann didn't probe.

Ten years earlier, pregnant with their first children, they'd met in childbirth classes. Bored by the endless questions of a few anxious women, Nora had glanced sideways at the woman seated to her right. Brown hair with blond highlights, short and spiky, framed her face and set off her blue eyes. Her fingernails were each painted a different color—pink, purple, yellow, red, and orange. Ann's nails, she later told Nora, were a symbol to get her through the everyday routines and demands of life. "A reminder that says, I've conformed this much, but I won't entirely." On a bad day, she said, "I look at them and they lift my spirits."

As the meeting dragged on, Ann had leaned close and whispered, "I can't stand these damn groups."

Nora smiled. "Me too." They bonded. Nora thought of Ann as luminous, almost sparkling. She wore clothes that were bright and cheerful, like her nails. Her scarves and earrings matched or contrasted in a good way. Nora, with long auburn hair that curled and frizzed and was never neat, had trouble matching clothes and wound up wearing tans, blacks, greys, whites she could mix and match. Like wearing a uniform.

Ann didn't have the inner angst she did; she possessed an innate kindness but didn't need to please others, could be definite and set boundaries, while Nora needed to ponder and weigh the pros and cons of each decision. When they were asked to join a neighborhood committee to study a proposed new housing development, neither of them was interested. Ann declined at once.

It took Nora a week to come up with an excuse that sounded plausible and acceptable. The contrast between them worked. They loved reading, shared books, but both hated book clubs and groups of any kind. They became sounding boards for each other. Brad and Ann's husband Nick eventually bonded, and the two families became close.

Ann was a high school English teacher. They had the same school schedules and summers off. Ann joked, "You have it easier. Kindergartners are fresh and spontaneous. I get them at the other end. Jaded." Nora had other friends at school and in the neighborhood, but none she could laugh with like she did with Ann. Brad said he always knew when she was on the phone with Ann by her laughter. No matter what happened, they found a nugget of irony.

Maybe someday we'll find humor in this too, Nora thought. The house buzzed with the excitement of the four children as Clare and Jack packed their overnight bags.

Once they left, Nora sat huddled on the couch and cried as she replayed Brad's words. Nothing made sense. Nothing in their lives should have led to this. Unhappy? Boxed in? She had imagined a marriage would wind down gradually. A slow leak, drip by drip, unheeded until the damage couldn't be ignored, until unhappiness was palpable. It was inconceivable that it could end in a sudden rupture like this. Typically, she looked to herself for reasons. Had she been oblivious to what simmered underneath the surface? Had she ignored the drips? Had she concocted an image of a happy family?

In the framework of their life, nothing unusual stood out. Brad coached soccer, helped with homework, rode bikes with

Clare and Jack, read to them—was fully involved. He and Nora divided everyday jobs. And he was a kind man. Whenever it snowed, he always shoveled their elderly neighbor's walk. A few weeks ago, he sat with a colleague whose wife was having surgery.

They had differences, yes, but didn't everyone? In the beginning, they had laughed at them. Brad, logical and analytical, was an expert at puzzles; he expected things to match and make sense. Nora hated puzzles. Early on, her lack of logic amused him. She couldn't follow directions and often got lost. When he gave her directions, he would say things like, "Go counterclockwise around the parking lot. The building you want will be at seven o'clock. Or go north or east…"

She would laugh and say, "Jesus, Brad. I have no idea what you're talking about. Just tell me right or left."

Or Brad would ask her what time she wanted him to make reservations for dinner. She would say, "How about seven fifteen?" which seemed like a perfect time to her.

He would shake his head and say, "No—either seven or seven thirty."

She would say, "Well, why did you ask me?"

Mostly, Nora didn't pay close attention to things unimportant to her: squeezing a toothpaste tube from the bottom or loading the dishwasher in the right way. According to Brad, she even hung the toilet paper in the wrong direction. She'd accepted it as part of the texture of their marriage. They worked it out, or so she had thought. No overt conflicts. For him, a tight face, sometimes reddened, with an overloaded dishwasher or a missing library book. She had stopped trying to meet his standards, ignored his frowns, and muttered *asshole* under her breath when she found him particularly rigid. Now she recalled an incident from a few months earlier.

Brad had complained when he couldn't find a CD. "Nothing's ever where it's supposed to be," he said, red-faced.

"Sometimes it sounds like you hate me," she'd replied and waited for his laugh, his hug, his apology. He'd left the room, and she'd forgotten about it. Had he become more rigid as time passed? Had she become more careless? When had they stopped laughing?

Brad had told her why he loved her on a warm night in the beginning of their senior year. They had started to date after the night of the party the spring before. They both had jobs in their hometowns that summer and barely saw each other, but they talked every day. Nora not only understood the feeling of an intense attraction to someone, but she also learned the thrill of being desired; it had been a magical spring and summer. That night in September, they sat on the grass outside her dorm. Brad smiled at her. "Do you know what I love about you?"

"What?"

"You're you."

Nora laughed. "What's that supposed to mean?"

"You're different." He cupped his hands around her face. "Kind and generous, cute, gullible, naïve..." He leaned back and smiled. "And ditzy. I love that you're so ditzy."

Ditzy, she thought now. When had he stopped being amused?

CHAPTER 6

Later, when it had gotten dark, she forced herself to eat a peanut butter sandwich and then went upstairs to get ready for bed. The solitude of the silent house felt strange, askew; she wished the children were home and in their beds. Her panic built. She ran through her fears of what could go wrong. Broken toilets, bugs, spiders, hurricanes, power outages… Where to turn off the water? The gas?

In the bathroom, she stood at the sink and ran a washcloth over her red and puffy eyes. The shine of her gold wedding band in the mirror startled her. She had never taken it off. Not once since they'd married. She got into bed, rocked back and forth, and wondered what Brad had told the therapist. *Could* there be another woman? His dresser faced the bed. She hadn't ever searched it; she'd never doubted him. The most she had done was pull out his flashlight or rolling lint brush from the top drawer. Now she got up and stood in front of the dresser for a minute. On top of it sat a tray with compartments that held odds and ends—paper clips, pens, loose change. She pulled open the first drawer. In it were a flashlight, a lint remover, and his white handkerchiefs. He had emptied his socks, boxers, and undershirts from the second drawer. The next two held the neatly folded T-shirts and sweaters he hadn't yet packed. In the last drawer, she found a thick manila envelope. She sat on the bed, removed the rubber band, and found several years of drawings, pictures, and cards from Jack and Clare. A surprise—she had always been the sentimental one.

At the bottom of the stack she found a card she'd given him last year on Valentine's Day. On the cover, a stick-figure drawing of a smiling couple holding hands. Red, pink, and purple hearts surrounded them with the words: *I've got you and you've got me.* On the inside: *Who could ask for anything more?* Her inscription read: *With love, always. Nora.* Why had he kept the silly card? Was it on purpose or did it get stuck in the stack of cards? She ripped it in half and tossed it in the trash.

Next, she opened his closet and checked each pocket of his navy blue and gray suits. Nothing. Not even a stray piece of paper, a pen, loose change. Hers were full of all sorts of things: wadded tissues, pieces of crayons or pencils.

She heard a strange noise and looked out her bedroom window at the darkness. After she tiptoed downstairs, she stared through the peephole at the front door, put on the double lock, walked around the first floor, closed the curtains to the French doors in the rear of the house, and latched the security bar. Then she rummaged through the liquor cabinet, grabbed a bottle of Brad's bourbon, poured a few inches into the glass he always used, and sat in the living room in the dark. Streetlights illuminated the yard. She checked outside each window for shadows or movement. No one. A few scattered lights on in the houses across the street. What was hidden in those houses, lurking underneath seemingly ordinary lives?

Each noise she had never paid attention to jarred her until she identified the source. The air conditioner cranking on and off and the chunking of the ice machine. Why was the dog next door barking?

Soon the heat and warmth of the drink calmed her, relaxed her enough that she might sleep. But in bed, she stared at the ceiling and pictured the Valentine card. Stick figures holding hands. She and Brad used to be connected like that, relying on each other. In the early years of their marriage, they wanted to be close, touching, hooked together. After Jack joined them, and then Clare, a new drawing emerged. Brad and Nora on the ends, separated by Jack and Clare in the middle. The years of babies and toddlers consumed Nora—colic, tantrums, fevers, rashes, sleepless nights. By the end of the day, all she wanted was to sink into bed, to be quiet and read with nothing expected of her. Yet, there were nights when she knew he wanted to talk or make love. He would lie in the bed and wait for her and she remembered saying things like, "Can we talk in the morning? I'm so tired." And by the time the children were older, and she wasn't as exhausted, their lives had coalesced into a pattern. A distance. Intimacy planned. Once the kids were in bed, they watched TV or read. Brad no longer waited for her; if in bed first, he would be engrossed in a book or magazine. But always a kiss and an "I love you," murmured before they curled into sleep. It was enough for her.

A sudden recognition caused her to sit up. It wasn't enough for him. Of course it wasn't. She had ignored the drips, let them accumulate, let the distance grow between them, hadn't been present enough to be aware of the unhappiness that had led him to a therapist. And yet she had prided herself on her intuitiveness, her sensitivity. As a kindergarten teacher for eighteen years, she had become adept at measuring the needs of her students, spending more time with the ones who struggled. Yet, she hadn't paid attention to him, hadn't known they were drifting. At some point, she had lost him.

By three in the morning, Nora had accepted the blame, sure she could convince him. He had loved her. It couldn't be too late. They could get counseling, regain their earlier relationship.

She got out of bed, grabbed the card from the trash, taped it together, and set it on her dresser. Then, back in bed, she stretched her hand across the empty side and fell asleep.

CHAPTER 7

Sunday morning she woke early, and after she brewed a pot of coffee, she sat in the kitchen with the phone by her side and her sliver of hope. The cloudy day cast a bleak light on the boxes of cereal, bags of pretzels, and the jar of peanut butter on the counter. Fruit flies circled the over-ripe bananas. Each time she waved them away, they circled back. She jumped when the phone rang.

"Okay if I come over?" Brad asked.

She looked at the clock. "Come in half an hour," she said.

Nora showered, put on lipstick and blush, and pulled her hair into a barrette. She moved the boxes of cereal and crackers left from the trip into a cabinet and put the bottle of bourbon away. Thick air hit her when she opened the door. Brad, hair uncombed, face unshaved, dressed in the clothes he'd worn yesterday, smelled of sweat. She hoped it had been a hard night for him too. The oddness of his dishevelment gave her hope. She tamped down her questions: *Where did you stay? Did you have breakfast?* When he gazed at the swarming fruit flies, she grabbed the bananas and threw them in the trash.

"Mind if I get coffee?" he asked.

The question sounded absurd. Like he was already a guest. "Help yourself. I made a pot."

"Where are Clare and Jack?"

"At Ann and Nick's. They spent the night."

When he had gotten his coffee, they sat across from each other at the island and were silent for a minute. He moved his mug back and forth. Finally, he looked at her. "Sorry I sprung it on you. I kept putting it off."

"Putting it off?" It was so unlike him. He wasn't a procrastinator. "For how long?"

"I'm not sure." He shrugged. "A few months."

She flinched. "Months?" This was August. All summer? Earlier? "How long have you been unhappy?"

Brad's eyes were on his mug, his voice low and quiet. "The past year—not miserable, just not myself."

The past year. The hard knot in her stomach grew. "I thought we were happy," she said quietly, almost to herself. But what was *happy*? Did she mean contentment with the way their lives had evolved? "I didn't even notice."

"I hid it." He gave a weak smile. "I can't explain it. I was sure it was a phase I'd get over."

"Listen." She touched his hand. "We've grown apart. I've gotten caught up with work, the kids."

He stared at the ceiling as if he were trying to recall something, or perhaps weighing his words. "I'm not sure what it is."

She jumped when the ice maker jangled and plopped. "We

can work on it. I'll go with you to your therapist."

He shook his head. "I need time, Nora. I need a break."

Had he stopped loving her? Or was he lying? She glanced into the family room, at their chairs angled next to each other, a small table in between, where each night they read or watched TV. She imagined herself sitting there at night by herself and him sitting with someone else in other chairs. "Tell me if you're having an affair."

He sounded offended. "No, I told you, no."

She looked away. For a few minutes, they sat in silence. It would be easier if it were another woman—better than the elusive torture of imagining reasons, of making it *her* failure.

Though repulsed by her tortured groveling, she continued. "Is it your job? Do you think you need a change?"

"No. My job's fine." In the tone he used when he tried to be patient as he explained something to her, he said, "I need time. I don't know what else to tell you. I need space. I can't do the job, the house, the kids, the therapy..." As he talked, he tapped his cup on the counter—a habit of his when he wanted to make a point, to make her listen—a habit that had always irritated her. And always made her want to hold his hand and say, *dammit, stop.*

Nora grabbed a napkin and wiped her eyes and face. Her tears had always evoked his concern and a tender response. Now she was afraid of no reaction. What had happened to him? He had become a person she didn't know, like he had already slipped away and occupied a different sphere. And it wasn't sudden, not for him. The drips had been pooling. He must have been slowly withdrawing from her. Already he was in full retreat, closed off while her anguish was only beginning. She turned away from him to shut out his face. Almost to herself, she said, "I don't know how you can do this to the kids, our family…"

"I want to make things easy, help…" He stood to get more coffee and leaned against the counter and looked at her. "I'll find a place big enough so their friends can come over."

She looked at him. "Their friends?"

He nodded. "When Jack and Clare stay with me."

"I can't believe you're already talking about friends of Jack and Clare coming to your apartment."

"Well, down the line. After we decide on how we'll divide the time," he said, his eyes fixed on hers. "I figure every other weekend, and one weekday overnight?"

He looked at her and waited like he had said something logical, to be expected, the next step. She sat mute and stared at him, no longer caring if her tears spilled over.

"But we can talk later," he said in a gentler tone.

What he was doing hit her full force. He wanted to share custody. It was happening too fast, yet in agonizing slow motion, her life unraveling. In hearing his plans to dismantle their life, she grasped the futility of her words. "You've really planned this."

With her sliver of hope crushed, she crumpled her napkin into a ball and pushed her cup away. He had plotted, he had planned, he hadn't given her a chance. For the past year, she'd gone about her life and this nightmare had lurked, waiting to pounce. "All this time, you faked it, made our lives a farce?"

"Not a farce. I tried. I wanted to make it work—"

"Do you think I'm happy all the time? That anyone is? Jesus, you sound pathetic, wallowing in your misery." A fierce, wounded anger took over. She slammed her cup into the sink hard enough to break it in pieces, hard enough to cause Brad to jump. She needed to get him out of the house. "Enough. I'm calling Ann to bring Jack and Clare home. You need to tell them. You lied yesterday." She pushed away from the island.

"I'll tell them." A nervous look crossed his face, as if he wasn't sure what she would do next. "I wasn't ready, wasn't sure what to say."

"And I'll be there to make sure you do." She kept her back to him and picked up the shattered fragments and threw them into the trash can. The odor of the bananas rose from the can and made her gag.

He stood and put his cup in the sink. "But first, I'd like to take a shower and get my shaving things and more clothes."

"Use the kids' bathroom. I'll empty bins for you."

"Thanks. I only need one."

In the basement, she grabbed five large Rubbermaid containers from the shelves and emptied them. Piles of Easter decorations, Halloween costumes, and shattered Christmas ornaments littered the floor. She carried the bins upstairs and lined them in the hall outside their bedroom and waited for him to finish.

After he showered and dressed, Brad glanced at the tubs and looked at her. "I don't have space for much until I get an apartment."

"You can store them in your van." A shudder ran through her. "I don't want your stuff in the bedroom."

She went downstairs, stood at the kitchen window, and eyed the sullen sky. It had started to rain and water dripped down the screen making patterns of crooked lines. Never had she felt so alone, so helpless, so on the edge of something she couldn't name.

CHAPTER 8

Nora left Brad in the bedroom to pack and waited on the covered porch for Ann to bring Jack and Clare home. The rain had gotten heavier and made puddles in the driveway. When Ann arrived, Nora opened an umbrella and went out to the car. Jack and Clare hopped out and ran into the house.

Ann smiled. "They'll be tired. They were up half the night." Then she looked closely at Nora's face and got out of the car. "What happened? The argument?"

"You're getting wet. Get back in the car. I'll tell you later." Nora looked toward the house. She didn't want Brad to talk to them without her. "I have to go back in." She hugged Ann, told her she loved her and would call later.

Brad had come down and sat in the family room with Clare and Jack. A repeat of yesterday, except this time she would be with them. Nora sat in her usual chair, Brad in his. "Dad wants to talk to us," Clare said to Nora as if an exciting event were about to happen.

Nora ran a finger over the dust on the table beside her as Brad gave his canned speech and counted off the bullet points on his fingers: "Sometimes, after people are together for a long time, they need to live apart; we'll always be your parents; we'll always love you; it has nothing to do with you; it's not your fault…"

The word "parents" jarred her. Sickened her. As if this were part of her decision to tear apart their lives. Clare glanced at her with a questioning look. Nora mouthed, "I love you." Jack's eyes jerked from Brad to Nora and back to Brad, a confused expression on his face. What could she say to comfort them that wouldn't make it worse, confuse them more? Not, "I'm sorry," as if it were her fault, or, "Dad wants this, not me." Her face flushed with the unfairness of it. In the room, silent except for the sound of the rain dripping from the gutters, Brad had finished his litany; his hands were quiet, folded on his lap. His mission complete. In a softer tone with a slight smile on his face, he said, "I'll see you all the time. I'll pick you up for dinner tomorrow." He looked at Nora. "Is that okay?"

She gave him a hard look. "Fine." Dizzy and nauseated, she stood and went into the kitchen to get a glass of water and listened to their voices, listened to Jack ask, "Why do you have to leave?" When Brad repeated the same spiel, her nausea increased. Maybe she would faint, fall on the floor, make a scene. She ran up to their bathroom and vomited, then, shaky and perspiring, leaned against the sink. She splashed cold water on her face and rinsed with mouthwash. Brad came upstairs with Jack and Clare to get containers he had packed and stacked in the hall.

Clare came into the bedroom. With an air of imparting important news, she said, "Daddy packed his clothes. In boxes. Out in the hall."

Nora nodded. She sat on the edge of the bed and held out her arms. "Do you want to come and sit with me?"

Jack and Brad had started carting the bins to the van. "No. I'm going out with them."

After Clare left, Nora closed the bedroom door partway to remain hidden from Brad until he finished. Finally, he called into the bedroom, "I need to get a cardboard wardrobe for the rest of my suits and shirts." He paused and waited.

She ignored him and waited for him to leave. When the house got quiet, she stood at her bedroom window. After Brad loaded the bins, he hugged Jack and Clare. They waved to him as he drove slowly down the street. In the gloom, rain dripping on them, cast into in a different role, it was like they were waving goodbye to a visitor. She couldn't believe he would drive away and leave them.

She started to go downstairs but stopped at the top of the stairs and took deep breaths. When Jack and Clare came inside, she went down. "Come sit with me," she said. They followed her into the family room. She sat between them on the couch and drew their damp bodies close.

Clare climbed into her lap. "Are you sad, Mommy?"

Acutely attuned to the feelings of those around her, Clare wore her emotions openly. Nora could read her more easily than Jack—her face radiated delight, concern, and sadness; she tried to re-imagine and deflect anything dark in her desire for everyone to be happy. After a few Disney movies when Clare obsessed for days asking questions like, "Why did he have to die? Why couldn't he find his mother?" Nora screened books and movies with sad endings, but now realized she had done her no favors as this reality edged in.

"I'm sad. But we're going to be all right."

Jack, so different from Clare, guarded his emotions—like Brad in that sense. But now he had an alert, watchful, almost fearful expression that reminded her of how he looked before his first swimming lesson at age four, trying to be brave. His voice cracked. "Why does he have to leave?"

"Oh, honey, I don't know." She pulled him closer, but he moved away and wiped his face on his sleeve.

Clare was quiet for a moment, as if she were hunting for a thread to grab hold of. Then her face took on a hopeful expression. She leaned over Nora to Jack. "Dad said we'll see him all the time. And we'll each have two bedrooms. And we get to decorate the new one."

Jack wasn't about to join in Clare's innocent optimism. He pushed her away. "Shut up, Clare."

Nora said, "There'll be lots of good things, but it will be different." It all sounded phony, like feel-good platitudes. "I want you to tell me how you're feeling. We can help each other."

Jack glared at her. "Why did you let him leave?"

Let him. As if she could have tied him up and kept him captive. Angry that Brad's lame explanation included her, she took slow breaths, afraid she might need to vomit again. "It's what Dad wants." Then, softly, she said, "I didn't want him to leave."

CHAPTER 9

That evening, everything seemed odd. At dinner time, with an empty refrigerator, Nora scrounged through cabinets and pulled out macaroni and cheese, applesauce, and milk boxes. Jack and Clare wandered in and out of the kitchen, pale and tired, probably both from the sleepover and the shock of the day. Listlessness replaced Jack's earlier anger and Clare's optimism. A pall of fatigue and disorientation hung over them.

As she spooned dinner onto their plates, she said, "Tomorrow I'll go to the store. You can help me make a list."

Jack asked, "Can we eat in the family room?"

He meant to watch TV. Nora, grateful for a respite, put on a cartoon and sat at the kitchen island and tried to eat what was left of the macaroni and cheese. As she ate, she counted the hours until she could collapse and be done with the day. Usually, she and Brad took turns with dishes, organizing baths, helping with homework, reading stories—evenings were full of purpose, talk, and bustle.

When the cartoon ended, Jack and Clare went upstairs to get ready for bed without their normal bickering. Usually, Jack was up later than Clare and watched another show or played a game, but tonight he wanted to go up and read. She went first into Clare's room and waited as she picked out two books for Nora to read. Both were Berenstain Bears stories, her favorites from a few years earlier. Clare had loved the stories about Brother and Sister and their adventures and challenges, always with Mama and Papa to provide security and love. Nora climbed into bed with her. "How are you doing, sweetie?"

For a minute, Clare looked down at the cover of one of the books, at a picture of the family gathered in a circle. Then her face brightened, and she looked up. "We'll see Dad tomorrow," she said, in a reassuring tone. "We're going out to dinner." Clare smiled at her. "Are you coming?"

"No, I'm not." What did she understand? Nora's eyes blurred as she hugged her. "I can't, but I'll be fine. You'll have fun."

Clare nodded. "But I want you to come."

She ached at Clare's need to worry about her. "I know, honey. It's hard. Confusing."

Hugging the stuffed panda she'd won at the arcade and her worn and flattened Pooh Bear, Clare was quiet as Nora read and she fell asleep before the end of the first book. Nora bent over and kissed her. "I love you to the moon and back," she whispered.

She moved to Jack's room. He held the latest Harry Potter novel he and Brad were reading together.

She sat on the side of his bed. "Do you want me to read to you?"

"No, thanks." He turned back to the book.

Nora had learned to wait, to try to enter backward to draw him out. His earlier anger seemed gone. "This is a hard night, isn't it?" She picked up his top sheet from the floor and covered him.

He shrugged and closed the book and let it drop to the floor. His face was screwed up in concentration like when he was determined to solve a math problem for homework. "Mom, do you think Dad will come back?"

"I don't know, but he'll be close by." She kissed his forehead. "You'll see him a lot."

He rolled over, away from her gaze. "I don't get why he had to leave."

A long pause settled between them. Nora knew she'd have to learn to navigate this terrain, learn how much to reveal. "I don't either, Jack." She swallowed hard. "But it's not your fault."

"It feels weird," he said into his pillow.

"It does." She leaned to hug him. "It's okay to feel sad and even angry at us."

With his face buried in the pillow, he asked, "Do you think he misses us?"

"Oh, honey. I know he misses you." She took a wad of tissue out of her pocket, already damp with her tears. "You'll see him tomorrow."

He rolled onto his back and faced her. "For dinner." Light from the hallway shone on his face. He yawned, stretched, and rubbed his eyes. She switched off the lamp and said, "I love you."

"I love you, too." He curled on his side and hugged his pillow.

Downstairs she poured herself a glass of bourbon and sat as she had the night before in the darkened living room. In the dark, as she sipped her drink, she called Ann and filled her in on the basics and listened to her shock and disbelief. Ann wanted to rush over, but Nora said, "No, don't come over. It's too late. I'm in a fog. I'll see you tomorrow night when Brad takes the kids." She wasn't ready to face anyone, even Ann, until the sharpness of the shock had ebbed. After the knot in her stomach eased. After she could think more clearly.

When her glass was empty, Nora went upstairs to their bedroom—*her* bedroom now. Everything reminded her of Brad. He still inhabited the house: his towels in the bathroom. His books and the current *New Yorker* magazines on his nightstand. The king-sized bed. She took the sheets off—she needed clean ones, without his scent. The last time they had made love in this bed was the night before they left for their vacation. It struck her now as odd. Why, if he planned to leave her? As a ceremonial last time? Nora, preoccupied with her mental list for the trip, had wanted to put Brad off. What if it was a test? What if he hadn't made up his mind, and her lack of interest propelled his decision?

CHAPTER 10

She slept in stretches, woke, touched the vacant void next to her. Waves of realization washed over her. What would be better? Moments of forgetfulness or a persistent awareness of his absence?

In the morning, still dark when she woke, she found herself invaded by a sense of foreboding. Her entire body felt limp. Thoughts of meals, lunches, and the empty refrigerator ran through her mind.

She dozed for a while and was wakened by Clare who had crawled into bed with her.

"Mommy, did Daddy take his pillow?"

Nora struggled awake. "No. It's in the closet."

"Why?" She had a look of bewilderment.

"He forgot to bring it." She pulled her close. "Did you have a nice sleep?"

"Can I call Dad?"

Nora dialed his cell and handed the phone to Clare. "Ask

him what time he'll pick you up tonight."

She went into the bathroom to grab her robe and listened. "Where did you go? Why did you leave your pillow in the closet? When are you coming to get us? I love you too, Daddy." She handed Nora the phone. "Five thirty. I'm telling Jack."

"Let him sleep, Clare," she said, while checking to make sure Brad had hung up. By the time she looked up, Clare had run into Jack's room.

"Jack, I just talked to Dad."

"Get out, Clare." His bedroom door slammed.

Clare ran crying to Nora, who held her and said, "It's okay, honey." But nothing was okay, and she thought, *I want my mommy, I want to be held and rocked and told everything will be all right.* When Clare stopped crying, Nora said, "Let's get breakfast." It would have to be the Cheerios that were left and milk boxes.

Jack stomped down the stairs, still angry at Clare for waking him. Both were cranky and whiny. They asked for orange juice, a different cereal, "real milk." Nora had a floating sensation, a numbness, as if watching the scene from a distance. On a normal day Brad would have the coffee made, and intervene with crabby moods, and come up with solutions.

Jack said, "I can't eat plain Cheerios."

"We can squeeze milk into your bowl." Nora cut into a milk box and helped them pour it. She looked at Jack. "Do you want to call—" she almost said "Dad," but the word sounded strange, making him still connected to her "—your father?"

"No." He ate his cereal without looking at her.

Nora patted his shoulder. He stiffened and pulled away. Was he angry at Brad or at her? Or at Clare for waking him or for calling Brad first? For a minute, the only sound was the chewing of Cheerios and spoons scraping bowls. Then Clare, as if trying to make amends, asked, "Jack, do you want to play basketball?"

Jack replied, "Leave me alone."

The injustice of what Brad had done to them angered her. *I should call him*, she thought, *ask him to come and deal with the mess he made.* Suppose she needed "time and space" and left him with the children? But she didn't think she could be that selfish, that self-absorbed. She sipped her coffee and stared outside, the same hazy sky as yesterday. A bee buzzed at the screen.

Jack looked up from his bowl. "Can I go to Eddie's?"

"I want to go too," Clare said.

"Let me think." Nora stared at the blank list in front of her. Already on the verge of bursting into tears, she hesitated to ask what food they wanted, afraid of another argument. She stood. "Okay, finish and clean up. I'll call Ann and see if I can drop you off while I go to the store. And we can invite Eddie and Maddie here tomorrow."

Clare asked, "Can I tell them about Dad?"

Tell them what? Did it matter? She nodded.

"No, Mom. Don't let her." Jack's face got red. Still mad? Or embarrassed?

"Then, can I tell them about my new room?"

"You're an idiot, Clare," Jack said.

"Stop," Nora said. "Jack, I can tell Ann to tell Eddie and Maddie. Would that work?"

"I guess." He stood and brought his bowl to the sink.

"Okay, then. Clare, you can tell Maddie about your new room."

After she dropped them at Ann's, she went to the supermarket and hoped she wouldn't see anyone she knew, anyone who would ask her about their vacation, ask her anything. Under harsh fluorescent lights, she roamed the aisles. She and Brad always planned menus for the week, and now the sight of foods she used to cook—chicken, ground beef for spaghetti and tacos, steak for special dinners—caused a wave of nausea. She glanced at purposeful shoppers as they filled their baskets and moved on. Chilled and shivering in the frozen food aisle, she eyed the shelves and finally grabbed an assortment of ready-made foods: lasagna, chicken tortillas, and mini pizzas. After she got milk, juice, and cereal, she added two bunches of pink and purple Peruvian lilies, Ann's favorites, to thank her. The woman at the checkout counter smiled. "The flowers are beautiful. Are you having a party?"

The words remained with her. A party. Life going on. She pictured flowers, music, and candles.

She forced herself through the rest of the day—picked up Clare and Jack from Ann's, cleaned the kitchen, scrubbed the counters, and finished putting away toilet paper and paper towels—she didn't want Brad to see the house a mess or to think she was wallowing in grief. The irritability of the morning had lifted; Jack and Clare were excited about dinner with Brad.

Against her will, knowing it was ridiculous, denial crept in again. Maybe he missed her. All afternoon, her hope battled with her anger. At five o'clock, a half hour before he was due to arrive, she showered, used a blow dryer to tame the frizz in her hair, clipped it back, put on lipstick and blush, picked a white sleeveless dress that looked good with her tan, and then sat in a chair in the living room to wait. Jack and Clare were already out front.

When Brad's minivan pulled into the driveway, she stood and waited for him to come to the door. The phone rang.

"Okay if I have them home by nine?"

Nora made her voice steady. "Sure. Have fun."

She watched as Jack and Clare hopped into the van and Brad drove off. She stood in the silence of the empty house feeling foolish and rejected, yet again. The sun had softened and filled the living room—the time of day she loved. On an ordinary summer evening, they would often grill, eat outside, play badminton, blow bubbles. For a few minutes, she let the light fall on her before she closed the Roman shades.

Memories flooded her mind of their early days, when Brad was lighter, less serious. Before the accident. When he whistled. When he loved to run. When his face lit up when he saw her. His big smile, sappy and exuberant in his love of her. Nora pictured his personality then—light-hearted, optimistic, flexible—the old Brad. After the death of his parents, he got an MBA and became an accountant, like his father. His temperament became altered, like a shade being drawn on one window in a room of four, blocking part of the light, a subtle dimming. Something you get used to over time.

CHAPTER 11

A shelf of the bookcase in their bedroom was devoted to the photo albums his mother had assembled of his childhood, a new one for each year, labeled by age. Nora would sit with Jack and Clare and point at the smiling faces of his parents: "Your Grandma Helene and your Grandad John." Reduced to those images, as if they lived their lives in perpetual happiness. Brad didn't speak much of them; when the children asked questions, Brad would share glimpses—his mother, a librarian, gave him his love of books; his father helped him with math. Superficial bits and pieces. But it was Nora who made sure to keep them alive in those albums.

Nora had never met his parents. The summer before their senior year was the last time Brad would see them. He had told them about her, promised he'd bring her home for Thanksgiving. She hadn't told him how she dreaded the trip or how nervous she was. A week before they were to leave for Boston, Brad walked her to her dorm, and at the door, held her and kissed her. "Someday, we'll have our own place," Brad said.

On an impulse, she blurted, "Let's stay here for the break. Your roommates will be gone. We'll have five days. All alone."

A smile had crossed his face. "Hey, good idea."

She hadn't expected that response and her guilt rose—he was an only child, and she imagined his parents' disappointment, perhaps their anger. "No, no. We should go. You said your mother loves to cook Thanksgiving dinner."

"She'll have lots of people to cook for. They always invite the neighbors. We can go after Christmas."

That week, in the apartment with mismatched furniture and blackened pots and pans, they cooked spaghetti, tacos, even a turkey. They closed the curtains and blinds and cocooned themselves, propelling them into a new phase in their relationship. She loved falling asleep next to him, waking up with his arms around her.

Soon after, on a Sunday night in December, during a party in his apartment, the call came. Nora and Brad had been standing next to each other, his arm around her, when his cell phone rang. He moved away to listen and stopped talking. His face changed. A foreign look passed over it—an expression she hadn't seen and couldn't identify. He took the phone into his bedroom and closed the door.

At some point, she'd gone into the bedroom and found him sobbing. His mother and father had been killed in a car accident, in a head-on collision by drunken teenagers. "Driving home from the fucking grocery store."

He didn't want her to come with him to Boston. Possibly, he blamed her for not insisting they go for Thanksgiving. She blamed herself. If she hadn't raised the idea, if she had insisted they go to Boston, Brad would have the memory of the last Thanksgiving. She would have met his parents. The tragedy preoccupied her. Remorse plagued her. The scene played over and over: Brad before the phone call—his arm around her as he joked and laughed with his roommates, his happy innocent face in the last moments before he became an orphan. She found herself obsessed with questions about their final moments. What did they buy at the grocery store? Did they see the car headed toward them? Did they have any inkling they would soon cease to exist?

When she had confessed her obsession to her roommates, one of them said, "But how is Brad?" As if she were trying to get consolation for *his* tragedy. Consolation she hadn't earned.

Brad didn't want to live with his roommates for the last semester of college. He and Nora rented a one-bedroom apartment. For weeks, night after night Brad watched TV, drank beer, skipped classes, and evaded her attempts to talk. Enclosed in his own pain and sorrow, he moved into a space she couldn't enter.

A framed picture of his parents on his dresser had become a magnet for her. Their fifty-year-old vibrant smiling faces. Faces that would never age. Brad had his father's deep brown eyes, his mother's wide smile. As Nora gazed at them, she felt her own loss. She would never meet them or have in-laws if she and Brad married. The children she and Brad might have had already lost a set of grandparents.

One day as she stood in the bedroom and stared at the picture, Brad had come up behind her. "What are you doing?"

Nora jumped like she had been caught doing something wrong. "Nothing, I'm just looking at them."

He took it from her. "You didn't know them, Nora." He opened a dresser drawer and stuck the frame in.

She wanted to say, "If we had gone to Boston, I would have." Instead, she said, "Well, tell me. I want to know what they were like."

"I have to go to class. I'll see you later."

She continued in her obsession with their death. After reading a book on the stages of grief, Nora decided that Brad was somewhere between denial and anger. One night, she sat next to him on the couch. "Can we turn off the TV for a minute?" she asked.

He flipped it off. "Why?"

She faced him. "I want to talk to you about your parents. I've read a book about the stages people go through. I don't think you've dealt with their death," she said gently.

"Really?" He stared at her. "And what should I be doing?"

"I think you may be in the stage of denial. Or anger. And it's okay if—"

"Dammit, Nora. You have no idea what you're talking about." He slammed his can of beer on the table. "You've read a book and you think you're an expert."

"Well, tell me, so I know. So I know what stage you're in." So sure, in her naiveté, she could help him navigate his grief.

"I'm going out," he said and left her sitting there.

In bed that night she stared at the cracks in the ceiling, listened as Brad's Big Ben clock ticked off the minutes, and checked the red numbers on her digital alarm clock.

At four o'clock the front door opened. Brad held on to the door frame and his dresser as he tripped into the room, then crawled into bed and put his arms around her. "I'm sorry. Can you please let me do it my way? I promise it'll get better."

As she held him, he sobbed. "It'll be okay," she said and stroked his hair. Like soothing a child.

After that night, Nora let him do it his way. Her fixation with the deaths faded. In a few weeks, Brad became more himself, returned to classes, and cut down on the beer. But he had changed. He quit track, stopped running, stopped whistling. And, as if to compensate for his promise to his parents about his grades, he became serious. Study replaced the parties; their weeks were quieter, and they became closer. Like a married couple. Settled. Safe. His need for predictability, hers for security—they met each other's needs in those ways. It was as if they had aged five years.

They turned their energy to mapping their lives, careers, and family. They would settle in Maryland close to the college. Brad wanted to get married right away. They planned a small wedding right after graduation. Nora wasn't like her sister who had perused bride magazines for years and dreamed of a big wedding. Getting married to Brad was all she wanted.

Nora and Brad picked simple gold bands, and the day after graduation, on a bright sunny day, with her mother and sister present, they got married at the county courthouse. Outside, after the ceremony, her sister took a picture of them smiling at each other in the sunlight, Brad in a navy blue suit and Nora in a beige sheath. Twenty-two years old. She had no doubts or qualms. It was as if she had gotten on a path with a map and her compass set as she marched into her future.

The photo of his parents, the one she had been drawn to after they died, imagining what they were like, memorizing their faces, hung on a wall of family pictures. Often, over the years, she stared at it. Had Brad harbored the guilt she had about that Thanksgiving? Had he blamed her? Whenever she brought it up, he remained elusive. Now she thought how odd it was she hadn't pursued it. All those years. She never knew when their birthdays were. After her initial obsession with them, she'd never even asked. As the first anniversary of their deaths approached, she suggested they go to Boston to the cemetery, and he said no. She'd let it go, but every year she remembered them on the day they died. December 12.

CHAPTER 12

Nora sat for a while in the living room and stared out the window after Brad left with the children. Ann had invited her for dinner that evening. When the bells chimed six times from a nearby church—their reliable peal rang each day at noon and six and gave her comfort in their constancy—she got a vase, the flowers, and a bottle of wine, and drove to Ann and Nick's house. Pale yellow stucco with cornflower blue trim, a long porch with matching blue rocking chairs, it stood out on a street with subdued brick colonials, black and grey shutters, and sculpted shrubbery.

Nick answered the door. Shorter than Ann, a bit stocky, he was as nondescript as Ann was startling. Easy and gentle, content to be in the background. He put an arm around her shoulder. "I'm sorry, Nora."

She gave him the wine and waved to Eddie and Maddie who were watching a movie in the den. In the kitchen, as she put water into the vase and arranged the lilies, they chatted about the kids;

she hoped he wouldn't ask her anything about Brad, wondering if he had seen cracks in their relationship, if he had seen it coming. Perhaps Brad had spoken to him about his unhappiness.

He handed her a whiskey sour. "She's outside—said you'd need this. And dinner is ready for whenever you want to eat. I made a pasta dish."

His gentle kindness brought tears to her eyes. On the deck, she set her glass and the vase on the table next to a platter of Brie and Greek olives.

Ann was watering pots of flowers that edged the deck, large pots full of annuals and perennials—yellow, purple, orange, pink—none of which Nora could name. She stopped when Nora came out and held her arms out. "Oh, Nora, I'm sorry."

Nora held on to her and wept. When she stepped back, she took a tissue from her pocket. "I've cried more in the past few days than in my entire life."

"Come and sit." Ann pulled two lounge chairs together, and they sat facing flashes of light that brightened the sky. Ann said, "I can't tell if it's heat lightning or a storm." She looked at Nora. "So. How are you doing?"

So many words came to mind. Horrible, desperate, terrified. Lost. "It's unreal. Like a bad dream."

"I don't get it," Ann said. "It's not like Brad. He's always been so steady."

Yes. Steady, safe, predictable. How had he entered the realm of feelings, he who was always buttoned up with his emotions, with his accountant's mind of facts and figures?

"And he never said a word?" Ann tapped her nails on the side of her glass, a habit she had when she was laser focused on searching for an answer. "Through the whole vacation?"

"I didn't notice a damn thing."

Ann leaned over and touched her hand. "I'm so sorry, Nora."

"What does Nick think?" She needed to know if he had been aware of Brad's unhappiness.

"He's shocked."

"Did Brad talk to him?"

Ann shook her head. "They don't talk about personal things. We're both pissed. Can't believe Brad sprung it on you. Did it to the kids."

Thinking of Jack and Clare brought another layer of sadness and an acute sense of what faced her. "Clare's worried about me. She was sure I'd be having dinner with them."

"Poor Clare." Ann looked at her with an amused expression. "But she found her bright spot. She told us she'll have her own room."

"Yeah. She works hard at finding the silver lining. Drives Jack crazy."

"Where did he take them?"

"I have no idea."

"So, he's definite about getting an apartment?"

"That's what he says. He figured he could live in the guest room until he found an apartment. It's crazy. Already talking about custody. The kids with him part of the time."

They stared at the sky for a few minutes as the wind picked up and clouds blew and concealed the stars. Thunder sounded in the distance.

Ann said, "I keep thinking. You and he were here for dinner before your vacation. Everything seemed fine."

"I know." Nora sipped the whiskey sour and shivered at its bittersweet tang. "You know those times in life when everything seems to run smoothly? When there are no major hiccups with the kids, when nothing is broken?"

Ann nodded. "Doesn't happen too often, but yes."

"That's how I felt at the beach."

They were quiet for a few minutes. Then Nora said, "I wonder if he's told anyone yet. Or what he'll say. Or what I'll tell people."

Ann's eyes were fixed on Nora. "Say you're separated. You don't have to say anything else. It's nobody's business."

"He said he's not having an affair."

Ann spread Brie on crackers and handed Nora one. "I'd like to strangle him, but I don't think he'd lie. He's too much of a straight arrow."

Nora said aloud what she'd been thinking. "I'd almost rather he was cheating. I'd have a reason." The piece of cracker she had bitten stuck in her throat and she crumbled the rest into her napkin. "We used to be closer. Passionate…" Nora wiggled around to face Ann. "That part became so predictable. With the kids and all. He might have needed more—"

"Shit, Nora. Do you think the passion lasts? If that were the case, we'd all be divorced."

"I'm driving myself crazy. Trying to find a reason."

Ann pointed at her glass. "You're not drinking it."

"It's giving me heartburn."

Ann dumped it into the bushes. "Do you want wine?"

"Do you have any bourbon?"

"Bourbon?" Ann's eyebrows raised.

"I've been drinking Brad's at night to relax."

"Nick has some. I'll get it."

When Ann left, Nora leaned back and stared at the sky. No longer heat lightning, but a jagged fork. She counted the seconds before the thunder. Fifteen. Still in the distance. But the wind blew harder and the strings of lights hanging across the deck swayed. The hurricane lamps at the corners of the railing flickered and cast a soft glow against the threatening sky.

She thought of Ann's words. A straight arrow. Was he? Who knew what was happening underneath? He'd shattered her illusions of their happy home. She had striven to create what had been lacking when she was a child, when she craved light, warmth, and harmony. Under the surface of her parents' predictable lives lay her father's obsessive need for order and structure, and her mother's surface acquiescence and simmering resentment and unhappiness. Nora's father had died of a heart attack when she was fifteen. She always thought of her mother's life as a "before" and "after." Miserable before. And then, after the months of sorrow and shock, her mother laughed and smiled more—her personality changed and expanded. No longer did they have rigid times for dinner, no longer did it matter if they ate pizza or hot dogs. No longer was daily life compressed into smothering routines. Remembering the years before he died and the endless meals in the tense kitchen under fluorescent lights, every flaw exposed, Nora lit candles every night at dinner and played music to soften the realities of daily life. She was sure she'd had the answers, knew better than her parents. And what difference had it made?

Ann returned with her drink. Nora took a sip and welcomed the warmth of the bourbon.

After a moment, Ann said, "So, you think he left because he wasn't getting enough sex?"

"I don't know." Nora smiled. "Could be part of it. Now I'm on something else."

"Tell me," Ann said as she bent and gathered the napkins that had blown off the table.

"You know how he's so exact, so detailed? Not mean like my father, but it reminded me how I hated the rigidness. In his job, Brad needed to be so precise and detailed; over the years I think it became more ingrained. He became more anal. And I stayed the same."

"Okay?"

"And the more anal he became I think the more I stopped trying to do things his way. I know I sometimes annoyed him, maybe more than I thought."

"Could be. So what? Everyone gets annoyed." Ann looked at her and put a hand on her arm. "You need to let it go."

Nora watched the row of cypress trees at the back of the yard swaying. She wished she could let it go. Wished she weren't plagued by questions. When had he made his decision? Had it come to him one day or was it a gradual recognition? Was there a before and after? "I relied on him, trusted him, was so sure of us. I want to understand."

"To understand how you made him unhappy?" Ann fixed her eyes on hers. "That's crazy. Why aren't you angry? Why are you blaming yourself?"

"I have been. It comes and goes."

Ann leaned toward her. "Listen, Nora. You need to stop. Stop looking for why. Stop blaming yourself. You are who you are."

"Meaning?"

"Brad's a detail person. You're not. You don't know north from south. You probably have a bit of dyslexia. You're a little flighty, impulsive. So what? It's what I love about you." Ann smiled. "Of course, you'd annoy him." Ann covered the cheese and crackers with a napkin as drops of rain fell. "He could be a jerk about those things. He needed a push back at times."

A push back. But she hadn't pushed back, not really, only in those little actions like murmuring "asshole" under her breath. Why? Because she accepted his needs as primary? Accepted that she was deficient in certain ways? Because she carried a cloud of guilt from her childhood when she couldn't measure up to her father's rigid demands? She swirled the ice in her glass and removed the clip from her hair to let the wind blow through it.

Ann's eyes flashed with anger. "Shit, Nora. You don't walk out on a family because you're annoyed by your wife. Because you like order and she doesn't."

Nora had worn herself out with her convoluted thoughts. A circle that went nowhere.

It started to rain, and Ann stood to gather the cheese and crackers. "Okay," she said, "let's list everything you did wrong: Not enough sex; Brad's anal and made you feel guilty; you refused to load the dishwasher right. What else?"

It was good to laugh again, to laugh at herself. Nora lifted her face to feel the rain. "He used to love that I was ditzy."

CHAPTER 13

That week, the weather continued hot and the air heavy. The milky sky cast a lethargic light on the dusty furniture, scattered toys, and unopened mail. In bed, unable to sleep, Nora tried to read. Brad's side grew cluttered with magazines, newspapers, and books—a painful reminder of her loss and her chaos.

The shift in her life brought a heightened sense of responsibility; being the sole parent in the house caused her to be vigilant. Every decision, fraught with hidden danger. Not since she was a child, terrified of disasters that lurked—tornadoes, hurricanes, earthquakes—had she experienced such fear. "You're afraid of your own shadow," her father had often said. Take deep breaths, she told herself, but couldn't expand her lungs.

Every night before she went to bed, she checked and double-checked to make sure the doors were locked. Awake often during the night, Nora went to her bedroom window and stared at the deserted street. She learned which houses kept porch lights on and which were darkened. She turned the digital clock to hide the red numbers. The times she fell into a deep sleep, she was woken by a noise. A car engine, a dog barking, an unidentified sound. She lay and listened. One night, hearing her neighbor dragging out trash cans to the street, something Brad always remembered to do, she had to get up and go out in her nightgown to put the cans out.

Once she had gotten through the nights, she forced herself out of bed. The smallest of things seemed huge. Showering, dressing, brushing her teeth. She had gotten in the habit of talking to herself when she was alone, just a few words, like a mini pep talk. She would say things like, "Okay, done," when she completed something or, "Oh well," when nothing seemed to go right. She forced herself to eat—a spoonful of peanut butter, a piece of cheese, a bite of the lasagna Ann brought.

Nora hoarded what energy she had for the children; she made time to play games with them and watched and listened to see how they were doing. Clare stayed close to her, following her around the house like she used to when she was younger. Jack walked around with his hands in his pockets, a mannerism of Brad's, but he wasn't as angry. He and Clare talked about when they would see Brad and their plans to see his apartment. When the phone rang, they fought to get to it to see if it was him. The few times Nora answered, he was pleasant, asked how she was doing. She wanted to say, "How do you think I'm doing?" For her, the daily calls were a painful reminder of her new reality. For Clare and Jack, the novelty of the week helped to postpone the realignment of their lives. That would come later, when they would have to get used to packing a suitcase to go to his apartment, when they would get confused about where their things were and would forget something important at one house or the other. But for the first week, they had an escape.

On Thursday, after another sleepless night, Nora took her coffee to the deck while Clare and Jack slept. The sun wasn't fully up, but the air was already thick with no breeze to sway and rustle the leaves. The heat and humidity even seemed to keep the birds from chirping. She swept her gaze over the drab garden: coneflowers with blackened tops, roses with yellow spots and withered blossoms, used and spent. Each year, Nora experienced a vague sadness as the last days of summer led into a new season and a new regime of the school year. Now, the sadness was accompanied by dread of what she faced as she headed into a foreign season.

She went into the house. The calendar sat open, a reminder that she needed to get organized for school. Two weeks left. Brad would be settled in his apartment. Yesterday they agreed on the new arrangement: The kids would be with him Wednesday nights and every other weekend.

For a minute, she stared at the dates. As she had done each day after he left, she reviewed the day a week earlier: Last Thursday we swam in the ocean, we had pizza for dinner, we flew kites. But it wasn't the idyllic picture she imagined it to be. He must have been plotting and planning.

On Saturday, they were to go to Pennsylvania, their annual end-of-summer visit to her family. "Cousin time" Jack and Clare called it. Last week, when her life was still intact, she had talked to her mother and sister and made plans. Fun activities for the children, dinners, day trips to a nearby lake. Now she wondered if she should call her mother, tell her what happened, and cancel the trip. She stared at the phone for a few minutes, then picked it up. As soon as she heard the excitement in her mother's voice, she hesitated. "We can't wait to see you. Becky went to a dollar store and bought light sticks and all kinds of things." Then her mother asked, "How are Brad and the kids?"

"Everyone's fine." Nora paused. It was easier just to go. Not to have to explain or to disappoint the children. "Jack and Clare are excited too. But Brad can't come. He has to work."

"Oh, no! Tell him I'll miss him."

Nora's mother adored Brad. In the summer before their senior year he drove from Boston to Pennsylvania to visit Nora several times and her mother took an immediate liking to him. After he asked Nora what her mother's favorite flowers and candy were, he brought pink roses one visit, dark chocolate caramels another. When there, he offered to mow the lawn, to change a smoke alarm battery, to fix a broken toilet.

Nora started a list of what she needed to do for the trip. Packing. Gifts. Where to start? Laundry. The duffel bags of dirty clothes waited. As she stuck a load in the washer, memories of Becky floated in and out.

Her sister had remained in the town and married Bill, her high school boyfriend. They had two children, close to the ages of Jack and Clare, and were teachers at the school where Becky had been homecoming queen and senior class president and Bill, a basketball star. Their athletic trophies sat in a glass cabinet in the entranceway. As children, she and Becky were close—best friends, they told each other. Only two years apart, they had shared toys, dolls, and secrets. It was when Becky was eleven and Nora thirteen when the changes began. Becky was ahead of her in physical and social development, got her period and needed a bra first. Nora, a skinny, long-legged, and awkward teenager, had been bewildered by Becky's new habits, like bleaching her long hair blond and tossing it over her shoulder as she laughed at the dumb jokes the neighborhood boys told. Their mother said once, "You girls used to be so close. Now you're like oil and water."

Once the girls she had been friends with during middle school hit puberty, they moved ahead without her, and like Becky, seemed to have an instinctive sense of how to be popular.

Becky would make stinging remarks about Nora's appearance. "You look like a giraffe," she told her once. "Even your neck is long and skinny."

After that, Nora often examined herself in her full-length mirror and pictured a giraffe. Curly, auburn hair, large brown eyes, an oval face, and a neck and legs too long for her body.

"You're a late bloomer," her mother said. "You'll grow into yourself. You have a beautiful face." And when Nora wept, because that made her feel worse, her mother said, "I keep telling you— you're too sensitive. You need a thicker skin."

As they got older, Becky had boyfriends and went on dates. Nora wondered if she was having sex. They no longer shared secrets. Nora had a few friends she made in high school—ones on the fringe like she was—and they spent their weekend nights watching movies and having sleepovers.

By her senior year of college, her body filled out, and she emerged, no longer giraffe-like. And she met Brad; she remembered Becky's surprise when she brought him home. "Wow, Nora. I can't believe it. And he's cute."

As the day wore on, Becky continued to occupy Nora's thoughts and she dreaded the trip. She never had developed a thicker skin, and she and Becky never returned to their earlier closeness. At thirty-eight, Becky's strong personality still overshadowed Nora's. When they were together, Nora regressed to her teenage self, grew silent, hurt at random comments Becky made. Each time, she promised herself she would rise above it, but each time she fell into the old pattern allowing her leftover resentment to surge.

Jack and Clare loved the visits. Becky took charge, organized games, was a fun and caring aunt. Brad and Becky enjoyed each other; they loved to discuss and analyze things that held no interest to Nora. Details about the history of the town, the businesses that had left, which overpass was built when—it could be anything. Bored, Nora's mind would wander, and she would think, "What a perfect match they'd be."

CHAPTER 14

On Saturday, Nora and the children drove the three hours to Pennsylvania. The sounds of Jack and Clare laughing and arguing over the video games they played filled the car. After her sleepless nights, Nora was tired and the bright sun glinting off the windshield made her squint. As she gripped the steering wheel and tried to keep awake, possibilities of how Becky would respond to her news filled her with unease. Her mother would be shocked and sad. But with Becky, she had no idea.

In the late afternoon, they arrived at Becky and Bill's split-level house in the same development Nora had grown up in, a few blocks from the house where her mother still lived. Jack and Clare jumped out and ran to the door to see Rebecca and Will. Bill came to the car, hugged her, and took suitcases out of the trunk. "A perfect night to sit on the deck and grill steaks," he said. "I'm sorry Brad can't be here."

She'd always appreciated his calm and thoughtful kindness.

She looked at him and smiled. "Something's different." She pointed to his wire-rimmed glasses. "Are they new?"

He smiled. "I'm getting older."

Becky, in an apron, met them at the door and gave Nora a quick hug. "I'm in the middle of a million things."

Nora called after her, "Hey, I like your hair." Becky's long blond hair had been cut short and spiky.

"Easier to deal with," she said.

Her mother came out of the kitchen and put her arms around her. "Hi, honey." Nora held on until her mother stepped back. "I've got to finish my potato salad. Get settled, then we can talk."

Upstairs in the guest room, the room she and Brad usually slept in, with twin beds and flowered comforters, she put her suitcase on the one Brad slept in. The late afternoon sun poured in. The room was still and hot. Nora splashed cold water on her face, changed into a clean shirt, and pulled the hair that had escaped back into her barrette. She smelled the charcoal and listened to the voices of Becky and Bill on the deck, and the shouts and laughter of Jack and Clare and their cousins. A wave of anger rose within her; Brad should be the one to tell them what he had done. As she headed downstairs, she gripped the banister to steady her shaky legs.

On the deck, Nora watched Becky and Bill as they moved around, getting dinner ready. Together for so long, they worked in sync. Bill opened the Chardonnay Nora brought and Becky bustled about from one thing to another, talking the whole time. As Nora observed them, so immersed in their lives, she thought of all she had taken for granted in her own. The days had rolled along, one after another, one season after another, life marked by rituals, holidays, and minor upsets here and there: a trip to the hospital for stitches, a bad grade, a power outage. Until now, nothing to interrupt the design of their lives.

Her mother came out and sat next to her. She smiled. "Jack and Clare have grown, just since June."

"Too bad Brad couldn't come," Becky said.

"How is he?" her mother asked. "What's he doing for dinner?"

The sudden pain evoked by the question surprised Nora. Her mother, who had cooked and served dinner for her father every night of their marriage, probably hoped she'd left a nice casserole for Brad to heat. Nora tried to picture what he might be doing in the hotel. Room service, a restaurant, carry-out? She shrugged. "I'm not sure what he'll have."

Before her mother could respond, Becky said with a chuckle, "No surprise there."

Nora ignored the comment and asked her mother about her book club. They chatted and sipped wine as they watched the children play in the yard—the boys at the basketball net, the girls on the swings. Bill stood at the grill checking the charcoal. The sun lowered and a cool breeze cleared the humid air and stirred the leaves of the large oak tree at the rear of the yard. She could wait to tell them. Maybe tomorrow.

Just then, Rebecca, their seven-year-old, ran to her mother. "Mom, did you hear about Uncle Brad?"

Becky had stood to light candles and was intent on arranging them. "What about him?"

"He moved to a hotel. And he's getting an apartment and Clare gets to decorate her room. She gets to have two bedrooms!"

Becky and her mother turned their attention to Nora. Then Becky's eyes widened. "Is she kidding?"

The suddenness caught Nora off guard. Of course, Clare would tell Rebecca. She felt heat in her face and as she straightened in her chair, she willed herself to focus. "No. She's not kidding." She paused, grasped for an explanation. "We separated. Last week." The word struck her as odd. Separated. Like separating laundry. Dividing something into pieces. Fragments.

"You, what?" Becky said. Then to Rebecca, "Go play with your cousins."

Her mother looked confused. "Separated?"

Nora tried to remember the words she had practiced. "Brad wants time..." She stopped and took a gulp of her wine. Time to do what? "I don't know what he wants."

"Are you serious?" Becky dragged a chair next to Nora.

"Yes, I'm serious." She slid her chair a few inches closer to her mother. She gulped the rest of her wine.

Her mother said, "Jesus, Mary and Joseph," the words she used for something dire.

Nora's hands trembled as she poured another glass of wine. The only sounds came from the laughter of the children in the yard, the bounce of the basketball, the creak of the swings, the sizzling of the grilling steaks. Becky started her interrogation. How long have you known? Where is he now? What happened? Is there someone else? Not satisfied with Nora's answers, Becky's voice rose in inflection as she asked more questions. With air quotes she said, "You mean out of the blue?" She looked at her mother and back to Nora. "You had no idea?"

"Not a clue."

"You don't know why?" Becky stared at Nora. "Nothing happened?"

Nora stared back at her. "I don't know why." Being expected to provide Brad's motives was like being punished for what she hadn't done. "Why don't you call and ask him?"

"Oh, honey." Her mother put a swollen, arthritic hand over Nora's.

Becky swung her head to their mother. "I can't believe he would do that." Again, as if Nora were mistaken.

"Enough, Becky," her mother said and put an arm around Nora. She looked toward the children. "How are the kids?"

"It's been hard. Confusing." Nora wiped her eyes on a napkin. She didn't want to cry.

Her mother's face was pale. "What will happen?"

"He'll get an apartment…"

Before she could finish, Bill came to the table. "The steaks are almost done. Everything ready, Becky?" When she didn't respond, he said, "Hey, what's wrong?"

"Brad. He left," Becky said.

"Left?" He set his can of beer on the table. "What do you mean?"

Becky stood and picked up the cheese plate. "He left. Moved out. No reason."

Bill ran his fingers through his hair. As a math teacher, he dealt with facts, solvable problems, not with things without a concrete solution. A pained expression crossed his face. He put an arm on her shoulder. "Jeez. I'm sorry, Nora."

His kindness, such a contrast to Becky's insistent questions, made her want to hug him. She squeezed his hand. "Thank you."

"You okay, Nora?" her mother said with a pained expression.

Before she could answer, Becky said, "Can you believe it, Bill? No reason."

Bill looked unsure of what to say. He pointed at the grill. "I better take the steaks off."

The flush had grown in Nora's face at Becky's last comment; she needed to get away before she ruined the dinner. She said to her mother, "Can you keep an eye on Jack and Clare? I'm fine, I'll be right back." She stood and walked past Becky, but then stopped and faced her. "Could you let it go? Just say you're sorry that he left and let it go?"

She wandered in the neighborhood, walked by the tidy yards. Life went on like a normal Saturday: men mowed their lawns, children rode bikes and kicked soccer balls, families were outside enjoying the evening—all innocent of the possibilities that might lurk around the corner. "Watch out," she whispered. "You may think you're happy, but just wait."

CHAPTER 15

When Nora came back from her walk, her mother and sister acted like nothing unusual had happened. Bill served the steaks and poured more wine. No longer the center of attention, Nora listened to the chatter of the children, smiled at their silly jokes, and made occasional comments. She kept her eyes from Becky. Her mother looked at her now and then with a weak smile or a pained expression. At the end of the evening, Nora walked her to her car. Her mother held her, whispered, "I love you. It will be okay." Like she had as a child, Nora cried on her shoulder.

A bitter residue of the day stayed with her that night. Becky's implied meaning—how could Brad have left without cause, without Nora having done something—stung, even though she'd been plagued with similar thoughts. Becky seemed more concerned about Brad. Nora had often joked that her mother and sister put him on a pedestal—Saint Brad. Once during the night, she looked for Brad in the other bed, listened for his snoring, and remembered.

It was still dark when she woke and as she lay there, a decision to steel herself formed: she would be calm and polite but wouldn't engage in further discussion about him; she wouldn't let Becky bait her. At seven, she tiptoed downstairs. Sun streamed into the kitchen, already bright with lemon-colored walls. An insistent color, trying too hard to be cheerful, as if it would change a sour mood. She emptied the dishwasher, careful to put the dishes and glasses back in their right place. Nora was looking at Rebecca and Will's artwork that covered the refrigerator door when Becky came in dressed in shorts and a T-shirt. Even those were yellow.

Nora braced herself. She pointed at the mugs she had put out. "I made coffee."

"Thanks." Becky picked up a mug and filled it. "I'm sorry. I didn't mean to upset you."

Nora waited for her to add, "But…" Becky had never apologized to her. After a minute, Nora said, "Thanks, it's okay."

"Are you going to try to work things out?"

Here it comes, Nora thought. Work things out. Apologize and atone for my failure. "No, I tried to talk to him. It's up to him."

Becky sipped her coffee and for a minute, didn't speak. Nora was on the verge of venturing further, saying something like, "I don't know what I'm going to do," when Becky stood. "Okay, let's get our day planned. Mom's coming at ten." She pulled out a box of pancake mix.

For the rest of the week Becky was unusually kind and solicitous. No underhanded comments, no more pointed questions. Nora assumed her mother or Bill must have talked to her. Still, she watched her, wondering what she was thinking. And she wished they could have a real conversation. One day, Nora asked her, "How are things with you? Your job?" Becky answered, "Everything's fine." As she did on the family visits, Becky stayed busy planning and organizing. On past trips, the frenetic schedule rankled Nora. She would argue, "It's too much in one day." Becky would push ahead and exert her control. For this visit, Nora was glad to follow the daily agenda without having to think or plan. A day trip to Hershey Park, a movie on a rainy day, a picnic to a nearby lake. Following Becky's assignments, she kept busy, making breakfast, packing lunches, buying extra sunscreen. By evening they were all tired. She slept nine hours a night, in bed soon after the children, falling asleep with no worries about whether doors were locked or about causes of strange noises.

Mostly they skirted around the subject of Brad. Her mother gave her pep talks, asked how she was doing. Nora tried to reassure her. "I'm okay, Mom. I'll get through it." Nora was conscious of the familiar tug from childhood of wanting her mother to be happy, not wanting to cause her pain.

On the last day of the visit, Nora managed to find a few minutes alone. The children were showering after the afternoon at the pool. Becky had gone to the store. Bill found her on the deck with a cup of tea. "Mind if I join you?"

"No. I'd love it." It was the truth. With Bill, she always experienced a sense of comfort.

"I don't want to interfere." He paused and looked away. "Have you worked out the separation agreement?"

"No," she said. "Honestly, I haven't thought about it."

"Probably something you should think about. Things like alimony, custody, your assets." He put his hand on hers. "I want to make sure you're protected. That you know your rights. And you don't want to be in limbo."

Alimony, assets. She hadn't thought of legal issues. Or Brad's intentions. Bill might think Brad was having an affair. Or that he would take advantage of her. Grateful that he had taken her side, that in his eyes Brad was the villain and not her, she said, "Thank you, Bill. I appreciate it."

"I'll help you find a lawyer if you think you need one."

CHAPTER 16

After the trip to Pennsylvania, Nora mulled over Bill's advice about a legal separation. Brad had suggested the arrangement with the children; she had been comfortable with the amount of time they would spend with him. There was no talk about finances or changes to their joint account. She didn't think to question him. She went back and forth over whether she should follow Bill's advice. Bill was right about being in limbo. She needed clarity. Why would she wait for Brad to make the next move?

The following Sunday, the day before the start of school, Brad had arranged to take Jack and Clare shopping for new backpacks and out to dinner. In the evening, she sat on the porch and waited for them to get home. The days were getting shorter as fall neared; the sun had edged down behind a row of oak trees that lined a neighbor's yard. One leaf and then another floated gently to the ground, the ones that were first to lose their grip. She had always marveled at how some leaves remained connected until the bitter cold. She shivered and went inside to get a sweater.

When she came out, Brad's van was in the driveway and he was giving high fives to Jack and Clare. When she reached them, he looked surprised at seeing her close up. In the past three weeks, their conversations about logistics had been by phone or email. After he said goodbye to Jack and Clare they ran in the house with their new backpacks.

She said, "I need to talk to you."

He shut the door to the van. "Is everything all right?"

Still unsure and worried about to pushing them toward an irrevocable path, she said, "We need to talk about a separation agreement."

He looked surprised. "Is there a problem?"

A problem. What was wrong with him? "Yeah, there's a problem. We're separated."

"We don't have to rush into it."

She was confused; she'd expected him to agree. "It's recommended that people get one—"

"Only if there's a problem. If people can't agree on things. Money, or the children, whatever."

He had a habit of interrupting her when she was trying to process a thought and choose her words. It always irritated her and made her feel foolish. But now, she was angry. "Hold on. It's like you want it both ways. To be separated but not have it official."

But Brad continued to list his reasons, counting them out on his fingers. "We have our joint account. No money problems. We agreed on the custody arrangement for the children. I don't think we need a court-ordered agreement."

He sounded sure of himself. Of course, he had thought it through. Nothing had changed financially; the arrangement with the children had worked out well. But he must know that a one-year separation was required before they could get divorced. Maybe to him this was temporary.

When she didn't answer, he said, "We're not adversaries." He looked closely at her. "At least I don't think we are?"

What are we? she wondered. He jangled his car keys, and she looked at his hands, startled to see the glint of his wedding ring. Why did he still have it on? Hers sat in a box on her dresser. She had taken it off when they got home from Pennsylvania. She rubbed the empty space on her finger. Why did he still wear his? And why didn't he want a formal agreement? Did he see it as a temporary separation?

Clare ran out. "Mom, can I show you my new backpack?"

Grateful to Clare for breaking into her fog of confusion, she said, "I have to go and get them ready for school. Thanks for getting them the backpacks."

Her head ached. Besides the surprise of seeing his ring, she was disturbed by the spark of hope it evoked. Their conversation had made things murkier, made her unsettled. And the next day loomed: the first day of school without Brad to help. After he left, she got the kids to bed and then laid out lunch bags, peanut butter and jelly sandwiches, and boxes of cereal for the morning. She lay in bed and her mind wandered through their conversation as she fell asleep.

It was a shock when the alarm rang at six thirty the next morning and she had to jump out of bed without taking a few minutes to ease into the day. Brad had been full of energy as soon as he woke. He always got Jack and Clare up, made coffee, put out breakfast, and allowed her to fumble until the fog lifted. Luckily, today Jack and Clare were in a hurry to get to school. Perhaps, because they had glimpsed Nora's disorientation, they packed their lunches and ate breakfast without arguing.

At school she was relieved to return to the security of the classroom where she could pretend her life hadn't been fractured. The sun slanted across the innocent faces of the eighteen children sitting in a circle on the orange rug in their new shoes and clothes. Ten boys and eight girls. She sat in the middle of the circle. "We'll go around and introduce ourselves. I'll start. I'm Mrs. Stanton." Startled, she paused for a minute. Mrs. Stanton seemed like an alias, a person she had once been. She gazed for a minute outside at the familiar oak trees bathed in the soft September sun, then turned back and forced a smile at the expectant children. After they finished the introductions, she stood. "Okay, everyone. Look for your names. I'll help you find your places." As she steered them to their desks, she wished for someone to help her find her name, her place, her new identity.

While they were busy with construction paper and crayons drawing a self-portrait for her to hang on the walls, Nora walked around the room and observed them, matching faces to names. Lucas, Alexander, James, Carlos, Samantha (no nickname, the parents had written), Frieda, Taneeka, Jasmine… A few jiggled and rocked, but most were serious and intent on their drawing. ⸺ had drawn faces with arms sticking out of the heads; others, w necks and bodies and several added suns, he stopped at the desk of a girl with a mass of ιose blue eyes focused on her and whose paper was blank. Alice. Nora pulled a chair next to hers. "Do you need help, Alice?"

Alice threaded her fingers through her hair. "I was thinking about my dog, Benny."

"Oh, you have a dog?"

Alice nodded. "But everyone thinks he's dead." She reached in the pocket of her dress and took out a creased and worn photograph. A white fluffy dog. "Here he is. He's not dead."

Oh, honey, Nora thought. She put an arm on her shoulder. "Do you want to draw your portrait with Benny in it?"

After Jack and Clare were in bed that night, Nora glanced at a photograph of Brad that hung on a wall of pictures in the hall. One she had taken on his fortieth birthday nine months earlier. He sat at the dining room table with his favorite lemon Bundt cake in front of him and smiled at the camera. At her. No hint of unhappiness. She thought of Alice. "See—he's still here," she whispered.

CHAPTER 17

Over time, Nora fell into the full knowledge of her loss as Jack and Clare adjusted and settled into their new routine. Clare was less wary and watchful; Jack's hands came out of his pockets. They had gotten used to moving between the two homes. Their days were full: hectic mornings, after-school activities, and visits at Brad's. Visits. That's how Nora pictured them. He planned fun things for them as if it were a mini vacation each time. At first, Clare would cling to Nora at the door, not understanding why she couldn't come. And Nora would tuck things into their suitcases: notes, a deck of cards, books of Mad Libs. But soon it became an anticipated treat. After they came home from being with him, they talked about what they had done—movies, bowling, dinners out. Like he was trying to make up for the horrible thing he had done. She found herself riddled with petty feelings of resentment that they were having fun without her and even jealousy that they might prefer to be with him.

When Brad picked up the kids, Nora stayed in the house. He didn't come to the door. Even if he wore the ring and didn't want to formalize their separation, nothing had changed. Their phone conversations remained brief and business-like. Neither mentioned a separation agreement.

When they were with him, she padded around the house in the stark novelty of the absolute silence, still unnerved by the blanket of quiet in the house. The silence she had often longed for was a reminder of her loss. A silence in which the relentless ticking of the wall clock in the kitchen echoed in the emptiness. She'd never lived alone. All her life she'd had someone there in case of an emergency: first her parents, then her college roommates, and then Brad. She continued to fear something might happen that she couldn't handle: a leak or a flood in the basement, a power outage, or worse, a tree would fall in a storm.

Sometimes in the evening, she stood and looked at the houses across the street as the sinking sun glinted off the windows. She wondered what her neighbors were doing, what they were having for dinner. Over the years she and Brad had taken part in neighborhood social events—progressive dinners every few months, occasional potluck meals. Nora didn't have any intimate friendships with any of the women like she had with Ann, and she assumed that loyalty to Brad had reduced invitations to dinners. Most knew only that they had separated. Not that he had left her. Perhaps they felt sorry for him, having to find an apartment and move out, not knowing that she was the one ejected from her life.

Each day, as night loomed and darkness set in, she experienced something like the homesickness she had experienced the first time she had gone to overnight camp. That empty longing. But she had never really known what loneliness meant. Yes, the cruel loneliness as a teenager, awkward and excluded. But not since Brad. Now she experienced the texture viscerally, surprised at the indescribable quality of the void.

The nights were saturated with stillness after Jack and Clare were in bed. She had trouble falling asleep and lay awake listening to the clicking of the chains on the ceiling fan and counted the days since he left. Like Alice with Benny, she experienced bouts of disbelief and denial that somehow brought her hope. He couldn't be gone for good. He still wore his ring. It must mean something. She fantasized scenarios of how one day he would look at her and his eyes would light up like they used to; he would smile that smile she had fallen in love with.

One night she took Brad's blue flannel robe that he had left on a hook in the closet and held it to her face. She started to wear it to bed over her pajamas. It helped her through the lonely nights. She drove by his apartment building once with Jack and Clare. "Show me which one." They pointed to three windows on the fourth floor, curtains closed, lights on, and a balcony with a chair and table. One chair. That gave her hope.

After that, she occasionally drove by and tried to picture the inside of his apartment. He didn't take any of their furniture—he hadn't asked, and she hadn't offered. Jack and Clare had told her how they each had picked their bed, desk, and dresser from IKEA: ivory for Clare and a dark wood for Jack's. She asked them about the other rooms. His bedroom. It was the smallest room, with space for a bed and a dresser. She stopped herself from asking what size bed he had.

Nora had offered to pick up Jack and Clare on Sundays after their weekends with him—she'd pictured him coming to the door and inviting her in for coffee or a glass of wine. But he'd said, "Thanks. It's easier for me to bring them to you. Nowhere for you to park."

CHAPTER 18

On a Saturday morning in early October, she looked at herself in the mirror. Not so different from when they met—a few wrinkles and strands of gray. But she was pale and haggard, and her hair had gotten thick and frizzy, full of split ends. It had been months since she had gotten a haircut. That afternoon, she went to the mall and bought new lipstick, blush, and mascara, and then had her hair trimmed at a Hair Cuttery.

The next day, before Jack's soccer game, Nora spent an hour getting ready. She carefully applied the makeup and used a hair dryer to smooth the frizz and allowed it to frame her face. Instead of her usual sweatshirt and jeans, she wore black leggings and a purple tunic top. She smiled at her reflection in the mirror.

The autumn day was cloudless with a warm sun shining on orange, yellow, and red bursts of color on the trees. A cheerful day. Full of possibility. At the last game, she had kept a distance and glanced occasionally at Brad. He had waved at her, and Clare ran back and forth between them. Now she walked to where Brad stood with Clare.

Clare's eyes got big. "Mom! You look like a movie star."

Nora hugged her and waited for Brad to look at her. Tried to check his fingers, but he had his hands in his pockets.

He glanced at her. "Hi, Nora. I was going to call you later."

At those words, her excitement rose. She smiled and waited. Waited for his face to light up.

There was no change in his expression. In a business-like tone, he asked, "Do you want me to arrange for the fall cleanup? Get the yard raked?"

It took a minute for her to adjust to his words and then to her sharp disappointment. He was concerned about the fucking yard. The yard he had always kept perfect: mowed, edged, fertilized, the beddings mulched and weeded. Jack had mowed the lawn a few times in September, but it wasn't neat or manicured and was littered with dead leaves. Her face reddened. "Sure, thanks," she said.

Brad's phone rang, and he took it out of his pocket and looked at the caller ID. She checked his left hand; the ring was gone. "Sorry, I've got to get this. I'll bring them home by eight. We're grabbing some dinner after the game."

Nora nodded, took a few steps sideways and grabbed her sunglasses to hide her tears. How foolish she was. When had he removed the ring? Why? She moved farther away. Clare came and stood next to her. "I like your haircut, Mommy." Oh, Clare. Did she pick up on Nora's disappointment? She bent down and hugged her. "We need to get you a haircut too."

Later, at home she decided, that's it. No more fantasizing. Time to buck up and accept it. It was then that she entered a new phase. No more swaying back and forth. In the bedroom, she took his robe off the hook of her door and threw it on the floor of the closet.

Without the energy that had been fueled by her hopes, she pushed herself through the next days: breakfast, work and school, home, dinner, homework, finally bed. Often, she resorted to carry-out—Chinese or pizza, and dinner in front of the TV. She turned down invitations from Ann.

The times Brad had the children, she gave in to the pull of lethargy, like sinking into quicksand. The raw pain of the rejection had ebbed, leaving in its wake a peculiar absence, a flatness, nothing yet to replace it. In a way, it was worse. Sunny days—too bright, too cheerful—exposed the empty spaces of the house, like a cruel reminder of what she had lost.

A weariness she had never known enveloped her. She became forgetful, would start to do something and forget or lose interest. One morning, she stood in the shower and stared at the bottles of shampoo and conditioner. *Did I wash my hair or just condition it?* She talked to herself. "It's Wednesday. The trash needs to go out."

One night she woke sweating in the midst of a dream. She was at a party and didn't recognize anyone; she was relieved when she saw Brad standing with a cluster of people. She tapped him on the shoulder. "Hi Brad." He looked at her blankly. "It's me," she said. "You *know* me."

"You must be thinking of someone else." He smiled politely and turned back to the group. She woke, sweating and embarrassed, feeling as she did as a teenager, alone and disregarded, but worse, as if she had been erased from Brad's awareness. She got up and turned on the lights and stood at the bookcase across from their bed that was lined with framed anniversary photographs of her and Brad. Eighteen of them. Each year Brad arranged a tripod and set the timer and hurried to get next to her before the camera clicked. Various poses but always touching, with his arm around her in many. They held hands, smiled at each other or at the tripod; in one, they kissed. But the last one, taken in May, three months before their separation, they stood, not touching, and smiled into the camera. She studied his smile. Not as wide as in the previous years.

She removed the pictures from the shelf and stacked them in an empty drawer of his dresser. Then she spotted their wedding picture that hung on a wall. She and Brad smiled in the soft May sunlight. If there was such a thing as pure bliss, it was in that moment. Around her neck hung the sterling silver heart on a delicate chain he had given her. She stared at her innocent face. How sure she had been of their future.

CHAPTER 19

A few weeks later, on a Wednesday night in mid-October when the children were with Brad, she invited Ann for dinner. In the days since the soccer game, they'd talked on the phone, but Nora had begged off seeing her, giving excuses about having a cold and not feeling well. She did have a stuffy nose and a cough, but mainly she'd lacked the energy.

A school meeting ran late, and she stopped at a Chinese restaurant and got some Moo Shu pork and fried rice and put it in the oven to keep warm. She moved around the kitchen, clearing the mess from breakfast. She had forgotten the chore chart Brad had made. With him there, it had been like clockwork. Jack and Clare had jobs: taking out trash and recycling, clearing and setting the table. She had let things slide. Magazines and mail littered tables; abandoned toys and games were strewn on the floor. She wiped sticky orange juice residue from the counter, rinsed the milk and soggy bits of cereal from the breakfast bowls, then grabbed plates and wine glasses from the cupboard and set them on the table with a bottle of red wine. Done.

She pulled on a heavy sweater and went to the porch and sat in one of the wicker rockers and waited. A few orange leaves drifted across the porch and she dully noticed that the yard had been raked, the grass edged, and flower beds mulched. Brad must have arranged to have it done that day.

By the time Ann arrived, the sun was sinking, and the air had chilled. They went inside and Ann poured wine while Nora switched on the gas fireplace and turned on lights. When they sat across from each other at the kitchen island, she examined Ann, who wore a crisped and pressed turquoise blouse with dangling earrings that matched and complemented her startling blue eyes. A contrast to her own tired and haggard face.

At the same time, Ann was scrutinizing Nora from across the table. After a minute, she said, "I've been worried about you. Are you okay?"

Nora shook her head. "No. I'm tired, drained, depleted..."

"From your cold?"

"Just everything."

Ann searched her face. "Did something happen?"

She was embarrassed to tell Ann of her foolish hopes. The last time they'd been together, Nora mentioned that Brad still wore his wedding ring. Ann had said, "Don't go there. He left. Who cares if he's wearing the frigging ring?" But Nora had gone there.

With a concerned expression, Ann asked, "Are you sleeping okay?"

"Sleeping is great. Just not enough." Now sleep came easily; she craved it.

"Have you seen Brad? Is he still wearing the ring?"

"He took it off."

Ann raised her eyebrows as if thinking *I told you.* "How did you find out?"

"I saw him at Jack's soccer game on Saturday."

"Close up? Did you talk?"

"A little. We stood near each other." She didn't say that she had stood next to him. Didn't say how she tried to attract him with her makeup and hairdo. Didn't mention his lack of response and her embarrassment. She didn't intend to tell her any of it until later, when she could laugh about her foolishness. Her silly illusions.

"Were you upset?"

"Oh, a little. You were right. I had hope." She thought for a minute. "One good thing… I stopped trying to find the reason he left." She shrugged. "I don't give a crap."

"That *is* a good thing."

"I don't know." She managed a weak smile. "I don't give a crap about anything." She had never known such a lack of purpose, of caring. And it frightened her. "I go to school, take care of Jack and Clare, feed them, get them to bed, like a robot…" She searched for words. "It's like I'm in a vacuum."

Ann stared at her glass and swirled the wine. "It's been how long? Two months?"

Nora counted back. "Two months on Saturday."

"Not long," Ann said. "It's normal."

"Normal. That's what I want. To be ordinary again. Capable. The house is a mess. The kids aren't helping now that Brad's not here to help remind them." She stared out at the dark night, then stood and closed the shade. "I hate that it's dark so early now," she murmured. "Are you ready to eat? I got some Chinese food."

"Not yet." Ann watched her for a minute with an intent expression. "I can't imagine what it must be like. I wish I could help."

Nora came back and pulled her chair closer. "You are. I don't know what I'd do without you."

"Listen," Ann said and pulled out a pamphlet from her purse. "There's a support group I've heard is good. For separated and divorced women."

They looked at each other, knew each other so well they could almost communicate without words. Ann's expression was tentative and hopeful. Nora imagined hers was incredulous.

"Ann…I hate groups. We both hate them."

"I know. I know." Then she went on like a salesperson pitching something amazing. "But you'd have people to talk with who are going through the same thing. Starts Saturday. At the church near the mall. Not far."

"Are you kidding?" Nora opened the brochure Ann put in front of her and stared at it.

Gain emotional support from people who understand. Learn how others are dealing with their loss.

You'll start as strangers in your group and end up as friends exchanging phone numbers for support.

"Jeez. A magic cure." Nora closed the brochure. "I don't think it's for me."

Ann smiled. "But it might help." When Nora didn't respond, she said, "You said you're exhausted, in a vacuum."

Nora was sorry she had shared her exhaustion and lethargy. Ann now felt responsible and thought she had to do something.

Ann grabbed her hand. "You can't go on like this, Nora. Go once. Just try it."

Nora looked at her for a minute. "Okay. If I go once, will you drop it?"

CHAPTER 20

On Saturday, a cold and rainy morning, Nora sat in the small hot room overlooking a church parking lot in an old worn brick building. Radiators hissed dry heat. Eight chairs in a tight circle. The leader, Loretta, asked each to say their name and how long they had been separated or divorced. As they took their turns, Nora studied faces: a few women looked pinched and pale, a few sad and sorrowful, a few blank and nondescript. At her turn, she said, "My husband left me in August. We're separated. We have two children. A boy and a girl. Six and ten."

Loretta congratulated them on their courage. "I know how hard it is. I've been there too," she said with an eager and sympathetic smile. "I'm sure you have a lot to share. Who wants to start?" She asked encouraging questions after each woman spoke. "Can you tell us what it was like?" Or made comments. "You were so brave. Think how far you've come!" She was perky, bubbly, wide-eyed, her voice an octave too high at times, her responses sounding canned from a psychology textbook. She wore different smiles and facial expressions to meet the various emotions.

Rain beat against the windows, rattling the screens as the women told their stories. One woman stared at her hands as she folded and unfolded a tissue into neat squares and spoke of her husband's infidelity. A few others said they drifted apart and made joint decisions to divorce. A young woman who looked to be in her early thirties left a controlling husband and was fighting for custody of her two children. An older woman, married for forty-five years, said her husband left her for another woman. She glanced around the room at the women and said with indignation, "What am I supposed to do now?" She shook her finger at the women. "Don't sign papers unless you have a lawyer check them. That's how my husband screwed me."

Nora shuddered, engulfed in a sinkhole of misery as each story brought sympathetic murmurings. She had nothing to share, nothing to chime in with. She wasn't willing to examine her pain and pull it out—to put her private anguish into words with strangers who would make it trivial. It was her shipwreck, and she didn't want sympathy or compassion.

After the women shared, Loretta looked at her with an expectant smile. "Can you tell us what it's been like for you, Nora? You separated in August?"

"Well..." She felt claustrophobic from the heat of the room and the gaze of the women. "I'm not sure I'm ready to talk about it."

Nurturing responses from several women popped up. The woman next to her patted her hand. And with a sympathetic smile, Loretta said, "Oh, it's okay, Nora. You don't need to share until you're ready. But know we're here for you." Others nodded in agreement.

Nora had trouble catching her breath. From the next room children sang "These Are a Few of My Favorite Things." She wished she were in that room. The women bonded with each other as they shared their stories. Nora was off limits by her own choosing. She wanted to escape the stifling room.

As she waited for the meeting to be over, in her mind she said to Ann, "See, I told you. I'm not a group person. Remember the childbirth class we hated?"

CHAPTER 21

Several weeks after the meeting, on a bitter November Sunday, what she would later name as her turnaround day, Nora woke shivering in her damp nightgown from the night sweats that had plagued her once she had turned forty. She glanced at the clock on her nightstand. Seven o'clock. Sundays, always a day of drudgery in Nora's mind—the end of the weekend, the laundry, grocery shopping, and cleaning— stretched endlessly. Now, they were worse, much worse, especially on the weekends the children spent with Brad. When he brought them home in the afternoon, they were often as tired and cranky as she.

Nora debated rolling over and going back to sleep but forced herself up and grabbed her robe from the floor. She emptied the overflowing hamper, gathered the clothes strewn on the floor of Clare and Jack's bedrooms, and headed to the laundry room. After starting the washing machine, she brewed a half a pot of coffee, more than her usual single cup.

With her coffee and newspaper, she sank into the couch and stared out the French doors at the trees, stark and bare, their branches swaying in the wind. The bird feeders were empty. At least she could feed the birds, she thought, but knew she wouldn't. The cloudy sky gave off a dull light in the room, the kind that exposes every crumb, smudge, and flaw: the accumulated stains on the faded seagrass rug; the comfortable but threadbare furniture. She remembered her excitement when they bought the house and furnished it—she had experienced the delight she had as a child with her playhouse, arranging and rearranging her miniature furniture. Now every chair, every table, every lamp added to her heartache and represented a chapter of her life that had ended. She couldn't remember the last time she had even lit a candle.

She yawned and rubbed her eyes. The newspaper sat unopened in her lap. The caffeine didn't work. She looked at the clock—she could sleep for two hours and then shower and straighten the house before the children got home. She took the phone off the hook, trudged upstairs, got into bed, and burrowed under the covers.

When the insistent ringing of the doorbell woke her, she didn't know what time it was. Jack yelled through the mail slot, "Mom, answer the door!"

She jumped up, tore off her nightgown and pulled on jeans and a turtleneck. In the bathroom, she squeezed a glob of toothpaste and rubbed it over her teeth with a finger and spit it out. She groaned at her image in the mirror: her pale face, puffy eyes, and frizzled hair. She heard the door open and footsteps in the foyer. Damn, Brad still had the key. When she got downstairs, he was gazing around the disheveled room. He hadn't been inside since he moved.

When he saw her, he said, "We called, but when you didn't answer…"

Clare grabbed her arm. "Mom, we went bowling."

"And to the movies," Jack said.

"Did you get your homework done?" As soon as she spoke, she regretted it.

"I'm sorry. I forgot. We were busy." Brad smiled at Clare and Jack. "We had fun."

Of course. Make her the bad one. He seemed relaxed, happy. Free from the grind of the daily routine. An unfamiliar red and black plaid flannel shirt. A red baseball cap. He hated shopping—she had usually bought his clothes. He seemed to be blossoming, his face fuller, less lined, while she had lost weight and felt withered and weary. She tried to hide her irritation.

After he left, Jack and Clare ran upstairs to do their homework, and she stood at the kitchen window. The trees were suddenly bare of leaves. She had missed their autumn evolution and exit. The purple and yellow pillows on the deck furniture—the pillows she'd meant to bring in—looked out of place, garish, in the bare landscape. As the sky dimmed, the colors faded and blended into the dark night.

She closed the shade and tried to think what they would have for dinner. Uncooked pieces of penne pasta littered the floor from two nights ago when the opened box had gotten knocked off the counter. She slid on a piece as she walked across the room. "Shit," she said, as she caught herself from falling. The refrigerator held a hodgepodge: an assortment of half-empty bottles and condiment jars; congealed General Tso's chicken from her carry-out meal the night before; a wilted bag of lettuce; a few wrinkled apples. She had made sure to buy milk, orange juice, cereal, peanut butter and jelly, and frozen dinners to throw in the microwave. The basics were all she could manage. A funny smell, an odor of food turning bad, hit her. She took out a jar of salad dressing and read the date—it had expired a year ago. When had she last cleaned the refrigerator? Bought fresh apples, salad, real food? For a few minutes, she stood at the open refrigerator as if searching for an explanation, then took a deep breath and began to empty its contents.

Jack came into the kitchen and looked at the littered counters. "Mom, what are you doing? When are we having dinner?"

"Soon. This is a mess." She dumped an old bottle of ranch dressing in the trash. "Make a peanut butter sandwich."

"It's been like that forever. Why now?" He wore an incredulous expression. "I don't want a sandwich."

Just then he reminded her of Brad. The way he'd sometimes gotten exasperated with her and make her feel inept. She stopped. "What's Dad's refrigerator like?"

"I don't know, it's fine. I'm going upstairs."

After she took the wilted lettuce and threw it in the trash, she called to him. "Jack, wait. Come back. Is there food? Salad, vegetables, eggs…?"

"Yeah, he always has all kinds of stuff."

She was embarrassed at what Brad had probably taken note of. The disarray. Her. As unkempt as the house, her hair a mess, her clothes wrinkled. Did he pity her?

Clare came in with her homework sheet. "Look at the

story I wrote about bowling." Then she glanced at the counters. "Mom, what happened?"

"I'm cleaning. As soon as I'm done, we'll order some pizza for dinner and I'll read your story."

"Can I watch TV?"

"One show." It had gotten dark, and she was determined to finish. After she switched on every light in the kitchen, she finished emptying the refrigerator and scrubbed the shelves and drawers, cleaned the counters, and gathered the stacks of newspapers and magazines and put them in the recycle bin.

Jack came back and rolled his eyes. "Mom," he whined, "I'm starved."

"I'm ordering pizza right now." She looked at his denim jeans. Stiff and not faded. "Are your pants new?"

"Yeah, Dad bought them; my other ones don't fit." He pointed at his grass-stained sneakers. "These don't fit either; my toes are squeezed."

She stared at him. His thick brown hair needed a trim.

"Mom, stop. You're creeping me out." He left the kitchen again.

"We'll get new shoes for you tomorrow," she called after him.

Her indifference scared her. When was the last time she had looked at schoolwork, checked their backpacks? Just last week the receptionist at the orthodontist's office had called to accuse her of another missed appointment for Jack.

After she ordered a pizza, she sat at the kitchen table with Clare while she read her story of her fun day with her father. As she listened, she was aware that she needed to accept the fact that she and Brad would have differing relationships with Jack and Clare. A large part of her adjustment had been the tedious daily routine without Brad to help. It was time to make changes. Jack and Clare needed to participate again in the chores; she also needed to build fun activities into her weekends with them. After they ate, she took Brad's chore chart off the refrigerator and revised it with them. They made a list together—Jack and Clare picked dinners they wanted that week—and planned a trip to the Baltimore Aquarium for the next weekend. "You can invite Eddie and Maddie to come and then have dinner and a sleepover," she said.

Once the house quieted, she got in bed and propped herself against the pillows. She lay back for a long time. Something had happened. A shift. A breakthrough from her emptiness. A vague awareness that she could adapt, maybe even be happy again. Not yet—she was suspended between her old life and what lay ahead, as if suspended between chapters—but freer to imagine new possibilities. Little things first. Getting her energy back, enjoying food and cooking again. Maybe she would sign up for yoga or Pilates.

A sudden determination filled her: she would stop accepting the limbo she had allowed Brad to orchestrate; she would get the house key from him and insist on a separation agreement.

A peace settled over her. It was past midnight when she turned off the light and fell into a deep sleep.

CHAPTER 22

The next day, Nora picked up the kids from school and took them to the grocery store and let them shop for the meals they had picked out for the week. She bought new condiments to replace the expired ones. Jack and Clare pick out the ingredients for their favorite food: spaghetti, tacos, hamburgers, and macaroni and cheese.

As they passed a bin full of turkeys, Clare said, "Mom. Thanksgiving's next week. We can get the turkey."

The word "turkey" was a shock. Nora, who always planned for Thanksgiving for weeks, didn't need to this year after having entered the unwelcome custody world of dividing the children for the holidays. She had negotiated to take the children to Pennsylvania on Christmas day by letting Brad have them for Thanksgiving. Now she felt the tears welling and anger rising at Brad for causing this.

Nora put an arm around Clare. "Remember, you're going to your father's for Thanksgiving."

Clare said, "Aren't you coming?"

Nora shook her head and tried to move Clare away from the turkeys.

"But it's Thanksgiving! Who's going to cook the turkey?"

"He knows how to cook. I'm sure it'll be fine."

"I want you to be with us. What are you going to eat?" Clare looked like she might cry.

"I'll be fine." Nora hugged her and held in her own tears. She would be alone. Ann and Nick were going to visit Ann's family. Nora's mother wanted her to come to Pennsylvania, but Nora didn't want to make the trip by herself. She didn't care whether she ate. What she cared about was the day she loved—loved cooking the meal, setting the table with her favorite tablecloth and napkins, having the family around the table.

Before they left the store, Nora slipped a TV dinner into the basket: turkey, stuffing, mashed potatoes, and cranberry sauce.

On Thanksgiving morning, Nora slept late and stayed in her pajamas and read. The day was drizzly and grey. In the empty space, she sat with her sadness and let it fill her. She wept on and off all day. Slept and wept. Not having to be stoic for Jack and Clare, she welcomed the release of the tears.

In the early darkness of late afternoon, she placed her TV dinner and a glass of Malbec on a tray and sat propped against the pillows on her bed and watched the news. After she finished dinner, she'd curl up in bed and read, and let the day be over. Tomorrow, she could look forward to Christmas with Jack and Clare and her family in Pennsylvania. She fell into a deep sleep and in the morning, woke with a rush of relief that it was over.

Brad had the kids until Sunday—she had two more days to herself. She wanted to decorate the house as they always did the day after Thanksgiving. She pulled out lights for the mantel and cleared the buffet table in the dining room for Jack and Clare to arrange the Christmas village when they got home.

Another tradition on this day was to buy and set up a Christmas tree. They didn't decorate it right away, but Brad strung the lights and Nora played Christmas music. She fought the crowds at the mall to find an artificial tree with lights already strung. Smaller than their usual trees, she got a five-foot-tall one with clear lights. She bought large silver and blue balls to replace the ornaments that had shattered when she emptied the bin for Brad to pack his clothes the day he moved out.

During December, Nora worked hard to be cheerful: She hung an advent calendar like they did every year; took the children to Santa. Even though Jack protested that he was too old, he gave in to Clare's begging. "You have to be in the picture with Santa," she said.

Although she would have preferred to skip it, Nora took Jack and Clare shopping for presents for Brad, just as she always had. In the past she had made suggestions—usually of gadgets or other things that he hinted at. Last year, it was a battery-operated screwdriver. This year she left it up to them.

In the men's department at Macy's, Jack held up a blue, peach, and yellow striped shirt. Nora debated. Should she tell him Brad hated striped shirts and would surely hate the bright colors? He generally wore subdued plaid shirts and khaki pants. Over the years, Nora had learned. One year, he'd returned a solid teal-colored shirt she'd gotten for his birthday.

She eyed the shirt and then the tie Clare picked—dotted with pink and purple flowers. She thought for a minute, smiled and said, "Wow. You guys are good. I bet he'll love them." Nora bit her lip to keep from laughing as she pictured Brad opening his presents. In the background, "Here Comes Santa Claus," played. Nora hummed along to the music.

PART TWO

We don't see things as they are, we see them as we are.
—— *Anaïs Nin*

CHAPTER 23

After swimming upstream during autumn and the dark cold of winter, the earth thawed. As the fog of Nora's grief lifted, she noticed a softening, a newfound ease in her life. It was as if she had turned brittle at the edges and been living in a dimmed world with the sun hidden behind the clouds. Now, with the change of seasons, as her eyes adjusted to the emerging light, she experienced a grace in the rhythm of her life. On a day when a few purple crocuses popped up in the yard, she even felt cheerful. It was like she had lived for months in a dull grey world of sensory deprivation and as the light emerged, She regained a resurgence of her lost energy along with a desire to climb out of her self-imposed hibernation.

With this fundamental shift, Nora entered a new passage. She was no longer that naïve woman on the boardwalk. She had stopped pitying herself—mostly. The traditional couples' holidays like New Year's Eve and Valentine's Day had been difficult, but her fantasies of getting back together with Brad had ebbed in the fall when she stopped watching his face for signs that he loved and missed her, stopped trying to understand why he had left her, stopped driving by his apartment. Neither of them had pursued the separation agreement and she let it go. They were cordial, but she kept herself at a distance, their interactions centered on schedules for Jack and Clare.

When the first snow of the season had come in the middle of January, schools closed. Nora had tried to recreate the day with their usual traditions. She and Jack and Clare shoveled snow, made a snowman, and drank hot chocolate in front of the fire.

She took pleasure in simple things: food, the smell of coffee, music. Once more she cooked for pleasure, and tried out new recipes—maple glazed salmon, Chicken Piccata, spinach lasagna— and she invited Ann and Nick for dinner. She made Jack and Clare's favorite lemon pudding cake. And she lit candles again.

Being alone no longer frightened her; she looked forward to time for reading, solitary walks, and doing yoga with no one interrupting her, to making decisions without needing to figure out what Brad wanted, or to check for his approval. No longer constrained by his expectations, Nora became almost grateful to Brad for the unintended consequences of his actions.

As she thought more about their relationship, she realized that when he teased her for not understanding something, he was condescending; he made her feel incompetent and she allowed it. Then she traced that feeling—a familiar one she'd grown up with—to how her father had made her feel. When Nora would be hurt by something he'd said, her sister made fun of her, telling her she had an inferiority complex.

Brad wasn't mean or harsh as her father had been, but the

subtle comments triggered the feelings of inferiority to creep in. Now, she could do what she pleased. She didn't have to hear him say, "Nora, it doesn't work that way," when his logical brain collided with her absent-minded one. And she didn't need to worry about being judged in other ways, like when she turned page corners down or underlined favorite passages of her books. Brad had once asked her why she didn't use a bookmark. "You're ruining the book." But they weren't library books, or his books. They were hers. Still, after he had said it, each time she folded a page she felt a twinge of guilt. But she had said nothing. So much she had never shared. So much they never shared. They aired their grievances in small ways or kept silent and held them within; they never really fought, never had a full-blown argument. Perhaps that was the flaw. The shadowy parts that lay underneath.

In March, she made a list of everything in the house she'd grown to dislike: the maroon front door and manicured shrubs on either side; the family room with the yellow chairs she and Brad had sat in for so many years; the threadbare green and gold plaid couch; the stained rug. First, she had the plants ripped out, replaced by an assortment of perennials that would bloom from spring to fall, the maroon door painted a soft aqua, and the black shutters a buttery white. Next, she went to IKEA and bought a slip-covered couch and chairs in a creamy beige color, a pale green seagrass rug, and tab-topped linen curtains. When she finished, the house had a light and airy feel.

One day she stood in their bedroom and stared at the heavy dark furniture—Brad's dresser, which he had refused to take, her matching mahogany dresser and the nightstands. All reminders. She remembered the day they'd picked them out. He'd liked the dark mahogany set. Nora gave in because he had let her pick the colors for the living room and family room. After he'd moved, she'd debated replacing the set but thought about how Ann took old furniture and painted it in bright colors. *I could do that,* she thought. Ann explained what she needed to do to prep the furniture. She'd gotten her supplies, spent days poring over paint samples and wound up with a soft teal color. Then, she bought a new comforter to replace the yellow and blue plaid one that Brad had chosen. Once she finished, it felt like a new bedroom. Hers.

In April, she boxed their old china, gave it away, got new dishes from Pier One—a colorful fiesta pattern—and new wine glasses and place mats. She likened it to the way real estate agents staged houses to sell—she'd re-staged hers, re-staged her life, ready to enter the next chapter.

CHAPTER 24

The months rolled by. As spring eased into summer and the end of school, she and the kids kept busy with swimming, soccer camp, and trips to Pennsylvania. Nora's sister called to plan visits and was kinder, even solicitous. Their relationship became easier. Brad took Jack and Clare to places they had always meant to go as a family: New York and the Statue of Liberty, Philadelphia and the Liberty Bell, which made her jealous. What bothered her more was that he took them to Boston to show them his old house, the schools he had attended, and the cemetery where his mother and father were buried—he knew Nora had always wanted to see the town he grew up in, to view the graves of his parents. They had talked about it, but never made plans. Why had it become important now?

No one mentioned a desire to return to the beach. One day in the beginning of August, Nora stared at a picture on the wall in the family room of Brad and the children on a boardwalk bench, smiling and sharing a large bucket of fries. She longed for the taste of the vinegar on the fries, the expanse of the ocean, and the salty air. But the visceral memories of the last day when Brad announced his unhappiness and decision to leave had remained, the details permanently etched in her memory. How happy she had been that morning, how unaware of what was to come. The before and the after. Despite that, a tangible longing to return to the ocean filled her. She went to the kitchen and studied the calendar. The following week, Brad planned to take Jack and Clare on a Busch Gardens vacation. Before she changed her mind, she searched for an available room and finally found one in a motel that faced the ocean on a quiet stretch of beach.

When she arrived, Nora drove to the cottage where they had spent nine summers, the first when Jack was one. In the late afternoon, the light softened as the sun ebbed. The familiar pink and purple petunias bloomed against the aqua siding. On the outside, nothing seemed to have changed. A barefoot boy and a girl who seemed to be near the ages of Jack and Clare played Frisbee on the lawn. She yearned to go back in time for a day. Yearned to examine the rooms to see if they were the same: the living room in a similar aqua blue shade as the outside siding, the shell lamps and beachy décor. Yearned to experience the sunbaked mellowness after hours spent at the beach—the scrub green pines against the blue sky as she stood in the outdoor shower. She gazed at the front porch where Jack and Clare had shucked corn, and she pictured their two heads examining the ears for any leftover silk. Suddenly, she realized the girl had stopped playing and was staring at her. Embarrassed, she smiled, waved, and drove to the hotel. For a few minutes, she sat in the car and let the mixed memories mingle. The happy times before the final horrible day. Her evolution over the past year in the path she had traveled from that day of disbelief.

That night after she checked in to the motel, she got a pizza and brought it back to her room. She opened the bottle of red wine she had brought and sat on the balcony of her hotel room. As it got dark, an orange moon rose and cast its luminous glow on the ocean. A gentle breeze blew. A breathtaking summer night. Perfect for the couple at the edge of the shore with their arms around each other. Watching them, she experienced a pang of sadness and loneliness. Although she wasn't ready to be entangled with someone new, she missed being touched, being held. Missed the idea of romance, the excitement that had ebbed from her marriage as the years passed.

CHAPTER 25

The next morning, Nora woke to the sound of rolling waves, the soothing noise that had lulled her to sleep. The breeze from the ocean blew open the curtains and allowed the sunrise to flood her room. After bringing her coffee to the balcony, she leaned back and closed her eyes. She had passed another milestone. She smiled and whispered, "I'm okay. I did it, I'm here."

At mid-morning, after breakfast, she took her chair and books close to the water. The tide was going out, the waves low and gentle. She read and swam and slept, enveloped by the warm sun and a mild breeze. For lunch, she got an Italian sub from the deli shop across the street from her hotel. A contented lethargy filled her. The surrounding activity brought happy memories. Children built castles, ran to the ocean for pails of water, and searched the sand for shells to put in their buckets. She smiled, remembering how she loved watching Jack and Clare.

Her phone rang. It was Brad. He usually gave his phone to one of the kids to call her. It was unusual for him to call unless there was a problem. "Hi," she said. "How's it going?"

"Fine. We had fun on the rides yesterday."

"Good." She smiled and pictured them on the roller coaster.

"But it's raining today. And supposed to rain again tomorrow."

"That's too bad." She set her book down. Enough of the polite conversation, always awkward for her. "Who wants to talk?"

"How's it there?"

"It's sunny, nice."

He cleared his throat. "Can we talk for a minute?"

"Okay?" She said it as a question.

His voice was low and hesitant. "Jack and Clare asked if we could come."

"What?" She pulled the phone close to her ear. "Come where?"

"To the beach."

What was he thinking? Stunned, she said, "Are you kidding? This is *my* time. My break. Your vacation with them."

"You can have your time. I'll take them to Funland, miniature golf—"

"Why don't you go home?" Nora made circles in the sand with her feet. It was absurd that he couldn't deal with them being bored. "Arrange playdates with Eddie and Maddie..."

"They miss the beach." He quickly added, "It would give us a chance to talk."

"Talk?" It took a minute for the oddness to sink in. For the irony to hit her. "Here? Do you realize it was a year ago?"

In a stronger voice, as if she had provided him a reason to

persuade her, he said, "That's part of the reason I'd like to come."

"Are you serious?" Nora stood and walked to an isolated area at the edge of the dunes.

"To explain."

She said sarcastically, "To explain why you had to leave me?"

"Sort of. The past year has been hard. But it got me to a different place. I understand more."

As if she should feel sorry for *him*. After she had emerged from the worst year of her life, she didn't care to listen to a rehash of his. "Why are you telling me this now? We've both had a hard year."

"It's so busy at home. And the kids do want to come."

Away from the cool breeze, she was hot and became more irritated. "I'll take them another time. Besides, there are no rooms available."

"I could check and see."

God, he was dense. She picked up a broken shell and threw it against the dune fence. "No, Brad. You can talk to me at home. Schedule a time. Let me speak to the kids."

After she talked to Jack and Clare and promised them a beach trip next summer, she turned her phone off. What the hell was wrong with him? Because he had come to a new awareness that he was impelled to share? What did he expect from her? Sympathy? She was far beyond the need for his apologies. Maybe he wanted absolution. To be cleared of responsibility for shattering their lives. Astounded at his selfishness, she whispered *asshole*.

Her face felt red, her body sticky and sweaty. She ran into the ocean and swam past the breaking waves to float. A lone red kite bobbed high in the blue sky. A cloud floated over the sun. Back at the chair, she wrapped a towel around herself. The sun had lowered and cast a soft light. The lifeguards blew their whistles and dragged their stands to the dunes. The family next to her packed their rolling carts and argued with their children to rinse the sand off their toys and buckets. After a few minutes of sitting there fuming, she walked on the sand until the sun lowered beyond the high-rise hotels and apartment buildings and it became chilly.

CHAPTER 26

After her walk and a shower, Nora was surprised at how hungry she was. She drove to a seafood restaurant and ordered a carry-out meal of crab cakes and coleslaw, then stopped at a liquor store and bought a bottle of Chardonnay. She brought her meal to the balcony. It was dark, and clouds moved across the sky and covered the moon. By the sound of the rising crash of the waves, she figured it must be high tide. It began to drizzle.

While she ate, she reflected on the surprise of Brad's call and his *hard year*, hoping it had been miserable. She speculated about what he needed to explain and what he meant by being in "a different place." She pictured the cottage. Seeing it again had evoked the familiar flood of questions that she had thought she was done with. How could she have been so clueless? Spending those weeks with Brad—the last two of their marriage—without any awareness of what loomed? How had he hidden what was happening underneath? He hated conflict; she knew that. Had he been so good at disguising his pain and unhappiness, or had she been so bad at noticing? And, had she been aware, could she have done something to change his mind?

By the time she had finished eating and poured a second glass of wine, her curiosity grew. Was he ready to tell her what had caused his unhappiness? Had he found what was missing? He hadn't bought a new car or a boat or changed jobs. Suppose he had found someone and wanted to talk about the divorce. Firm the date. He had piqued her interest. She waited until ten o'clock when she figured Jack and Clare would be asleep, and then she called. "Are the kids in bed?"

"Yeah. Did you want to talk to them?" He sounded hurt, perhaps angry that she had refused to listen to him earlier.

"No. I want to talk to you. To hear what was suddenly so important."

"It wasn't sudden. I'd hoped we'd have time after Jack's party. I hinted at coming in, but you were in a hurry."

She tried to remember the day of Jack's eleventh birthday the month before. Brad was friendly, but she hadn't thought much about it—she had long since stopped trying to attract him or to see if he had changed.

"Okay. I'm listening."

"Now? On the phone?"

She sipped her wine and stared at the ocean. "Yes, now."

"Well. I wanted to tell you about the past year. Are you sure you want to hear it now?"

"That's why I called."

"As I told you when I left, it wasn't about you or us. It was like it started out of nowhere. At first, I figured, no big deal—you know, a mid-life crisis or whatever. But it got to the point where

I felt lost. For so long, I couldn't figure out what was wrong with me. I didn't know why I was so unhappy."

Nora listened as he rambled, like a volcano that had erupted and was now spilling. She leaned back in her chair and put her feet on the railing and let the warm drizzle cover her. It was like hearing a story and filling in the blanks, waiting to learn the outcome. At a distance, as if it had happened to someone else.

"I felt trapped. I couldn't concentrate. It wasn't fair to you. I needed to be alone, to have time. So, I found a good therapist." After a few months of intense sessions, he said, his therapist asked questions about his parents, their sudden deaths, and how it affected him. And once he started talking about it, he couldn't stop thinking about it. She helped him to understand that he had never really grieved the death of his parents. "I knew that the day they died it was like an earthquake."

"I remember. It was horrible." She thought of the look on his face when he learned of their deaths. "And I remember how you closed me out."

"I couldn't talk about it. I was overcome with all kinds of horrible thoughts. I imagined them in the car. Pictured their faces. Wondered how bad it hurt. Over and over. I kept thinking of the randomness—how easily something bad could happen. It stuck with me. I needed to build a wall, a barrier just to get through, to protect myself."

Nora was struck by how similar their obsessions were after the tragedy and the questions she had kept inside: What had his parents bought from the grocery store? Did the food spill all over the car? Did they see the car heading toward them? He had told her the teenagers had had their licenses taken away; that they had to attend classes. Over the years, she had wondered about them. What had they done with their lives? Had they changed afterward like Brad had, closing off pieces of themselves, leaving the carefree part behind?

Brad went on. "After we got married, it was easier. Work, the kids. I thought I was content, happy. I got used to the fear, tamped it down. Still, I think I was always on guard, needing to be in control. But then, a few years ago, something happened. Patricia—that's my therapist—helped me see the stuff that had gotten buried. What happens is, it can start leaking into other areas. Leaking. That's the word she used. She suggested the trip to the cemetery."

So, that's why he went to Boston. Nora had mistrusted his relationship with his therapist, resentful that he shared his emotions with her, but now she thought more favorably of her. "How did it go?"

"It was hard. I even cried a little. But with Jack and Clare, I didn't want to be too morbid."

"When they got home, they wanted to see pictures of your parents again, so I pulled out the album," she said.

"Thanks, Nora. I'd like to borrow the album and look at it."

"Well, it's yours. You can take it."

Then he talked about driving by his house and school, realizing that he had cut off ties to Boston after the funeral, hadn't kept in touch with his high school friends. "I may try to look a few of them up."

She sipped her wine. "I'm glad it's working out. The therapy. Your parents. All of that." And she really was. Happy for him and vindicated in some way, learning it hadn't been about her. "I have a question to ask you. Last summer. Why did you do it on the last day? On the boardwalk of all places."

"I couldn't face telling you before the vacation. Or during it and ruining it. And the thought of going home and doing it there… I knew however I did it, it would be awful."

"Awful for me or awful for you?"

"Both of us. I know it was for you and the past year for me was hell, but it got better. It's like something's lifted."

It felt like something had lifted in her as well. "I'm kind of glad you called. It clears some things up."

"I'm sorry for what I put you through."

"Well, I hated you. But I've gotten through. I'm happy." It felt good to say it, to feel it, to tell him.

"I hope you don't hate me anymore?"

"No. I don't remember when I stopped, but no." She asked, "Why did you keep the wedding ring on at first?"

"I guess it was hard to take it off. It had been so long."

The drizzle gave way to rain, and she watched the spatters on the rail of the balcony. Then what made him take it off? "So, have you dated?" she asked.

"Yeah, for a few months. Someone from the office. It was nothing."

Even though she'd imagined him dating, his acknowledgment of it stung. "From the office," she repeated almost to herself to allow it to register. "Had I met her?"

"No, she started last year."

"Hold on a minute. I need to go inside. It's raining."

After she pulled the sliding glass door closed, she sat on the bed and stared at the phone. She reasoned with herself. Why wouldn't he have dated? But the idea that he had, while supposedly needing the time and space apart from her to work through his issues, felt like another betrayal. Forget the mid-life crisis. His therapy. His finding himself. The fact that he'd dated while she went through the difficult adjustment for her and for the kids now seemed terribly unfair. Because she needed to create stability for Jack and Clare, she wouldn't have entertained thoughts of dating.

"Nora. Are you there?"

"I'm here."

"Have you?"

"Have I what?"

"Dated?"

"No," Nora said. "No, I haven't."

He sounded relieved. "Part of why I wanted to come is…" He paused, and then said, "I miss you."

When she didn't answer, he went on. "Yesterday I was watching Jack on the roller coaster and for a second I looked for you. To smile at you like we used to when they were on rides. And I missed it. Missed you. Missed us."

She stood and paced the room. He missed her. Missed *us*. But there was no *us*.

"Brad. I really don't know what you want."

"We're not divorced. We could try again."

Did he think he got to leave when he wanted—take a sabbatical from their marriage and return when he wanted? Did he expect her to be the same Nora? The sensible, responsible one with no fantasies of life outside their marriage?

"Try what again?" She felt the heat rise in her face. "I told you. I'm happy now. I'm not the same."

"Neither of us is the same. And it would be better for Jack and Clare. And financially for all of us."

Of course, he had lined up all the reasons. "Did your therapist suggest this?"

"We talked about it."

Fury rose. She hated the therapist again. "Tell her she's got a lot more work to do. Just because you've found yourself, or whatever the hell you did, you can't suddenly decide what you want and think it's what I want."

"Okay, I'm sorry. I didn't mean to hurt you."

"No. No. You don't get it. You have no clue." She paused. "Do you know how horrible it's been for me? How selfish this is? You have no idea where I am in my life, who I am. I've moved on."

With her hands shaking, she ended the call.

To clear her mind, she drank a glass of cold water, splashed some on her face, and then sat on the floor and leaned against the bed. His timing stunk. Did he think she'd still be pining for him? Perhaps if he had asked her six months ago, she would have been the same Nora, waiting for him with open arms. He had missed the points when he could have interrupted her journey, points when she would have been receptive. If she had known he'd want to come back to her after he "found himself," would she have endured, waited, kept herself fixated on him? It was as if he'd robbed her and wanted to return what he had taken. After getting through the trauma and the awful months, she had emerged to arrive at a place she was learning to inhabit, able to think of him without desire and longing. The distance between that Nora on the boardwalk bench a year ago and this Nora was too far. It was too late.

CHAPTER 27

When Brad brought Jack and Clare home on Sunday, to Nora's relief he acted cool and nonchalant, as if nothing out of the ordinary had occurred. She had steeled herself, determined to remain civil but remote. Clare jumped out of the car first and ran to Nora, throwing her arms around her. Jack followed, dragging his suitcase, and gave her a quick hug. After Brad helped carry their bags to the door—wearing a baseball hat and sunglasses that obscured his eyes—he glanced at her. "Clare has a sore throat and an earache. She may have an ear infection. I've given her Motrin." He hugged each of them. "It was fun. I'll see you guys on Wednesday." That was it. Nothing in his tone or demeanor connected with the words he had spoken on the phone.

Nora had packed and left after Brad's unexpected intrusion—like an uninvited guest, he had crashed her peaceful vacation. On the ride home, a familiar feeling returned. The guilt was not about her denial of Brad, but about Jack and Clare and what was best for them. Since their separation, she had followed the advice she read in books, magazine articles, and blogs on the effects of divorce on children: she never said bad things about Brad, listened when they wanted to talk, and watched for signs of trauma. She had the name of a therapist ready in case. Although they seemed happy and adjusted, she knew they missed Brad. She would overhear them on the phone with him: Clare at the end of each call saying, "I miss you, Daddy. I love you." With Jack, it was more about plans for the next visit. Dinner, a game, or a movie. Aware that it would be easier for her and the children, she was mindful of the choice she was making, mindful that she might be shielding herself to prevent being hurt again, closing off the possibility of feeling anything for him.

The night after Brad brought home the children, Nora woke after a vivid dream. It was Christmas morning, and they all were sitting on the floor in front of the tree opening presents. Jack was a few years older and looked to be about as tall as Brad; Clare had pimples and wore braces—both seemed bored and unhappy. Brad's eyes were on her after he handed her a large box wrapped in purple paper and tied with a yellow ribbon. As she untied the bow and ripped the paper off, she sensed Brad watching her from a distance, not connected in any meaningful way, almost like a stranger. Disappointed when she woke before discovering what the box contained, she lay in bed for a while and wondered what the dream meant, if it was a sign. A warning of what it might be like to return to him. Perhaps a truth about their marriage: the disconnect and the distance. Even the children were unhappy.

On Wednesday evening, five days after her trip, she and Ann had their usual weekly dinner at their favorite neighborhood

Italian restaurant. In the days leading up to the dinner, the dream stayed with her and as she pictured the scene and the tension in that room, it helped to free her from the notion that she was responsible for Jack and Clare's happiness. Or Brad's. Or anyone's.

She and Ann sat outside on the patio they loved: tables with umbrellas, candles stuck in wine bottles, and red and white checked vinyl tablecloths. It was a hot and humid night, but the sun had started to sink, and a slight breeze blew. Ann and Nora had been there enough times that their waiter knew to bring a carafe of Chianti after they sat.

Nora had told Ann a sketch of what had happened, but they hadn't had a chance to talk at length.

Ann asked, "Are you okay?"

"I am," Nora said, although she was sure she didn't look it. Her blouse was wrinkled, just pulled from the dryer, and her hair frizzed in the humidity. After they ordered seafood linguine— their usual—Nora related what had happened and the range of emotions she had experienced. Irritation, curiosity, empathy, and fury at the end. "I was so pissed off; I didn't even have to plan what to say like I usually do."

"Good." Ann pumped her fist in the air. "So that was the whole point? He told you about his hard year and his therapy? And now he wants to get back together?"

"Yeah, like he could just decide, and I'd be waiting."

"Jeez. What happened when he brought them home?"

Nora shrugged. "Oh, nothing. We both acted like it hadn't happened. I think he was hurt or embarrassed."

"He should be embarrassed," Ann said. "It sounds like he

gave you a sob story about his parents to get you all involved. I'm glad you didn't get drawn in."

The streetlights came on. As the sun lowered, Nora stared at the faint traces of pink that remained in the sky. Ann's words seemed harsh. Nora hadn't thought of it as a sob story; she'd been glad that he had faced the trauma and was dealing with it. On one level, she was protective of Brad. He was a good father. Had been a good husband. She didn't want him to look worse in Ann's sight, didn't want her judging him more than she already had. Not for his clumsy attempt.

"I think he meant well," Nora said. "As mad as I was, I don't think he was using that to lure me back."

"I can't believe he did it on your vacation. Wanted to bring the kids. And then unloaded on the phone."

"That was me. I called him because I was so curious about what he wanted. I'm glad he was able to open up about his parents." She paused for a minute to thank the waiter after he set down their salads. "But then the surprise of him wanting to get back together, that even being a possibility. It's like I was heading in one direction and he threw a roadblock. Later, I started to think about Jack and Clare. What's best for them. Making that decision. What it would mean for them to not have a splintered family. They miss him."

"It's because of him." Ann tapped her nails on the table. "So, you're feeling guilty?"

"I was," she said. "About the kids." Nora rubbed her fingers across the sticky plastic tablecloth, brushed some crumbs to the floor. "I drove myself crazy. I started to worry about the future. Raising them as they get older, carting them from one place to another, waiting up for them at night."

"I get that." Ann poured more wine in their glasses. "I'm dreading those years."

Nora waited for the waiter to clear their salads and serve their dinner. "Even stupid things, like if one of us gets married, maybe to someone with children. Blended families, divided holidays, on and on. The finality of it. The future. The unknown."

Ann had an amused smile. "Sounds like you're making a case to get back together."

"No. No." She glanced at a couple at the table next to them, eating their food, not talking, not looking at each other. It looked like such an effort. Earlier that day when she had a headache and opened the cabinet to get a Motrin, she had noticed Brad's contact lens solution. As she stared at the bottle, she remembered the daily routines, sharing the bathroom, sharing the house, watching Brad's expressions to monitor his moods, anticipating his impatience with her for one thing or another; being constrained by his timetable and expectations.

She told Ann her dream—Jack and Clare looking bored and unhappy and Brad cold and distant. "It put an end to my doubts. I can't go backwards even for Jack and Clare, for some fantasy of everyone living happily ever after. I've made the decision for me and for what I need. I've closed the door."

"Good," Ann said. "I hope you're done with the damn guilt."

"For now," Nora said. "Until something else comes up. It's in my genes." She laughed. "But I'll remember the dream. My new mantra is, I'm not responsible to make things right for everyone."

They were quiet for a minute while they ate. Nora hadn't eaten since breakfast and was hungry.

Ann looked up from her food and smiled. "Think of it, Nora. You're free. I'm jealous in a way."

"You're jealous? Please."

"You get a new life, a different life. Opportunities. Choices."

Nora searched Ann's face. "Are you and Nick okay?"

"We are, but sometimes when it gets old and boring, times when the spark is flickering really low…" She shrugged. "I love him. I'd never do anything, but there are those drudge days."

"Yeah, I remember." Nora looked around, surprised that the patio had emptied, and the background chatter had ceased. The quiet couple was gone. The candles on the tables still flickered in the dark night. A strong cool breeze blew the heavy humid air away and Nora brushed her damp hair from her face. "Okay. Enough about me," she said. "I want to hear about your vacation."

"In a minute." Ann held up her wine glass. "Here's to us. You can date, and I can live vicariously through you."

Nora smiled and clinked her glass with Ann's. "I'm not sure I'm ready for another relationship. Not sure I'm strong enough. This made me see how vulnerable I am, how easily I can get thrown off center."

"Listen, Nora, you're strong, stronger than you know. I've been watching you—you're finding yourself, becoming you, becoming Nora." Ann smiled. "Hey, it sounds like the title of a book."

CHAPTER 28

In September, Nora and Brad returned to their usual routines—schedules, school, and soccer. Jack was now eleven, and Clare, seven. Nora and Brad remained cordial but chillier. One evening in October, Nora was cooking dinner for Ann and Nick—maple-glazed salmon and roasted potatoes. They sat at the island sipping Chardonnay. The children had eaten pizza in the family room and were watching TV. It was still warm for October and Nora had opened the windows in the kitchen to allow a breeze in as she cut up vegetables for a salad. She and Ann had been talking about a PTA meeting they had attended.

During a lull in their conversation, Nick said, "There's this man at work, a lawyer in my department. I've known him for a while. Real nice guy."

Nora was half listening, but noticed Ann and Nick exchanging glances.

"Anyway, the other day we were at lunch and he was joking that he's the only bachelor in the firm and I thought—"

Nora gave Ann a look. "This is you."

"Honestly, it was his idea."

"Really." Nora smiled and turned back to the cucumber she was slicing.

"You could try it," Ann said. "What's his name, Nick?"

"Andrew."

Nora said, "Have you seen him, Ann?"

"No, Nick says he's in his forties, blondish hair, lean."

"I like guys with dark hair." Nora looked at Nick. "Why is he still a bachelor? Does he live with his mother?"

"No, he has a condo in DC. He works hard. Long hours. Probably doesn't have time to meet people." Then Nick said, "He drives a silver Mercedes."

"A Mercedes. Like I care."

Ann looked at her and shrugged. "So, you may not like the car, or the color of his hair. But what do you have to lose?"

"A free night. I'm enjoying my nights without the kids." But really, what did she have to lose? A night at home reading a book?

She was nervous in the days leading up to the date. She didn't know what type of restaurant they were going to. Casual or dressy? On the night—a Wednesday when Jack and Clare were with Brad—her bed was lined with dresses, pants, blouses, sweaters, and shawls. She had her closet divided into sections: her clothes for school, easy to mix and match and divided by season; a small section of dressy clothes for the rare occasions that she and Brad had had something fancy to attend; a middle section of clothes that she wore for dinners and movies. In the end, she picked black pants, a satin grey blouse, silver hoop earrings, and black heels. She observed her reflection at the mirror. With the heels, she was at least five feet, eight inches. What if he was short? She switched to flats. Then she ran through topics to discuss. She wished she had asked Nick more about him. Wished she hadn't said yes. She wondered whether he was a Democrat, so they could talk politics. She and Brad had the same values, goals, opinions. By the time Andrew arrived, she was dreading the evening.

When the doorbell rang, she took a deep breath and answered the door to the chilly October evening. Medium height—good thing she didn't wear the heels—thin, his reddish blond hair neatly trimmed and pale blue eyes. He wore a navy blue suit, a white shirt, and a solid maroon tie. She tried to gauge if he looked nervous. He had a pleasant smile and shook her hand. "Great to meet you."

She grabbed her coat and followed him out to his Mercedes. The ride to the restaurant was awkward with perfunctory comments about the weather, how it had turned sharply colder, the traffic getting worse all the time. She had always hated having to make conversation. Why had she said yes?

The restaurant, with white tablecloths, a bud vase with red roses, and candles reminded Nora of the type she and Brad would have picked for their anniversary, for a special night. Full of promise. But she knew soon enough what kind of night it would be. When they were settled, their server came to the table and asked for drink orders, then stood waiting, while Andrew perused the wine list. After a few minutes, Nora made eye contact with the waiter, smiled at him, embarrassed to keep him standing there. To liberate him and her, she said, "I'd like a martini, extra dry, up with a twist." The drink she and Brad had when they were at a restaurant like this.

Andrew looked up from the wine list. He seemed startled. "Oh. Well. Give me a scotch on the rocks. Chivas."

In the quiet restaurant, his voice sounded loud; he talked a lot, without her needing to ask much. Nora sipped her martini and listened. She tried to find the positive—she hated that she often judged quickly on first impressions. Just because he kept the server waiting didn't mean he was without empathy. He could just be nervous.

As her mind wandered through the thicket of his details, she tried to retain words and phrases about his job, his golf games, or his last ski trip. With each of her questions, he answered at length. He didn't seem perceptive enough to sense her growing boredom. He asked a few perfunctory questions. Had she been anywhere interesting lately? "To the beach. To Pennsylvania to visit my family." How old were her children? "My son, Jack, is eleven. Clare is seven." Did she play golf? "No."

He didn't ask anything more about the children or her trips, and she tried to think of what to add. She groped. "Have you read any good books lately?"

"No. By the time I get home, it's late. I watch the news." He picked up his menu. "Ready to order?"

She was about to say no, she hadn't looked at the menu, but he was waving his arm for their server.

"I'll have crab cakes." It was the first thing she read on the menu.

"And you, sir?"

"Steak. Medium rare. I want it pink in the middle. Not red. Not well done." He looked at Nora. "What kind of wine do you want? White with your crab cakes?"

She didn't care. "Whatever you want. Or a glass of Chardonnay is fine for me." Again, the waiter stood there while Andrew deliberated. *Please*, she thought, *just order the fucking wine.*

Finally, he ordered a glass of Pinot Noir for him along with her glass of white. As she observed him treating the server as if he were invisible, she missed the comfort of being with Brad who was always kind. She found herself overly thanking anyone who refilled their water, brought bread, served their salads. After Andrew pierced a piece of lettuce, she gazed at a blob of salad dressing on his lower lip, wondered when he might wipe it off, wondered why his eyebrows were so bushy with his hair so short and tidy.

She checked her watch. They had been there for forty-two minutes. It seemed like hours; she felt trapped, even claustrophobic. She glanced at a couple a few tables away. They held hands with their eyes locked. She caught herself straining to hear what they were saying, but the table was too far.

Andrew said, "Is something wrong? Are you always this quiet?"

"No." She switched her attention back to him. "I'm just tired. Thinking of school tomorrow."

"You really like working with five-year-olds?"

"Oh, I love it, love watching them, their faces when—"

"Yeah, my nephew is five. Five or six. It's a fun age."

They could talk about children. She could ask him if he had other nieces or nephews. "It is," she said. "They're so open and curious. Like sponges."

He gave a short laugh. "But after a few minutes, I'm bored out of my mind."

As the night wore on her eyes grew heavy. When their entrees arrived, he ate slowly and deliberately. Thankfully, his steak was done right. Nora ate quickly and finished first and waited impatiently. Finally, he finished and crossed his knife and fork across his plate.

The waiter cleared the table and asked about dessert. Andrew said, "I never eat it. Do you want something?"

She shook her head. "No, I'm full."

When the check arrived, Nora pulled out her American Express card to share the bill. She didn't want to feel that she owed him anything.

"No, I got it." He smiled at her and placed his hand over hers. "You can invite me in for a nightcap."

She flinched and after a few seconds removed her hand. "Sorry, but I have a really early day tomorrow."

After Andrew paid, he stood and turned from the table. Nora pulled out a twenty-dollar bill and slipped it under her water glass.

CHAPTER 29

At the end of December, after Nora returned from Christmas with her family, the children were with Brad for several days. Nora spent another New Year's Eve alone. She tried to read but couldn't concentrate and wound up watching the celebration at Times Square until ten when she went to bed. Emily, who also taught kindergarten at her school, had invited Nora to a New Year's Day brunch. Her husband had a group of friends he played soccer with on weekends, and one of them was having the party. Emily was pregnant and about to start maternity leave and begged Nora to come to the brunch. "It'll be all the guys from his team and a few couples I don't know. We can hang out together." Nora wasn't sure she wanted to make the effort, but the usual let-down following Christmas was so much worse this year.

Nora was nervous; she hadn't been to a party since Brad left, and she'd never enjoyed being in groups. The thought of going alone and attempting to meet new people and make conversation unnerved her.

New Year's morning, Nora pulled out the same outfit she had worn for her date with Andrew. When she arrived at the party, Emily came and greeted her and introduced her to her husband and the host who directed her to the bar and the buffet. After she got a mimosa, she glanced around the room. The first thing she noticed was a man in the center of a group—tall and muscular with shaggy brown hair, in faded jeans and a black T-shirt—animated as he talked and gestured, everyone laughing. *The life of the party*, she thought. He glanced her way, caught her eye, and held her gaze for what seemed minutes, but was probably only a few seconds, enough for her to feel a spark, an intent.

A memory surfaced. In her second year of teaching kindergarten, some teachers at her school had invited her to join them for a drink after work on Fridays. Tom, a third-grade teacher, often sat next to her at the bar, listened to her, focused his eyes on her in a way that awakened something dormant—a feeling she had once shared with Brad until their lives settled into the routine of jobs and careers. She remembered the pang of regret when she recognized the loss. She and Tom never touched, but still she felt guilt—guilt for what his look aroused in her—as if she were being disloyal to Brad in some more important way than if they were physically intimate. The next year Tom transferred to another school and Nora never saw him again. Once she got pregnant with Jack, her life moved on.

Nora turned and moved to the buffet table with Emily and got a slice of quiche and some fruit salad. They sat together on a couch and Emily talked about names she was thinking of for the baby. Nora noticed the man who had earlier glanced at her standing across from them. Emily looked up. "Hi, Jim. How are you?"

"Good, what about you? I hear your life is about to become exciting."

"It sure is," Emily said. "This is my friend Nora. She teaches at my school."

"Hi Nora," he said.

She smiled and said, "Hi Jim." His eyes on hers brought the same anticipatory spark as it had when she first noticed him. She felt herself blush, and embarrassed, turned back to Emily. People mingled around Jim and talked. Nora only half-listened to Emily, aware of his voice, his laugh, his bold personality, and aware of a thrill of excitement. When she stood to leave and was pulling on her coat, he followed her. "I'll walk you to your car."

The cold air felt good. She had parked half a block away and as they talked they realized they lived forty-five minutes apart, he in Virginia across the Potomac River from her house in Maryland. When they got to her car, Jim leaned against it and looked at her. "We need to figure out how we can meet for dinner," he said, as if it were a forgone conclusion. "I want to know more about you."

That did it. Besides the undeniable attraction, Nora liked that he was so sure of himself.

They exchanged numbers and after Nora got in the car, he stood as she drove off and waved. Nora wondered if he would really call. She pictured him with someone as charismatic and outgoing as he was. Was he interested in her because she was the only woman there without a partner?

The next day Brad dropped the kids off in the morning. The Christmas break was over, and Nora had a busy day: doing laundry, getting the children to pack their backpacks, and shopping for school lunches. When Jim called that evening, she was folding laundry in her bedroom and had almost forgotten.

The evenings were Brad's time to call and Jack answered the phone. He called up to her. "Mom, some man wants to talk to you."

Damn, she thought when she realized. She should have given Jim her cell phone number.

"Hi Nora, it's Jim. It sounds like you might be busy?"

"No, just doing laundry, getting the kids ready for school." She laughed. "My life is pretty boring."

"Do you have a minute? Can we make plans for dinner?"

She told him she would be available on Saturday and Jim suggested a restaurant in DC, halfway between his apartment in Virginia and her home in Maryland. "A pub-restaurant where we go after our games," he said.

After she gave Jim her cell phone to use instead of the land line, she called Emily to ask about him. She didn't want to get her hopes up. What if he had a bad reputation?

"Jim Bradley?" Emily said. "He's a nice guy, fun. He's divorced, no children… Hey, did he ask you out? I could tell he was attracted to you."

Thoughts of Jim popped up all week. Nora mapped out the restaurant so she wouldn't get lost. She tried to imagine what they would talk about, remembering the awkward disaster her date with Andrew. *I'm too old for this,* she thought.

On Saturday morning she went through her closet and laid out clothes. What should she wear to a pub? She decided on jeans, boots, a sweater and a scarf. She carefully dried her hair to smooth out the frizz and let it hang loose and frame her face.

The restaurant was a simple drive from her house. Jim waited for her in the parking lot and had a booth set aside for them. He knew the owners and was friendly with the servers. It warm and cozy with paneled walls and padded booths and soft lighting with imitation Tiffany lamps and tea lights on the tables. Nora relaxed right away, thinking how it already felt like the opposite of her date with Andrew.

Jim had a few beers and a hamburger; Nora had a glass of wine and a crab cake sandwich.

Over dinner, they shared their stories. Jim was forty-eight, seven years older than her, a building contractor. He had dropped out of college after two years to start a construction business with a friend, had divorced eight years ago after being married for seven. Amicable, he said. It just didn't work out. "We wanted different things."

He asked her more questions about her teaching career, her children, where she was from. No one had shown such interest in her for so long. He looked at her at one point and said, "You have beautiful hair. The color matches your eyes."

At the end of the evening, he casually put his arm around her as they walked to her car. Just that touch thrilled Nora. He asked when they could see each other again. When she explained her situation with the kids, he said, "Not until two weeks from now?"

Nora wanted to see him sooner too and thought through the possibilities. She could cancel her dinner with Ann. "How about Wednesday?"

He smiled. "That's better. I can pick you up and we can go somewhere in your neighborhood."

Nora wasn't ready to have him at the house or to go to a local restaurant with him. "Let's do this again. I like it and it's easy for me to get to."

Elated at the thought of seeing Jim again, and thrilled that he wanted to see her, she called Ann and made an excuse about skipping their dinner. When she got to the restaurant the following Wednesday, Jim was at the bar and got up when he saw her and gave her a hug. As on the first night, he was fun and easy to be with. Witty with a dry sense of humor, he kidded with their server. She loved the way his eyes crinkled with amusement, his infectious laugh, his intent gaze on her as they talked about themselves, their families and where they grew up.

After dinner, he held her hand as he walked her to her car. His hand felt different from Brad's. Larger and callused. A worker's hand. That night, when he hugged her, they held on to each other for a minute. He had a big frame, with a body more muscular than Brad's. It felt good to be touched and held.

CHAPTER 30

That night, Jim called to make sure she got home okay and to invite her to a party on the upcoming Saturday afternoon at a friend's house to watch a football game. It was her weekend to have the kids, so she arranged for them to go to Ann's to play with Maddie and Eddie. At school she found herself smiling on and off all day.

Nervous the day of the party about fitting in with his friends and making conversation, she worried about being a drag on him. Right away, Jim put her at ease. He held her hand and walked her around to introduce her. Everyone was friendly and made her feel welcome. Jim was still as big a presence as he had been at the earlier party as he drew her into the circle.

It was dark when she left the party to go home. Jim came out with her. "I wish you could stay."

"I do too, but I have to pick up the kids."

He held her face in his hands and they kissed, gentle at first and then more insistent. The depth of her desire surprised her—she hadn't kissed many men before Brad, and the kisses with him had lost the novelty. After that, Jim called or texted every few days at first, then every night. Because of Nora's situation, they couldn't see each other as often as they would have otherwise. He would write things like, "Wish I could see you tonight," or "I'm counting the days."

Nora marveled at the dramatic switch in her life. At home, she played music and hummed to herself, basking in feeling wanted, attractive, young again. She kept her phone close and checked it often. Even in school she kept it near and smiled inwardly when she heard the vibration of a new text and couldn't wait for a break in her classroom schedule to read it.

After Ann started questioning her about the canceled Wednesday dinners, Nora told her about Jim. Ann, of course, wanted to meet him. "Let's see where it all goes," Nora said. "It's too early to tell."

For several weeks, they met at the restaurant whenever Nora could arrange it. On a frigid January evening, when they finished dinner, Jim covered her hands with his. "Come home with me. Your kids are with their father for the weekend, right?"

Nora had known from the start that this was where they were headed. Warm glances and the lure of their attraction had overshadowed their conversations. Jim awakened an intense longing in her, a sign of the extent of her loneliness in the eighteen months since Brad had abandoned her, in the eighteen months since she had been touched.

But that night, as she followed him to his house, gripping the steering wheel and staying close to his car, her stomach hurt, and she had trouble catching a deep breath. All desire had left her, and the thought of fleeing entered her mind. Home to her bed, free from the frightening unknown of being with someone other than Brad, the only person she'd been intimate with other than a few earlier fumbled encounters. But stepping back to her celibate life, alone and undesired, because she was afraid? No.

She followed him and parked in a visitor's spot in front of his three-story apartment complex, a modern, cream-colored stucco building lined with balconies. He held her hand on the elevator ride to the third floor. When he went to the kitchen to open a bottle of wine, Nora glanced around the large living room and dining room—a brown leather couch and two matching recliners, glass coffee tables and end tables. Big windows. No curtains. On the refrigerator door, multiple magnets held carry-out menus. A bookcase with stacks of magazines, remotes for the TV, and a CD player. No books. Did it matter? The thought made her smile. The attraction had nothing to do with books. Nora stopped at a table with framed photographs. Several were of Jim and his friends; she recognized a few of them from the party. And a few looked to be family pictures.

Jim set the goblets and a bottle of Pinot Noir on the glass table and switched on the gas fireplace, then stood next to her.

She pointed to a photo. "Is that your family?"

He nodded. "My parents and my sister. Those are her children. She did the grandchildren thing, so I didn't have to." He laughed. "I get to play with them and then leave."

Framed photographs of his construction jobs lined an entire wall—before and after pictures. She crossed the living room to examine them. "Jim, these are amazing. You should have a website." She asked him about his projects, knowing she was stalling.

Finally, he took her hand and drew her to the leather couch. They sat next to each other and stared at the flames as they sipped their wine. By the time he put his arm around her, the wine had calmed her, and she leaned against him. He turned to her, took her wine glass and set it on the table, took her face in his hands and kissed her. They had kissed before, leaning against her car at the end of the evening, leaving both wanting more. She was ready when he took her hand and drew her into his bedroom to the queen-sized bed that took up much of the room.

She stopped him. "I need to use the bathroom."

"Sure." He pointed to it. "Let me know if you need anything."

Inside the bathroom, her anxiety resurfaced, and she leaned against the door and took deep breaths. A huge mirror ran from the ceiling and across the length of the double-sink vanity. White and black tiles covered the floor and walls in a geometric pattern. His toothbrush and toothpaste and a can of shaving cream sat on the counter. Although she saw no signs of another woman, thoughts of his sex life led her to a new set of worries: pregnancy, herpes, HIV, protection, condoms.

Her mouth was dry, and she turned on the faucet and drank handfuls of water, then picked up the toothpaste and squeezed a dab on a finger and rubbed it across her teeth. After she undressed and hung her clothes on a hook on the back of the door, she uncoiled the braid in her hair and pulled her fingers through and let it hang free. The mirror showed her forty-two-year-old body—breasts that had started to sag and arms less toned. She grabbed a thick white bath towel from a set on the shelves and after she wrapped it around her, she stood and held the cold doorknob. *You can do this*, she told herself. The fear she experienced reminded her of standing at the edge of a diving board when she was learning to dive. The fear, but also the excitement. She took a deep breath and opened the door.

Jim had undressed, had pulled the comforter to the floor and waited in bed. A light on the dresser gave the room a soft glow. Nora got into bed, then unwrapped the towel and slid it to the floor. He looked at her with an amused smile. "Are you okay? We don't have to do this."

"A little nervous." She didn't know how to ask about condoms. "I'm not on birth control—"

"Nora." He pointed to his nightstand where a pack of condoms lay opened. He leaned over and pulled her to him. "Don't worry. Everything will be okay," as if she were a child in need of comfort.

That first night, he slowly and gently eased Nora through her awkwardness and self-consciousness. The chemistry between them was as she had anticipated, their intimacy full of the passion she had imagined. Afterwards her body felt limp, as if something within her had uncoiled and released. When she stood to get her clothes, he had pulled her back. "No, stay." She spent the night, surprised at how easily she fell asleep, how nice it was to have the warmth of his body touching hers and yet, how strange it was to be with another man.

CHAPTER 31

After that night, Nora spent weekends with Jim when Brad had the children. She kept a bag packed, hidden in her closet with a change of clothes, a book to read when Jim watched TV; she kept a toothbrush and shampoo at his apartment. Every other Saturday, Nora left with her suitcase as if taking a trip. As she moved into a sphere so removed and secret from her ordinary life, it felt clandestine, like she was a character in a novel. Often, she wondered what her mother and sister would think about Jim. And Brad. Would he care?

Nora and Jim developed routines on those weekends. Saturday dinners at restaurants in his neighborhood or carry-out at his apartment. Sunday afternoon parties with his friends to watch football games and the Super Bowl. It was so different from the life she and Brad led where their routines revolved around the children and dinners mainly with Ann and Nick. She became more and more comfortable with his friends at the parties. One of them took a picture of her and Jim one day when they got soaked coming from the car in a cold, drenching rain. Nora was shivering and Jim had his arms around her; they were laughing as she leaned against his body. He had the photo printed and framed and set it on a shelf in his apartment.

Some nights she brought dinner—a lasagna or other casserole she made at home. As if she were recreating a part of her life that had vanished, she even brought candles and place mats for the table. One night, as she leaned over the table to light the candles, she turned to see Jim watching her with an amused smile.

She smiled. "Are you making fun of me?"

He shook his head. "Do you do this at home? Light candles and all?"

"I used to. I like the soft glow. I still light a small one at dinner with the kids."

"I like it. I've never lit a candle."

One night after dinner, they sat by the fire and talked about their marriages. He told her about his wife, Lisa, a real estate agent who, when she turned thirty-five, decided she wanted kids. "I was okay with it, even though we both had decided earlier that we didn't want them. Then she couldn't get pregnant and it changed everything. They checked me but it wasn't me. It turned out we would need all kinds of expensive procedures having to do with in-vitro stuff. I was turning forty-two. I just wasn't into what it was going to take. I'd read enough stories about it taking years."

As she listened, Nora felt sorry for Lisa. She thought about Brad's vasectomy and how she had regretted it when Clare was a toddler. "That must have been so hard for her," she said.

"Yeah. It was."

Listening to his story about his wife intrigued Nora. "That's why you got divorced?"

"That, but other things too. She was happy just to stay home when she was off. She worked on the weekends and I worked all week. Our lives veered apart."

Nora said, "Then you moved here?"

He nodded. "She kept the house. Anyway, she got remarried a few years later and turns out she got pregnant right away. She has two kids now. We're friendly; we keep in touch. I told her—maybe the tests were wrong. Maybe it was me." He laughed. "Who knows?" He put his arm around her. "Okay. Tell me about you."

After Nora gave him a brief sketch of their marriage, she said, "My husband had a mid-life crisis of sorts."

He hugged her and said, "I'm glad you got divorced. His loss, my gain."

When he said divorced, Nora was about to correct him but decided it didn't matter. She had forgotten the divorce instructions that sat in a drawer in her dresser; she had meant to discuss it with Brad when the one-year separation period had passed.

Nora looked at the photograph of her and Jim. No sign of him and his wife. She wondered if there had been revolving photos of past women on that shelf. It was as if Jim took each day as it came and kept himself unencumbered from prior entanglements. It made her feel freer to keep him in a separate space.

CHAPTER 32

Through January and February, Nora kept Jim separate from the rest of her life. She made up excuses to Brad about why Jack and Clare needed to call her on her cell phone the weekends they were at his house. A few times he looked at her with raised eyebrows and a questioning expression, which made her inwardly smile.

With her normal world suspended, she sailed through things that previously annoyed her or seemed like drudgery. Too engrossed in juggling her schedule as she planned for the next time she would see Jim, she could more easily ignore the squabbles of the children. She went through her closet and picked out the clothing she used to wear that she had pushed aside and now had a reason to shop for new clothes. Ann laughed at her secrecy. At the end of February, she reminded Nora that it had been two months and she had yet to meet Jim. "It sounds like you're still married and having an affair."

Nora had thought for a minute and then laughed. "But it is an affair. I *am* still married."

"Nick and I still want to meet him," Ann said.

It was unnatural it for her to have such a big part of her life separate from Ann. But Jim was so different from Brad. She had trouble imagining the four of them together and Jim taking over the conversation and having nothing to talk about that would interest Nick. He and Brad had their topics—books, politics, sometimes sports—that occupied them during their dinners together. But after she thought about it more, Nora realized how lopsided her relationship with Jim was. Because she kept him in a separate sphere, their social time had been with his friends. Nora finally agreed to a dinner at her and Ann's regular Italian restaurant.

They met on a chilly night in the beginning of March. For the first time, Jim came to her house to pick her up. Still protective of her private space, she debated waiting out front for him, but they had been dating for two months and she had been at his apartment so often that it seemed silly of her. She brought him in and showed him around the first floor.

"Really nice, Nora."

As she was showing Jim the family room, he stopped at the picture wall in the den and stood for a minute.

Nora pointed out Jack and Clare, and he nodded. "Cute kids. Clare looks like you. Does Jack look like your ex?"

Nora nodded. "That's what people say."

Jim smiled. "Now I can picture where you live."

His comment made her uneasy, and she wasn't sure why. It was as if she crossed a barrier.

As they drove to the restaurant, Jim said, "Ann and Nick, right?"

Nora nodded. "Are you nervous about meeting them?"

"I just want to make sure I got their names right."

Part of Jim's charm was how he remembered names and used them often. They were quiet for the rest of the drive. Nora was still confused. Why did she feel uncomfortable having him in her house and seeing the family pictures? Did she feel as if it were a betrayal of Brad? It was drizzling, and the only sound was the scrape of the windshield wipers.

When they got to the restaurant, Ann and Nick were in a booth next to each other and stood through the introductions. Nora had only seen Jim on his turf with his friends, comfortable, laughing and joking. At the restaurant, she figured he would be out of his element; he was used to his where the servers and bartenders knew him. But he was normal Jim. It was she who felt uncomfortable bringing him into her realm.

"Nice restaurant," Jim said, after they sat. "Ann, Nora said you come here often."

"It's our hangout," Ann said with a smile. "Nick rarely gets to come."

Their server, Richard, used to seeing just Ann and Nora, looked surprised to see the four of them. He introduced himself and from then on Jim called him by name, just like he did with the servers at his favorite restaurant. It made her a little uncomfortable, but it was so much better than being with Andrew, who had ignored the server.

After Jim and Nick ordered a beer and Ann and Nora their usual carafe of chianti, Nora showed Jim the menu. "Ann and I get the seafood linguini."

"I'll get the same," he said.

Ann eased into her bubbly self and talked about how she and Nora met and how the kids were like brothers and sisters. Jim asked more questions and laughed with Ann. But Nora had never seen Nick so erect, his expression so tense; he was shy to begin with, and Nora was sure he missed Brad.

Nora brought up the work Jim did in construction. She told them about the wall in his apartment with framed photographs of his before and after jobs.

Jim turned to her and put an arm around her. "Thank you." He said to Ann, "I should have her do commercials."

Nora went on. "He plays soccer every weekend," she said, hoping to encourage a common interest with Nick.

Nick asked Jim about where he played soccer and then what project he was working on now. They both ordered another beer. Nora had told Jim that Nick was a lawyer, and Jim asked him questions about the law he practiced. Jim shared a funny story that had them all laughing.

Nora sipped her wine and felt herself relaxing. She caught Ann's eye and her twinkle of amusement.

"He's cute," Ann said the next day. "I can see the attraction. The two of you seem happy. I approve. Nick does too, although he was surprised that you found someone so different from Brad."

"Me too. I was thinking how inexperienced I am with dating. I don't have much to compare."

"Do you think you'll introduce him to Jack and Clare?"

"I doubt it," Nora said. She would think about the possibility, but she knew a long-term relationship wasn't realistic. Early in their relationship, she had accepted the probable impermanence of it. After Jim had told her about his wife and their divorce,

Nora didn't think he'd want permanent ties with anyone, especially a woman with children. Their lives were too dissimilar—she couldn't imagine Jim taking on the daily responsibility of a family.

Now she smiled at Ann and said, "I love the excitement, but it's like I have two lives. I just can't see combining them."

CHAPTER 33

Throughout March, Nora loved having the weekends to look forward to, loved the calls and texts between them. That's why it was such a surprise when spring came, and soccer started for Jack and Clare. Jim played on weekends as well with his friends. On some Saturdays, Nora was late getting to his apartment, or she had to rush home on Sunday to attend games. He—at first kiddingly—complained, "Do you have to go to *every* game?" And another time, "It would be nice if you could attend one of *my* games."

Although she refused to admit it to herself at first, as he became more possessive and jealous of her time with the kids, she felt claustrophobic. Now it upset him when she didn't respond right away to his emails and texts. "I texted an hour ago. What are you doing?"

Then at a party, in the middle of April, one of his friends commented in an offhand manner, "Finally, he's settling down with someone."

"Has he had a lot of girlfriends?" Nora asked.

"No one special."

That unnerved her. Nora had enjoyed the relationship without thinking of the future, sure that her photograph would eventually be replaced. The *settling down* words not only caught her off guard but made her assess their relationship and ask herself what she was doing. She didn't love him—she loved being with him, loved being wanted and desired and held. Loved having that part of her life restored after the three years of absence of touch. Loved feeling young again. Loved the freedom of having such an adventure, so different from her mundane life. She'd figured he felt the same. Although he had started to end his phone calls and texts with a breezy, "Luv you," she didn't take it as a serious commitment.

Even if she loved him, it would be impossible. His pushing for more of her time magnified the contrast between her life and his. He didn't want children or responsibilities; she had children and responsibilities.

A turning point came when she had to cancel one night because Clare had a high fever and she wanted to be home with her. He asked, "Why can't her father take care of her?" It felt callous to her; without children, he was free from those obligations and unable to understand the worry of a sick child.

One realization led to another. The weekends were with his friends and revolved around his interests. She realized she missed the depth of what she had known with Brad. Their history. The shared past. The children. What first attracted her to Jim—his big personality and charisma—now seemed superficial.

The more Jim pushed for more of her, the more uneasy she became about hiding that part of her life from Jack and Clare.

Each time she took the suitcase out of its hiding place, the unease made her dread packing, dread Jim's complaining about her skipping parts of their weekend. It was with a sense of sadness and regret when she finally accepted the truth. Jim wanted more of her while she wanted less of him.

As crocuses and daffodils budded and bloomed, her desire for Jim ebbed. She started to make excuses about not spending the night. As the passion had worn off, their relationship felt like work. Jim felt to her like another responsibility.

CHAPTER 34

It became clear to Nora that it wasn't fair to Jim to continue the relationship. Now it was just a question of when and how to summon the energy to face him and to end it. Because Jim had been pushing for them to spend more time together, Nora had earlier promised him they could spend a week together in the summer when Brad would have one of his vacation weeks. On their last night together, the night Nora was planning to tell him, they sat on his couch after dinner and he excitedly showed her pictures of a cabin in the place he wanted to rent. A calendar sat on the coffee table with the dates circled. "I'm planning to take the whole week off," he said.

Nora listened and looked at his face with a sinking feeling. She couldn't do it now and decided to wait until morning. He was kind and solicitous when she told him she wasn't feeling well and wanted to go to bed. It made her feel worse. When he got in bed that night, she was curled on her side pretending to be asleep. Once his breathing turned even, she let her tears wet the pillow. Tears for him, for her, for what had been and for what couldn't be.

After a fitful sleep, Nora woke with a stone-like weight in her chest. She stared blankly at the grey light as it edged through the slatted blinds. When Jim stirred and rolled over, she again pretended to be asleep. He got up and showered and then made coffee. When he came back with hers, he sat on her side of the bed. "Are feeling better? What do you want for breakfast?"

"I'm okay, but I'm not hungry. You go ahead." In the dull light of the bedroom, she listened to the drone of the TV in the living room and the clatter of the frying pan. The odor of bacon permeated the room and blanketed her with nausea. She felt awful; she was doing exactly what Brad had done to her, springing it on him. And yet, as she made that comparison, she realized how absurd it was. How could she even compare the two? Brad did it after eighteen years; this was merely five months. Still, it felt as if she had been pretending something she wasn't and leading him on.

After she dragged herself out of bed, she sorted through their scattered clothes and laid his on a chair. She showered, dressed, packed her shampoo and conditioner, and threw her toothbrush in the trash. She sat on the edge of the bed for a minute, wishing she could disappear. Although she had been rehearsing what she would say for the past week—not the truth, but a benign explanation about her need to spend more time with Jack and Clare—she was unsure what to expect since he had become so possessive. Would he try to stop her? She stood, steeled herself, and walked into the living room. The blinds were closed to keep the glare of the sun off the TV. She stood for a minute and saw the room as if for the first time in a while. Dim. Dark.

Jim sat in front of the TV, his eyes glued to ESPN, watching a soccer game from somewhere, his plate on his lap with a few crusts of bread and curds of eggs. When he saw her, he pointed to his plate. "You want some?"

"Just more coffee." After she went to the kitchen to pour another cup, she sat on the couch next to him and touched his shoulder. "Can we talk for a minute?"

He muted the sound on the TV and turned his attention to her. "You okay?"

She gazed at a commercial on the screen—a car careening around a cliff. "I think we need to take a break."

"A break?" He sounded confused. "You mean us?"

She nodded and faced him. She studied his face for any shift in expression, any look of anger, disappointment, or sadness, but couldn't tell.

He switched off the TV. "Why?"

Then she said, "I just think it's time. You're busy, I'm busy…"

He cleared his throat. "Did I upset you?"

She shook her head. "I'm not upset. You didn't do anything." She had tears in her eyes as she looked at his face. A baffled expression replaced his usual upbeat one.

"Then I don't understand. Why now?"

"I have the responsibility of the kids." She glanced around the room as if searching for something lost. "They're getting older, taking up more of my time on the weekends…"

They looked at each other in silence. "I wish you had told me earlier."

She looked away. "I'm sorry," she said quietly, almost to herself. She felt chilled as she listened to the humming of the air conditioner. She wiped her eyes on her sleeve and stood. "I think I should go."

She went into the bedroom and picked up her overnight bag. He followed her to the door. As she reached out to hug him, he stepped back and shook his head.

In a grey drizzle, she hurried down the sidewalk, tripped on a curb by the parking lot, and grabbed hold of a lamp post to keep from falling. At the car, red-faced, she got in and fumbled for her keys. He watched at the door as she drove off.

CHAPTER 35

Nora was disoriented initially, feeling like she'd been away for a long time. She unpacked her overnight bag and set it on a shelf in the back of her closet and pushed thoughts of Jim to a separate corner of her mind. She had wandered out of her realm and was now home again. Not having to hide, not having to pack and drive to Virginia every other weekend, her life would be easier, less complicated. But an unease at the note they ended on nagged at her. She wished it had gone differently, wished she had handled it differently. She should have raised it earlier when she realized that a long-term relationship wasn't going to work for her.

A few days later, she was flipping hamburgers for dinner when Jim called. "Can we talk? Can you meet me for dinner?"

She turned the flame of the burner off. "No, I have the kids."

"Maybe this weekend?"

"No, I don't think so," she said, thrown off balance and trying to think of how to respond.

In an unfamiliar pleading tone, he said, "Just give me a chance. Tell me what I've done wrong."

Jack and Clare were in the family room playing a video game She went outside and took a deep breath. "Jim, I told you. You did nothing wrong. I'm sorry. I have too much going on with work and the kids."

"I'd love to meet your kids and get to know them. I can be involved, play soccer with them, make your life easier."

"You never wanted kids."

"This is different. I'm ready. Really," he said, almost as if to convince himself.

Just then, Jack came outside. "Mom, I'm hungry."

She gestured to him to go back in. "Jim, I have to go. I'm cooking dinner."

"Think about it."

She wanted to be kind but definite. "It's not going to work for me," she said and added, "I'm sorry," before she hung up.

She *was* sorry. Reminded of her reaction when Brad blindsided her—her denial and efforts to discover what she had done wrong—she felt empathy for Jim. She remembered when she would drive by Brad's apartment and stare at his windows during the early time after he left her.

Throughout that week, his texts and emails came every few days. Nora ignored them, hoping that would discourage him. His messages were benign: *How are you doing…I hope you change your mind…I miss you…*

One morning, Jim called as she was getting dressed for school. "I was cleaning yesterday and found a pair of your earrings on the dresser."

In her hurry to leave that last morning, she hadn't put them on. "That's okay. You can throw them away."

"No, they're nice. They look like sterling silver."

"Really, it's okay. I have other ones. Donate them to a thrift store."

"No. Let's meet for dinner. Just a friendly dinner. We're still friends, right?"

She could tell he wasn't going to let it go. "We can meet at the coffee shop down the street from your apartment. I'll have a few minutes before I have to pick up the kids."

"When?"

"Today." She needed to get it over with.

That afternoon, she rushed from school to get there on time. He was in a booth sipping coffee. Instead of his usual T-shirt and shorts, he wore a celery green oxford shirt and khaki pants as if dressed up for an important meeting. On the middle of the table sat her earrings in a small zip-lock bag along with a box wrapped with silver paper and a lavender ribbon.

He stood and reached out to hug her, but she backed away and slid into the seat across from him.

He sat and faced her. "What would you like?"

"Nothing, thanks. I don't have time. I'll sit for a minute."

He pushed the box across the table. "This is a necklace to go with your earrings."

She felt like crying. "Jim," she said, "I can't accept that."

He smiled and pushed the box closer to her. "It's just a gift. A reminder that we had something good. Didn't we?"

The sadness in his eyes was something she had never seen. She felt terrible. "We did, and I'm sorry but I don't need a present."

She stood and picked up the earrings. "Thanks for bringing them. I have to get home."

"Take it, please." He held up the box. "A remembrance of our time together."

"If you promise to move on," she said. "Agree it's over."

"Okay. But if you change your mind…"

As she drove home, she let the tears flow. There were things she would miss about him. His sense of humor, his friends, and the warmth of being touched and wanted.

That night, she opened the box. The necklace was beautiful, a flat woven delicate silver. She put the box in the back of her drawer with the earrings.

CHAPTER 36

In the next few weeks, Nora felt heavy with fatigue and nausea. Probably a mild virus or the stress of breaking off the relationship. She got a substitute teacher for her class one day and slept, then forced herself back for the last week of school, still tired and queasy. The days were lengthening. With the lingering light, Jack and Clare were up later than usual. Each night she longed for bed. She had wondered if it would be hard to get used to the weekends when Jack and Clare were at Brad's and she was alone, but she was so tired that she slept much of the time.

In her classroom on the last day of school, she opened the windows to a cool breeze. As each year ended, she experienced both anticipation for the summer break and the nostalgia of knowing she would miss the children she had grown so fond of. Flowers, cards, and gift bags covered her desk. The children were gathered in a circle on the rug, angles of sunlight touching the faces and expressions she had memorized over the year. She smiled, thinking of seeing them in the fall, watching them as they matured and edged forward.

After she read a book about a bear navigating the seasons—saying goodbye to one and welcoming the next—she pointed to the calendar on the wall. "Tomorrow is June twenty-first. What season will that be?"

She smiled as they yelled, "Summer!" She paused. Something nibbled in the back of her mind as she thought of the seasons. Winter and spring with Jim. Summer already. When the children were in the cafeteria for lunch, she sat at her desk and opened her calendar. When was her last period? She had no idea. With a dawning sense of unease, she pictured the full box of tampons under her sink.

That night, the small plastic bag from CVS sat on her bed where she had flung it when she got home from work. Nora opened the bag and held the box in her sweaty hands. She shut and locked the bedroom door and hoped Clare and Jack would play in the yard. The smell and taste of the hamburgers they'd had for dinner nauseated her. During the meal she'd been irritable, impatient for it to be over, tired as Jack taunted Clare until he caused her to break into tears. She sat on the bed. It was still light. The evening sun poured into the room. Birds chirped. From across the street, a dog barked.

With sweaty hands, she opened the test kit and read the directions three times, then carried it into the bathroom. She dipped the test strip into the cup of urine, then watched as the color emerged. *Pink.* After she re-checked the instructions to make sure, she sank to the floor. "Stupid, stupid. What have I done?" Cold fear intermingled with the nausea. How could she be pregnant? She remembered only once that Jim had forgotten to use a condom. One night. But she hadn't worried, sure that at almost forty-three, her fertility had diminished. When was that? She vaguely remembered the windows in the room being open but that could have been any time from March on. She stood at the mirror sideways to look for a bulge; she'd had a slight one ever since Clare was born and now couldn't tell if it was larger. Her breasts were also sore—another sign ignored. What surprised her most was how oblivious she had been of her body, how she hadn't paid attention. She thought about Jim's wife who couldn't get pregnant. And for Nora, one lousy time without a condom. Carrying the test strip, she went to the bedroom and sunk onto the bed. Just then, the phone rang.

"Hi," Brad said. "Okay if I pick up Jack early for his soccer game on Saturday? We want to have time to practice."

His voice added an extra dimension to her dread, her wish that she had never met Jim, that she could erase the past five months. "Okay. Great."

She threw the test and results in the plastic bag, knotted it and carried it down to the trash. In the kitchen, Jack and Clare had cleared the dishes, loaded the dishwasher, and were in the backyard playing badminton. As she watched them, she was filled with dread at what she faced.

CHAPTER 37

In bed that night, she decided she would have an abortion. Soon. She didn't know how far along she was. No one would know about Jim. Her life would return to normal. When she woke the next morning, she put her hands on her abdomen. A baby who could be four, six, eight weeks old. Sorrow filled her. What if she did have the baby?

No. She couldn't expose her affair for all to see. How could she have Jim's baby? But why couldn't she? He would never have to know. But in another hour, she was googling Planned Parenthood clinics. She wrote the number on an index card and stuck it in the drawer of her nightstand.

She didn't sleep much that night. Tuesday morning, she was blanketed with nausea and fatigue and the feeling of being utterly alone. After pulling out the clinic number and staring at it for a few minutes, she scheduled an appointment for an abortion on Friday.

But then at breakfast as Jack and Clare ate, she studied them and as she imagined what the baby might look like, it reminded her of the longing she'd had for another child. When Clare was six months old, Brad had raised the possibility of a vasectomy and she agreed, so exhausted that his reasons made sense: she hated the side effects of birth control pills; they had planned to stop at two. But she hadn't anticipated the pangs that would come after Clare had passed the baby and toddler stage. How feelings of loss would rise in her as she gazed at mothers and babies. Was it because Jack and Clare had gotten older and didn't run to her with delight the minute they saw her? Because she was no longer the center of their universe? Once, when she was in her mid-thirties, she had asked Brad, "Do you ever feel sorry that we won't have another child?"

Brad had a puzzled expression. "It's so much easier now that they're older. Can you imagine starting over?" Of course, she could. She hadn't tried to explain. Hadn't brought it up again. She wondered what would have happened if she and Brad had had more children. Would they still be together?

She decided to make an appointment with her doctor for a pregnancy test to be sure; she got appointments for the test that afternoon and on Thursday for the results. Since it was the first day of summer vacation, she called Ann to arrange alternate play dates for the week.

On the afternoon of her appointment to get the results, Nora sat between two pregnant women in the only available chair in the crowded waiting room. She shivered in the harsh glare of the fluorescent lights and the chill of the air conditioning. As she pulled her sweater around her, she glanced at the young woman next to her and noticed her wedding band. Nora rubbed her fingers over her ringless left hand. She was relieved when she was ushered to an examining room to wait for the doctor.

She paced the small examining room. At the mirror, she stared at her reflection. She looked pale and tired. Perhaps, the doctor might say, "Oh Nora, you're almost forty-three. It would be too dangerous." And that would make her decision. She forced herself back to her chair and told herself to calm down.

When her doctor came in, he smiled and shook her hand. He'd been her gynecologist since she was pregnant with Jack. From the beginning, he had said, "Just call me Jeffrey." With his gentle demeanor and observant blue eyes, he had always reminded her of a country doctor. Now about sixty, his hair had turned white, and he wore wire-rimmed glasses.

He sat across from her on a stool. "How are you, Nora? Still teaching?"

"I am. Almost twenty years now."

"And the kids? How are they?"

"Good. Getting big. Clare's eight and Jack's twelve." She tried to keep her voice steady, willing the pleasantries to be over.

"It's hard to believe they've gotten that old."

She nodded, quiet, waiting, working to keep her hands steady.

He held up a piece of paper. "Our test confirmed it. You *are* pregnant. Does Brad know?"

Nora wondered if he had forgotten about Brad's vasectomy. "It's not Brad's." She pulled a tissue from her pocket and dabbed at the perspiration on her upper lip. "We separated about two years ago." *Please don't ask whose it is.*

He nodded, glanced at her chart, and then slid his glasses down and looked over them. "When was your last period?"

More embarrassed, she said, "I don't know. Maybe in

April…" That was the best she could come up with after studying the calendar countless times.

"Oh." He was quiet for a minute and seemed to count with his fingers. "Okay." He was silent as he paged through her chart.

He closed the chart. His eyes were soft and kind. "There are some increased risks, so I'll need to monitor you, watch you for any early signs of complications. At your age, there can be an increase in genetic problems but there are tests we can do. First, we'll schedule a sonogram—find out how far along you are."

He gave her the papers to give to the receptionist to make the sonogram appointment as if there were no need for further discussion about options.

CHAPTER 38

The night after her doctor's appointment, when Jack and Clare were asleep, Nora sat in bed with a cup of chamomile tea as rain pounded against the windows from a summer storm. She held the two appointment cards in her hand. One for the sonogram and one for an abortion.

The sensible thing would be to have an abortion and cancel the other appointment. No one would have to know. Her life would remain uncomplicated. She set the two cards by the phone. She found herself struck again with an overwhelming feeling of loneliness. She turned off the lights and crawled into bed. Her dreams were full of clutter and chaos.

In the morning, Nora wandered to the backyard and turned a chair to face the sun. The air smelled new. Last night's storm had cleared the heaviness, replacing it with a soft summer breeze. As she sat there, she pictured a sandbox next to the swing set they'd had for ten years. A sprinkler and plastic pool for the summers. Would she feel regret over what could have been? Then she pictured Jim—his nose, eyes, mouth, and smile—and imagined what the baby might look like.

Ann was coming for dinner that night after Brad picked up Jack and Clare for their Wednesday night with him. Nora needed Ann to be her weather vane as she discussed her options. When Ann arrived, Nora led her into the kitchen where she had opened a bottle of Chardonnay. She poured a glass of wine for Ann and ice water for herself. After they sat across from each other at the kitchen table, Ann asked why she wasn't having wine. It gave Nora an easy way to share her news.

Ann was wide-eyed. "So that's why you've been feeling sick." Then she looked closely at Nora. "So... Wow. I'm assuming it's Jim's?"

Nora nodded.

Ann paused, quiet as if waiting for the news to digest. Her usual bubbly demeanor was reduced to a pensive thoughtfulness. After she took a sip of her wine, she scraped off a glob of oatmeal stuck to the table from breakfast. She looked at Nora. "How did it happen? I mean I know, but wow."

"Stop saying wow." Nora looked at the little pile of oatmeal Ann had made and got a sponge to wipe it up. She met Ann's eyes. "One stupid night."

Then Ann began to interrogate. How did she find out, when did she find out, when did she have her last period?

Nora was embarrassed to tell her she had lost track of her periods. Ann tapped her fingernails on the counter and murmured, "You're still nauseated. Probably still in the first three months."

Nora put her hands over Ann's. "Can you stop that please?" This was the first time that Ann's tapping grated.

"Stop what?"

"The damned tapping."

Ann said, "Sorry. It helps me think."

Nora's mouth was dry, and she gulped some water. "I have an appointment for an abortion."

Ann's eyes widened. "When?"

"Wednesday."

"You already decided?"

"I have an appointment for a sonogram too."

"A sonogram?" She looked confused.

"I can't make up my mind." Nora held her hands over her abdomen. "It's like a part of me now, and I can't imagine what I'll feel afterward if I have the abortion. And yet having it will be an enormous challenge. Plus, I'd be close to sixty when the baby's a teenager."

For a few minutes, they sat in silence. The sun had sunk enough that the kitchen was dim. Nora walked around pulling down shades and lighting lamps. She cast a sidelong gaze at Ann's face. She half-expected Ann to say, *Nora, you can't have the baby. It's crazy. Jim's baby? Think of Brad and the children. You'll ruin your life. Think of your age.*

Finally, Ann spoke. "It sounds to me like you've made the decision."

Ann always got to the heart of things. Nora sat down and faced Ann. "I don't think I can go through with the abortion."

Ann nodded and sipped her wine for a minute. It was unusual for her to be this quiet. Nora felt a sense of relief with having decided.

"What will you do about Jim?" Ann said.

Nora winced at the thought. What would she do? "Nothing

right now. I need some time to get used to it myself. Maybe I won't even tell him."

"He doesn't have any weird medical problems?"

"Not that I know of. He's healthy. His parents are still alive. He's never mentioned anything."

"What if he finds out and wants to be involved?"

"I honestly don't think he would. He's never wanted kids."

Nora wanted Ann to stop asking questions about Jim. She got up and put out the bowl of chicken salad she'd made earlier, tossed a salad, and opened a box of croissants and set them in a basket. They were quiet again for a few minutes.

Ann cut open a croissant and filled it with chicken salad. "Well, you've wanted a baby for years."

Nora smiled. "Yeah, but not this way." When Clare and Maddie were three, she had asked Ann, "Do you ever think about having another child?" Ann had replied, "No more for me. I'm done." Nora had marveled at her surety.

"Does your doctor have any idea of your due date?"

Nora shook her head. "Not until I get the sonogram."

"Have you told anyone else?"

"God, no. I can't imagine telling Brad." Nora tried to joke. "Hey Brad, I'm pregnant. I'm not seeing the guy anymore, but I'm having his baby."

Ann laughed. "Well, he doesn't get a say. He'll just have to accept it."

Nora said, "I can't think about him right now."

"I'll help you get through this." Ann reached over and hugged Nora. "I can be your doula."

"Yes. You can come to childbirth classes," Nora said. "That would serve you right for forcing me to go to the divorce group."

CHAPTER 39

By July, Nora's tests and sonograms had remained normal; she was due in the middle of January. Once the first three months had passed, Nora knew it was time to face the challenges. She would tell Brad first. Then her mother and sister. Last, Jack and Clare.

On the morning she had arranged to tell Brad, Nora woke to the sound of a siren blaring in the distance. A heavy feeling of dread had been with her since she called him a few days before. The bedroom was dim in the early morning light and the house was quiet; Jack and Clare were at a sleepover at Eddie and Maddie's. The sheets on her side of the king-sized bed were in a wrinkled ball. During the night, she had been hot and restless with dueling dreams of Jim and Brad.

As she lay in bed, she replayed her awkward conversation with Brad. "Would you have time on Sunday morning to come for coffee? Around ten?"

"Coffee? Sure."

"Jack and Clare will be at a sleepover with Eddie and Maddie."

He sounded concerned. "Is everything okay? Is there a problem?"

Right then, she had felt the leaden weight of her decision. What was it? A problem? A predicament? "Just something I need to talk to you about," was what she had answered. It would have been easier if he hadn't become friendlier, if the distance between them hadn't narrowed. If he hadn't been hinting at having dinner for the past few weeks. She felt a sense of sorrow at the loss.

The top of the sun became visible over the houses and trees and lightened the sky. The leaden weight grew as she wondered what she would say. All the words she had practiced disappeared. Should she come out with it right away? Lead up to it? She remembered Ann's words of advice: "You decided, Nora. There's no way to sugarcoat it. And remember, he's the one who left you."

She showered and dressed and checked her image. Her face looked pale and tired, gaunt even. She put on lipstick, blush and mascara and pulled her thick curly hair into a ponytail. After Brad had left, she usually wore it loose, free. Today she wanted to look neat, put together, sane, responsible.

She wandered downstairs, pulled open blinds and curtains and walked from room to room picking up books, games, and newspapers. It was cool for the beginning of July and she opened windows. At ten, when the doorbell rang, she jumped. Right on time. Brad looked good—tanned, his hair longer, the way she loved it, and ruffled from the breeze—and was wearing a blue oxford shirt and khakis, as if it were an occasion of some sort. As if *he* needed to dress up.

After she brought a mug of coffee, they sat and faced each other in chairs in the family room.

"So, what's happening?" He looked at her. Closely. Expectantly.

In the last moment before she told him, she hesitated. It was like she was about to step across a line, close a door. "I have to tell you something…" She imagined Ann's voice in her ear. *For God's sake Nora, just do it.*

He sat up. "Are you okay?"

His look of concern made her want to cry. "I had a relationship with someone for about five months."

His eyes widened a bit, but he didn't speak. His expression was quizzical, surprised, perhaps alarmed.

She quickly added, "But we're not dating anymore." Why did she say that? Was she trying not to hurt him? Protect his feelings? She sounded as inept as she felt.

Brad waited and watched her. Maybe glad to hear she was no longer dating; he didn't look as alarmed.

"So, here's the thing…" *Say it, just say it.* She took a deep breath and said in a low voice, "I'm pregnant."

"What?" Brad stiffened and sat up in his chair. He glanced down at her abdomen. "Did you say pregnant?"

She nodded. His glance filled her with embarrassment.

"Jesus, Nora." He put his mug on the coffee table and looked at her with a bewildered expression. "I don't know what to say."

She remembered their excitement and happiness when they had learned she was first expecting. How Brad had been fully involved, had taken pictures of her every week through the nine months to chronicle the changes and had insisted on accompanying her to doctor's appointments.

Now her voice was shaky as she pushed herself to finish. "I'm going to have the baby."

They looked at each other for a minute. Both trapped for an instant after she shared her news and he tried to absorb it. Then he looked down at his hands, his expression camouflaged. In disappointment, sadness, or anger, she couldn't tell. She swallowed an urge to apologize.

He stood and walked to the French doors and stared at the yard for a minute. "The lawn looks good."

"Yes, they mulched a few weeks ago," she said to the back of his head, grateful for the interlude, relieved that she had said the words, had gotten through that much. The house was silent. The only noise came from the hum of the refrigerator and the breeze blowing against the blinds in the kitchen. Clouds moved back and forth over the sun causing the room to brighten one minute and darken the next.

He faced her, his expression serious and intent. "What are you planning to do about Jack and Clare?"

What was she planning to do? Nothing really, other than share her news with them and deal with their reactions. She had decided to wait to tell them until the fatigue and nausea passed and until she was ready for it to be public—she couldn't ask them to keep it a secret. But she knew that she would put it off for as long as possible, imagining the shame she would feel at telling Jack and seeing his embarrassment. At twelve, he was entering the worst time to hear that his mother was pregnant. An unwed mother. Clare, on the other hand, would be delighted to have a brother or sister.

Nora threaded her fingers through her hair. The clip that held it in place fell out. "I'm planning to wait a few weeks to tell them."

"That's not what I meant." He walked back to his chair and sat. "Do you understand how hard it will be for them?"

It reminded her of how he would point out her lack of logic as if it were something she had overlooked. She wondered if he would start tapping his knuckles on the table. "I know it'll be hard. For everyone. I'm sorry." Her apology had popped out as if it were an involuntary tic.

"You don't need to apologize to me. It's them I'm worried about."

"Do you think *I'm* not worried about them?" She felt a wave of nausea and craned her head to see the clock on the stove. Twenty after ten. She wanted this to be over.

"It's none of my business…" He paused and looked at the wall of pictures. Still full of ones of him and the children. "The guy you were dating. He's the father?"

"Yes." Her face reddened. She stopped herself from saying he was the only one she had been with. "And it's not your business."

He held his hands up. "I'm sorry. I didn't mean that." He rubbed his hands over his face, through his hair. "I'm just trying to understand."

It looked like his eyes had filled with tears but from across the room, she couldn't tell.

"What does your mom think? And Becky?"

"I haven't told them yet." While no prude, her mother would question Nora's judgment, would worry about how she would manage. With Becky, she had no idea. Since her separation from Brad, they were on easier terms, yet Becky's critical edge remained;

she would probably think Nora was crazy.

"Have you thought it through?" He looked at her, kindly now, and spoke in a soft tone. "It's not just about you, Nora. Others will be affected." It was like he was still trying to discover the strand of logic that would make her come to her senses. Trying to reason with her like she was a wayward child. "It'll be hard for Jack and Clare to understand."

Angry now, she said, "Please don't talk down to me." She took a deep breath. "I've thought about it. I decided. There are different ways to look at it. Clare and Jack are resilient. Life is messy."

He stood. "It doesn't have to be."

She wondered if he was suggesting an abortion and she put her hands over the baby within her to protect it from Brad's negativity. "You're right. But I'm choosing it."

"Okay. Okay," he said, his voice flat and resigned. "Let me know when you plan to tell them."

After the front door closed, Nora sat and stared outside at the orange and yellow buds on the daylilies about to burst into bloom. Although shaken and sapped of her energy, she was relieved. So relieved. She patted her abdomen and whispered, "Okay. We got that done. We did it."

CHAPTER 40

In the weeks after telling Brad, her relationship with him had
become strained. He no longer got out of the car for pick-ups
and drop-offs, and she remained in the house. She experienced a mixture of feelings: thankful that he knew but shame and
embarrassment at his response.

Toward the end of July, it had been over a month since
Jim called. Nora still thought about him—how could she not?
Every day was a reminder. The whole affair felt surreal, as if
she had veered off the rails of her life for an escapade and
now was in the midst of another adventure. Her nausea and
fatigue had passed, and she had energy and felt excited about
the baby. Still she wrestled with when to tell Jim, wanting to
wait until there was enough of a distance, until she was sure he
had moved on.

Nora spent lazy days at the pool with Ann and the kids,
enjoying the interlude before she would have to share the news
next with her mother and sister. She planned to tell Jack and Clare

later, two weeks before school started. That way she'd have time to help them adjust before school started.

Nora tried to imagine how each of them would react. Clare still played with her American Girl dolls, and she would probably be excited to have a real baby. She had no concept of sex. When her friend's mother had a baby, Clare asked why they couldn't have one, as if it would magically happen by deciding or wishing. But Jack, at twelve, would know. She and Brad had been open with him, had gone through the awkward talks, and last year, discussed the curriculum for his health class on sexuality: heavy on abstinence as the best option, and the importance of protection. The irony was not lost on her.

By the start of August, she was over three months pregnant. One day she stood in front of the mirror after her shower, looked at her reflection, and wondered if there was a slight bulge. *Too early*, she thought, but she had gained weight and needed to buy larger pants and tops that were loose-fitting. Time to tell her mother and Becky.

On a weekend when Jack and Clare were with Brad, Nora drove the familiar trip from Maryland to the small town in Pennsylvania, skirting Baltimore and York on the major interstates, then on four-lane roads through rolling farmland dotted with new developments, and finally to the two-lane road leading to the house where her mother still lived.

As she drove, the impact of what she was about to do hit her full force. She hadn't even told them she was dating. To distract herself, she put on an audiotape of a Sue Grafton mystery but couldn't follow the plot or the characters. After switching to a classical music station, she tried yoga breathing but remained twitchy and nervous. Even though she was certain of her decision and no longer wobbled back and forth, she dreaded going home to report her affair and its consequences.

It was four o'clock when she arrived at the split-level home—three bedrooms and two baths—which had seemed huge when Nora was ten. Inside, her mother embraced her and said how happy she was to see her. Becky gave her a quick hug. "I only have an hour before I have to pick up the kids."

"But they're all coming back for dinner," her mother said with a pleased smile.

As she carried her suitcase upstairs to her old bedroom, Nora reminded herself to ask Becky not to tell her children until she told Jack and Clare. Now she wondered whether it was a bad idea to tell her mother and sister first.

In her room, except for her bookcase, now filled with her mother's books, nothing was changed. The ballerina wallpaper and the blue carpeting. Her dresser and desk. To be in this room, in this situation was like being a teenager again, but a teenager in trouble, a teenager who had done something reckless. She heard her mother and sister downstairs, their voices too low to hear the words.

Nora stood at the window and stared out at what used to be a vast expanse of farmland and cornfield and was now a development of cookie-cutter houses, all split-levels. The maple tree she had watched grow from a spindly sapling was still there, giving shade to the front yard. Across the street, a mother pushed a toddler on a swing. Nora pictured a husband waiting in the house, the table set for dinner. Children in the yards across the street ran and played in a sprinkler in the late afternoon. A normal Saturday.

Becky yelled up the stairs, "Nora, we haven't got all day."

In the kitchen, her mother and Becky sat on one side of the rectangular table and she took a seat facing them and the wall behind them. Her mother was letting her hair go grey and sitting next to Becky with her bright blond hair and tanned face, she looked pale. She would be turning seventy in the fall and had left her job as a librarian in June.

"How's retirement, Mom?" Nora asked.

"I love it. I sleep late and have lots of time to read."

Nora smiled. "I saw your books in the bedroom."

"I'm running out of room."

Nora wanted to stay in that innocent conversation and talk about novels. But her mother got up to check on the dinner and Becky sat engrossed with her cell phone. Texting or emailing, Nora wasn't sure which. At the oven, her mother pulled out a large casserole dish with a pot roast, a dinner Nora and Becky had loved as children. But it was a heavy meal she had grown to dislike and which she couldn't imagine eating on this summer day.

The meal evoked memories of her childhood. Nora pictured the platter. It would have potatoes, onions, and carrots piled around the sliced meat. And for a moment, she visualized the room as it had been. Although her mother had remodeled it after her father died, making it light and airy with bright white cabinets and quartz countertops, then it had been dark. Remembering the brown Formica table in the room of walnut cupboards and the harsh fluorescent lights could still depress her if she dwelt on them.

Glasses of iced tea and a plate of cookies sat on the table.

Nora glanced at the cookies—Oreos—she hated Oreos. Had her mother forgotten? Becky was the one who loved them. Being home, even for a few minutes, evoked unattractive petty thoughts—wanting to be the favorite, wanting to be cherished, wanting her mother to remember that she loved vanilla crème cookies. *How silly,* she thought, yet when her mother passed her the plate of Oreos, the realization that, yes, she had forgotten caused tears to spill over. *I can't believe I'm crying over cookies,* she thought, picking up a napkin and wiping her face.

Her mother looked alarmed and put a hand over Nora's. "What's wrong, honey?"

"I'm just tired from the drive."

Becky turned off her cell phone and looked at Nora for a few seconds, then said, "Are you okay? You wanted to tell us something?"

Becky had asked her why it couldn't wait a few weeks until the family vacation and Nora figured she was still annoyed about that. "I don't know where to begin," Nora said. "No, don't look like that, Mom, no one's sick, Jack and Clare are fine." Nora took a deep breath. It was like she was making a pitch, selling something. "I met a guy, and we dated for about five months."

Before she could add that they no longer were together, Nora's mother smiled and nodded. "I'm glad you met someone."

Becky said, "Five months? And you never mentioned him?"

With no window to look out, no escape for her eyes, Nora focused on Becky's dangling earrings. Dolphins? She couldn't tell. "No. I didn't tell anyone. Except Ann. I didn't want to tell Jack and Clare, didn't want to complicate their lives again. They're settled, happy." She added, "We're not seeing each other anymore."

"Why are you telling us now?" A twinge of Becky's hard edge emerged. Perhaps hurt or irritated that Nora had told Ann and not her. Over the years, Nora detected what she assumed was jealousy at the closeness she and Ann had. What she and Becky once had as kids. It was the tone she used in comments like, "So, how's your friend Ann?"

"Becky, let Nora tell us."

Nora took a deep breath before she took the plunge. "So, this is the hard and embarrassing part."

Becky eyed her. Her mother wore a worried expression, the pained look she wore of empathy whenever one of them had been hurt.

Nora wiped her sweaty palms on her napkin. "I'm pregnant."

"What?" Becky's eyes widened.

Her mother's face turned paler and she put a hand over her mouth so quickly that it seemed an involuntary response. Becky put a protective arm around their mother. The kitchen window faced west, and the sun slanted on Becky's face like a spotlight. Her hazel eyes seemed to change colors depending on the light and now flashed a greenish hue. In a tone of shock and disbelief, she said, "Wait a minute. You're pregnant and not seeing the guy anymore?"

Nora looked away from their shocked faces and stared at the condensation that had formed under her glass of tea. "We didn't have much in common. We broke up a few months ago—"

Becky asked, "Because of the pregnancy?"

"No. Before I knew." She needed to get it over with. "I'm almost four months. I'm keeping the baby."

They stared at her, wide-eyed. The room was silent. Nora's

throat was dry, and she took a sip of her iced tea, lukewarm and weakened from the melted ice. The house felt suffocating. The open windows gave no relief as the late afternoon sun poured in and the oven heated the room. Her blouse stuck to her chest.

Then her mother looked down at her hands and whispered, "Jesus, Mary and Joseph."

Wounding her mother caused a raw ache inside of her. "Mom, I'm sorry." Nora covered her mother's hands with hers. "When I found out, I was shocked, couldn't believe it, but one day I woke up and I knew what I wanted to do. I know how ridiculous it sounds, and how hard it will be. But I'm happy." After she finished, she felt a sense of relief, even a hope, that they might understand and be happy for her.

Becky had straightened in her chair, picked up her iced tea, and sipped it while staring at Nora. Quiet and thoughtful for a minute.

"How are you feeling, honey?" Her mother looked at her with the same expression that Nora knew so well. Deep brown eyes that held compassion, that always seemed so wise—as if she were aware of something no one else was, as if to say, *everything will be okay.*

"I'm better now." Her mother's kindness brought tears to Nora and reminded her of how, just as she was doing now, her mother had often rescued Nora with a kind word, a glance, a touch after her father had interrogated her for some infraction.

"What about the guy?" Becky asked. "What's his name again? "Jim."

"Does he want you to keep it?"

"Becky, Nora's probably tired," her mother said. "Let's drop it."

"It's okay, Mom." She was determined to get Becky's questions over with. "He doesn't want kids. I don't think he'll be involved." Nora didn't mention that she hadn't told him. *And it's a baby, not an it,* she wanted to add.

"What about Brad?"

"I told him."

"What did he say?"

Nora had always felt that Becky still harbored sympathy for Brad. Nora tried to keep her tone even. She stared at Becky. "Obviously, he doesn't think it's a great idea."

"Boy. This will be weird for him."

Her mother sighed as she wiped cookie crumbs into her napkin.

"I suppose it will." Nora jiggled her legs and forced herself to remain in the warm kitchen with the aroma of the pot roast increasing her nausea.

"And the kids?"

"I'll tell them next week. Don't tell Rebecca and Will." Nora wiped her forehead with a napkin and stood up and walked to the sink and leaned over it toward the window to get some air. She turned from the window. "It is what it is, Becky. I've thought about all of it. It's done. I'm having the baby. Like Mom used to say, no crying over spilled milk."

Becky's expression softened, and she smiled at Nora with a glimmer of amusement. "And like Dad used to say, don't shut the barn door after the horse has bolted."

And just like that, the room lightened. They all laughed. Nora came back and sat.

Her mother relaxed and smiled. "When is the baby due?"

"The middle of January."

"Now that I'm retired, I can come and help." Her mother smiled. "Another grandchild. That'll make five."

Becky picked up a cookie and held it for a minute in midair, then put it back and gazed down at her hands. She moved her fingers as if counting, then gazed at Nora. "Do you know that when this child is seventeen, you'll be sixty?"

Her mother gave Becky a look.

"Thanks, Becky," Nora said. "I hadn't thought of that."

"I'm just saying it's like you're starting out all over. Diapers, toilet training, tantrums..."

Nora laughed. The worst was over.

"I have one more question."

"Jesus, Becky. One more. I feel like I'm going to confession."

"Did you ever love him?"

"Or was it just a sordid romance?" She smiled at Becky. "Is that what you mean?"

Becky laughed. "No. Just wondering."

Nora thought for a minute. "I loved the attention. Being with him. He was nice, fun. We'd go out when the kids were with Brad. Dinner, movies. Maybe in the beginning I thought it might turn into something different. Maybe I misjudged what I wanted." She was surprised at the tears that ran down her face.

Her mother left her chair and came to Nora's side of the table and sat next to her. She gave her a tissue and then put her arms around her and held her as she sobbed, smoothing her hair down like she used to do when Nora was a child.

CHAPTER 41

After Nora got back from Pennsylvania, it was time to tell Jack and Clare. She picked a Saturday morning. At eight o'clock, when Nora woke, the house was quiet. Pale sunlight peeked through the sides of the closed curtains. Jack and Clare were still asleep. At seven, when she first woke, it was still dim and she had turned over and gone back to sleep. During the night, she had been startled awake, panicked by some dream, the fragments of which eluded her. Her heart raced, and she sat on the side of the bed to pull in deep breaths.

All week she had been anxious as she anticipated this day. She wanted to hold on to this moment before they knew, before she would alter their landscape and set into motion a new chapter of their lives. She got up and opened the blinds, then went to the kitchen and made a cup of herbal tea. Back in bed, she propped herself against the pillows.

As Nora sipped her tea, she thought of Ann's words when Nora expressed her dread of his reaction. "Jack won't be happy.

He's mad at you anyway." Ann had laughed about the changes in Jack and Eddie: "They've gone to the dark side. They'll be back in a few years." Nora wished she shared Ann's optimism. When Jack turned twelve, when sprinklings of pimples erupted on his forehead and chin, he became private, less talkative, even curt at times. Nora had found it difficult to navigate this new stage by herself.

Brad spent his time with the kids doing fun things: restaurant dinners, movies, and the mall. He was free from the daily parenting routines—the meals, baths, laundry, chores, homework. Nora had become the enforcer of everything Jack rebelled against. His room was a mess. She had to nag him to take out the trash and help around the house. Before, with confidence, she had sailed through the various stages of childhood, but now, with Jack, she felt incapable. And lately, it had only gotten worse.

The door to Clare's room creaked open, and she padded down the hall and climbed into bed with Nora, their favorite way to begin a Saturday. It used to be Jack on one side, Clare on the other.

"Hi honey." Nora scooted over and knocked a few books and magazines to the floor.

Clare crawled under the comforter and snuggled next to her. Nora bent and kissed her on her forehead, smiled at her sleepy face framed by her curly brown hair. As she breathed in Clare's sweet smell, she closed her eyes and had started to doze when Clare sat up. "Can we make pancakes? I'm hungry."

In the kitchen, Nora pulled up the shades. Bright sunlight poured into the kitchen. A beautiful day. The sound of a lawnmower made her wish they could have a regular Saturday morning. Do something as ordinary as yard work, chores, grocery shopping. Clare climbed on a stool next to her and helped to stir the batter and pour measured amounts on to the griddle. The pancake batter puddled on the pan until each one formed its shape. The sound of the TV emerged from the family room; Jack had woken and was stretched across the couch. Nora debated. On a normal day, she would have said something. She didn't want him watching TV for hours and was trying to set limits. But this wasn't a normal day.

Ten minutes later, Nora set the pancakes, syrup and butter on the island, and glanced at Jack to gauge his mood. Unreadable. His hair was long and shaggy; the bangs partially obscured his eyes. He refused to get it cut. He grunted when she asked how he slept. A ratty T-shirt and long, baggy shorts replaced the flannel pajamas he used to wear. He looked almost like a stranger. *Who are you?* she thought. *Why now?*

After Jack grabbed half the pancakes, Clare whined, "Mom, he took too much."

Nora sighed. "It's okay. We can make more."

Jack's cell phone beeped with a text message. The phone was something she and Brad had argued about. Nora wanted to wait a year, but Brad, always trying to please these days, thought Jack should have it. She relented after Brad made a list of rules: Jack would have limited access to various sites; the phone had to be off after bedtime and at meals.

Nora put a hand on his. "Can you turn it off till we're finished?"

A look of annoyance passed over his face. "Why?"

"We're having breakfast." She went to the refrigerator and got a container of orange juice and filled two glasses. "And I need to talk to both of you."

He ignored her and scrolled through his text messages.

She leaned over and touched his hand again. "Jack."

"What?"

"I asked you to turn it off."

Clare's eyes moved back and forth between Nora and Jack.

"Fine." Jack slid the phone across the countertop and picked up his fork and stuffed a mouthful of pancakes in.

Nora looked at them in this last moment before they knew, then said, "So, I have something important I want to share with you." She stopped and took a deep breath. "I'm pregnant. I'm going to have a baby." The words sounded stilted, forced, and still so foreign. She hadn't meant to just blurt it out, had planned to explain to them about her relationship with Jim. But the thicket of words she would have to travel to get to the main point suddenly felt like miles.

Only then, did Jack look at her. "What?"

"A baby?" Clare's eyes got big. "A real one?"

Nora nodded. "A real one."

"Like Amy's mother?" Clare twirled a piece of hair as she always did when she was excited.

Nora nodded again.

"Wow!" Clare beamed. "Jack, a baby."

He ignored Clare and stared at Nora, watchful, as if trying to decipher the meaning of her words.

Suddenly, she realized it was absurd that she hadn't told them separately. She had thought about it but wasn't sure who to tell first. Not Clare who wouldn't be able to wait to blurt it out. Jack? Perhaps she was afraid of his response.

"When?" Clare asked.

"In January," Nora said, as she waited for a response from Jack who continued to stare at her.

"Not until then?" Clare asked.

"We'll have lots of time to get ready. You can help." Nora put an arm around Clare. "Honey, why don't you go and watch something on TV for a few minutes?"

"I'm not done eating."

"You can take your breakfast."

Clare hesitated, looking torn between staying and getting to eat in front of the TV, then grabbed her plate and ran to the family room.

Nora's palms were cold and clammy as she faced Jack.

He asked, "You and Dad are having a baby?" His expression had brightened a bit, perhaps at the thought of she and Brad reconciling, becoming a family again.

"No, not Dad."

Jack's eyes were fixed on hers. "What the hell?" One of his new expressions.

She spoke softly and slowly. "I dated a man, and we were close…" The euphemism sounded ridiculous. She wished she could crawl into a corner and hide. "We had a relationship."

"You had sex?" Jack's face had turned red. "With someone else?"

Nora struggled to think of an answer. To say it was about love would be a farce. She simply said, "Yes, I did." She wondered if her face was as red as Jack's.

Jack's expression held a combination of confusion and embarrassment, and she envisioned his shame at having a mother who would do such a thing. Would he try to picture her having sex? Sex with an unknown stranger? When Nora learned about sex as a teenager and tried to picture it, she thought it was disgusting and gross, and then was appalled and embarrassed that her parents had really done it. She wanted to comfort him as if he were younger, push the hair out of his eyes, say, everything will be okay, you'll go through this, you'll hate me for a while, but then it will all work out.

Then, as a new idea seemed to form, Jack's eyes got bigger. "Does Dad know?"

She nodded. "I told him."

Jack stared down at the napkin he was shredding. Then he stood and pushed his plate away. "I'm not hungry." He grabbed his phone and left the room.

The clock in the kitchen was ticking. His pancakes sat on the plate with congealed butter and pooled syrup. She knew to leave Jack alone, knew it would be useless to follow him. Unable to offer anything to soften or alleviate his confusion, or to expiate her actions, she needed to allow him his space. Her tiredness mingled with the sting of Jack's rejection but also with relief that she had done it. That part was over. Gently she placed her palms over her belly.

Clare called from the family room. "Mom." Her eyes glowed. "Will the baby live here?"

Nora went and sat next to her and smiled at her innocent exuberance. "Yes, honey."

"Where?"

"In the guest room, next to your bedroom."

"Is it a boy or a girl?"

Just then, the phone rang. It was Brad. Jack had just called and asked if he could spend the night with him. "He's really upset. Is it okay for me to come and get him?"

Nora went back into the kitchen. So now Brad and Jack were aligned in judgment of her? "I know he's upset. But I'd like to try to talk to him."

"Nora, I think you should let him be for now, let it sink in."

"We're leaving for Pennsylvania in a few days. He has to pack and get ready."

"I'll bring him home first thing tomorrow."

As she cleared the table and wiped the counters, she told herself to let it go. It was okay; he'd be back tomorrow.

Jack's heavy footsteps running down the stairs, caused glasses in a hall cabinet to rattle. He stood at the doorway from the kitchen and glanced at her as he put on his backpack. "Dad's here. I'm spending the night at his house."

Clare said, "I want to go too."

"No, not today. You can invite Maddie over."

Nora went to stand next to Jack. "I'd like to talk to you," she said.

"He's waiting. I have to go." He backed away from her and turned to leave.

Clare followed him. "I want to see Dad. Can I tell him about the baby?"

Nora said quietly, "He already knows." But Clare had already gone out the door. Nora stood at the window in the living room and watched her run to the car. Jack had gotten in and sat in the front seat staring away from the house. After Brad got out and hugged her, Clare waved her arms about excitedly. Although Nora couldn't hear her words, she could tell by Clare's expression that her voice lifted in excitement as she talked. Brad looked down at her with a tight smile and nodded.

CHAPTER 42

The day passed peacefully. Clare's thrilled response to learning she'd soon have a baby brother or sister kept her occupied with imaginary scenarios with her dolls. That night, once she got Clare to bed, Nora's thoughts returned to Jack. His reaction wasn't entirely a surprise. At his age he had entered a different sphere where she was already an annoyance, sometimes an embarrassment. Still, she hadn't anticipated the extent of his anger. She wondered how Brad was handling it with him. Were they discussing her? Jack's reddened face played out in chaotic dreams as she moved in and out of sleep.

In the morning, she woke when it was still dark, unsettled and upset from her dreams. She dragged herself out of bed thinking of all she needed to do in the two weeks before she would have to set up her classroom for the start of school. Tomorrow they were scheduled to go to Pennsylvania for their annual visit. She gathered laundry from her hamper, tiptoed past Clare's room and stopped at Jack's room and stared at the piles of clothes on the floor. Jack had begun to do his own laundry when he turned eleven. She had been nagging him all week about cleaning his room and doing his laundry so they could pack. As she stood amidst the clutter, she could see no solution, not to the mess, not to his unhappiness with her.

In the kitchen she made coffee and fixed oatmeal for Clare who had woken and come downstairs carrying one of her dolls—a baby, swaddled in a blanket. Once Clare was eating, Nora began to move through her list of tasks, not able to finish one before she thought of another, her mind disordered and chaotic. Clothes to be packed in piles on her bed; the counter in the kitchen lined with bags of pretzels and snacks along with juice boxes and wine she had bought for the trip. She stopped to take a break and sat with Clare who was at the kitchen table humming as she colored a picture to take to Pennsylvania—a drawing of herself and Jack and their two cousins in a circle under a clear blue sky, their arms in the air reaching for a Frisbee. Nora watched as Clare added a smiling sun. She let herself be calmed by the serenity and simplicity of the cheerful image.

When the phone rang, she saw it was Brad. "Hi. What time are you bringing Jack home?"

"I need to talk to you. Is this a good time?"

She felt an uneasy jolt. Talk about what? "Just a minute." She moved upstairs. "Okay. Go ahead."

"Jack's having a rough time with this."

As if she weren't aware. As if she didn't feel guilty enough. "I know."

"He doesn't want to go on the trip."

"What?" It took a minute for his words to connect, for

the meaning to sink in. "What are you talking about? We're leaving tomorrow."

"I tried to talk to him. He's definite."

"I don't care if he's definite. He can't make that decision."

"Nora, he's confused." He cleared his throat. "He's embarrassed."

She thought Brad was probably pleased at Jack's reaction, embarrassed along with him by her and her illicit behavior. His tone was measured and calm as if he were trying to be a go-between. She tried to picture him and wished he had done this in person, so she could study his face. Had he decided it might be easier on the phone? She paced the hall, furious, trying to decide how to respond, trying to keep her tone as measured as his. "He'll have to deal with it at some point."

"He needs time."

She went into Jack's room, glanced at the floor scattered with clothes, shoes, and books, the bed unmade, dirty dishes on the desk, and shut the door so Clare couldn't hear her. "You do realize he was already angry and unhappy before this."

"That's beside the point."

"I don't think so." She picked up a plate, sticky with peanut butter. "It's something we need to address."

"Right now, this is what we're dealing with."

Yes, she thought. *This. Me.* She was getting more annoyed and now didn't care how loud her voice was. "Letting him decide won't help anything. And there are other people involved. Becky bought tickets for Will and Jack to go rock climbing."

He said something she missed—his voice had lowered, and she wondered if Jack was listening—and she had to ask him to repeat it.

"What I said was, if you try to force him, he'll be miserable. It'll be miserable for everyone."

"I'd like to speak to him."

"He won't want to."

She tried to calm herself. "Can you put him on?"

"He's in the shower." Brad made an exasperated noise. One of his loud sighs, so familiar when he used to get impatient with her, when she wasn't agreeing with his logic. "Listen. He won't change his mind. You can't force him to go."

He's a child. We're the parents, she thought. But Brad wasn't going to budge in his support of Jack's decision. A weariness settled over her. Brad had become softer, more indulgent with the children after he moved out and had less time with them. Nora had always been the one to give in, to worry about their feelings; Brad had an easier time saying no and sticking to it and he would sometimes smile and say, "You're too soft. Wait until they're teenagers. You'll have to toughen up." Just when she needed him to be tough with Jack, to set limits, they had switched roles.

She slammed down the phone and sat on the bed, feeling queasy and boxed in. If she tried to fight the two of them, she might make Jack angrier.

After pushing a pile of clothes aside, she stretched out on the bed and tried to calm herself with deep breaths. When that didn't work, she called Ann and after she vented for a few minutes, she invited her and Maddie over. "Help, I need a break from myself."

"Give me fifteen minutes," Ann said.

Soon Ann and Maddie arrived, and they all went out front, so Clare and Maddie could ride their matching purple scooters on the sidewalk. Ann and Nora sat in rocking chairs and were quiet for a few minutes, watching the girls zoom to one end of the block and back to the other, smiling and waving each time they passed the house. It had been a stretch of sunny days, no clouds, warm but not stifling for the middle of August. Sunlight filtered through the tall oaks and elms that lined the street.

Ann said, "We still have a few easy years with these two."

Nora nodded. "Yeah. You should have seen Clare trying to get Jack excited about the baby."

Ann looked at her. "How are you doing?"

"I'm just worn out. Jack's response was worse than I expected. He was horrified." She unclasped her hair from its barrette and ran her fingers through it. "I didn't do it right. I couldn't figure out how to say it."

"But I think he'd react the same no matter what you said."

"Probably."

Ann reached over and patted her hand. "You did it."

Nora nodded. "I'm so glad to have it over with." She turned her chair to face Ann. "At first I felt guilty and embarrassed when Brad called and said Jack wanted to spend the night with him. But then I was relieved to have a break from his anger for the night and to give Clare a chance to be happy about the baby. Hopefully give him a chance to get used to it. I didn't envision this."

Ann's eyes followed the girls, and she waved when they passed by. She said quietly, as if not sure how Nora might take it, "It might be good he's not going on the trip."

"Yeah, but it might make it worse. Jack was so difficult already, and Brad didn't see it. Now Jack will think he can do whatever the hell he wants. I can't imagine what will happen when I get back. Suppose he wants to live with Brad?"

Ann rocked the chair back and forth and was quiet. Then she turned to Nora. "Remember Laura?"

Nora nodded. Laura was a friend who had divorced, remarried, and moved from Boston to their neighborhood with her new husband. Several years ago, when her eldest daughter was fourteen, she'd become belligerent. "Impossible to live with," Laura had said. When her daughter decided she hated her mother and wanted to move back to Boston with her father, Laura gave in, and her daughter moved and lived with him for two years. Now at sixteen, she'd returned home, and she and her mother had regained their pre-teen closeness.

Ann said, "Remember how Laura says it was the best thing that could have happened? Her ex had to handle the anger. He became the bad guy."

Nora nodded. Laura had become visibly more relaxed once she agreed to let her daughter move.

"Hell, I wish at times that Eddie had somewhere to go," Ann said. "You know how I'm jealous of the break you get every other weekend."

She bent sideways, away from Ann, and pinched the dead blossoms from the geranium plant that sat next to her chair and piled the broken stems onto the ground. Then, as she fought back tears, she faced Ann. "Really? You want to trade places? It's no fun being the single parent most of the time."

"Are you crying? God, I'm sorry. That was a stupid thing to say." She grabbed a tissue from her pocket and handed it to Nora. "I just wish I could help."

"I know." She wiped her eyes. "It's okay. I'm a wreck. What will he be like after he's been with Brad for a week? It scares me." She pulled her fingers through her hair and re-clasped it. "Other people have affairs. One affair—I get pregnant and screw up my life."

"You're going to get away for a week. It'll give you a break. When you get back, I'll help with Jack. He and Eddie can have lots of sleepovers."

"If he wants to live with Brad, I'm not sure I'll have the energy to fight them." Already she thought of them as a unit, aligned against her.

CHAPTER 43

After Ann left, Nora called Becky to tell her that Jack wouldn't be coming; she explained that his soccer practice started early, and he needed to stay. It was halfway true—Jack had only gotten lukewarm permission from his coach to skip the first week. Although Becky was annoyed initially, by the time Nora and Clare arrived she was fine; she'd arranged for Will to invite his best friend to spend the week with them.

The week turned out to be a pleasant and peaceful hiatus. Becky had let go of her anger at Nora's decision and even seemed excited. "I had so much fun buying baby clothes again." Her mother had replaced her worry and concern with a joy that seemed genuine. She smiled and hugged Clare. "Now you'll have a new brother or sister, and I'll have five grandchildren."

Becky had scheduled activities for the children each day; Nora didn't have to think or plan. After the adrenalin of the past months, Nora gave in to her exhaustion. One day Becky took the children to the pool, and she read and slept for hours. She was aware that the week would have had a different atmosphere with Jack—he would have been uncomfortable with Clare talking constantly about the baby.

After they got home on Sunday morning, she unpacked, dropped Clare at Maddie's for a playdate, and sorted the mail while she waited for Brad to return with Jack. When the car pulled in the driveway, she opened the front door and waited. Jack mumbled, "Hello," and walked past her.

She called after him, "How was your week?"

"Fine." He headed upstairs.

When she saw Brad walk to the door, she knew. She took a deep breath.

"Can we talk?" He had a set expression.

Nora steeled herself. "Do you want to come in?"

"No, out here is fine."

Nora closed the front door and waited. Brad took off his baseball cap and stared down at his sneakers. Then he looked at her. "Jack wants to live with me."

For a minute she didn't respond. Let him wait and wonder what she would say.

Brad watched her. Then he repeated it. "He'd like to move in with me."

Ready and surprised at her calm, Nora steadied her voice. "Pennsylvania was one thing. We have a custody arrangement."

"It's not a legal one."

"We can make it a legal one. He can't decide."

"I think he's old enough to decide what he wants."

"He's twelve." She was furious at Brad and what he had done. He didn't care about what Jack wanted a few years ago when he moved out.

In an exasperated tone, he said, "We don't need to fight about this. Or make it harder."

"What are you talking about? It is hard. Suppose he decides he doesn't want to go to school, or do his homework, or whatever."

"That's far-fetched."

"I don't think so."

"I don't see what the problem is. It's not as if it's unusual for a kid to live with his father."

"It's something we need to decide together." Nora walked to the edge of the porch to gather her thoughts. It felt as if Brad were encouraging Jack to punish her. She turned to him. "You didn't give a damn about what you put him and Clare through when you left. And now you're so worried about him being upset?"

"Nora," he said with clear exasperation, "that's a ridiculous comparison. Besides, I don't know how you'll stop him. He's upstairs packing."

Worn out and depleted now, Nora wondered if Brad understood the responsibility he would entail. "If he does, you'll have to take time off, get him to soccer practice every day." She wasn't going to help him. "And school—you'll need to get him to the bus every morning. And I want him to come home for dinner once a week."

"I think I can handle it." Brad, hands stuffed into his pockets, turned his gaze away from her to somewhere across the street.

Nora looked in that direction. Lights were lit in the houses as it began to grow dark, as the days shortened. Fall was coming. Brad continued to look away. Was it the broken limb on their neighbor's Bradford pear? A tree that Brad had often said needed trimming. Or a neighbor walking a German shepherd?

Nora left Brad on the porch and slammed the door. She went upstairs to Jack's room and stood in the doorway. Jack had two large duffel bags on his bed and was picking up piles of clothes from the floor and stuffing them in. He ignored her as he emptied socks and underwear from his dresser drawers, heaping the clean on top of the dirty. With a bit of revenge, she imagined the familiar odor of his room permeating Brad's apartment. When he glanced at her, she said, "Can you stop for a minute?"

He stopped and waited with a pained expression, and she moved a few inches closer. "I didn't intend or plan what happened. But it did. I understand why you're so upset with me. I love you."

Nora thought it was the tears suddenly spilling over her cheeks that caused his expression to soften a bit—not much, but enough. Something she could hold on to. She hugged him briefly before he had a chance to push back.

After they left, Nora kept busy with the energy of her grief. She cleaned Jack's room, washed his sheets and comforter, and remade the bed. It would be ready when he came back.

CHAPTER 44

I n the next week, Nora felt numb. The sight of the dining room table littered with supplies for her classroom—posters of seasons, colors, days of the week, the alphabet—overwhelmed her.

Clare spent the first day crying and asking why Jack had to leave. It reminded Nora of when Brad left, of trying to find comforting words and facile explanations. "You'll see him a lot," Nora said. "Every Wednesday, every other weekend. Plus, he's going to come home one night for dinner every week."

Clare said, "It's not the same."

And it wasn't the same even though it was easier for Nora to not have to deal with his reaction to her pregnancy on top of his already teenage behavior. Every night, his absence at dinner was a reminder. The house had a subdued atmosphere without the teasing and the arguments as well as the sound of their laughter when Jack agreed to play with Clare, without the sound of Jack running up and down the steps. Nora would repeat to herself, "Laura's daughter came back." And she tried to fill the space by arranging play dates for Clare and Maddie and bringing Clare with her to get her classroom ready.

Because of the stress of Jack leaving, Nora didn't have much of an appetite and forced herself to make and eat healthy foods. Over the months of her pregnancy, Nora's appetite had been as erratic as her anxiety level. Some days she pushed herself to eat, other days she was starving and gave in to whatever cravings she had. Chocolate mint ice cream was the one thing she could eat no matter what level her anxiety was. Over the summer she had gained about twelve pounds and her clothes no longer fit. By the time she returned to school in September, she was wearing maternity clothes. No one questioned her; besides Emily, who was out on maternity leave, Nora only had a few friends at the school who knew superficial details of her past relationship with Jim and hadn't delved further.

After Nora had an ultrasound and learned that the baby was a girl, she decided to keep it a surprise. In October, when she was six months pregnant, her colleagues at school had a shower for her. That same month, Ann had enlisted Clare to help plan a small surprise; they invited Nora's mother and sister, who arrived laden with presents: fleece blankets, baby clothes, a teddy bear, all in generic yellows and greens, were wrapped and placed in a baby stroller. Clare was beside herself with excitement as she watched Nora's surprise.

The contagious joy of celebrating her pregnancy set the tone for Nora's week—hopeful and excited about the upcoming months, of setting up the nursery. She hired someone to paint the walls of the guest room a soft celery color and the trim a creamy yellow; she hung framed drawings of animals—a giraffe, elephant, and zebra. She and Clare packed the dresser with diapers, blankets, and baby clothes in yellow and green. Nora hid a box of outfits in pink and lavender. Nick assembled the crib. The room was ready.

The hardest part of her pregnancy was the loss of her relationship with Jack. Although they had agreed he would come one night a week for dinner, the meals turned out to be strained: Jack, polite but distant, barely spoke a word; Clare chattered and tried hard to engage him; Nora was often so fatigued by the evening that it was hard to stay at the table. When Jack began to make excuses why he couldn't come—homework or soccer practice—she let him be, bided her time for now and let the visits lapse.

But during the soccer season, she attended each of his games; she needed to be there, whether she was wanted or not, acknowledged or not, to convey an unspoken message—I'm still your mother, I love you no matter what. You'll come home someday. Your bed is ready.

Nora would pick a spot several feet from where Brad watched with other parents. Back in the spring before her pregnancy, they had stood near each other. Talked and chatted. It seemed so long ago.

Now, they stood apart and had only necessary interactions. At the start of the season, Clare wondered why they couldn't stand with Brad. Nora had said, "I can see better from here, but you can go." After that, Clare would point out where Brad was. "Dad's down there," perhaps hoping that Nora would come to her senses, and then she would run back and forth between them.

On the Saturdays Clare spent with Brad, Nora stood by herself at the soccer field and waited for Clare to see her, to come to her. *Poor Clare*, she thought. Her desire to bring everyone together, make everyone happy. She still had trouble understanding why Jack had moved in with Brad. On one level Clare had known Jack wasn't thrilled about the baby—which she wasn't able to fathom—but she didn't connect that with his leaving. As if she needed to keep her up to date, Clare would come home and tell Nora of their arguments. "Jack said I was a jerk. For no reason."

On a Saturday, soon after they had finished the nursery, Clare beamed at her. "I'm going to tell Dad about the baby's room!"

Nora looked over at Brad who stood with another father. He wore an old plaid flannel jacket she had given him for Christmas one year. She wondered if he remembered. After Clare ran to him, her arms waved about, her voice rose in excitement. Brad nodded with a tight smile on his face just as he had when Clare first told him about the baby. Another thing Nora hadn't anticipated: Clare's excitement interacting with Brad's disapproval.

She sighed and turned to the game. Her eyes followed Jack as he kicked the ball down the field. In years past, he would glance at her, catch her eye, and grin. She would smile and wave. Once, after she'd blown a kiss, Brad said, "For god's sake, Nora. It's a game. You'll embarrass him." Now, Jack didn't look her way.

Later in the season her feet were swollen, and she had to wear her sneakers unlaced. Attending the games had been easier before she started to show. Once Nora had filled her maternity clothes, there was no hiding the fact that she was pregnant and that she and Brad were not together. Often one of her former students or their parents would be at a game and would run up to see her and stand with her. Because Brad had always been more involved with the soccer team—he helped to coach some years—he had a closer relationship with the parents. Nora had always been on the periphery, but it hadn't mattered. She'd been with him.

At the last game of the season she stood self-conscious, on the fringe, like she had as a teenager. The day was cloudy and chilly; she had tears in her eyes from the wind. Her back hurt. She wanted to be home and warm. At the end of the game, when Brad and Clare congratulated Jack on the win and the goals he had scored, she moved closer. "Good game, Jack," she said.

He glanced her way and said, "Thanks."

Brad hugged Clare and then he and Jack left and walked to the parking lot. Nora stood for a minute. Lights were on in houses across from the field. Families together. Normal life. She forced a smile at Clare and took her hand as they walked to the car. When they came near a woman pushing a baby in a carriage, Clare stopped, pointed to Nora's belly, and said, "We're having one too."

The woman smiled at Clare, looked at Nora, and glanced down at her abdomen. "That's great," she said. "Soon?"

Nora smiled. "In January." In this small exchange, with no need to explain or justify, Nora felt, for a moment, like any pregnant woman.

CHAPTER 45

When the baby began to kick, Clare was thrilled, her eyes wide with wonder. "Can he feel me touch him?"

Nora smiled and said, "It could be she."

Clare switched genders. "She's awake. Can she hear me?"

Nora got out the albums Brad had created for her pregnancies with Jack and Clare—he had taken monthly pictures of Nora to chronicle their growth. He had loved to look at her body, touch her abdomen, feel the baby kick. Ann and her family were excited and supportive, but they couldn't fill that void of the intimate connection she'd had with Brad. The shared excitement of marking each stage together. Brad was so attentive, spoiling her, urging her to take naps on weekends, cooking and doing the grocery shopping when she couldn't bear the thought of food. Now she found herself weepy at odd times. Lonely. But it wasn't until one night in the end of her seventh month that fear kicked in.

That night, once Clare was in bed asleep, Nora put on her nightgown and robe and sat in the baby's room in the gliding rocker her mother and sister had given her. The new lamp she had bought had a lemon-yellow shade that gave off a warm and soothing glow. Calm and happy, she went to bed and fell into a deep sleep.

In the dark and silent bedroom, in the middle of the night, Nora woke with a start. The digital clock read 2:47. Her eyes circled the room, and she listened for a noise, for what had caused her to be so wide awake. She decided it was pressure on her bladder. After she went to the bathroom, she walked around the bedroom to try to relax. The only noise was the wind blowing the branches of the tall magnolia tree in the front yard. The neighborhood was quiet, the houses across the street dark and peaceful.

She walked to Clare's room to check on her. She slept as she always did, with her arms stretched out as though she were welcoming someone. Nora smiled. At the door to Jack's room, she felt the familiar pang of loss she'd experienced since he moved out. At his last soccer game, she had caught his mortified look when he glanced at her large and swollen body.

She went into his room, sat on the bed, picked up his pillow and held it to her face; she pictured him as he usually slept—curled up on his side with his arms wrapped around his chest. The sweaty gym smell had dissipated. As she sat in the darkness, aware of the mess she had made, she wept for Jack, for herself, even for Jim. She had removed him from the equation, as if he were a sperm donor.

Back in her bed, she closed her eyes. Restless, and uncomfortable, she rolled from one side to the other to find a comfortable spot. After a few minutes, she counted backwards from one hundred. Then she felt pressure and tightness low in her back. One of the signs? She couldn't recall what that indicated. Then another sensation, this time in the front. A contraction? She placed her hands over her abdomen to feel for the tightening she remembered that signaled the start of one. It was only the baby moving and kicking. "Everything's okay," she whispered to herself and the baby. "Go back to sleep."

When she closed her eyes, she took long slow breaths to lull herself and the baby back to sleep, but then thoughts of Jim popped up again. Thoughts of something unfinished, a thread hanging. What would she say about him in future years when questions arose? What if there were medical or psychiatric problems? A gene that could be passed on, something that could be fatal. Odd now, she thought, that she hadn't explored taking birth control pills. He had been prepared with a drawer full of condoms and she had passively let him be in charge, as if it made the affair less real if she wasn't the one to take the preventive steps. She remembered thinking that condoms would protect against other things. They hadn't discussed it.

Nora sat up and turned on her bedside lamp to close out the darkness. After she propped herself against two pillows, she picked up a notepad from her nightstand where she had jotted down names for the baby. She had written a list of the girls in her kindergarten class: Sara, Alice, Megan, Katy, Naomi, Seneca, Emma. Names she loved. She picked her favorites. Emma Stanton, Naomi Stanton, Alice Stanton. Her throat became dry as she was hit with a sudden shock. A baby with Brad's last name? Brad, who turned his gaze away from her swollen body when they saw each other? How had she not thought of that? Maybe she could change her last name from Stanton to Tobin, her maiden name. But she and the baby would have a different name than Clare and Jack. Disclaiming them in a way. Possibly angering Jack even more.

Her doubts and fears gave rise to a sense of dread. Doom even. Had she rationalized it all? Talked herself into this alternative reality? Made some huge mistake, an error that would be disastrous?

She turned off the light and, in the darkness, trying to quiet her mind, she recited anxious pleas. *Breathe. Let it go. Help. Help.*

CHAPTER 46

Later she would think of that sleepless night as a portent—
as if her preoccupation with Jim during the night had
somehow caused the serendipitous meeting.

A few days later, on a Sunday when Brad had the children,
she and Ann took the subway downtown to an exhibit at the
National Gallery of Art. Nora and Ann stood at a painting by
Mary Cassatt titled *Mother and Child* when she heard Jim's familiar voice behind her. She turned and they stared at each other for
a minute.

"Nora, hello. What a surprise." He glanced down at Nora's
pregnant body.

Nora froze. She could feel her face turn red and she instinc-
tively smoothed her maternity blouse.

Jim put his arm around a young woman next to him, pretty,
with long blond hair. "This is Megan."

"Hi, nice to meet you," Nora said and then touched Ann on
her shoulder to get her attention. "Jim, do you remember Ann?"

Ann turned from the painting and her eyes widened. "Jim, hi. How are you?"

"Good," he said. "It's nice to see you again."

At that point Megan was looking from Nora to Ann as if she were trying to figure out the connection.

Jim took Megan's hand and said, "Well, we better get going."

Nora and Ann wandered around the museum for a while longer, solitary as they moved from one exhibit to another. Nora was rattled by Jim seeing her at this point in her pregnancy when she was huge and ungainly.

Once they were seated on the subway to go home, Nora said, "God. I can't believe that happened."

"I guess he found someone," Ann said. "He looks happy. But she looks like she could be his daughter." Then she looked at Nora. "Are you okay? Was it weird seeing him with her?"

"No. I'm glad. But now he knows I'm pregnant. I should have told him. What if he asks if it's his?"

"It could be anyone's baby."

"He can count. What if he wants to share custody?"

"Nora, you said he never wanted kids—relax."

"That's easy for you to say."

Ann grew serious again. She put an arm around Nora's shoulder. "Nora, I'm sorry. I know it was a shock."

It was a shock. Jim had emerged from the compartment she had put him in. In bed that night, Nora's worries rotated through a stream of scenarios. What if she told him it was his and he wanted to be involved? But the thought of navigating birthdays and holidays and balancing custody arrangements with him and with Brad was unfathomable. She could ignore the situation and not do anything. But what if he called and asked? She could lie. Tell him it wasn't his. That she was seeing someone else at the same time. She could say she and Brad had gotten back together. But the child might do a search to find her father when she became an adult. Too many lies would catch up with her.

During the night she slept fitfully and woke when it was still dark, knowing she needed to tell him. When she called him the next morning and asked if she could see him, he was friendly. Told her he'd been glad to see her and sure, he'd love to get a chance to talk.

CHAPTER 47

On a sunny and frigid November Sunday when Clare was at Brad's, she drove the familiar route, her palms sweaty and her throat dry. Would he question how she got pregnant from that one time? How improbable was that? Would he be upset that she was keeping the baby?

When she arrived, she sat in her car for a minute and stared at the door, remembering the day she left and how he had stood at the door watching. She rang the bell, and he opened the door right away.

He smiled—a polite and awkward smile, and, like they were meeting for the first time, said, "Come in. Can I take your coat?"

He looked the same. Handsome, rugged, in a T-shirt and jeans. She remembered the attraction, the initial thrill that felt so distant now. She asked to use the bathroom, both from need and from curiosity, hoping that Megan and her toothbrush had taken up residence. Nora glanced in the bedroom on her way to the bathroom. The bed was neatly made; no clothes were strewn about. A second toothbrush, a second set of towels in the same spot hers had been. Relieved, she went back. Jim sat on the only chair, leaving her to sit on the couch where they shared their first kiss.

"Do you want coffee?"

"I'd love water."

"Ice?"

"No. Thanks."

While he was in the kitchen, she looked around the room for signs of anything new. Was there anything left of her? The place mats and napkins and the candles she brought were still on the table. Nothing seemed different. Familiar and yet not, as if she'd been away for years instead of months. Sunlight glinted off the television bringing memories of the lonely Sundays when his attention was turned to the screen. The room had a startling stillness, waiting for what was to come next.

When he returned, he sat in the chair across from her.

Nora said, "It was nice to meet Megan."

"She's a great gal. So…" He paused to sip his coffee and then said, "How are you?"

"Well, as you can see, I'm pregnant. I thought I should let you know." After she said it, she thought it absurd that she sounded so formal. She left unspoken that it was his.

He nodded and leaned forward, his elbows resting on his knees. He didn't say anything for a minute. Alarmed? She wasn't sure.

"When are you due?"

"In January. A few more months."

He looked down at his hands as if counting the months on his fingers.

"Seven months," she said.

He stared at her for a minute. "I'm surprised. I thought we were careful."

She nodded. "We were. It was that one night." In case he thought she had gotten pregnant by someone else, she added, "I wasn't with anyone else."

"I didn't mean that." His expression softened. "I'm sorry. I—"

"You don't need to be." She wanted to get this part over with—to free them. "I just thought it was the right thing to let you know. I don't want child support. I'm assuming you're fine with not being involved?"

He looked apologetic. "Not at this point in my life…" He shrugged. "I'm close to fifty."

She felt almost giddy with relief. "I know. It was my decision to have the baby."

"Listen, I can help financially."

"No. No." She didn't want any involvement. "Just one thing," she said. "Your medical history. Is there anything I need to know?"

"I don't think so." He thought for a minute. "No cancer or anything like that. My mother has diabetes, but it's under control. My father's overweight. He might have high blood pressure. But that's all."

For a minute, they were quiet. She was relaxed enough now to concentrate on his face. The father of her child. To memorize the size of his nose, the way he smiled, his brown eyes, his ears, imagining what features the baby might have.

He looked at her, thoughtful, perhaps worried. "What will you say if he asks?" he said. "About his father?"

"She. It's a girl." His questions brought a feeling of tenderness toward him and a wistful sadness. "What would you like me to say?"

He shook his head. "I don't know. I was just wondering."

"I'll say that it was someone…" She found herself tearing up. "I'll say her father is a nice, kind man."

He smiled, and it looked to her that his eyes had filled.

Nora felt free to ask, "Are you worried she might try to find you when she's an adult?"

He sipped his coffee and was quiet for a minute. "No. If she wants to look me up…" He smiled. "If I'm still around."

An idea crossed her mind. "The necklace you gave me. It's beautiful. If it's okay with you, I'd like to give it to her when she turns sixteen."

"I'd like that," he said.

At that point, the baby kicked, and Nora wished she could say, "Do you want to feel how hard she kicks? I think she'll be a soccer player."

After they talked for a few minutes, inconsequential things— he had started to play soccer on weekends, his business was doing well—there seemed to be nothing more to say.

After she stood to leave, she stopped at the bookcase, surprised to see that he had kept the photo of her leaning against him with his arms around her. No picture of Megan yet.

"Do you remember that day?" he said. "How hard it was raining, and we were dripping wet?"

"I do." She smiled at him. "I remember."

At the door, they looked at each other. They hugged, and he held her for a minute. "Call me if you need anything."

CHAPTER 48

In the beginning of December, when she was eight months pregnant, Nora signed up for a one-day childbirth class at the hospital where she would deliver. In the class thirteen years ago when she was pregnant with Jack, when she met Ann and they bonded over their impatience with the endless questions of a few women, she was flanked by Brad on one side and Ann on the other. This time, she sat between sets of couples and listened to chatter of the women around her. Nine women and their partners, eager with notebooks and pens. Young and bubbly. Smiling eyes, smiling faces. As she studied them, she figured she was the oldest. Certainly one of the largest. Several looked like they had gained minimal weight with bellies the size of a soccer ball, unlike the basketball that she carried. She had given in to her cravings for peanut butter cups and chocolate mint ice cream and weighed more already than she had by the end of her other pregnancies.

As she waited for class to start, she questioned her decision to spend a precious Saturday stuck in a classroom. An overhead fluorescent bulb blinked rapidly, nervously, annoyingly. She caught a vaguely familiar woman staring at her and gave her a half smile. Someone in the neighborhood who knew she and Brad had separated? She tried to figure out where she had seen her.

The loud thump of the instructor's bag when she arrived and dropped it on the table caused Nora to jump. The woman gave a brief nod and surveyed the room and introduced herself—her name was Judith—and shared her credentials: years as a labor and delivery nurse followed by becoming accredited as an instructor. She looked to be in her fifties; her face plain and sturdy, her voice slow and deliberate, but louder than needed in the small room.

Her gaze flickered around the circle. "Let's introduce ourselves. Your name, your due date, and whether this is your first baby."

The sharing revealed that it was the first pregnancy for the other women. She felt singled out, old, alien for being alone. After Nora had said, "This is my third," Judith smiled at her. "You can help me. Share your experience. Will you have a partner?"

"I have a friend who'll be with me," she said to reassure Judith and the women in the circle whose eyes were fixed on her. She hadn't told Ann about the class. No need for two of them to give up their Saturday.

Nora was relieved when Judith launched into a PowerPoint presentation with descriptions of early labor, false labor, Braxton-Hicks contractions, what to watch for, how to recognize the onset of true labor. Since she wouldn't have Brad to help her decide, she was especially attuned to the part about when to call the doctor: persistent low back pain, contractions at regular intervals that become longer and stronger, breakage of the amniotic sac resulting in a trickle or a gush of fluid.

Margaret Farrell Kirby

After Judith finished, it was time for a bathroom break. Nora stood in line and listened to the women talking, sounding more nervous now than earlier. A few women asked her questions about her experience. Had she had an epidural? She said, "Yes, for both. I'm a chicken with pain." How long was her labor? Twenty hours with Jack, but she didn't tell them that. "I can't remember a lot of details, but afterward the main thing you remember is the absolute joy."

Once they were back in the classroom, the chatter continued. Judith clapped her hands. "You'll have time at lunch to talk. We have lots to cover. Now we'll discuss the role of your partners."

Nora remembered how Brad had listened to each instruction and was so intent on doing it right—he timed contractions, rubbed her back, breathed with her. She remembered finally saying, "Please, don't talk; don't touch me." She didn't want a coach, didn't want any attention during the contractions; in between she wanted to rest; she wanted his presence—not his voice or his back rubs.

As Judith talked, the coaches took notes. "In the days and weeks before your baby's due date, make sure both you and your partner make a list of what you need. Don't forget a camera or video camera. Feel free to personalize the room. You can bring aromatherapy balls, or scented oils, lotion for back and foot massages. Her favorite music, a yoga ball..."

It sounded like planning a trip to a spa. Nora remembered the searing pain—nothing else mattered. The purple yoga ball Brad had brought sat in the corner of the room. No way would she move from the bed or do anything to bring on another contraction. Nora imagined all of them going home to their secure lives, packing suitcases with lotions, aromatherapy, CD players....

The large white and black wall clock seemed to stall. Another hour to sit in this chair. The woman on her right kept jiggling charms on her bracelet as she took notes—as irritating as the blinking fluorescent light. As she doodled on her legal pad, Nora shifted in her seat, arched her back to relieve the tight ache in her hip, and wiggled her swollen feet. Finally, at noon, Judith said, "Time for lunch. There's a cafeteria on the second floor. We can pull tables together and get to know each other. This afternoon we can practice breathing exercises. We'll do some role-playing." She looked at Nora. "We'll pick someone to be your partner. You can show us techniques that helped you the most."

Nora wanted to say, "Forget it. Forget all the props. You'll go through hell no matter what, and then it'll be over. And it will be wonderful."

CHAPTER 49

On January 15, the last day of school before Nora would start maternity leave, the room mothers organized an afternoon party—the children had decorated cookies and cut out snowflakes and snowmen—and they told her to sit. "You don't need to do a thing." She felt touched by their kindness. All day she had experienced strange sensations as if the baby couldn't settle and was squirming to get comfortable. It felt good to rest and let the children come to her with their contagious excitement and their offerings of cookies and snowflakes. In a lovely surprise, the room mothers presented her with a soft yellow blanket, and a stuffed teddy bear along with notes to the baby the children had written. At the end of the party, Nora said, "This means a lot. I'll miss you and I'll send pictures of the baby. We'll come and visit." She stood at the door and hugged each child. "I'll be back in April."

By the time school ended, she had begun to feel cramping and pressure in her lower back. Maybe this was the start. *Early but not too early*, she thought as she drove home. She had weekly visits now and at the last one, Jeffrey had said, "The baby's in position. It could be soon."

If she were to go into labor now, it would be okay. She was ready to have the baby, to be able to wear shoes, to not worry about her blood pressure. The only problem was that Ann, her "doula," was leaving for the weekend to visit her parents in New Jersey. "Do you want me to stay?" she had asked when Nora talked to her.

"No. I'm sure it's false labor. I'm not due for weeks."

"I'll be back Sunday," Ann said. "Call me if anything happens and I'll get in the car and be home in five hours. Nick's home if there's a problem."

Later, Nora wished she had said to Ann, "I feel like it's starting. Don't go."

That night, Clare was at Brad's. Nora wished she had someone with her as the feeling of pressure persisted. She kept herself busy making up a bed in the guest room for her mother who would be with her for the first few weeks after the birth. After she laid out towels, vacuumed the room and cleaned the bathroom, she packed her suitcase and set it by the front door.

She went to bed early and slept but was woken at five with a strong contraction. In ten minutes, another. By six when the light filtered into the room, they were getting stronger, eight minutes apart. Should she wait to call the doctor? To call Nick? She needed Ann to sit with her and help her decide when it was time; she needed someone.

After she showered and dressed, she sat with her Timex watch on her lap. When the contractions were seven minutes apart and stronger, she called the doctor.

"It sounds like the real thing," Jeffrey said. "Has your water broken?"

"Not yet."

"We'll take care of it at the hospital. I'll see you soon."

She called Nick, re-checked the contents of her suitcase, got several towels to sit on in his car, and waited. It was a sunny morning. Hopefully, this would be the birthdate. January 16th.

At eight, when Nick pulled in the driveway, he left the car running and rushed to the door looking nervous and disheveled, his shirt buttoned wrong. He looked odd wearing glasses; he hadn't taken the time to put in his contact lenses. By then, the contractions were more frequent, and she was worrying they might not make it to the hospital. Nick drove slowly, as if she might have the baby in the car if he moved too quickly. His anxiety added to hers. On the fifteen-minute drive, he eyed her frequently. Nora glanced at his worried face, at his knuckles tight on the steering wheel.

"I called Ann. She's getting ready to leave," he said. "She should be home by one or two."

"I'll be okay. I hate for her to have to come home."

"I'd never be able to stop her. You know that." As he drove, he tried to make small talk. "What a beautiful day. Look at that sky."

Nora didn't want to look anywhere. She kept her hand over her abdomen, hoping to slow the contractions. *Drive faster, please,* she thought. Brad had gone through yellow lights as he sped her to the hospital for each birth. When they arrived at the entrance, Nick exhaled, jumped out, walked her inside, and handed her over to the receptionist. He turned to Nora. "I'll park and be back." Before she could tell him she was fine and to go home, he had left.

A hospital volunteer got her a wheelchair, took her to her room on the fourth floor. Once in bed, in her hospital gown—decorated with pink and blue elephants and giraffes—Nora watched as the nurse hooked up monitors that would display and time her contractions, and measure her blood pressure and the baby's heartbeat. Robin. Kind blue eyes, strawberry blond hair, and freckles, probably in her forties. Calm, efficient, and confident. Nora sighed, relieved, safe. Sun poured in through the tops of the trees and made the room less institutional, almost cheerful.

She and Robin looked at the monitor together. Six minutes apart. Robin smiled. "All set. Your doctor will be here soon." At the door, she turned back. "Is there someone in the waiting room you'd like me to get?"

"No, thanks." Then she remembered Nick. "Yes. There's a man who may be there. His name is Nick." She felt she needed to explain and added, "A friend."

After a few minutes he came to the doorway, looking unsure of what to do next.

"Thanks, Nick. You can go." She smiled. "I really appreciate it."

He stepped from one foot to the other as if he couldn't remain still. "I hate to leave you alone."

"Everything's fine. Clare's at Brad's for the weekend. I called my mother. She's coming today. And Ann will be here." She held a hand up as she took a deep breath through a contraction and then smiled. "I'll be busy. Nothing you can do. I'll call." She blew him a kiss.

She didn't want the worry of Nick sitting by her bed, watching her, making small talk, trying to comfort her.

A few minutes later, her cell phone rang, Ann's voice bright and clear. "Perfect timing, Nora. Daytime and a Saturday. I'm in the car, on the way."

"You don't have to. I'm tucked in my bed and I have a nice nurse. I'll be fine." And at that point, she was.

"No way. I'm coming. I'll be there this afternoon."

"Poor Nick. He was so nervous."

"He's gone home to get a shower, then he'll be back."

Another contraction. "I have to go. I'll call."

As soon as she hung up, Jeffrey arrived. After he examined her, he said, "You're doing well, Nora. Your blood pressure's okay. You're about five centimeters dilated. I'll break the sac and then we can do an epidural."

"I want to try without it." She figured her labor would be quicker with the third child. With Clare, she had trouble pushing at the end because of the epidural. She would be brave and withstand the pain.

"Okay. But after I do this, the contractions will get stronger. Let us know if you change your mind."

She felt in control. And at first, she was. Scared, yes. Serenely scared, she thought. Able to breathe her way through each contraction. Robin was in and out to check on her, to monitor her heartbeat, the baby's, her blood pressure. Bringing ice chips. Cold washcloths.

One time, as she left the room, Robin asked, "Do you want me to see if your friend is still in the waiting room?"

"Yes. If he's there could you tell him I'm doing fine? His wife will be here later." Nora thought she caught a look of concern on her face, or perhaps a look of pity, and she wondered how many women gave birth alone.

A new stage of labor caught her by surprise, shattering her calm resolve. The contractions grew stronger and closer, four minutes apart, lasting more than a minute. Nora had forgotten the excruciating pain and dug her nails into her palm and bit on a washcloth as they reached their peak. She remembered Brad's face, pale and stricken with fear as he tried to hide his worry. Now, as the pain engulfed her, so did fear. Dark thoughts crept in. What if she died and left Jack and Clare motherless? She wished she had held Clare close for a minute before Brad picked her up—rather than the quick hug she gave her and the hurried I love you. The last time Jack let her hold him was before she mortified him with her pregnancy. Brad didn't even know she was in labor, wouldn't know if there was an emergency.

Between the contractions, she tried to focus on an object. Anything. She was getting hot and as she stared out the window, a large rectangle of glass, she wished she could open it a crack. When had hospitals become so closed, so suffocating, trapping the stale air inside with the odor of illness?

Robin came in and wiped Nora's sweaty forehead and the edges of her face where her hair was wet and matted in clumps. "Can you try to take deep breaths, Nora? It'll help."

As she lay there, her mind traveled back to her previous labors, both merged into a blur, but with Brad sitting next to her bed. A quiet and comforting presence after she had pleaded for him to stop the coaching crap. She imagined him in the chair now, pretending that he was there.

At eleven o'clock, Jeffrey examined her. She had been there close to three hours. "You're moving along. Dilating nicely."

Nicely. Such a word when everything felt wrong. Not nice.

She would be punished. She visualized her monitor's alarm ringing and a voice over the intercom: "Code Blue: Delivery Room." Now she longed for Ann to be with her—to talk her down, to say, "Nora, for God's sake you're having a baby, not a heart attack," or something that would pull her out of the pit she had sunk into. Why hadn't she agreed to an epidural? Had she felt a need to punish herself? She pushed the call button.

"I changed my mind," Nora said. "I want an epidural." She couldn't remember ever being so frightened, ever being in so much pain. So cold, she was shaking uncontrollably. Tears ran down her face. She looked up to see Jeffrey in his scrubs, watching her, watching the monitors. "I'm afraid I'm going to die. If something bad happens, will you call Brad?"

He put a hand on hers. "You're doing fine, Nora. The baby's fine." He pulled another blanket out of a cabinet and covered her. "The anesthesiologist is on the way. First, I need to examine you."

When he finished, he looked at her. "Nora, it's time. The baby's ready. Robin, let's set her up." He patted her arm. "Hold on. We're almost there."

Everything moved quickly after that. Another nurse in the room. A blur. The insistent voices: push, push, harder, bear down, bear down. The final push. The ripping apart. Then the release. Her body soaked with the effort. The moment before the cry. Her baby girl cradled on her chest. Euphoria. She was alive. The baby was alive.

In her daze, she heard Jeffrey's voice. "It happened so fast. I couldn't prevent the tear. I have to put in a few stitches."

While he did, a nurse took the baby from her to wash, measure, and assess her. A few minutes later, she came back and announced, "Seven pounds, eleven ounces. Twenty-one inches. A tall one."

Nora couldn't stop the shaking or the tears.

After he had finished the repair, Jeffrey looked at her with concern. "You're both fine, Nora. You did good." He gave her a tissue, stood, and got another blanket. "The shaking will stop. It's normal."

After she wiped her face and blew her nose, she smiled at him. "I'm fine. Crying because I'm happy." She looked up at him. "Thank you for not laughing at me during my neurotic breakdown."

"Thank you for not dying." He smiled. "Jeez, Nora."

"I was terrified."

"Luckily, it was a quick labor," he said. "Imagine if it lasted though the long dark night."

CHAPTER 50

fter she had washed and put on a fresh gown, Nora held her daughter in her lap and examined her nose, mouth, ears, and chin. Touched the dark fuzz on her head. Whispered, "You're here. We did it." Her blue eyes opened and closed with an unfocused look. To Nora's relief, nothing stood out, although she wasn't sure what she was looking for at this point. Jim's nose or his chin? Tall. She would probably be tall.

As she stared at her, memories of Brad popped up. The two of them marking the birth of Jack. Sharing their tears and joy. She needed to let him know, let the kids know, but the thought of telling Brad the news was too much.

Later, Ann and Nick arrived with a vase of pink Peruvian lilies. Amid hugs and tears, they took turns holding the baby. They made plans: Ann would meet Nora's mother at the house with a key, help her unload her suitcases, and bring her back; Nick would call Brad, tell him the news, and arrange for Ann to pick up Jack and Clare and bring them to meet the baby.

Nick went out to the corridor to call Brad. When he came back, Nora asked, "What did he say?"

Nick looked at her blankly and shrugged. "He'll tell the kids and have them get ready."

"You told him it's a girl?"

He nodded. "He asked how you were doing. I told him you were fine."

That's what she wanted to know. It mattered that Brad asked about her. It mattered that Ann would bring Jack to see the baby.

After Ann and Nick left, Nora thought about Jack and wondered how he would respond to seeing the baby. She hadn't seen him since Christmas when he had come to open his presents and have dinner. She was big and uncomfortable and too close to her delivery date to travel to Pennsylvania as they had the past two years. Clare had set the tone with her enthusiasm to have him home. While Nora fixed dinner, Jack and Clare played one of the video games she had given him. She made the dinner they had always had as a family on Christmas—a roast fillet, twice-baked potatoes, and creamed spinach. She lit candles. They drank sparkling apple cider. He didn't talk much to her but wasn't as sullen as she had expected; he even helped to clear the table and load the dishwasher, organizing it just the way Brad had. After dinner, Clare insisted that Jack come upstairs to see the nursery. Nora had wondered if he had gone into his room.

While Nora waited for Ann to bring the children, she and the baby slept on and off in between her attempts to breastfeed. In late afternoon, as she moved the baby from one breast to the other, a movement at the door caused Nora to look up to see her mother with Ann, Clare, and Jack. After the hugs and embraces—Jack allowed Nora to hug him briefly—Clare climbed in bed next to her. Nora placed the baby in her lap, and they all watched as Clare studied her face. "Lily. She looks like a Lily." She looked up at Nora. "Can that be her name?"

"It's a beautiful name." Nora glanced around. "What do you all think?"

"I love it, Clare," her mother said. "It's beautiful."

Ann bent down to examine the baby. "You're right. A perfect name."

Jack stood in a corner of the room. Nora glanced at him. "Jack?"

"It's fine."

"Lily it is," Nora said. "And Tobin for her middle name." She looked at her mother. "For Nana."

"Lily Tobin." Her mother had tears in her eyes. "I'm honored."

"Jack, would you like to hold her?" Nora asked.

He shook his head and went to the cushioned window seat that lined the long window—a bed for a partner to spend the night—flopped down and pulled out his cell phone.

Her mother said, "Jack, you've become a teenager since I last saw you."

When his face flushed—any singling out embarrassed him— her mother smiled at him and said, "You have no idea how moody your mother was."

Nora stared at Jack's sullen face, his long hair hanging over his eyes as if to further shield him. When he glanced at her, she smiled; he returned a half smile. A bit of a bond, Nora thought. She sighed inwardly for him, ached for him. For his embarrassment, confusion, for whatever roiled inside of him.

"Clare, can I hold Lily?" her mother asked, and then gathered her and carried her to the window seat and sat next to Jack. She whispered something to him. He shrugged and let her put the baby in his lap and help arrange his arms around her head. Nora couldn't see his expression as he looked down at Lily. Ann took a picture of them. After a few minutes, Clare insisted it was her turn again.

Ann held up her camera. "Move closer together, everyone." They sat in a row on the seat: Clare cooing at Lily, her mother smiling at the camera, and Jack looking down at his cell phone. Ann said, "Jack, put the phone down and look up."

Nora sipped a cup of tea, watching as Ann snapped the photos. The scene felt blurred, but pleasantly so. A tableau, as if from a distance. With another child to inhabit their photographs.

Ann stopped. "Now, we need you in the photo, Nora. Okay, guys, gather around the bed." She took Lily from Clare and brought her to Nora. Her mother sat in a chair next to her, Jack stood on the opposite side and Clare got into bed with her. Ann looked at them. "Not enough light," she said. The sun no longer streamed in; the view from the window was of a darkening sky. Ann went around and switched on lights, bringing a sharper focus to the room. "Okay everyone, smile. Jack, that means you."

When Ann finished and put her camera down, Clare looked at Lily. "Is my daddy her daddy?"

Shit. The room became silent. Tense. Nora's stomach knotted. When Clare was seven, the mother of a girl in her class was pregnant and it was all she could talk about. "She has a baby inside of her, Mom!" she'd said, and Nora had replied, "Yes, Clare.

Babies grow in a place inside their mother called the uterus." She'd said: "The sperm from the man and the egg from a woman come together. That's how your daddy and I had you and Jack."

"An egg?" Clare laughed. "Like the kind we eat?"

Nora had laughed with her, then showed her the pictures of the egg and the sperm, the woman and the man, and tried to explain. Clare glanced at the page, but it became clear she'd lost interest in the book and the discussion. She didn't seem to wonder about how the sperm got inside the woman. "Can we have one?" was all she asked. Again, and again. The various explanations, such as "parents must decide how many children they could take care of," hadn't mollified her. A year later, when Nora had become pregnant, Clare was thrilled. And Nora had broached the subject again. "Remember how we talked about how babies are made?"

Clare nodded.

"Do you remember how a baby gets in?"

"The egg and the sperm meet each other. But how will it get out?"

When Nora said that when the baby finished growing, he or she would leave the uterus through the birth canal and come out through the vagina, Clare's eyes had widened. "How big will it be? Will it hurt?"

Clare was excited about the getting out part, not the getting in. Nora had let it drop. Easier to let her remain comfortable in the sphere of her innocence. And easier for Nora.

Now, with no idea of how to answer her question about the daddy, Nora said, "No honey, he's not."

"Where is the daddy?"

Jack murmured, "Jesus Christ."

Her mother's eyes widened, and she cleared her throat.

Nora's mind was working in different directions. First, she said, "Jack, watch your language." Then, "Clare, he's…he's away." Away. What a ridiculous answer. She cast a brief glance at her mother's widened eyes and Jack's reddened face and then at Ann, who looked down at the floor.

"On a trip?" Clare's mouth was half open as she gazed upward—her thinking expression. "Will she have to live with him sometimes?"

"Idiot," Jack said.

"I'm not an idiot." Clare cried and wiped her tears on her sleeve. "You are."

He stood. "Can we leave? I have homework."

Embarrassed at her inept answer and the impossibility of providing a plausible one, Nora said, "Clare, I need to get something from the bathroom. Come with me." She turned to her mother. "Mom, would you take Lily?"

In the bathroom she shut the door, closed the toilet seat and gathered Clare on her lap.

"It's okay, honey. I'm glad you asked. Lily's father is a nice man, but he won't be involved with her like your daddy is with you."

"Why?" Clare had buried her face in Nora's shoulder.

"It will be different. Sometimes that's how it is with families. Not all the same. But she'll have all of us." Nora waited a minute and wondered what else to tell her.

Clare moved back and smiled at Nora. "Okay," she said. "Can I hold her again?"

"You go back," Nora said. "I'll be out in a minute."

Nora had to pee and was sore from the stitches. By now, her euphoria had ebbed. Worn out and chastened by the reality of what she faced, she was gripped by fear and the realization that she had done something that would alter their lives forever.

When she finished and opened the door, Ann was waiting; she came inside and closed the door behind her. "Clare cracks me up," she said. "You can almost see what goes through her mind. And Jack. I can only imagine..." She stopped and looked at her. "Oh, Nora. I'm sorry. I didn't mean to joke about it. It'll be okay."

"God, I don't know how I can do this."

"You're tired. It's all new. Clare will be fine. Jack, he's at that jerky age."

"But still. I wonder if he'd be as miserable if I hadn't gotten pregnant."

"He'd find something else. Eddie was pissed off yesterday because we ran out of orange juice. I wanted to smack him."

Ann was right. Jack had been jerky before she had gotten pregnant. Nora hugged her. "I love you. Thank you for today." But it had been too much. All she wanted now was to have all of them leave so she could give her attention to Lily. "I need to nurse her. I'd rather be alone, without embarrassing Jack even more."

When they came into the room, Jack was at one end of the window seat, hunched over his phone and Clare and her mother at the other. Lily was in Clare's lap. Ann said, "Hey guys, we have to leave and let your mom rest." Ann turned to Nora's mother. "You need to get unpacked, get some rest yourself."

After her mother brought Lily to Nora, Clare climbed into bed and lay next to them. "I don't want to go."

"We'll go to my house and order a pizza," Ann said. "I'll bring you back tomorrow."

When Clare didn't move, her mother took her hand. "C'mon, honey. We'll have some hot chocolate with the pizza."

Nora hugged Clare. "I love you and I'll see you tomorrow. We'll be coming home. You can show Lily her room."

They gathered at the door and Nora blew kisses and waved. Jack had already gone out in the hall and was out of sight. Her mother came back and sat on the edge of the bed. "I talked to Ann. Clare's spending the night there. I'm coming back and sleeping with you."

"Oh, Mom. You don't have to. You won't get any sleep," Nora said, then burst into tears. Yes, she wanted her mother to stay.

Her mother picked up Lily and placed her in the bassinet, then held out her arms to Nora. Nora sobbed on her shoulder.

"You'll be fine. Clare and Jack will be fine. It'll all work out." Her mother cupped Nora's chin in her hand. "She's beautiful. She looks just like you."

PART THREE

And the day came when the risk to remain tight in a bud was more painful than the risk it took to blossom.

— *Anaïs Nin*

CHAPTER 51

Nora would think of those winter weeks of January and February as a distinct period, an interlude in her life. The days after Lily's birth unfolded in the blur a newborn baby brings. Nursing every two hours, changing diapers, rocking, snatching sleep in between. Intense, exhausting, and exhilarating all at once.

For the first two weeks, her mother was there to help with Clare and with meals, and most important to Nora, to be another adult presence. When she left and Nora had to face being alone, she found she missed Brad. Missed having him with her during the long nights of intermittent wakefulness. Missed him when Lily had a rash on her cheeks or a sniffle, a cry that was a little different. They had worried about those things together.

After Clare got on the school bus in the morning, Nora and Lily were cocooned in the house for the day. Afraid to venture out with a fragile newborn in the cold, gray, and often icy days, Nora arranged for a grocery delivery service. At times she found herself both bored—with a vague lack of purpose to her days—and blearily sleep deprived. Fatigue accumulated, and she lost track of the days. Often when Lily napped, she went back to bed with her Kindle or a newspaper and fell asleep reading. She looked forward to Clare's arrival home from school and her bubbly presence. Clare loved to help with Lily, to run upstairs for another diaper or a clean burp cloth, and she learned how to hold and rock her, talking to her in soothing tones when she cried. "It'll be all right," she would whisper. As the weeks passed, Lily slept for longer periods; her eyes focused, and she started to smile. Nora's life became easier as her body recovered, and she felt more confident.

Jack's absence still felt like a missing piece. She touched base with Brad each week to check in, to see how he was. Brad gave short noncommittal answers—fine, nothing new; when Nora asked to speak to Jack, he often was "not available" according to Brad. Other times when she insisted he call her back, the conversations were brief and lasted until Nora had run out of questions.

So, it was a surprise when Brad reached out for her help. It was a sunny and unusually warm day in early March, when Lily was close to two months old. Brad called and asked if he could talk to her when he came to drop off Clare. Alarmed, Nora asked why. "Just a homework issue with Jack," Brad said. Unusual, she thought. But he didn't sound worried, and she went about her day.

When they arrived, Clare had Brad's hand. "Mom guess what! Dad's coming in!" She brought him into the family room where Lily was in her porta-crib watching a mobile that hung above her. Her wispy brown hair had grown, and her eyes were becoming brown. "Look, Dad. She's smiling at you," Clare said. As Brad stared at Lily, Nora wondered if he was examining her, trying to picture her father.

Brad smiled at Lily and then at Clare. "She's a cutie, Clare."

Clare said, "I think her mouth looks like mine."

Brad nodded and smiled again. Then he looked at Nora as if signaling he wanted to move on to the purpose of his visit.

Once she had Clare settled with her favorite movie, *The Little Mermaid*, in a chair next to Lily's porta-crib, she and Brad sat across from each other in the living room. She had opened the windows and a light breeze blew against the curtains. Nora hadn't seen Brad up close since the fall soccer games. He had a cut on the side of his face from shaving; his dark brown hair had silvery strands around the edges; his eyes looked tired. Strange to have him sitting here, she thought. A guest. A Sunday afternoon visitor.

"I forgot," she said. "Do you want coffee or tea?"

"No, thanks."

"What's Jack doing? Is he at Eddie's?"

He shook his head. "Doing homework. He's grounded."

"Grounded?" Over the years, they had confined their discipline to removal of TV privileges for a day. Nothing yet to require grounding.

He looked at her with a strained expression. "I got a note from his math teacher. She said he hasn't been turning in his homework; he flunked a test." He cleared his throat. "He could flunk the class."

Flunk the class? He was close to the end of seventh grade. Twelve, almost thirteen. Nora taught in a different school than the local one the children went to and wasn't familiar with their teachers. "Why wasn't I notified too?"

He shrugged. "His teacher emailed. I responded."

"Why didn't you send me the email?"

"I figured we could talk about it."

She tried to keep the irritation out of her voice. "Have you gotten other emails?"

"No. Nothing." He fiddled with the cork coasters on the side table.

"Have you been checking his homework? His backpack?"

He had a sheepish expression. "Obviously, I should have been."

"I thought you helped him with his math?"

He looked away. "He hasn't wanted me to." Then, as if admitting defeat, he said, "He's been hard to deal with."

"What do you mean?"

He didn't answer right away.

In one sense she felt a twinge of pleasure—she wasn't the only one Jack was difficult with. But how had it had gotten to this point without her awareness?

Brad's eyes traveled around the room and came back to her. "He spends a lot of time in his room, stays up late on his phone. Then he doesn't want to get up for school. He's mad at me when I drag him out of bed."

Nora felt so removed from Jack and what he may have been going through. Struck with an acute sense that she had abdicated her responsibility and that she had let Brad set the tone, she asked, "Are other things going on? He's not into marijuana or anything, is he?"

"Oh, no. It's more the phone, video games, stuff like that."

That's normal, she thought, relieved, and surprised that Brad sounded so helpless. When Jack entered adolescence, after Brad had left her and she was the one who dealt with him most of the time, Brad hadn't understood how hard it had been. Hadn't understood that Jack was difficult *before* she became pregnant. She wondered why Brad had let it reach this point. Wondered why she hadn't insisted on regular updates. "I had a rule about the phone," she said. "He had to give it to me at bedtime. And a rule about homework before TV."

"The problem is, sometimes I'm not home from work until six or seven. He's by himself. I figured he did his homework then. Then I get dinner, we eat, and he goes to his room."

That surprised her too. She had jealously envisioned Jack and Brad's relationship—lots of talking, playing chess, and watching movies, but with Brad also keeping track of school and grades. "How long is he grounded?"

"For today. Until he finishes his homework. His teacher wants to meet tomorrow. After school, at three. Can you come?"

"Of course, I'll come. And I'll tell her to include me on the emails." It had gotten chilly, and she stood to close the window. "From now on you need to fill me in." Tired now, she wanted him to leave. It was getting dark, and she needed to get dinner for Clare and nurse Lily.

"One more thing," he said.

"What?"

He cleared his throat. With an uncertain expression, his voice low and tentative, he asked, "Do you think we could go back to the old schedule?"

She sat back down. "What schedule?"

His eyes locked on hers. "You know. The custody arrangement.

How we used to have it."

It took her a minute to grasp what he meant. "You mean Jack moving back here?"

He nodded. "With me on Wednesdays and every other weekend. If it works for you..."

Nora stared at him. It was so unexpected that it stunned her.

When she didn't respond, he sounded more eager to make his case. "I think it might help him. So, he's not alone as much." He gave a weak smile. "And it would help me. I hadn't expected how hard it would be—"

"Really? I tried telling you how difficult it was."

"I know."

She tried to think, to frame her feelings into a response. Angrier now, not only that he hadn't told her of the problems, but that he changed his mind about where Jack should live when things got difficult for him, she asked, "What about Jack? Does he know about this?"

"Not yet."

"What if he doesn't agree?"

His voice grew stronger. "I don't think he gets a choice."

"Because *you're* having problems now?" Nora felt the heat in her face. "You let him decide before."

Brad looked around the room as if searching for an answer. Then he turned to her. "He was upset and confused. I thought it would be easier for all of us."

"And now? You think he won't be angry, that he won't be upset and confused again?" She stood. "I have to check on Lily."

After Nora saw that Lily was asleep and Clare immersed in her movie, she went into the kitchen to get a glass of water.

She imagined Jack back in the house, the children together, having that part of the family whole again. Imagined him playing basketball with Eddie. Clowning around with Clare. Bonding with Lily. Dinners, always a reminder of his absence, would feel more normal. But as much as Nora would love to have him back, the thought also filled her with anxiety. Her maternity leave was ending, and she was scheduled to return to school in a month. Lily would be in day care. It would already be a time of transition.

She went back to the living room. Brad stood at the window and stared out. The streetlights had come on and solar lights lit the dogwood tree in the front yard. He turned when he saw her. "The dogwood's getting ready to bloom. I remember planting that. I think when Jack was a baby?"

"I'm not sure." *I don't give a damn*, she thought. What a stupid question to ask her now. After they were back in their chairs, she said, "I'm happy for him to move back. But I have conditions. And we need to think about him and what he needs."

He nodded.

"What reason are you going to give him?"

"The truth. That I work long hours and it would be better for him to be here. And that he's failing math."

"We need to be consistent in how we deal with him. You need to give me reports of your time with him and share anything that comes from the school. You need to help him with his math."

"I agree." His expression relaxed, and he leaned back in the chair and listened as she listed her expectations.

"Phone calls. Meetings on Sunday every week. The three of us." He must be desperate, she thought—he kept nodding to whatever she said. "We'll set boundaries and consequences together."

By the time she finished, she heard Lily waking. "I have to get her," she said.

He said, "I'm sorry. I should have let you know sooner."

"Yes, you should have," she said, and stood and waited for him to leave.

After he left, as she nursed Lily, she tried to sort her feelings. She couldn't fully blame Brad. It occurred to her that for the past eight months, consumed by her pregnancy and the birth, she had allowed Jack to keep her at a distance. She had to admit it had been easier for her. And so, she had accepted Jack's noncommittal answers when she asked about school. He'd always been a good student, and she'd seen his first two report cards, which were fine. But she had let him be in a compartment separate from her, assuming he was happy and doing well in school. Between Nora and Brad, Jack had fallen through the cracks.

The next afternoon, she got a babysitter for Lily. It was raining as she drove to the school listening to the scrape of the windshield wipers. After she parked, got out, and was locking her car, Brad pulled in next to her. He caught up with her and tried to hold his umbrella over her, but she walked in front of him and put the hood of her raincoat over her head.

In the classroom, she and Brad sat across the desk from Mrs. Samuel. Nora guessed her to be in her fifties; she had taught at the school long enough to have a reputation for being firm, nononsense, but fair. She looked up over her glasses.

"Thank you for coming in." She glanced at Brad. "As I told you, Mr. Stanton, I'm concerned about Jack. He did well in the beginning of the year, but he seems to have lost interest. I talked to his other teachers and they feel the same."

Nora looked at Brad. "You said you didn't get other reports."

"I didn't." He shook his head.

"His grades in those classes are okay," Mrs. Samuel said, "but his teachers have all noticed a difference. A lack of motivation."

"I wish we would have been told," Nora said, feeling a combination of irritation at Mrs. Samuel and guilt at her own culpability. She felt like one of the parents she and Ann complained to each other about. On one side of the spectrum were those who hovered and were overly involved, wanting to meet at the slightest hint of a problem; on the other side, those who, for whatever reason, seemed distant and detached, not responding to emails or suggestions.

Again, Mrs. Samuel focused on Brad. The parent in charge. The one she communicated with. "Have you been aware of anything at home?"

Nora felt like an appendage in the room. Mrs. Samuel must know they were separated, and that Jack lived with his father.

"I have," Brad said. "He's quieter. In his room a lot. He doesn't want me to help him with the math homework."

Mrs. Samuel, still looking at Brad, said, "What do you think might be the problem?"

"Honestly, I don't know." He turned to Nora.

Did he think she had an answer? Or was he trying to include her? Or imply that she was the problem, that Jack's behavior was linked to her pregnancy? But as she looked at his face, she saw something else—a plea for help. He seemed baffled, at a loss.

She leaned toward Mrs. Samuel. "Have you noticed anything else besides his grades?"

Mrs. Samuel glanced down at her notes for a minute and back at Nora. "He is quieter. He used to raise his hand to answer questions. He doesn't interact as much with the other kids. But it's hard to tell with one class."

"Do you think he needs tutoring?" Nora asked.

"I'm not sure that's the problem." Now she looked at Nora. "It would be good to set him up with the guidance counselor."

CHAPTER 52

Nora wasn't sure how Brad convinced him, but Jack acquiesced with the move. A week after Brad had come to the house to report the problem, he helped Jack move his things back.

Nora gave Jack space and didn't expect too much in the first week. She insisted he eat dinner with her and Clare, which he did grudgingly, taking turns with Clare to clear the table and do the dishes before he left for his room. Clare was thrilled to have him home. She followed him around the first few days, and he put up with her at first, but then would escape to his room. Each night when Nora went in to say goodnight, he was either in bed reading or at his computer. "What time do you usually turn off the light?" she had asked after the first few nights. "When I'm done," he said, whatever that meant. Done with what? When she asked him about homework, he gave evasive answers. His room was already a mess. She picked up a dish or two when she left.

It was in the second week of his being home when she had

to keep knocking at his door to get him up for school, and when she got an email from his social studies teacher. He wasn't turning in his homework and had flunked a test. She went to his room that evening to talk about new rules, about bedtime, homework, and his phone.

He rolled his eyes. "Oh, man. I need to go back to Dad's."

"Go ahead and call him."

Nora left his room and a few minutes later, Brad called. "What's going on?"

"He's flunked a social studies test. He isn't doing his homework. I don't know what time he goes to bed. I have trouble getting him up. He needs structure. And if he's living here, he's going to treat me with respect."

"I'll talk to him now. And on Sunday when we meet."

For the first meeting they sat at the kitchen table while Lily napped, and Clare played video games. After Nora talked to Ann about their guidelines for Eddie, she made a list of rules: Jack needed to bring the phone to her bedroom at night; he needed to get himself up in the morning—she gave him an alarm clock; he needed to review his homework assignments each day with her or Brad; they would request weekly updates from his teachers.

Jack had his head down as she talked and when she finished, he looked at Brad. "Dad, this is crazy."

"Sorry, Jack, but this is the way it's going to be. When you come on Wednesdays, I'll help you with your math. We'll get a tutor if you need one. And if things don't improve, I'll keep your phone until they do."

Nora continued, "Your room needs to be cleaned and

vacuumed once a week. You and Clare will take turns cleaning your bathroom. No more dirty dishes in your room."

After she and Brad had presented a united front with Jack, and listed his choices and consequences, he grudgingly complied. After that, things got a little better. He set his alarm clock and was up on time in the morning and showed her his homework at night. At the Sunday meetings, Nora encouraged Jack to talk about how he was feeling about school, but as soon as they were finished talking about school and homework, he gathered up his things and left the room. She and Brad would talk for a few minutes afterward. They kept their focus on Jack. Brad left shortly after they finished. Each week, Nora was ready for him to go. She was tired from the meeting and her head was full of all she needed to do that day—cook dinner, feed Lily, organize lunches for the week, go through the bedtime ritual with the three children.

Eventually, she saw glimpses of Jack's old self as he teased Clare and sometimes agreed to play a video game with her. Lily grew to recognize him and smiled with delight when he came near her; he couldn't help but smile back at her. To get him out of his room, Nora would ask him to keep an eye on Lily; she'd make up reasons: she needed to shower, do laundry, fix dinner. At night she would go into his room like she used to, sit on the side of his bed, ask how his day was, tell him she loved him and make do with his one-word answers and his pulling away from her hugs. He still didn't initiate conversations or call her Mom.

Just give him time, she told herself. But having him near, being able to see the subtle changes as he grew taller, as his voice lowered, gave Nora a feeling of regaining something that had been lost. He would be tall like Brad but hadn't filled out yet, making him gangly and awkward. He still had the sprinkling of acne. She slipped a tube of acne cream in the medicine chest.

Mrs. Samuel called after a few weeks to report that Jack was doing his homework and pulling up his grades, but she suggested again that he meet with the guidance counselor—she felt he was still quieter, still somewhat withdrawn. Nora talked to Jack about it, but he was adamant in his refusal. "She's weird," he said, "plus, everyone would know."

Nora and Brad talked and agreed. They would give Jack a choice: either meet with the school counselor or with a private therapist. He agreed to see a therapist and Nora got a referral for one who worked with adolescents. Dr. Friedman. Nora spoke to him on the phone of their concerns: Jack's isolation, lack of motivation, and possible depression. She asked if he'd like to meet with Brad and her first. "No," he said. "I'd like to meet with Jack and get his take on the problems."

After he had met with Jack twice, Nora and Brad had an appointment with him. A tall man, with thin, wire-framed glasses and black hair turning grey, he was probably in his fifties and reminded Nora of Fred Rogers, who always comforted her when she was a child watching his TV shows. She and Brad sat next to each other on club chairs facing his. High on the eleventh floor of an office building, the room had big windows giving a view of the tops of tall trees and the Washington Monument in the distance. By then it was close to the end of April. The leaves on the trees were full and green.

Dr. Friedman smiled at them. "I got permission from Jack to share a few things with you."

Nora and Brad sat stiffly in their chairs and waited.

"So," he said, "it sounds like Jack's been through a lot."

Nora and Brad nodded at the same time. Feeling guilty at the mess they had made, she had nothing to say.

Dr. Friedman looked at his notes. "How long have you been divorced?"

"We're not divorced," Brad said. "Separated."

He sounded surprised. "But he thinks you're divorced?"

Brad glanced at Nora for a second and said, "I guess he does."

Like a piece of unfinished business, their status had been left hanging, undiscussed and unpursued by either of them. It revealed the gap in their communication with each other and with Jack and made her feel even worse. She couldn't tell her truth: *I had an affair and forgot about the divorce. Then I got pregnant. I was too busy.*

Dr. Friedman looked at Nora. "Jack said you have a baby?"

She felt her face flush. "Yes. Three months old. A daughter."

Please don't ask about the father.

With a gentle smile, he said, "He's had a lot to deal with."

They both nodded again in unison. It felt like they were in the principal's office. She could see out of the corner of her eye Brad jiggling his knees.

Dr. Friedman was kind, his tone soft.

"Can we talk about your relationship?"

"Of course," Brad said.

Nora stiffened.

"He doesn't seem to understand why you're not together. Or, what happened. That might be part of why he's angry." He closed the chart. "Have you explained things to him?"

The room was silent. She looked at Brad who was staring at

something on the floor. And she waited. But Brad didn't speak. "We tried," she finally said. "It was hard to explain." Dr. Friedman silently glanced from her to Brad and back to her. Finally, she said in a faint voice, "I didn't even know why Brad left."

At that, Brad leaned forward and faced the doctor. "I was going through a tough time. I was in therapy and I felt the only way I could…" He trailed off and shook his head. "It was a hard decision. Probably a selfish one."

Dr. Friedman said, "And how are you doing now, Brad?"

"Better," he said. "Much better."

"Good. I think it would be helpful if you try to include him more. In your decisions. In how you're feeling, some of what you went through. So, he doesn't wonder, or make up his own scenarios. He's old enough."

Nora had all kinds of thoughts running through her mind. They could have done things so differently.

Dr. Friedman was ending the session. "I think we need to meet with Jack the next time. In the meantime," he said, "think about how you handle hard situations." He gave a gentle smile. "Sometimes it's easier to avoid conflict. We may not try to hide things, but at the same time we don't reveal them. They stay buried but simmering. Do you think that might be the case?"

CHAPTER 53

Nora was anxious at the first family session. Her palms were sweaty, and her stomach hurt. Jack and Brad sat on the loveseat and Nora in a chair next to them, all facing Dr. Friedman and the window behind him. Jack, looking embarrassed and uncomfortable, sat hunched over in his chair, his face already a light shade of pink as Dr. Friedman led him through what they had discussed and planned in their private meetings.

He began by saying, "Jack, as we've talked, you've shared some things you're confused about. We're going to help your parents understand what those are." He smiled gently at Jack. "One is your confusion when your father left. Can you let your parents know how you felt?"

Jack's face had turned redder and his response was immediate, as if he had practiced the words. "I had no clue. It was a shock." He looked at Brad. "You just left." Then he turned to Nora. "And you said you didn't know why."

"I didn't." She heard the rebuke in his voice—an accusation

that she knew more and hadn't told him. As she looked at the sky, grey and overcast today, she thought of the unfairness of it. "It was a shock to me, too. I thought everything was fine." Yet, it sounded like she was making up an excuse for missing signs that she should have seen.

Brad glanced at Nora for a second and then at Jack. "Your mom didn't know. I didn't even know why. I was confused too."

As Brad spoke, she imagined Dr. Friedman wondering how a marriage could fall apart just like that, without either person knowing why.

"Can you tell us more about that?" he asked Brad.

All eyes were on Brad. His expression seemed vulnerable to her, but perhaps it was because she felt so vulnerable. *I want this to be over*, she thought as she snuck a glance at her watch and listened to a clock softly ticking, and to Brad talking about being unhappy, but not sure why, and how his therapist had led him to understand how his buried feelings about his parents' deaths had affected him. The same story she had heard when she was at the beach last August and Brad had called, proposing that they think about getting back together. As Brad spoke, Dr. Friedman kept his eyes on him. He would nod, or say a word to prod him on, like a signal, Nora thought. She remained quiet, and the knot in her stomach eased as the spotlight was on Brad. She half listened and stared out at the clouds that had formed.

"Remember the day we went to the cemetery?" Brad asked Jack. "I didn't tell you, but it was the first time I had gone since their funeral."

Jack looked surprised. "Why?"

"It was too hard before. After they died, I couldn't face it.

It was easier to think and analyze rather than feel." He smiled. "That's probably why I became an accountant."

Dr. Friedman said, "Thank you, Brad. You were brave to get help and brave to share your feelings with us."

Nora thought, yes, he went through a lot; he'd changed and become more open and accessible to his feelings. Yet he sounded like a martyr.

Dr. Friedman turned to Jack. "Do you see how easy it is to bury things? No one wants to feel the pain." Then his eyes zeroed in on her. "Nora, you said you saw no signs?"

She nodded.

"Jack said he didn't remember any big arguments. Did you and Brad hide your disagreements from the kids?"

Nora thought for a minute about how to answer. Her eyes traveled from Dr. Friedman's plaid shirt, a muted peach and green, to the thickening clouds; she found it too hard to look into his searching eyes. No, she and Brad didn't have loud disagreements, unlike her parents. Nora remembered how she would hide her head under her pillow to block out the noise of their arguments, feeling somehow responsible. She thought of the times she said nothing when she had been annoyed with Brad and how she'd assumed that the things that bothered her weren't worthy of mention. She didn't want Jack and Clare to worry about the atmosphere in the house as she had as a child. But it was too hard to explain, or to say anything except to admit that yes, they had rarely argued. She wouldn't make excuses about her behavior, wouldn't blame it on her childhood, wouldn't make *herself* a martyr.

Finally, she said, "We didn't argue. If we had disagreements, we hid them—not only from the kids, but from ourselves."

Brad had been watching her as she spoke. He nodded and said, "I guess we both kept things inside."

Whenever Dr. Friedman smiled, his eyes seemed to sparkle. "So, you worked hard at making everything seem fine?"

"I really thought everything was fine," Nora said. "But I realized afterward that we lived on the surface. As Brad said, he didn't share his feelings. I didn't like conflict and I kept things inside." Nora had brought a light sweater, and she pulled it around her shoulders. She hoped he wouldn't ask more of her.

Still looking at Nora, Dr. Friedman said, "Do you want to tell us anything more about that? Anything that might help Jack?"

She turned to Jack, who was looking at her. "I don't know. I need to think about it more..."

The room was quiet while Dr. Friedman waited for her to elaborate. "It became a pattern. Living on the surface. We were busy; it was easy to do."

Dr. Friedman nodded. She hoped he had finished with her. But no. He looked down at his notes again. "Jack shared his feelings about the baby."

At the word *baby*, she stiffened and felt herself get hot. The pit of dread felt like a stone. She took off her sweater and waited.

He threaded his words kindly. "Jack and I talked and tried to figure out why he was so upset. He had a lot of confusion. We talked about some reasons for that. I think he feels better about it now. Is that right, Jack?"

Jack nodded but didn't look at her.

"He expressed some resentment about Clare."

"Clare?" She had been expecting something about how she

had embarrassed him when she got pregnant, something about sex or betrayal.

"He thinks you favor her," he said to Nora. "Jack, can you tell your mother why?"

Jack had tears in his eyes. "She's always crying and complaining about me." He wiped his face on his sleeve. "You always listen to her." Dr. Friedman handed him a tissue.

This, she hadn't envisioned. She wished she could have time to let it sink in. Did she really favor Clare? Reflexively, she said, "Oh, I'm sorry, Jack. I had no idea."

The room was quiet. Dr. Friedman waited for Nora to say more. Rain had started and was making designs on the screens. Nora tried to picture Clare and Jack's interactions and her response to each of them. Clare was easier in some ways because she wore her emotions, making it less difficult to understand what she was feeling, unlike Jack who kept his feelings inside. Easier because she was younger and at a different stage. Nora thought of a typical scenario and proposed it as a question. "She looks up to you and tries to get your attention and bothers you, then you get annoyed. Then she gets hurt and because she's crying, I respond to her?"

Jack nodded, and Brad said something about sibling rivalry being normal.

Dr. Friedman responded, "It may be normal, but it doesn't make it easier."

Jack had bent to tie his sneaker; she couldn't tell if he was crying. Nora thought of her jealousy as a child. "Jack," she said, "when I was your age, I was shy and quiet. Aunt Becky was the opposite. She got all the attention. I remember being so jealous of her. And because I was older than her, I would get blamed when we had an argument. Is that part of how you feel about Clare?"

Jack looked up and shrugged. "I guess so."

Then Dr. Friedman spoke again about Lily. He explained that the baby had become another threat when Jack found out Nora was pregnant. Another way that Jack felt like he would be in third place. The resentment of Clare had gotten tied to the baby. He looked at Jack. "Did I say that right?"

Jack nodded. His face had relaxed and was back to a normal color.

"Is there anything you want to add to what your mother said about Clare?"

Jack shook his head.

"Okay. Our time is up." He looked at Nora. "It sounds like you've had first-hand experience with what he's feeling."

"I have," she said, and turned to Jack. "I'm glad you told me."

"Jack has come a long way," Dr. Friedman said. He looked at Jack with a sparkle in his eyes. "Do you want to talk about how you feel now about Lily?"

Jack's expression brightened. "It's okay. I like her. She's fun."

To Nora, Dr. Friedman said, "Now he understands she's not a threat. You've done a good job."

Nora felt so grateful to Dr. Friedman, she wanted to hug him.

CHAPTER 54

After the sessions with Dr. Friedman, Nora paid attention to her interactions with Jack and Clare, careful not to respond too quickly to Clare's tears, and she tried to help them learn to share their feelings with each other. Slowly Jack's attitude towards her softened. With small steps. Baby steps. He invited Eddie to the house. Laughter and the sounds of the bouncing basketball returned. She became *Mom* again. It happened one morning when Lily was giggling as Jack played Peek-a-Boo with her. "Look, Mom. Watch her!"

Mom. He hadn't used the word in so long that it sounded foreign after his clipped questions and one-word answers. Another day, he woke with a fever, headache, and cough. She brought him ginger ale and sat on the side of his bed; she laid her cheek on his brow to see how hot his forehead was—just like she used to.

She returned to school in April. Only a week later, she found herself weeping at the end of the day. It was too much. Besides the challenges with Jack, she had to transition Lily to day care and pump enough milk to make bottles to last the day. "I can't do it," she said to Ann one day. "I am so tired."

Ann said, "You're trying to do too much. Working, taking care of Lily, and dealing with Jack. Jesus. I couldn't do it." Then she said, "Can't you have Brad do more with Jack and Clare?"

"He's offered to help but I don't want to ask him for anything," Nora said. "We do our meetings on Sundays and I get through that." Brad had been going out of his way to be accommodating. He had asked her if she needed him to help Jack with his math on other nights besides Wednesdays or if she wanted him to take Jack and Clare out to dinner on another night to give her a break.

"You need to get over that and let him help. That's like cutting off your nose, or whatever the cliché is."

Ann was right. After she swallowed her irritation with Brad and asked him to take Jack and Clare on Mondays, he agreed to get off work early and pick them up for after-school care, feed them, help with homework. On the weekends they were with Nora, he offered to take them to a movie or a museum.

Nora examined other options to simplify her life. Although she was hoping to wait until Lily was at least six months old to stop breast feeding, she started the process of weaning her. And she talked to her principal about being overwhelmed; she agreed to allow Nora to cut back to part-time for the rest of the school year. The woman who had substituted for her when she was on maternity leave, who the children were used to, would fill in. After a few weeks, she felt better, more able to cope.

Through the weeks of May, Nora noticed a thawing in her relationship with Brad. As they developed a bond to help Jack, the distance between them narrowed and the relationship shifted and became lighter and easier. Brad didn't rush out of the house after the Sunday meetings; he even stayed for coffee. They talked every few days to discuss Jack's progress and attitude.

Brad was more relaxed, and he smiled more. Nora caught herself watching him and observing him with Lily. At four months old, she smiled and even laughed and had grown to recognize Brad. Nora would catch him glancing at her and making faces to make her giggle.

One day it startled her to hear a familiar sound after Brad left to walk to his car. It took her a minute to realize that he was whistling the same off-key tune she knew so intimately from their college days. He seemed more like an earlier version of himself. The one she had fallen in love with. Perhaps it was the therapy? Or being separated from her? Or a new relationship which caused him to regain his old spontaneity. To whistle again.

When he dropped off the children on one Sunday afternoon near the end of May, she stood at the front door while he helped to unload their duffel bags. His shirt hung out casually and his hair was longer, not as manicured. Earlier, she turned on the sprinkler in the front yard to water a bed of geraniums she had planted. Brad followed Jack and Clare into the spray. Soon they were soaked and laughing. As she came out to the yard, he smiled and waved to her and turned to leave. She said, "I'll get a towel to put on your seat."

"No need. It'll dry."

After he left, she thought how weird, how different. He used to insist that no one sit on the seats after the pool without a towel.

One night, Nora had a vivid dream about Brad. They were

together—somewhere she couldn't place—talking and laughing. It took her by surprise and puzzled her. His presence felt so familiar and right.

A few nights later, she had another dream about him. They were with other people—no one she knew—at opposite ends of a room. When Brad glanced her way and saw her, his expression shifted, and he smiled as he if suddenly recognized her. His gaze stayed on her for a minute, reminding her of the night they met. The unexpected thrill she felt was with her when she woke, and, in the half light, in that gauzy period between sleep and wakefulness, she held onto the feeling, held on to that image of him all day. This too took her by surprise, the dreams, and the longing. It was as if the old Brad, the one she had fallen in love with, had emerged out of hiding and returned in a newer version. She wondered if he had ever dreamed of her, wondered if he harbored any remnants of love for her.

She imagined inviting him for dinner on a Sunday when he brought Jack and Clare home. She would say, "Hey, I have a beef stew in the crock pot. Do you want to stay?" Beef stew had been his favorite. She would set the table in the dining room, count out four place mats, put an Eva Cassidy CD in the Bose, light candles, and ask him to open the wine. Should she seat him in his old spot at the head? She pictured the candle glow, the laughter, the softness of the room. Like in her dream, he would look across the table at her and his face would light up. They would sip wine and talk far into the night.

One night, she called him to invite him for dinner. He can just say no, she figured. After he answered, and they discussed mundane logistics about the kids, she said, "Would you like to come for dinner next Sunday? I'll make beef stew."

"Dinner?" He sounded surprised. "Let me check. Hold on."

She could hear a rustling of papers and the TV in the background.

"Sorry, Nora. I have plans. Another time?"

She hung up, chastened by her silly fantasy. He was probably dating and had made a new life. She lay still for a while, disappointed and deflated. Had she really thought he would remain stagnant as she moved on, dated and had an affair?

In the morning, she stood in the kitchen and watched as birds fluttered at the feeder and the sun edged above the trees. When she heard Jack and Clare's pounding footsteps as they raced each other downstairs, she turned and ladled oatmeal into bowls, and set out plates of quartered apples and sliced toast. While they ate, she asked casually, "Have you met anyone at Dad's apartment?"

Jack had a mouthful of oatmeal and mumbled, "Some lady once. I think she forgot something."

Clare took a bite of her apple and turned to Jack. "Remember when she came to drop off the spaghetti?"

Nora took a bite of toast to stop herself from asking the questions that arose. *What does she look like? Do you know her name? Was the spaghetti good? Better than mine?*

Maybe that was why he was whistling.

CHAPTER 55

On a warm and sunny afternoon in the beginning of June, Nora carried Lily to the door to wave goodbye to Brad after their Sunday meeting with Jack. Brad stopped and pulled up a few weeds from the garden bed.

He went to the trash can to throw away the weeds and came back to the porch but seemed reluctant to leave. He cleared his throat and said, "Hey, does the dinner offer still stand?"

"The dinner offer?" She had tamped down her expectations about him.

"I thought I smelled stew."

"It's in the crock pot." She smiled at him. "Do you want to stay?"

"Do you have enough?"

"Plenty." The Sunday stew had become a habit—easy to throw together with leftovers for a few nights during the week. The kids had tired of meatloaf and macaroni and cheese.

They went inside, and she told Jack and Clare that he was staying for dinner.

"Yay!" Clare said. "Can I set the table, Mom?"

Jack ran downstairs. "Dad, do you want to shoot some balls?"

Brad looked at Nora. "Do you need help?"

"No, go ahead."

After she put Lily in a baby swing, she turned off the air conditioner and opened the kitchen window above the sink to let in the cooler evening air. Brad and Jack's laughter carried in from the basketball net. Clare hummed as she folded napkins into triangles and counted out four place mats. "Mom, Dad, Jack, me," she murmured. "I put Dad where he always sits."

Always. As if he had never left. Nora thought how hard it must have been for Clare to get used to the empty places—first Brad's and then Jack's—and the quiet nights. She hugged Clare. "The table looks great. Why don't you go out and play?"

Nora cut up tomatoes and cucumbers for a salad and put the sourdough rolls in the oven. When she finished in the kitchen, she stuck an Eva Cassidy CD in the Bose, dimmed the chandelier, and lit candles, just as she'd imagined. She stood back and surveyed the room, and it occurred to her that the last time they all sat at this table was a few nights before their last trip to the beach, a spaghetti dinner with Ann and Nick and the kids—it would be three years in August. Three years since that summer when she had thought their lives were perfect.

Brad came in. He grabbed a paper towel and wiped his forehead. "They beat me."

His hair had curled in the heat, and he had a big smile. She thought of how Jack's smile had returned and reminded her of Brad's.

"Beer, wine, water?" she asked.

"Water first and then wine would be great."

After she poured ice water for him, she took out wine glasses and a bottle of Merlot. "Could you open it?"

He pointed to a drawer. "Is the opener still there?"

She nodded and watched as he went to the drawer and wondered if he remembered where the dishes and glasses were. Wondered if he noticed the teal canisters she had bought to replace the white chipped ones. They stood for a minute sipping their wine. Feeling awkward, Nora grasped for something to say. Their conversations over the past few months had centered primarily on Jack and how he was doing. They hadn't delved into the sessions with Dr. Friedman that had involved them and their patterns with each other. "I think Jack's feeling better about Clare," she said.

"Good. He seems better. Anything new at your school?"

Anything new? The new teacher, the principal that some complained about, all small and petty stuff. There really wasn't anything much to share. "Nope. The usual. The kids get smarter each year. I'm glad it's almost summer. How's your job?"

"Oh, fine. Some turnover…"

Their conversation reminded her of asking Jack or Clare, "How was your day?" Not expecting much. She felt like she and Brad were groping to fill in the silence. She turned back to the dinner and Brad looked at Lily in her swing as she smiled and babbled. The oven timer went off, and she pulled the rolls out of the oven, put them in a basket and asked him to put it on the buffet table in the dining room next to the salad. She stirred the stew and checked the carrots and potatoes. "Everything's ready." She called out the window, "Clare and Jack, dinner. Come and wash your hands." She put Lily in her highchair and brought it into the dining room.

Brad carried the plates and the crock pot to the buffet. When everyone had filled their plates and gathered around the table, he glanced at the place mats. "Where should I sit?"

Nora pointed to his chair. "Clare set you at the head."

Brad said, "I can sit anywhere."

"Dad." Clare took him by the hand. "You have to sit in your seat."

Nora sat at the place Clare had set for her at the opposite end of the table. She and Brad in their usual places. Lily, in her high-chair next to Nora, chewed on a teething ring. Once they were busy eating, Nora's tension lessened. The chattering of Jack and Clare erased the awkward silence. She watched Brad as he inclined his head toward the kids and listened to them. He laughed as Clare moved her arms in the air as she explained something that had happened at school. He and Jack laughed at a silly joke. Nora hadn't remembered Brad being so fully present or so lighthearted; at dinner he'd usually been distracted and serious.

The sun had lowered, and the candles glowed in the dimming light, softening the edges of the room. Lulled by the wine, Nora took in the scene as if from a distance. It felt so right. Everything seemed so simple. She wondered what Brad was feeling. Occasionally he glanced toward her. Did his eyes light up or did she imagine it? Wish it?

Jack touched her arm. "Mom, Dad's talking to you."

"Oh, sorry." She turned to Brad. "What did you say?"

"I was just saying the dinner's great." He smiled. "I always loved your stew."

"Thanks. I'm glad you still like it."

Lily whined and started to cry. It was past her bedtime. Nora scooped her up. "I need to feed her and get her to bed. There's more food. Help yourself."

"We'll clean up. Right, guys?" Brad said.

As Nora sank into the peace and stillness of the nighttime ritual of Lily's end-of-the-day bottle, she listened to the noises from downstairs. The sounds of dishes and laughter. A toilet flushing. The garbage disposal running. After she rocked Lily and sang "Rock-a-bye Baby," she kissed her and put her in the crib. Lily smiled sleepily up at her. After Nora turned on the monitor and the night light, she slipped out and went downstairs.

Jack and Clare were outside at the basketball net. Brad was in the family room sipping wine and staring at the pictures on the wall. Not wanting to intrude, Nora quietly set the monitor on the kitchen counter and stood and watching Jack and Clare. She turned when Brad came into the kitchen.

"The dishes are done. We put away the leftovers." He put his wine glass in the sink. "I should go."

She checked her watch, eight o'clock; she didn't want the evening to end. "Stay. There's more wine." As soon as she spoke, she thought he might be in a hurry to leave; maybe the dinner felt different to him. It could be a sense of obligation that had caused him to accept the invitation. But he smiled and nodded. She poured more wine in their glasses and then opened the French doors and allowed the cool air in. They sat across from each other in the armchairs that she had bought to replace the ones they had sat in for so many years. Brad picked the one that was in the same place where his had been.

"I like this," he said, patting the arms of the chair. "It's a lot more comfortable than the old ones."

Nora nodded. "It was time. They were worn out."

Brad looked at her with a pensive expression. "I think she's helped Jack."

"Who?"

He pointed to the kitchen where Lily's sing-song voice came through the monitor as she edged into sleep. "Lily. She makes him laugh. He's happier, more cooperative."

Jack was happier. Even his acne had cleared up. But Brad attributing part of it to Lily astounded her and gave her the impetus to ask, "What's it like for you? To be around her?"

He swirled the wine in his glass and was silent for a minute. "It's okay, good. Hard at first, but my therapist helped."

"Really. How?"

"To understand why I was so upset." With a smile at Nora, he said, "She asked me, 'Weren't you the one who left her?' I thought about that. It wasn't like you got pregnant in the middle of our marriage."

The house was quiet; Lily had fallen asleep.

"So," she said, "did you figure it out?"

"I was hurt." He looked thoughtful. "Maybe jealous."

Nora's pleasure at hearing that he had been jealous surprised her. "But now?"

"I've let it go. All the stuff with Jack and needing your help... And the sessions with Dr. Friedman. I got to thinking of what I put you and the kids through." He looked at her. "Weird, isn't it? It's made me understand what really matters."

Nora was about to ask him what he meant when Jack and

Clare came in. Brad looked at his watch. "Oh, time to go. I have an early morning meeting tomorrow."

Crap, she thought with a stab of disappointment. She wanted to hear more. And she especially wanted to ask, what *does* really matter?

In bed that night—pleased, content, and wired all at once—she couldn't settle; it was like she had overloaded on caffeine. She replayed the scenes of the evening: his interactions with Lily, the ease and comfort of the meal, the warmth she felt having him there. At eleven she turned off the light and was falling asleep when the phone rang.

Brad said, "Did I wake you?"

"I'm not asleep yet."

"I was wondering." He hesitated. "Can we have dinner together at my place? Next Saturday? Can you get a babysitter?"

She sat up. "What?"

"Dinner at my place. I'll grill steaks."

CHAPTER 56

Although the warmth and closeness she felt Sunday evening stayed with her during the week, so did an undercurrent of curiosity about where it was leading. When Brad invited her for dinner at his apartment, she wondered what was happening between them, whether he had the same feeling of attraction she did or if she was again deluding herself, not only about him—thinking he had changed—but creating another fantasy and setting herself up for disappointment.

She kept it to herself. A dinner, that was all. She didn't want to make a big deal of it. Ann knew Brad was back in Nora's life because of Jack and that things were going well, that Brad was comfortable being in the house with Lily, but this was all Nora would share until she was sure. Ann had heard enough of the back-and-forth Nora and Brad had gone through in the three years since he left.

That week, she replayed cautionary advice Ann had given her in the past. "Really, a mid-life crisis, as an excuse to do what he did?" Nora could imagine Ann questioning her motives now, saying, "What the hell is wrong with you? You were glad to be free, to become your own person." She thought of how she would respond. "We're both different. I'm stronger; I can be my own person. He's easier, freer, lighter. Like he used to be when we first met." But as she remembered other snippets of words Ann had said before, "Are you sure you want to go down that road?" Nora thought, *No, I'm not sure of anything.*

On Saturday evening as she drove to his apartment, she was nervous. She'd changed outfits several times and wound up wearing her go-to summer outfit—a white sundress and a lavender shawl. It felt like she was going on a blind date, with no idea of what to expect. Although Brad had offered to pick her up, she declined, not wanting to try explaining to Jack and Clare why they couldn't come. She had called Sophie, a neighborhood college student home for the summer who, when she was in high school, had babysat Jack and Clare. After the school year ended, Nora hired her three mornings a week to babysit Lily, so Nora could take Jack and Clare to the pool, or to a museum, or shopping. Lily had gotten used to her and had no problem now when Nora left.

As she drove, she hoped Jack and Clare hadn't told Brad that she'd asked them to show her where he lived. Or that she'd asked if another woman had been there. It felt unreal to know she would soon be inside, not driving by to stare up at the windows and try to visualize the interior. He said he'd meet her in front of the apartment building at seven. When she got there, he was sitting on a bench in front of the main entrance and came to the car to show her where to park. As they walked from her car, he pointed.

"I'm on the fourth floor. That's my apartment with the lights on." She nodded as if she hadn't seen it before. In the elevator, Brad chatted with an older couple, something about the trees that were being pruned in the complex. At the fourth floor, as they were getting off, he introduced her, "This is my friend, Nora." She smiled at the couple while thinking it funny to be called his friend.

Inside his apartment, Brad said, "I'll show you around."

She followed him from the combination dining room and living room down a short hall to the bedrooms. Jack's room had soccer pictures on the walls and a navy blue comforter on the bed; Clare's room was all pinks and purples. "I got bunk beds, so they could have a friend spend the night." Brad watched her as if wanting to see her reaction, perhaps get her approval. She glanced at a small room that must be his—sparse, his desk from home, a double bed. He pointed to a closed door. "Here's the bathroom, if you need it."

In the kitchen, Brad pointed to open bottles of Chardonnay and Pinot Noir on the counter—the ones that had been their favorites. "Help yourself." A salad bowl with a bottle of ranch dressing, a bag of romaine, and two steaks sat on the counter next to a store-bought apple pie. "I have potatoes in the oven. I'm still not much of a cook."

"Trust me, this is a treat." And it was. She felt the tension ebb, eased by the normality of the scene and by his efforts to make a nice dinner. He'd never liked to cook, wasn't good at multi- tasking and putting together a meal—he'd get caught up on doing one task at a time perfectly, precisely, like cutting a cucumber or carrot or potato into equal parts. As she poured a glass of Chardonnay, she glanced at the round glass-topped dining room table set for two with the white earthenware plates Brad had taken from the basement. Their first set of dishes after they married. In the center stood two tall candles in glass holders. She smiled, pleased that he remembered how she hated the glare of harsh artificial lights.

"I'll be back after I light the grill." He went out the sliding glass doors that led to the balcony.

While he was outside, she tried to take in much as she could of the rooms where Clare and Jack spent their times apart from her. Against one wall, a loveseat with a framed print of Boston Harbor hanging above it and two chairs on either side. A TV mounted on the opposite wall over a gas fireplace. She perused the built-in shelves lined with the books he had always liked: biographies, mysteries, historical novels. Framed photographs sat on other shelves. A few of Jack and Clare with Brad—ones she'd never seen, which gave her a pang of sadness at being left out of a part of their lives. A photo of her with Jack and Clare on a boardwalk bench eating French fries—the same scene of the one she had with Brad in it. He must have taken it when he moved. She picked up the picture of his parents she remembered so well. The one he had hidden from her when he caught her studying it soon after they died.

She turned to see him standing next to her. "They weren't much older than I am," he said.

"It must seem weird. Do you wonder what they'd look like now?"

"I feel like they'll always be fifty. Fixed in my mind." He moved away. "Let's get our wine and sit outside."

Nora stared at the picture once more before she returned it to the shelf. On the balcony, Brad had set out Brie and crackers and lit a candle in a hurricane lantern. The apartment was high enough above the parking lot and trees to have a view of the pink and purple horizon as the sun set. They sat for a minute and looked at the sky as the sliver of the moon emerged. The evening was cool, and she pulled her shawl around her. Still fixed on the picture of his parents, she wanted to talk more about the day that was etched in her mind along with her guilt and regret. A guilt that had waned over the years, not as raw as in the beginning, but still there, underneath.

"Every year, I remembered. The date."

"The twelfth of December," he said.

"That Thanksgiving. When we were supposed to go. Did you blame me?"

"Blame you?"

"I was the one who had the idea."

He looked confused. "Idea?"

"Not to go to Boston."

"But I wanted to." His voice was gentle. "I wish they'd had time to meet you. I felt bad that they never did."

"Me too. I would have met them if—"

"Nora, you don't need to feel guilty. It's the way it was." He smiled. "Think of it. If we hadn't had that week, we could have drifted apart."

Although he had absolved her of any blame from that Thanksgiving, she wanted to say, "We *did* drift apart. You drifted away."

They sat in silence, staring out at the emerging night, at the flickering fireflies. The sounds of talking and laughter drifted up from a balcony below. Brad cut a slice of Brie, put it on a cracker, and handed it to her.

"Do you sit out here often?" she asked.

313

"Not much. I grill hamburgers and hot dogs for the kids." He stood. "Time to put the steaks on. Still like yours medium rare?"

She nodded. "Do you want me to toss the salad?"

"Sure. Thanks."

After she went inside, she returned to the bookshelf and looked once more at the picture of his parents. She whispered, "I'm sorry."

In the kitchen, as she tossed the salad, she could hear Brad whistling a new tune, one she couldn't place. After he brought the steaks in, he bustled about: he took the potatoes out of the oven, poured more wine, and put a tub of butter on the table. Classical music played from a radio in the kitchen. It had gotten dark outside. Brad stood and switched on the glass globe light that hung above the table and dimmed it. They were quiet as they buttered their potatoes and cut into their steaks.

"I hope your steak is okay?"

"Perfect."

After they ate in silence for a few minutes, she asked, "How's your job?"

"It gets stifling. Assets, liabilities, financial transactions." He grinned. "I've always been jealous of how you loved your job, like you were meant for it. You always knew what you wanted."

"I'm not sure I was that certain," she said. "Are you really tired of what you're doing?"

"There's an opportunity for me to move into a different department, where I can do strategic planning, be more vision and goal oriented." He smiled.

The evening felt magical, unreal, the same feeling she'd had at the Sunday dinner. Comfortable, easy, right. She thought of the price they had paid to get to this point, aware that this was a beginning; there was a lot left unsaid, still buried.

When they finished eating, Nora stood to help Brad clear the table. "I'll take care of it," he said as he carried their dishes to the kitchen. "It'll take me a minute."

She went to use the bathroom. The three toothbrushes in a holder—blue, green, and purple—matched the colors of the bath towels and washcloths. She smiled. Just like Brad to have a logical system of color-coding. She wondered if the woman he had dated ever slept here. And if she kept a toothbrush in the holder like she had at Jim's.

She wandered from the bathroom to a table in the corner of the living room with a jigsaw puzzle spread out and partially done. She remembered how Brad had worked on them to relax at the end of a day. At home and on their vacations, a game table sat in a corner, spread with the pieces of a puzzle in varying stages of completion. He and Jack and Clare would spend hours doing them, dozens of puzzles over the years that he would give to Goodwill when they finished. He had glued and framed two of them that he and the children loved—one of an amusement park and the other a Harry Potter scene—and they still hung at home in the family room.

As she stood there, she studied the pattern that had emerged in the puzzle he was working on. A seascape with changing colors: the blue-gray of the ocean at one end gradually lightening to an aqua color as the water got shallower, and the waves broke on the shore. She looked at the unmatched pieces and picked up one—a piece that looked like sand—and found its space. Proud of herself, she picked up another and was fitting it in when Brad stood next to her. "You hated doing these."

"I know. I never really tried."

He stood next to her and soon more of the picture emerged.

He turned to her. "Look. The waves are gentle. Calm. The way you like them."

She stopped and looked at him. In that moment it was like she saw the whole of him, the old Brad, the middle of the marriage Brad, and now this Brad. This Nora. And wondered what it meant and where it would lead.

CHAPTER 57

In the days after the dinner at Brad's apartment, Nora replayed images of the evening: sitting on the balcony watching the fireflies; standing close at the puzzle table; their quick and awkward hug at the door, the first time they had touched in three years. On Thursday, when he picked up Jack and Clare for the weekend, she was aware of a current between them when their eyes lingered on each other for a few seconds. Right then, she'd asked him if he wanted to stay for dinner when he bought the kids home, aware that it would be the third dinner in three weeks, no longer a casual meal, but an intentional edging into a different relationship.

His smile got bigger. "I'll bring dessert," he said, "and I'd love to take a bike ride with Jack and Clare before dinner." Brad's bike was still in the garage. On Sunday afternoons in nice weather the three of them had often ridden along a bike path that ran through a wooded area near their home. She loved that he wanted to do it again.

Sunday morning was humid and overcast. Nora lowered the setting on the air conditioner to remove the mugginess from the house. Lily sat in her highchair chewing on a teething biscuit and watching Nora as she cut up an onion and garlic and mixed it with tomato puree and placed it in the crock pot along with the Italian sausages she had seared. She played one of Lily's CDs and sang along to "Twinkle, Twinkle, Little Star." When she finished the sauce, she put Lily in her crib for a nap, made a fresh pot of coffee and laid out a plate of croissants and strawberries. She had invited Ann over, ready to tell her about Brad now that he was becoming more of a presence in her life, now that she was sure that something was happening between them.

The first thing Ann did when she arrived—as she did each time—was to search for Lily.

"Sorry. She's taking her morning nap." Nora pointed to a magnet on the refrigerator that held a picture she had taken of Ann bouncing Lily on her knee, both looking in each other's eyes and laughing. "She looks at the picture and points at you and says, 'in' for Ann."

Ann laughed. "I adore her." She stood at the refrigerator and stared at the picture. "She looks like a combination of you, Jack, and Clare."

Lily's wispy hair had grown curly and blondish brown like Clare's, her eyes a deep brown, the color of Nora's and Jack's. Each time someone commented on who Lily resembled, Nora pictured Jim, thankful that nothing startling stood out. "It's lucky that Jim didn't have blue eyes and bright red hair," she said.

"It smells good," Ann said. "What are you cooking?"

"Spaghetti sauce for dinner. Brad's staying when he brings

the kids home. They're planning to go on a bike ride." She looked out the window. "But it's supposed to rain."

"Hopefully, it'll cool things off. It's so damned humid." Ann didn't seem surprised that Brad was staying for dinner, perhaps assuming it was part of their weekly plan with Jack.

Nora picked up a strawberry and held it for a minute, studying its textured skin, as she thought of how to start. She casually said, "So, I had dinner at Brad's last Saturday."

"With the kids?"

"No. I got a babysitter." She watched Ann. "Sophie. He had dinner here a few Sundays ago. Then he invited me to his place."

Now Ann looked surprised. "Any special occasion?"

"No," she said. "Not really."

"Was it weird?"

"It was nice. He has a nice balcony and he grilled steak. I liked seeing his apartment and Jack and Clare's bedrooms…" She could tell by Ann's expression she was dubious. "I thought of you after he invited me and wondered what you'd think." She smiled. "I even pretended I was talking to you, telling you about the dinners."

Ann asked with an amused expression, "Why didn't you just call me?"

"I figured you were sick of hearing the back-and-forth, us connecting and disconnecting. All the crap over the years."

"That's crazy. You hear all my crap," she said. "So, tell me, what did I say?"

"Oh, you gave me advice, warning me like you did before about being able to trust him, and asking me why I would get involved with him after what he did."

"And what did you say?"

"I didn't answer you." Nora laughed. "Not out loud, anyway."

"Well then, what were you thinking?"

Nora buttered a croissant and took a bite. "It reminds me of when we were dating. He pays more attention, focuses on me and on the kids in a way he hadn't in the last years. He makes me laugh. He's lighter and freer like when we first met." As if she was listing selling points, she added, "I'm attracted to him the way I was before it became routine. I like being with him."

Ann was silent. No nail tapping or jiggling, unusual for her to be so still.

Nora added, "He whistles again."

Ann looked at her quizzically.

Nora knew she couldn't convey the importance his whistling meant to her—an indication of the old Brad, the way he was before his parents' deaths dimmed that part of him. Needing another piece of evidence, Nora pointed at the picture of Lily. "He's great with her."

"That's nice," Ann said, then paused. "But I want to ask you…" She paused again. "When he wanted to get back with you—how long ago was that?"

"Two years ago," Nora said. "Almost exactly."

Ann nodded. "I understand that he may be different, fun to be with. But two years ago, after he drew you in, talking about the therapy, his parents, all of that, you didn't think you could trust him again. What's different now?"

Nora wasn't clear herself on what had tipped the balance, but something had shifted; she believed him, trusted that an essential part of them had lasted and endured. How to explain her feeling of comfort, and mutual re-attraction, without sounding foolishly sentimental, or even deluded?

"A lot happened in the two years. Jim, Lily…" She ran a finger around the rim of her cup. "And I wasn't ready then. I don't think he was either."

Ann had no discernible expression that Nora could read. "I'm not making excuses for him," she said. "What he did three years ago and how he did it was horrible. We've talked about it. I believe him when he said he felt he had no choice. I could turn away, not risk, not try again."

Ann asked, "Do you think he wants to come back?"

"You mean live here?"

Ann nodded.

"I have no idea," she said. "We have a long way to go before I'd even think about that." Nora had wondered about it, got as far as imagining what it would be like having another adult in the house, how good it would be for Jack and Clare. But she didn't want a relationship based on nostalgia, on the lure of being drawn back into a family. And it was too soon to know where they were headed.

Nora added, "I'm taking it slow—on my terms. For now, just this." She pointed at the slow cooker. "Meals together, letting it unfold. Believe me, I'm keeping myself…" She thought for a minute. "Not on guard, but cautious, I guess."

"Listen," Ann said gently. "You don't have to convince me. If you're happy, I'm happy. But…" She put her hand on Nora's. "I'm glad you're taking it slow."

CHAPTER 58

At five o'clock Brad arrived wearing a T-shirt, shorts, and sneakers and carrying a cake pan covered with foil. He smiled at Nora. "Dessert. We made it this afternoon." Jack and Clare left their duffel bags in the hall and ran to see Lily, each trying to outdo the other to get her attention.

Nora and Brad laughed as Lily crawled from one to the other. "I think she missed you guys," he said. He looked at Nora. "We should go. I think we can do it before the rain starts."

As she watched from the kitchen window as they got the bikes from the garage and Brad checked the tires and pumped air, she thought of Ann saying earlier, "If you're happy, I'm happy." She *was* happy with a depth she hadn't experienced in a long time.

After they left, she washed a cucumber and set it on the cutting board while Lily sat on the floor banging a wooden spoon on a pot. Nora heard a commotion at the front door.

Jack burst in yelling, "Mom, there's blood everywhere. Dad fell off his bike."

Nora wasn't sure if she needed to call 911, if "blood everywhere" was as dire as it sounded. She picked up Lily, strapped her in her bouncy seat, and said to Jack, "Stay here and watch her." She grabbed a bunch of paper towels and ran out. The bikes were lying on the sidewalk in front of the house. The rain had started again, and the road was wet. Brad limped up the driveway, blood dribbling from his knees, smiling at her, red-faced. "I slid and lost control."

As usual, when Clare was anxious, she wore it on her face—her chin scrunched up the way it did when she was about to cry. "Do we have to go to the hospital?"

"It's okay, honey," Nora said. "Brad, sit on the stoop, let me see." She looked at his knees and applied pressure over the cuts and abrasions. "Good. You don't need stitches."

Brad said, "See, Clare, I'm fine."

When the rain got heavier, Nora stood. "Let's go in the house so I can clean it." Inside, she said to Brad, "Let's go upstairs. I have everything there. Clare, go with Jack to watch Lily. I'll be right back."

As they got to the bedroom door, Brad glanced around. It was the first time he'd seen it since he moved out.

She waited for him to notice the furniture she had painted and the teal comforter that replaced their yellow and white striped one.

"I like the furniture. You had it painted?"

"No, I did it."

"Really?" He looked closer at the top of his dresser.

"I'm impressed."

In the bathroom, he sat on the toilet and she knelt on the floor and washed his knees with warm water and then with peroxide, gently removing the pebbles and pieces of leaves stuck to his wounds. As she patted his knees with pads of gauze to dry them, she felt his eyes on her and looked up at him, startled by his expression. Tender, warm, searching, so known, so intimate. Flustered by the interplay of her emotions—touched, attracted, and elated all at once—she felt her face turn hot and she lowered her eyes to his knees. "Does it hurt much?"

"No." He smiled. "I forgot how good you are at this."

She didn't look at him as she covered his knees with gauze pads and adhesive tape. When she finished, she went to the sink to wash her hands and then into the hall where Brad was looking at the line of pictures. She wondered if he noticed the missing ones of their wedding and anniversaries. After she had removed them, she replaced the empty spaces with photos of the children. But she hadn't entirely erased him. She'd kept the family ones. He was quiet as he studied the wall.

When they walked by Lily's room he stopped. "Nice. I like the green and purple."

As they walked by Jack and Clare's bedrooms, still with the same sturdy furniture he had assembled, he said, "I remember the hours it took to put together the desk and dressers."

She pointed to the mess on Jack's floor. "His room at your house is so much neater."

"Not usually. I cleaned it up before you came for dinner."

At the top of the steps he stopped and looked at her as if he wanted to say something.

Lily had started to cry. Jack called up, "Mom. She wants to get out."

"I know," she called down. "I'm coming."

Brad smiled and pointed to his knee. "Thanks for doing this."

Downstairs, Nora picked up Lily and put her in her high-chair with a sippy cup of milk and Cheerios. Brad offered to chop the cucumber for the salad. As she heated the water for the pasta, she watched as he peeled and diced it—straight and even—each piece uniform. His preciseness didn't trigger a visceral response as it often had. Instead, she found it endearing. While Jack and Clare set the table, she buttered the bread, sprinkled it with garlic and cheese and put it in the oven.

During dinner Brad was as attentive as he had been at the first dinner, relating to each of them with their interests in mind and making Lily giggle as he played "Peek-a-Boo." Once, when he caught Nora's eyes on him, his expression shifted and brightened. Another time, she looked up from feeding Lily to see him watching her with the same intimate expression, the same searching look that had crossed his face in the bathroom. He smiled, and she smiled back and kept her eyes on his for a few seconds.

At seven thirty, while Nora put Lily to bed, Brad and the children cleared the table and did the dishes. As she listened to the noises from downstairs, she thought of how it contrasted with the quieter evenings with just her and the children, of the times she experienced the emptiness and loneliness as the sole adult faced with the tedious tasks of dinner and bedtime rituals.

While she was rocking Lily, Nora thought of how easy the dinner was, how simple it had seemed. No bickering between Jack and Clare. Although Jack's mood and attitude had improved with the therapy, and his anger at her had ebbed, he was still self-absorbed at times, still sullen and irritated at the littlest things. But for the weekly Sunday dinners, he was polite and upbeat.

Of course, she knew that if the dinners continued, they wouldn't always be this serene. Everyone was on their best behavior; the novelty of having Brad there for dinner hadn't yet ebbed.

When she came down, she found them in the kitchen. The steady rain and the warmth of the lights gave an aura of comfort to the room. Watching them made her smile—Brad cutting the brownies, Clare putting one on each plate, and Jack putting scoops of ice cream on top—each intent on their task. Clare said, "Mom, we made you brownies." Brad smiled. "Still your favorite?"

She nodded, pleased that he remembered. After dessert, they sat on the floor in the family room and played Scrabble like they often did after dinner and, as he did before, Brad came up with obscure words that they challenged. At nine thirty, when Nora went upstairs with Clare to get her to bed, Brad played a video game with Jack.

After she returned from putting Clare to bed, Brad said, "It's late. I'd better get going." Then he cleared his throat and as if he were overstepping a boundary, he asked, "Would it be okay if I kiss Clare goodnight?"

"Sure. She'd like that."

When he came back, he smiled at Nora. "She's almost asleep."

After he said goodnight to Jack, she and Brad went out on the porch. They stood for a minute under the roof, watching the rain.

He turned to her. "Thank you for dinner, and for bandaging my knees."

As they looked at each other, she wanted to touch him, to hold him, to have him hold her. He put his hands on the sides of her face, pulled back a few curls that had escaped, leaned in and they kissed. Gentle at first, familiar—it felt right, like coming home—and then more insistent, enlivened with a hunger that had gotten buried. Then he put his arms around her, and she reached up to hug him and put her head on his shoulder. They stood like that for a minute. He smelled of the aftershave she remembered, a comforting scent of sandalwood she had loved.

CHAPTER 59

The kiss on the porch after what Nora thought of as the "sausage dinner night"—finding it easier to remember what they ate rather than the date it occurred—propelled them even closer, adding a physical attraction to their relationship that reminded her of the electric tension she had felt when they were first falling in love, not with the intensity of that, but also not with the lower wattage the desire had become by the time Brad left.

After that dinner, Nora found herself thinking about where their relationship was leading and whether she would be able to believe that he wouldn't have another crisis that would make him unhappy. Would she be holding that trauma in the back of her mind?

On a Sunday in the first week of July, Brad had to go to Florida for a conference. On his first night there, he called from his hotel room, having gotten into the habit of calling each night when the children were in bed. Besides going over schedules, they'd talked about their work, how she was doing yoga early in the mornings, how he had started jogging again, sort of filling in the gaps, splicing the missing pieces of their lives.

That night, she lay in bed in the dark, the windows opened and the breeze billowing the curtains, the old-fashioned streetlights giving off a dim glow in the room. Brad said, "It's Sunday night. I wish I were having dinner with you."

"Me too," she said. She'd already gotten used to the different texture of the week, anticipating and planning the meal, looking forward to his company. The evening had felt washed out, empty without him.

"I miss you," he said.

The warmth of his words made her smile. She tried to picture him and wondered if he was in bed. In a chair? Lights on or off? A smile on his face?

There was a beat of silence. "I love you," he said.

Although she had expected the words and was thrilled to hear him say them out loud, and although she was sure of her love for him, she needed more than the mere words. Far easier in the dark, without having to face him and watch his reaction, she asked, "Love me how? Like you used to?"

"Like I used to love you. Like I love you now." He added, as if she knew where the conversation was headed, "I never stopped loving you, Nora. I never wanted anyone but you. I missed you. There were so many times I wanted to tell you that."

She knew he didn't see his leaving as rejecting her but as a struggle to dig out, to save his life. But she needed to address her concerns. "When you say you always loved me... I guess in your own way, you did. I *do* believe you felt you had no other choice." She thought about degrees of love, what it meant to really love someone, and tried to pinpoint what she was feeling. "But still, you cared more about what you were going through than what you were about to put me through. Like you didn't love me enough to at least try."

"I did love you. But I couldn't *really* love you. I wasn't there, and I felt horrible. I still do. When I think about it now, I think why the hell didn't I talk to you, get help way earlier. It seems ridiculous."

"I'm still not sure what you mean by love. How is it different?"

"Because I'm different."

It was true. She thought of the night at his house, standing at the puzzle table and looking at him, thinking him a fuller dimension of himself, with qualities of the early Brad woven in, and wondered if she seemed different to him, if he saw her as stronger and more resilient. "I'm not the same twenty-year-old girl you fell in love with. Or the forty-year-old woman you left," she said. It was important to her he know this.

"I love the Nora then and the Nora now."

She could hear the smile in his voice.

"Actually, I crave you."

"Crave me?"

"Like craving something elemental, you know, like food, water, something needed to survive?"

CHAPTER 60

After that they talked most nights, and before they hung up, Brad said, "I love you." It took longer for Nora to feel sure enough to say the words. She thought of the two of them as being reassembled with missing pieces of their puzzle gradually filled in. Nora asked him about the woman Jack and Clare had mentioned. The one who had brought the spaghetti. Brad had been patient during her questioning and laughed when she asked how the sauce was. "Not as good as yours."

Nora was surprised that Brad hadn't asked about Jim, as if it were a taboo topic. He knew the basics from when Nora told him she was pregnant—that she'd a relationship for five months, but they were no longer together, and she was keeping the baby. After that, the only time Jim was mentioned was when Brad shared insights from his therapy and his hurt and anger about her pregnancy.

Nora remembered the words of Dr. Friedman. *We may not try to hide things, but at the same time we don't reveal them. They stay buried but simmering.*

It was a missing piece in their emerging relationship. One evening after dinner when the children were in bed, Brad sat on the couch and patted the seat beside him. It was dark by then, and Nora switched on a light and sat in a chair facing him.

"Is something wrong?"

"I want to tell you more about Jim."

He looked surprised. "Okay... Sure."

"Do you have any questions about him? We've never talked much about it."

He was silent for a minute. His expression changed from relaxed to attentive. "I assume he knows?"

Nora nodded.

He looked at a photo of Lily that sat on a table across from him. "Doesn't he want to be involved?"

"It's complicated. He never wanted kids. He's almost fifty."

"Do you want him involved?"

She shook her head. "No. It's easier. Maybe when she's older."

"Did you love him?"

She answered, "No, I didn't love him." She waited for him to ask more. How long they had been together; why she decided to keep the baby—the things she would have been curious about. But he smiled and said, "How about a glass of wine?"

"Not yet." Nora felt compelled to make excuses for Jim, for herself. More importantly, she wanted Brad to have a positive impression of Lily's father. She explained that she had run into him downtown with his new girlfriend. And then went to see him and talk about her pregnancy. "He's a nice man. He was willing to help financially, but I didn't want him to."

"He sounds like a nice guy. Do you miss him?"

"He is a nice guy, but I don't miss him." She moved to the couch and sat next to him. He put his arm around her, and she leaned into him. "I'd love that glass of wine now."

CHAPTER 61

By the end of July, Brad was joining them for dinner several times a week. She cooked, or they ordered pizza, or he grilled hamburgers. It sometimes felt as if he had never left. Other times she was startled upon hearing his voice in another room, surprised that he was there. And then, a happy feeling would wash over her. One day she watched him across the street, talking and smiling with a neighbor, an older man whose sidewalk Brad had shoveled in the wintry weather—another reunion of sorts. When he saw something that needed fixing, he got his tools from the garage and whistled as he took care of it. He did the things he knew she hated doing: killing spiders; sweeping out the garage; weeding the garden.

By then, Nora had invited Ann and Nick and their family for dinner, hoping that Ann would let go of her mistrust of Brad. In the beginning of the first dinner it was strained, but the noise and exuberance of the children drowned out any obvious discomfort. At first, Nora was aware of Ann's eyes on

Brad like a laser, beaming in on his interactions with her, and was pleased that he didn't seem conscious of her scrutiny as he chatted and laughed with Nick. By the end of the evening, when Ann and Nora sat on the deck while Brad and Nick played soccer with the kids, Ann said, "Well, he sure seems happy and in love with you. Nick will be thrilled. We can have dinners again."

The children took his increasing presence in stride. Nora found herself saying, "Dad's coming tonight," rather than "your dad" or "your father."

Her doubts started the night Brad suggested getting back together and telling Jack and Clare. "They see us together all the time. I'm on a month-to-month lease. We're not divorced; it would be easy. Why don't we at least make a plan?"

Nora wasn't sure. She didn't know why. Of course, it had been in the back of her mind. Clearly, they were headed in that direction. It was the word *plan* that threw her. Once he proposed it, she became obsessed with what it would actually mean. She'd been enjoying being with him—the family dinners, the attraction, the renewal of their love for each other—and was happy, without the full commitment.

Now, in bed she would look at his side, imagine him there instead of the books she was reading. Wonderful, yes, but the solitary nights reading in bed once the kids were asleep had become a favorite part of her day. Also, in the years since he left, she had started a habit of getting up early before the children and spending twenty minutes doing yoga, loving the quiet still-ness. Brad would be there, needing to shower, dress. She loved the bookends of her days: the nights in bed reading and the morning solitude.

One Saturday night, when Brad was leaving, Clare pulled on his sleeve. "Why can't you stay?"

That night on the phone, he said, "Clare's right. Why not? It's silly to have two places."

He was right. It was getting ridiculous moving Jack and Clare back and forth each week, not to mention how impractical it was financially. All she could think of to say was, "It has to be more than that," she said. "More than making our lives easier."

"It is more than that. I love you. I want to be with you."

"Yes, but it's such a big thing. Final. Permanent."

"I hope so."

When she didn't respond, he said, "What do you want, Nora?"

"I want to be with you. I love you," she said. "I love that we'll be a family again. It's all happening so quickly. I need..." She looked around the bedroom that had been hers for three years. "I need to have time to myself. To do yoga in the morning. At night I might want to get in bed and read a book as soon as the kids are asleep."

He sounded relieved. "I think I can handle that. We'll figure it out."

She thought of all the good things his presence would mean and the happiness she felt when she was with him. But a part of her was not ready to say yes. The logistics with the children were part of it. She and Brad had little time to be alone; they joked that they were like teenagers kissing on the porch at night. And for a while, that was all Nora wanted. Just as she took her time to say "I love you," she needed to be sure before they took that next step. Brad was eager to move ahead; he kidded about feeling like a horny teenager. She wrestled with herself, thinking her reasons were silly, but still she put him off.

One weekend when Jack and Clare had a sleepover planned with Eddie and Maddie, Nora invited Brad to spend the night. They would have a romantic dinner after Lily was asleep. Nora bought a new nightgown—a silky cream sheath unlike anything she had worn during their marriage. After the children were born, she wore flannel pajamas in the winter or T-shirts in the summer. That night, Nora and Brad were sitting by the fire when Ann called. Clare was throwing up and wanted to come home. "Oh, well," Brad said with a smile. "Almost."

CHAPTER 62

In the middle of August, when Nora needed to go to school to attend meetings and get her classroom ready, she started Lily in day care. Brad took time off to be with Jack and Clare. Nora was preoccupied with planning for the fall and thinking of the challenges of the first weeks of school. Just thinking about the daily schedule of getting Jack and Clare to school and Lily to day care wore her out.

Brad was pushing her to set a date for him to move in and she continued to vacillate. One day she would feel ready to take the leap. On another day, her doubts would revisit along with a fear of putting something in motion that she might regret.

One night, Ann called to invite them for dinner. "I think Nick and Brad have gotten into a cooking competition," Ann said. "After the gourmet meal Brad made last week, Nick's been looking for recipes."

Nora was in her bedroom folding laundry after she had gotten the kids to bed.

"I'm sure we'd love to come. Today's Thursday, right? Did you say on Sunday?"

"You sound distracted."

"I am. Brad's pushing to move back and I can't make up my mind."

"Why?" Ann said. "I figured it would happen any day the way things have been going."

Nora shut the bedroom door and sat on the side of the bed. "I got used to making decisions on my own. Like what to eat, what time to eat. It's like I was in control of the remote for three years and now I'll have to share it."

"Yeah, that's kind of how it is." Ann laughed.

"It is like a perfect world. Having two places. Not getting sick of each other."

"How long do you think Brad would be okay with that arrangement?"

"Not long." Nora laughed.

"Besides the reality of married life, what is it that you're really afraid of?"

"I don't know. Maybe it's a combination—me and my freedom but also a nagging flashback of being blindsided by him. Maybe I'm worried about that. Remember how I blamed myself when he left?"

"When you twisted yourself into believing that you had made him unhappy?"

"Yeah. Twisted and tormented myself." Nora paused for a minute. "I don't know. I don't want to be watching his moods, his reactions."

Ann paused for a second, then said, "Do you really think you're responsible for his moods, like a magic fairy with the power to make everyone happy.? Do you think your life will be perfect, no arguments? If I worried about Nick being annoyed, I'd have an ulcer." She laughed. "You're not responsible for his happiness."

"It's crazy, I know."

"He seems more laid back. Easier," Ann said. "And he seems so happy with you. He adores Lily."

"Listen to you." Nora gave a weak laugh. "Not long ago, you thought we were moving too fast."

"You convinced me," Ann said. "You were sure he had dealt with whatever it was. You trusted him, forgave him."

"I do trust him. I have forgiven him. It's more about me." Nora got up and paced the room. "I don't want to go backwards. I'm not sure I'm strong enough—"

"Nora. Think of all you've gone through in the past three years. Dealing with life on your own. Making the decision to have Lily. Having to tell people and face all of that. Jesus. You're a hell of a lot stronger than I am."

"I don't feel so strong right now."

"How do you feel when you're with him?" Ann asked.

Nora closed her eyes and thought for a minute.

"Loved. Happy."

"Maybe that's your answer."

"We aren't living together. It'll be different." Nora smiled. "Remember when Brad left? You said I could be ditzy and not piss anyone off? I loved that. I want to be myself. I still have memories of feeling stupid because my brain doesn't work like his. When I couldn't figure how things work."

"I watched you at dinner last week. You were just as ditzy. He seemed fine."

"That was one night."

"I have an idea," Ann said. "Jack and Clare can stay with us for a weekend sometime and Brad can move in for a few days. Think of it—you have leverage now. You can set your conditions. Try it out. That would give you four days to be your ditzy self."

After they ended the conversation, Nora leaned back against the pillow and listened to the cicadas. Or were they locusts or katydids? She never could keep them straight.

CHAPTER 63

Nora knew she wasn't ready to have Brad move back for a trial. She put him off by telling him she needed to get ready for school and Lily used to day care. Brad stopped asking and Nora was able to put it in the back of her mind until the night that became a turning point. An ordinary night. They planned a cookout on the Saturday before the first week of school. Nora was looking forward to a relaxing evening.

The day started out warm and sunny. Brad came in the afternoon and while Lily napped, they all played badminton and softball in the backyard. The hamburgers and hot dogs were ready to grill; the picnic table, with an orange and yellow striped tablecloth, was set for dinner.

But the day turned in a different direction for her soon after Brad put the food on the grill, as clouds moved in and blocked the sun, causing a sudden chill in the air. Everything that one minute had been sparkling in the sun took on a drearier cast.

Nora picked up the napkins that blew off the deck and

looked up at the sky; she shivered in the cool breeze. "It's getting cloudy," she said to Brad. "Should we eat inside?"

"Up to you," he said, as he flipped the hamburgers.

She went inside to get Lily who had woken from her nap, then carried her outside, stood for a minute, and stared up again at the increasing clouds and then at Brad who was taking the food off the grill. "What do you think?" she asked.

He held the platter of grilled meat. "Nora," he said, with a tone of impatience, "if you think it's too chilly, tell me; we can move everything in."

Sensing his impatience, she glanced at the table with everything laid. Unable to decide, she said, "I don't know what would be easier." Lily began to cry.

"Okay," Brad said, "let's move inside." He carried the platter into the kitchen and called Jack and Clare to help. They picked everything up and moved it in and set it on the kitchen table. The hamburgers and hot dogs, ketchup, mustard, pickles, were crowded in the middle of the kitchen table. They sat close together with Lily's highchair squeezed next to Nora. She wished she'd suggested eating in the dining room. More space. The noise of the forks scraping across the plates irritated her. After Clare kicked her feet against the rung of her chair for the third time, Nora said, "Stop it, Clare."

Tears filled Clare's eyes. Nora sighed. *Let this meal be over*, she thought. With no room for Jack's elbows, he knocked his glass of milk to the floor. Shards of glass flew across the room. Lily got scared and cried again at the sound of the glass breaking. While she comforted Lily, Brad quietly swept up the glass and mopped the milk. While they ate, Nora watched Brad—no evidence of his earlier annoyance. No one seemed to notice her bad mood. Her head throbbed.

By the time they finished dinner, Nora wanted to put Lily to bed and go to bed herself. It was Brad's weekend with the kids, and she couldn't wait for them to leave, wanting to be alone.

Clare had cleared the table and Jack and Brad loaded the dishwasher while Nora put Lily to bed. When she came back to the kitchen Brad said, "Why don't we sit and have a glass of wine? Maybe we can talk about setting a date?"

Brad hadn't noticed the shift in her; they'd had two different experiences. She said, "I'm tired. I think everyone is."

He looked concerned. "Do you think you're getting sick?"

"No, I just need to sleep."

"Okay. It was a long day," he said. "How about if I bring pizza tomorrow night when I bring them home?"

As he left that night, she stood on the porch and waved. It was drizzling, and in the distance were rumbles of thunder. She turned away, drained and strangely uneasy. Something nagged at her; she carried the aftertaste of her indecisiveness, his impatience, and an elusive feeling she couldn't name.

After Lily was asleep, she undressed and put on a nightgown before she collapsed into bed, falling into a deep sleep, and waking at two in the morning hot and clammy. She opened the window and got back in bed and lay there staring at the ceiling fan, listening to the rain that beat against the screen, some of it blowing in upon her and cooling her. Wide awake, she faced the questions she had buried earlier, and that now swirled through her mind, magnified in the dark of the night.

What had happened to her? It wasn't easy for her to define.

She'd gotten cold and wanted to eat inside. Why hadn't she said so? If Brad hadn't been there, she would have made a quick decision. And even though it was so small a thing, petty really, something that shouldn't have been anything but a blip in the evening, it seemed much larger. Soon she had gotten herself into such a funk that every thought that crossed her mind gave her pause, adding to her disquiet.

As she pictured Brad's face and his flicker of impatience at her indecision, she thought how easily they could revert to the pattern of their marriage. She had convinced herself Brad had changed, wasn't as uptight. But what if he hadn't? Once they were together every day, would he get annoyed, tell her she was being impractical about one thing or another? And what if she hadn't changed either? What if she couldn't stand her ground and say what she was thinking? What if she wasn't even sure of what her desires were?

CHAPTER 64

It rained all night and into the next day. Brad took Jack and Clare to a movie, and Nora stayed home and napped when Lily napped. By the time Brad came with pizza and wine, the rain had ended, the sun was out, and there was a blurry hint of a rainbow. During the meal, she was conscious of the dissonance within her and wrestled with herself. Was she making a big deal out of nothing?

Brad noticed nothing of her unease. A big smile crinkled his eyes as he made jokes with Jack and Clare and played Peek-a-Boo with Lily.

After she put Lily to bed, she went to her room and sat on her side of the bed. She wasn't ready. She needed to let him know. When she went downstairs, Brad was in the kitchen washing the colander. Jack and Clare were outside playing basketball.

"I want to talk. Let's sit down." She went into the family room and sat on one end of the couch; he followed and sat next to her.

He looked alarmed. "What's wrong?"

How to explain the doubts the scene on the deck had raised? She felt a tightening in her chest. "I don't know. Worries…"

His face took on a serious expression. "About what?"

"About starting over. Living together. It seems so final."

"Is that a bad thing?"

She took a deep breath. "The other night when it got cloudy and chilly, when I asked you if you wanted to eat inside…" She stopped. It sounded so silly now. She looked down at her sweater and pulled on a loose thread.

His eyes softened, perhaps in amusement, perhaps in relief. "And then we did," he said. "I thought everything was fine. A little chaotic maybe."

Jack and Clare's laughter from outside distracted her. Nora stood and closed the doors and then sat in a chair across from him. "I was trying to figure out what you wanted. Then I thought you got annoyed."

"I don't remember being annoyed." He looked up at the ceiling as if trying to recall. "I remember I wanted you to say what *you* wanted. Lily was crying. Someone had to decide."

She nodded. "I should have said I was cold. That it looked like rain. And after, I wondered why I didn't."

"I wish you would have, but it was no big deal." He smiled gently. "We'll get irritated with each other." He shrugged.

"It's life."

Logical as always, as if the problem were simply about annoyances and irritations. She struggled to find the words to explain what she still didn't fully understand. "I've gotten used to making my own decisions, doing things my own way. Even if they aren't the way you would do them."

He looked surprised. "But you could have made that decision."

"I should have. That's the point. I wondered why I was so concerned about what you were feeling. Watching your face. It reminded me of how I used to watch my mother's face. I always felt responsible if she seemed unhappy."

"I never knew that." Brad looked surprised and watched her closely.

She studied him for a minute. "I don't want to try to read your moods. And I don't want to feel inferior if I don't do things the way you would."

"Jesus, Nora. I know I can be a little anal, but making you feel inferior? The thing about where to eat started all of this?"

"It brought it all back. It even triggered memories of the day on the boardwalk when you suddenly told me you were unhappy."

"I was never unhappy with you."

Now, as she heard those words, something clicked. "You were *unhappy*. Period. I had no idea. Of course, I was sure it was me. I blamed myself. Looked for reasons. I need to be sure about myself, strong enough about what I want."

Then, as if something clicked for him, he said, "Are you saying you don't want to get back together?"

"I'm not saying that. I'm just not ready."

"Nora…I don't know how to convince you." He was quiet for a moment. "Is it going to hang over my head forever?"

When she didn't answer, he asked, "Do you think we should see Dr. Friedman again?"

Nora thought of having Dr. Friedman's eyes on her as she tried to sort her feelings. "I don't know. Maybe."

They were quiet. She looked at the set of pictures that hung on the wall. Smiling family photos. How ridiculous that she'd assumed responsibility for his unhappiness. A role she had fallen into from the beginning when his parents died in the accident. When he was unable to share his feelings with her and she began to watch his face for nuances in his tone and expression.

She looked at him. "Think about it. If I had suddenly told you *I* was miserable and wanted to separate, think about how you'd feel."

He nodded. "You're right. I can't imagine. But I feel like I can't win." He shook his head. "Every time I get annoyed, you'll wonder if I'm unhappy?"

Yes, possibly she would. That was the problem. Her problem.

He sounded frustrated. "What do you want me to do? Read your mind? Explain my every annoyance, every time…"

"Nothing. I don't know." She listened to the thumping of the basketball and fiddled with her hair, twisting strands around her fingers.

"You want some perfect world that doesn't exist." When she didn't answer, he said, "Maybe you don't want us?"

Mindful on some level that he was right, aware that she was expecting something impossible, she said, "I do want us." That she knew. But she also knew that once he moved back in, it would be final. She had to be sure of herself.

Brad stood and crossed the room and stopped at the French doors. Nora watched his profile as he stared outside, his hands in his pockets. He spoke quietly. "I wonder if you know what you want."

"I just need a little more time."

When he turned back, his face held an expression of resignation. He sounded deflated. "Okay. I don't want to push you. We should take a break. Give us time to think." He opened the door to the yard. "I'm going outside to say good night to the kids."

Nora went to the kitchen and wiped the counters, cleaned the sink, then wiped the counters again, needing to do something with her hands. As she watched Brad throw basketballs with Jack and Clare, watched how right it seemed, how happy they were to have his presence, she felt an uncomfortable sorrow and a feeling of loneliness. It was as if she had been collecting evidence to build a case, but for what? To close herself in a protective shell, invulnerable, waiting for the perfect world?

No kiss on the porch. A quick good night hug. She watched as his car drove into the distance until the lights disappeared and the street was dark.

CHAPTER 65

On Monday, Nora woke feeling worn out after sleeping sporadically and questioning herself each time she woke. She dragged herself through the day—getting Jack and Clare up and to school and Lily to day care before her workday began and back home to dinner, baths, and bedtime rituals. The way the evening with Brad had ended unsettled her, and she called him once the kids were in bed.

"Can we talk for a minute?" Nora said.

"Okay," he said in a cool and distant tone.

"I'm not sure what you mean about a break, but I want us to keep talking. I'd like you to still come for dinner and see the kids."

"I don't know. That would be hard for me." He cleared his throat. "Besides, you said you need time to think."

"I do…about the moving in part. But I know I want to be with you. And the kids will be confused if you stop coming."

He didn't answer right away. Then he said, "Okay. I'll come on Sundays for dinner."

After they said goodnight—no 'I love you'—she called Ann to get the number of a therapist a friend of theirs had gone to and liked. "I have no desire to do this, but I need help. I have to make up my mind."

Ann was surprised, but pleased. "That's a good idea. Her name is Ellen Barton. She's easy to talk to, direct, gets right to the heart of things. Plus, her sessions are ninety minutes, so it's not rushed."

Nora was intimidated about the thought of the long sessions. But the next morning, she took a deep breath and dialed the number. Nora was able to get an appointment for Thursday morning; she got a substitute for her class at school. Nervous about filling up the time, she got a notepad and wrote a timeline of what had happened and jotted down some notes to look at if she got stuck.

Ellen, who looked to be in her fifties, had a mixture of grey and black hair pulled into a bun which would have made her look severe if it weren't for her kind brown eyes and gentle smile. Her office was in her home in a small room off the living room. On one side were two chairs facing each other with a round coffee table between them; a couch lined another wall. She directed Nora to a chair with a view toward the garden and sat across from her. The window framed a crepe myrtle tree with several purple blooms still hanging. Soft morning sunlight illuminated the room.

"Tell me what brought you here, Nora," Ellen said with a welcoming smile.

Nora, with her notepad clutched in her sweaty palms, explained that she and her husband had been separated for three years and were in the process of reuniting but that she was having doubts. Ellen began by asking questions about why they'd separated. After Nora explained about Brad's unhappiness and her shock at hearing it, Ellen encouraged her to talk about what it had been like to be blindsided. Nora shared the trauma of her shock, grief, and depression.

While Nora talked, Ellen wrote notes, with an occasional nod, or question of clarification. After Nora described how she had eventually adjusted and adapted, Ellen asked, "What was that like? How long did that take?"

"The first days and weeks were awful. I thought once I got through those it would be easier. But after the adrenalin of the shock ebbed and my anger subsided, it was almost worse. Fatigue and lethargy. Emptiness. No appetite. I couldn't focus and wasn't fully available for my children. I was depressed but couldn't do anything about it. A support group just made it worse. It took months before I felt like myself again."

"What does that mean?" Ellen asked. "Feeling like yourself?"

"Energy. Feeling hungry again. Enjoying simple things like a cup of coffee. And realizing that I'd found a freedom I'd never known," Nora said. "Then, after a year he wanted to get back together. He had been in therapy." Nora told her about the sudden death of his parents in a car accident when Nora and Brad were seniors in college and how he had closed off part of himself.

"How did you feel when he asked you? Was it a surprise?"

"A total surprise. It was as if he thought I'd be just waiting. I got angry and said no."

Then Nora talked about dating Jim, breaking up, finding she was pregnant, and deciding to have the baby.

Ellen asked questions about how Brad and the kids felt about her pregnancy. Nora talked of Brad's anger and Jack moving in with him; she finished by explaining how Jack wound up back at home with her. Her saga felt like a Cliff Notes version of her life.

Ellen put down her pen. "It sounds like you've been through a lot of loss and trauma."

Nora nodded. Laid out chronologically, it felt to her like a soap opera.

Ellen looked down at her notes for a minute. "How was your relationship with Brad before he left?"

Nora said, "I have to think." She fiddled with a strand of her hair that had escaped from her barrette.

"Take your time," Ellen said.

She was an oasis of calm with a presence about her that put Nora at ease. She didn't fix her eyes on Nora during her silent moments the way Dr. Friedman had. Instead, Ellen glanced down at her notes and waited. Nora heard a door open and someone padding quietly through the house. Ellen wore a wedding ring, and Nora wondered if it was her husband. Wondered what their relationship was like.

Nora finally said, "I was sure we were happy. He was a good husband, a good father. It was such a busy life with the kids and work that I never thought much about our relationship. It was like we floated along on the current." Nora stopped again to think. "But after he left, I looked at our marriage and realized so much was on the surface; there was so much we never discussed. So much we never shared."

Ellen said, "Besides being busy, were there other reasons for that?"

Nora thought again for a minute and then spoke about her lack of self-confidence in high school and college. How Brad was the first person she fell in love with, the first person who fell in love with her. "He wanted me. It felt like such a big deal. By the time we got married, I hadn't developed a strong identity. During our marriage, I don't think I ever felt entitled to recognize my own wants and needs."

Ellen said, "Can you tell me more about that?"

"I didn't bring up unpleasant things. If there were things that bothered me, I kept them to myself." A breeze blew off a blossom of the crepe myrtle. Nora watched as the petals fell to the ground. She looked at Ellen. "As I mentioned, he became different after his parents died. He kept feelings inside. That's why it was such a shock when he said he was unhappy."

"Can you give me an example of things that bothered you about him?"

"Before his parents were killed in the accident, Brad was light and spontaneous." Nora talked about how he shut down. "I read books about the stages of grief and tried to talk to him. It just made him angry, and I stopped trying. He became more serious, more orderly, rigid at times. I think that's why he became an accountant—because it's so black and white."

Nora looked down at her notes and doodled for a minute. The things that bothered her felt so petty now. "Brad was so exact. Precise in how he did things. He counted and knew the number of glasses in the dishwasher. That sounds silly, but it was things like that. If we made reservations, it could never be like seven: fifteen. It had to be on the hour or half hour. Although I got used to it, I didn't realize until after he left how much freer I felt. His tendencies reminded me of my father, who had rigid standards, although Brad was nothing like him—my father was nasty and domineering—but that triggered my resentment. He made me feel inferior with his comments about how I did things the wrong way."

"But you never told Brad? You never said anything?"

Nora shook her head. "Just muttered *asshole* under my breath. I know I annoyed him too—I'm at the other extreme. Not that I'm messy, I don't pay a lot of attention to details. Little things like that. Nothing huge. But it was a presence in our marriage."

Ellen had her notes in front of her. "You mentioned your father. You used the words nasty and domineering."

Nora nodded.

"Was he abusive in any way?"

"Not physically. I guess he was psychologically abusive. He yelled a lot. We never did things the way he wanted them done. He and my mother argued. My sister and I hated him."

"How did that affect you? Your mother? The atmosphere in the house?"

Nora was silent for a minute. She thought of her father's obsessive need for order and structure, and her mother's unhappiness that simmered under her acquiescence, their daily life compressed into smothering routines. Nora spilled out what she had never fully shared with anyone, not even Ann. The guilt from not being able to measure up to her father's stringent demands; covering her head with her pillow at night when they argued; the endless meals under fluorescent lights with every flaw exposed.

As she spoke, it surprised her to feel the tears running down her face. "I felt like I was suffocating."

Ellen pushed the tissues closer to her. "Okay," she said gently. "Do you want to take a break?"

Nora shook her head. "I want to talk about what happened

after my father died." She spoke about the change in her mother, the way the house had a light and airy feel. "It's not the same at all but it was similar in a way for me. My own liberation after Brad left. I redecorated the house, got rid of things I hated. I made it light and airy for me. But I feel bad even comparing it."

"No," Ellen said. "It's an important insight to realize that Brad's similar tendencies—without the mean and domineering part—triggered the constricted feeling in you."

Nora held a tissue to her eyes to blot the tears that continued to well and took another tissue from the box and blew her nose. "We got married right away after we graduated. We were both so young. I think what happened…how he couldn't share his pain with me set the tone on how we dealt with our feelings during our marriage."

"Do you think trauma from your childhood contributed?"

"I never thought of mine as trauma, but it did in different ways." Nora said. She talked about how she had worked to create a house different from her childhood one. "I craved warmth and harmony. I lit candles every night at dinner and played music… As if that would make a happy home."

"And when Brad was suddenly unhappy, besides the shock, it must have been a repudiation of all you had done to make the atmosphere different in your home from the one you grew up in."

"Exactly. I was sure our marriage was so different."

"I'm curious about something," Ellen said. "You said that Brad wanted to get back together after a year, and you said no. What drew you to reconciling now?"

"Brad's lighter now, easier. More like he was when I first met him. We had to spend time together because of Jack. We found a doctor and in our family sessions we talked about ourselves—how we buried conflict and kept our feelings inside. He talked about his therapy and the ways it helped him. It's like we both kept the blinds partially closed. Like the sheer curtains that give privacy but also block some of the light."

Ellen smiled. "That's a good analogy, Nora."

"We've had lots of dinners; the children are thrilled to have him back, and he's grown to love Lily. His therapy helped him to deal with his hurt and jealousy."

"You said that Jack has grown to accept Lily too?"

"Lily won him over. It's hard to be in a bad mood around her."

Ellen looked at the clock. "We need to finish for today. Next time we can talk about the doubts you're having."

At the door, she gave Nora her card. "You did a lot of emotional work today. If you need to call me before our next appointment, this is my after-hours number."

CHAPTER 66

Nora was both shaken and exhausted after sharing so much of her past three years, as well as of her childhood memories. But, after a few days, she felt as if something had been lifted. At night when everyone was asleep, she sat with a pad of paper to list her doubts and fears. She questioned herself. Did she want to date again? No. She pictured Brad dating and marrying someone else, and Jack and Clare with a stepmother. After the first meeting, Nora told Brad she was seeing a therapist and trying to sort things out. He didn't push for details, only said he hoped it would help.

At her next appointment, Nora sat in the same seat. The window was open a few inches, and the day was cool. The room felt chilly; she wished she had worn a sweater.

After Ellen asked if she'd had any repercussions after their meeting, Nora said, "I felt as if a weight had lifted."

"If you're ready, we can talk about your doubts about Brad moving back?"

Nora nodded.

"You say he's changed, not as rigid as he was?"

"He's not. But when he talked about making a definite plan to move back, my reaction surprised me…" She still wasn't sure. "I loved being with him, loved being a family again even though we had separate places. He came to my house most nights for dinner."

"What scared you?"

"First, it was the idea of it being permanent. I'm comfortable with myself, my freedom." She paused. Faint sounds came from another room and Nora wondered if it was the person she'd heard the last time. "It's the thought of having someone in the house all the time. I had never been alone, and it terrified me after Brad left. But then I got used to it and realized I liked time by myself and making my own decisions. His leaving gave me that gift. I finally know more of who I am, what I want."

Ellen nodded. "You learned that you enjoy solitude." She smiled as if she understood. "A crisis can be an unexpected opportunity to discover those things. Many people don't have the chance you did to dig down and find that about yourself."

Nora nodded. "I did dig down and I was confident but…" She smiled. "I think had a remission."

Ellen laughed.

Nora told her about the evening on the deck that raised doubts about herself.

"Did he do something in particular?" Ellen asked.

"No, not at all. He got a little impatient at one point, but it was more me worrying about what he wanted. It made me afraid that I'll fall back into the old pattern. I think of the everyday decisions I'll need to make with him once he moves back."

"Are you afraid about being blindsided again?

Nora thought about the things she'd shared with Ann and with Brad. "I'm not so much afraid of him wanting to leave; it's more me. I don't want to be checking his reactions. Watching his face. Not be strong enough about what I want. That night, I couldn't decide. I didn't know if it was going to rain and get chilly. I wanted to know what Brad wanted."

"Have you talked about it with him?"

Nora nodded.

"What did he say?"

"He doesn't know how to convince me. I told him about you and how I'm trying to work through my confusion."

"What you're doing is good practice—you're not trying to make Brad happy. You don't need to feel guilty about letting him wait to move back in. You said no. You didn't capitulate to what he wanted. You told him the reason."

"I did," Nora said.

Ellen said, "It's not fair to expect Brad to figure out what you want. There will be times like that night on the deck when there is no good answer. When you won't be able to decide. When you won't agree. And that's okay; it is what it is."

Nora thought about Ellen's words for a minute and how she had tied herself in knots over something so small. Ellen was right; it wasn't fair to Brad. She said, "I think it was part of me wanting everything to be perfect."

Ellen nodded. "Yes. Your happy home. Sort of Pollyannaish." She smiled. "I don't mean that negatively. It's the legacy not only of your childhood but the old expectation that women should be people pleasers."

"Yeah." Nora laughed. "That's what I don't want to be. A Brad pleaser."

"Yes. Let Brad worry about *your* happiness."

Nora said, "You sound just like my friend, Ann."

She smiled and said, "She sounds like a good friend."

Nora nodded. "And a good role model. She's able to let things go—she deals with something and she's done."

Then Ellen became serious. "You know there will be much harder things you have to face besides the everyday moods and irritations. You and Brad need to keep working on sharing and allowing yourselves to be vulnerable."

Nora nodded. "It's like we shared a home and a life, but not what mattered most."

"Exactly," Ellen said. "But you don't need to share every little thing. I'm a believer in keeping a part of yourself sacred." She smiled. "There are times we all need those sheer curtains." Ellen got up to close the window. The drizzle had turned to a steady rain. She stood at the window for a minute. When she sat down, she smiled at Nora. "I have an idea," she said. "What if you and Brad practice? Have him move in for a few days, a week, whatever. Try it out. Practice saying what you want; carve out time for yourself."

"Ann suggested it, and I thought about it," Nora said, "but I was afraid that once he was in the house…" She trailed off.

"You can make it clear to him you won't make the final decision until you're ready. Until you're ready to say yes while keeping the essential part of you." Then Ellen looked closely at Nora. "You need to realize what you've accomplished after he left. Besides the grief and loss, you were pretty much the primary parent while working full time. You even redecorated the house. And then Jim.

The decision that he wasn't right for you, your determination to have the baby, going through your pregnancy alone, losing Jack." She shook her head. "Goodness, Nora. You're way stronger than you think."

CHAPTER 67

Through the therapy with Ellen, Nora gained more trust in herself. As she braided her thoughts and Ellen's words, she found herself believing in the possibility of a life balanced with her needs and Brad's. She thought about his presence in a different way, in a positive way. His steadiness. Their similar interests. His love for the children. The security and predictability she would have. She pictured ordinary days: cooking on the grill; playing badminton in the backyard; a fire in the fireplace.

But she also knew their lives would get busy and cluttered and she would have to work to accept the imperfect, the flaws, the everyday annoyances, and to acknowledge and voice her disagreements. It would be good to practice. She called Ann to take her up on her offer for a weekend sleepover for Jack and Clare. "I have a great idea," Ann said. "There's a long weekend coming up in October and we're going camping. It will give you a longer time—four days."

Nora and Brad hadn't talked much about themselves since the night they started their break four weeks earlier. She had only told him she was seeing a therapist; now she called him to talk about how it had helped her to put her doubts in a larger context. "I think she did for me what your therapist did for you. And she suggested we have a trial period. Live together for a few days. Ann and Nick will take Jack and Clare."

"I'd love to," he said, "but it sounds as though I'll be on trial."

Nora said, "It's more of a test for me."

Nora spent the next week helping Jack and Clare to pack for their trip and busying herself with preparing for Brad. Early on the Friday morning of the long weekend, Nora sat in the kitchen and sipped her coffee while Lily slept. The weather forecast was for a string of lovely October days. Jack and Clare had left with Ann and Nick for their camping trip yesterday afternoon to give them a four-day weekend. Nora got a substitute teacher to fill in for her.

Brad was taking the day off from work and was due to arrive at ten. She watched the birds flutter around the feeder and wondered if Brad was as nervous as she. If this were a trial, a test, how would they measure it, rate it? Would it ease her concerns? The scene on the deck seemed distant and silly to her now. Nora had written down a few of Ellen's words that had resonated with her and put them in her nightstand drawer, and she finished her coffee and went upstairs to read them.

You won't like everything about him; he won't like everything about you. Sometimes we expect too much from our relationships, sometimes not enough. You don't need to share every little thing. There are times we all need those sheer curtains.

Nora glanced around the room that had been her bedroom for three years. She was used to Brad's presence on the first floor but imagining him in this space intensified her anxiety. She busied herself with the logistics of preparing the room like she would for a guest. Yesterday, she cleaned the bathroom and hung towels on the bar that had been his and slid aside her clothes that had crept into his side of the closet. As she surveyed the bedroom, her eyes focused on the bed and the night before they left for the beach when she was unaware it would be their last night in it. When she heard Lily waking and singing, she hurried to move her books from the bed and change the sheets, and as she slid his pillow into its case, she tried to imagine what it would be like, not only the physical intimacy—which was both scary and exciting—but his presence next to her, filling the empty space she'd grown accustomed to.

Once finished, she got Lily dressed and fed and was out front with her when Brad arrived, a duffel bag in one hand, a bunch of yellow roses in the other. Touched that he remembered her favorite flowers, some of her tension ebbed. At first, it was awkward, especially when they went to the bedroom for him to unpack. Nora put Lily on the floor to crawl around and closed the gate at the top of the stairs. Brad seemed like a guest, careful not to get in her way. He set his toothbrush and shaving supplies on a side of the vanity and asked if it was okay to hang a few things in the closet. "Just a couple of shirts."

She left him there to finish and brought Lily downstairs. As she arranged the roses in the vase he had given her on one of their anniversaries, she recalled the times when he filled it often and wondered when it had happened that he forgot, and she forgot, and the vase remained empty.

Later that morning, they went to the grocery store to buy food for the weekend. Brad surprised her; he decided he wanted to learn to cook and brought recipes he wanted to try for their three dinners—chicken fajitas, lemon fettucine, blackened tuna steaks—and held a list of ingredients. "I need to learn how to do more than open a bag of lettuce and throw a steak on the grill."

Nora pushed Lily in the cart as he filled the basket, marveling at how easy it was to shop with him and keep her attention on Lily who was trying to climb out of the cart. For lunch, they made a picnic and walked to the park. When they finished eating, she sat on a bench in the sun while Brad pushed Lily on the baby swing, both smiling. Watching them, Nora experienced a feeling of joy at how the relationship between them had evolved. An unexpected gift she would have thought impossible when she became pregnant and faced Brad's anger.

In the afternoon while Lily napped, Nora brought the baby monitor outside. They pulled two lounge chairs out of the garage and sat in the backyard under a maple tree, one Brad had planted when they moved in and was now tall and wide, its leaves today a brilliant red and yellow. "I feel like I'm on vacation," Brad said.

They lay back and read and sipped iced tea. Nora closed her eyes and listened to the rustling of the leaves. Brad was right. It was like a holiday, a retreat, she thought, no longer worried about how they would pass the time. They'd never gone on a real honeymoon. A few times her mother came and babysat, and they took weekend trips to the Poconos or to the beach. But she couldn't remember the last time, or at what point in their marriage, when planning time together stopped being a priority.

After a while Brad put down his book, took off his sunglasses, and turned to her. "I was thinking…"

She turned a corner down on the page she was reading and waited. His face reminded her of Jack's, when he was curious about something and his eyes got bigger.

"Why did your therapist suggest this?"

"Remember when I told you how I felt responsible for my mother being happy? And how I did the same with you during our marriage?"

He nodded. "Reading my moods. Worrying about me."

"In my therapy, we dove into that. My childhood, your parents dying, the night on the deck, all of it. It helped." She smiled. "Ellen said at one point, 'Let Brad worry about your happiness.'"

"Really? Jeez." He reached over and took her hand. "I was thinking about what you'd said about how I've made you feel at times when I'm anal. Just kick me when I do."

"I will. But so far you haven't."

"So, this *is* a test. Am I passing?"

Nora laughed. "I told you on the phone. It's more a test for me. To see if I can know and say what I want without worrying. Just relax and be you."

"Ha. Easy for you to say."

They were quiet again. Nora put her head back and let the sun warm her face.

Brad put his arm on her shoulder. "What if we had gotten divorced?" he asked. "Do you think we'd be sitting here? Or would we have moved on?"

Such an un-Brad-like question, she thought. He wouldn't have asked something so abstract before, at least not out loud to her. "I don't know." She took off her sunglasses and faced him. "I was ready with the papers. I set them aside and forgot."

"Well, I was glad you did," he said. "I didn't bring it up because I really didn't want us to get divorced." He swirled the ice around in his glass. "Though I thought about it when you got pregnant."

"And you said nothing?"

"You were going through the pregnancy and Jack was moving in with me. I figured I'd wait." He took her hand. "I'm glad I did."

It surprised her to hear that he had been concerned about her. Another possibility occurred to her. "Suppose we hadn't separated? Do you think we'd be sitting here?"

He shrugged. "Why wouldn't we?"

"I don't know. I think we were doing the motions. Even before whatever was going on with you. We took each other for granted. I didn't even know how much until months after you left, and I realized the illusions I had of a happy marriage."

"Really?" He swung around and sat on the side of his chair. "You felt like that?"

"Not until you left. I had a lot of time to think. We were so young when we got married. We both had our baggage…"

A yellow leaf fell in her hair and he reached over and picked it up. "It's funny. I never thought you had any baggage."

"Oh, yeah. It wasn't only you."

They were quiet for a minute.

He said, "So many things could have happened."

"So many things *did* happen," she said.

CHAPTER 68

That evening, she fed Lily and put her to bed while Brad cooked. When she came down, he was on the deck lighting the candles in the lanterns. A platter filled with his fajita dinner sat next to a bottle of red wine on the kitchen counter. He arranged bowls with sour cream and shredded cheddar cheese. Although he never cooked much, Brad had always helped with the prep and the cleanup, so it hadn't bothered her. But now, she thought of it as a nice addition to the new Brad. She stood at the window and watched him. The sun had lowered and slanted on his face. When he looked up, he saw her and smiled.

They lingered over dinner and sipped wine, their conversation easy. By the time they finished dinner and cleaned up the kitchen, it was dark, and Nora felt shy and nervous again as the hour for bed drew closer.

Upstairs, they stood for a minute at the bed. He looked at her. "Are you okay with this?" he asked as if sensing her anxiety. "I can sleep in Jack's room."

"I'm okay. Just a little nervous."

He said, "I have an idea. Let's pretend we're at camp." They turned off the lights, opened the windows, and pulled back the curtains making the room open and airy. She went to the bathroom to undress and put on the silky nightgown she had saved. When she came out, Brad stood at the bed and held out his arms. After they kissed, he held her face in his hands. "God, I missed you." As Nora gave in to longing and desire, intimacy came easy, both familiar and new, more than the rote habit it had become during their marriage.

During the night, the moon shone on the bed and the wind chimes that hung under the eaves gave off a soft tinkling sound. Nora woke often, surprised that he was next to her, and put her arm on him where the empty space had been. *I'm happy*, she thought, with a sense of relief.

They woke to the sounds of birds chirping and cool air blowing on them through the open windows in the sun-drenched room. They smiled sleepily at each other and listened to Lily babble as she woke. It reminded Nora of the early idyllic time when Jack was that age, when it was easy, just the three of them. She got Lily and brought her back to bed. Lily, who had started saying Ba when she saw Brad, crawled to him.

"I think she's trying to say Brad," Nora said.

He grinned at Lily and then turned to Nora. "I feel like I…" He hesitated for a second, then said, "I'm not sure of my role. Are you okay with me picking her up, helping?"

"If you'll be living here, she's part of the deal."

"I'd forgotten how much fun it is." He picked up Lily and held her over his head, causing her to giggle with delight.

Nora smiled at them, relieved at how comfortable he seemed, how normal it felt. When they went downstairs, Nora sat Lily in her highchair and sprinkled Cheerios on the tray. Brad offered to make breakfast. He loved mornings and had always loved to eat first thing. And Nora would force herself to help cook and then sit and eat with him and Jack and Clare, not hungry, not ready for conversation. Once he left, she got in the habit of fixing breakfast for Jack and Clare and having something later.

Nora took out the eggs from the refrigerator and sat them next to the English muffins. "Help yourself. I'll get a smoothie or cereal when I get hungry." She added, "I've always hated breakfast."

He looked surprised, and a little confused. "Why didn't I know?"

She shrugged. "Oh, because I guess it's what I assumed my role was. To eat breakfast with the family."

"Well, I wish I'd known. All those breakfasts."

"It's okay. I never told you."

He smiled. "I'm glad you're saying what you want." He opened the carton of eggs. "Does Lily like scrambled eggs?"

"Loves them," Nora said. "Can you watch her while I do yoga?"

"Sure. I'll feed her."

Later, they took Lily outside and sat on the grass. Brad asked, "Is it okay if I weed a little?"

Nora looked at the flower beds and pictured them from his perspective. Sad and neglected. Weeds mixed in. Roses that needed to be dead headed. Although she felt no guilt or need to apologize, she asked him, "Does it bother you that I let them go?"

"The plants?"

She nodded. "It's a mess out here."

"It's not your thing." He went to the shed and got a small shovel and his old gardening gloves. His face was serious and intent on the weeds until Lily crawled over to him and he broke into a wide smile.

That day passed. A trip to the park. Books in the afternoon. Cooking. Their normal world suspended. The weather remained perfect. At night after Lily was in bed, they ate on the deck watching the sun sink and the stars emerge. They talked more about Lily and even the possibility of Brad adopting her.

The third morning, while Brad took Lily for a walk, Nora did yoga and reviewed pieces of their weekend, moments of risk and trust, images of him—playing with Lily, cooking dinner, changing a light bulb too high for her reach, like she was gathering snapshots for a photo album. She pictured him yesterday, talking on the phone with a colleague whose wife was sick and offering to bring food. This wasn't what real life would be like; it resembled a mini honeymoon. Life would become mundane, but Nora felt comfortable and sure of herself.

In bed that night, he said, "I'll miss you. I hate to leave."

"Maybe you don't need to."

He leaned over to her and smiled. "So, I passed the test?"

"We passed the test."

"Can we tell the kids?"

Nora nodded. "I was thinking earlier, why not just stay at night? Move your things in gradually?" She picked up his left hand. "Do you still have your ring?"

He nodded. "In my top drawer. I hope you still have yours?"

She took it out of her jewelry box. The wide gold band inscribed with their wedding date. She hadn't had an engagement ring. They married quickly after they finished school and she hadn't wanted one; she loved the simple band.

He held it for a minute. "Should I propose? Put it on you?"

Once it was on, she wouldn't want to remove it. "After we tell the kids."

On the last morning when she woke, it was still dark. It had gotten chilly during the night and she pulled the comforter over her and looked at him for a minute, his face relaxed and his breathing quiet and even, thinking of the thread that connected them over the years and through the jagged journey they had taken to get to this point. She got up quietly so as not to wake him and went out to get the newspaper. The moon was still visible over the house. She stood for a minute and looked up at the bedroom, at the windows opened wide and smiled as she pictured Brad in the bed.

CHAPTER 69

"We have something to tell you," Nora said to Jack and Clare who had returned earlier that afternoon from their camping trip with Ann and Nick. While Lily was napping, she and Brad led them into the living room.

"Let's sit," Nora said. Jack and Clare sat in chairs across from the couch where Nora and Brad sat. When Brad left three years ago, Clare had been six and Jack ten. Since then, their faces and bodies had changed but their essential temperaments hadn't all that much. Clare's face lit up with anticipation, while Jack, always warier and less optimistic than Clare, sat straight and tense, his expression worried. Nora wondered if the sudden announcements of Brad's leaving and her pregnancy filtered through his mind. She put her hand on his and said, "It's a good thing, Jack." She waited for Brad to take the lead, to close the loop, to reunite what he had divided.

He started out sounding stilted at first and appearing as tense as Jack. "Your mother and I decided that we want to be together." He glanced at Nora. "So, I'll be moving back."

For a minute, the room was silent until Clare asked, "You're coming home? Here?"

"Yes." Brad smiled at Nora. "I'm coming home."

Jack seemed less tense, his face and shoulders relaxed.

Clare looked from Brad to Nora. "Tonight?" When Nora smiled and nodded, she said to him, "You won't leave?"

"No, I won't leave."

"We don't have to go to your apartment anymore?" Jack asked. Nora could sense pleasure in his expression despite his noncommittal façade.

"No," Brad said. "We'll need to pack and move things out."

For a minute, Clare stared off in the distance, her eyes not seeming to focus on anything but the thoughts churning in her mind, then asked, "What will happen to my bunk bed?"

Brad said, "Well, I guess we'll sell it or give it away."

"But I want to keep it."

"I'm not sure we have room for it," Nora said. "But we'll see."

"Jack," Brad said, "are there things you want to keep?"

Jack looked away for a minute and then said, "My desk. The one I have is too small."

"What about the puzzle table?" Clare asked.

"If it's okay, we'll set it up here," Brad said, looking to Nora.

Nora felt tears welling. She'd assumed that with Brad around as much as he'd been, his moving home wouldn't mean a big change for them. Now she realized that it would be like moving a part of their lives too. They had memories and routines she knew nothing about.

"We'll put it where it used to be," she said.

"Let's go upstairs to your bedrooms and see what'll fit," Brad said.

In Jack's room, he and Brad talked about moving furniture to accommodate the desk. It seemed so long ago—the night Brad had left when she sat on the side of Jack's bed, his pain and her pain mingling.

Then in Clare's room they decided they could move one of the twin beds to the basement, to save for Lily, making room for the bunk beds. "Then I can have two friends spend the night," she said. Nora pictured Clare the night Brad left standing at her bookcase and finding an old book, wanting the comfort of the Berenstain Bears.

She stepped out of the room and stood in the hall for a minute. As the painful memories of that night washed over her, and of the long road it took to get to tonight, Brad came out to stand next to her. "Are you okay?"

She nodded. "Let's take them into our room," she said. She would have to get used to thinking of it as "our" room. That morning, Brad had gone to his apartment and packed clothes for the week. He'd brought a small box that held his wedding ring and Nora set it next to her ring on her dresser. She wanted Jack and Clare with them when they put them on. And she wanted them to see evidence of Brad's presence in the bedroom, his books on his nightstand, his suitcase on a chair waiting to be unpacked.

Perhaps it was the solemn tone of her voice that made Jack and Clare stand quietly, as if both recognized it as an important moment when she showed them the rings that sat on her dresser.

"Dad and I are going to put them on again and we wanted you with us," she said. She handed Jack her camera. She planned to retrieve and rehang their anniversary pictures and wanted photos to mark this day.

Brad slipped her ring on her finger—it still fit perfectly—and he leaned in and kissed her. Nora put his ring on him and let her hand linger on his for a minute, then smiled up at him.

"Mommy, you're crying," Clare said. "Are you sad?"

"No, I'm happy, Clare. Sometimes I cry when I'm happy."

She and Brad put their arms around each other and smiled at the camera. Then she reached her arms out to Jack and Clare. "Group hug," she said. Jack groaned but allowed her to draw him into the circle.

CHAPTER 70

It was already getting dark that evening when they arrived at their favorite pizza restaurant. The dinner went well for a while. Lily, content and rested from her nap, sat in her highchair, chewed on a teething biscuit, and played with a set of plastic cups. Their server, who looked to be in her twenties, took their order. Her name tag read "Christie," and Clare said, "Both of our names start with C, and we both have ponytails."

"We do," Christie said with a smile. "What's your name?"

As Christie and Clare talked, Nora looked at Jack. A few years ago, before the moodiness set in, he would have smiled and joined in. Clare's bubbly antics wouldn't have bothered him; now, ready to pounce at the slightest offense, he winced as she chatted, oblivious to his annoyance and embarrassment.

Christie came back with glasses of chianti for Brad and Nora, Sprite for Jack and Clare, and milk for Lily which Nora poured into her sippy cup. At the next table, a boy who looked to be five or six laughed as he told knock-knock jokes to his parents.

The mother caught Nora's glance and smiled at her. Brad and Nora sipped their wine and listened to Clare's stories of the spiders in their tents. Jack told them about cooking over the campfire, burning the hot dogs, and the hikes they took. They laughed at the story of Ann screaming for Nick when a spider crawled on her sleeping bag. Nora glanced often at her ring; she'd always loved how it glinted in the light. While she fed Lily a jar of baby food, she half listened to Brad telling Jack and Clare about his experiences at boy scout camp. *I'm happy*, she thought. Their trial weekend had worked out and erased any of her lingering doubts. She thought about planning a party with her family and Nick and Ann. A celebration.

The trouble started when Christie, after setting the pizza on the table, asked how old Lily was. Clare said, "Nine months. She'll be a year in January."

Just then, Lily looked at Brad and said "Ba-ba." Christie smiled and said, "Oh that's so cute. Ba-ba rather than da-da."

Clare leaned over and grabbed her sleeve. She said in a faint voice, almost a whisper, as if she didn't want Lily to know, "He's not her daddy."

Jack's eyes widened. "Shut up, Clare."

Nora gave him a warning glance as tears ran down Clare's cheeks.

Christie's face reddened. "Anything else you need?"

"We're fine, thanks." Brad's face had also turned red—with hurt or embarrassment or a combination, Nora couldn't tell. He looked toward Clare, and with a pained expression put an arm around her. "It's okay, Clare."

Clare's voice had a higher pitch, the tone she used when

explaining something that should be obvious. "But I want you to be her daddy. Why can't you?"

Brad pulled her closer and said again, "It's okay, honey."

Jack, staring hard at Clare, said, "Because he's not!"

"You don't know anything," Clare said.

Nora, pulled from her happy contentment, was struck with the realization that Lily would always be a reminder of her relationship with Jim. And, as much as Jack adored Lily, he wasn't over his embarrassment, wasn't ready to forget Nora's transgression.

"Okay, guys. It's complicated," Nora said. "We'll talk about it later."

Nora looked at Brad, caught in the middle of the messy and painful reality. *I wish*, she thought, *I wish you were her father.*

Brad cut slices of pizza and passed them. "Pepperoni for Jack, plain for Clare. Nora?"

"Plain, thanks." Jack bent over his plate and ate, but Clare was staring at her plate, the tears still coming. "Clare, I think you're tired from the weekend. Try to eat your pizza," Nora said and handed her a tissue.

When Clare's tears turned to sobs, Jack muttered, "Baby."

Brad's face tightened, and he turned to Jack. "Enough," he said. "Stop it."

Nora sighed and stood. She said to Brad, "Would you give Lily a few small pieces of the plain pizza?" She led Clare to the ladies' room and held her as she sobbed. "It's okay, honey."

As she patted Clare's back, she remembered her questions in the hospital after Lily's birth and how, afterwards, she had sat down with her and tried to explain. "Children in families don't always have the same father," she had said, and it was enough to placate her then. But that was before Brad had become so involved in Lily's life, giving her a different layer of confusion.

Now, as she dampened a paper towel and patted Clare's face, she said, "He'll be like her daddy. He cares for her the way he does you and Jack."

"Then why can't she call him Daddy?"

"We'll see. Maybe she can."

Nora held Clare and rubbed her back until her breathing evened and she stopped crying, then said, "Let's go back and eat. I'm hungry."

After they sat, Brad tapped Jack on the shoulder and gave him a pointed look. Jack squirmed in his seat, then said, "Sorry, Clare."

Clare, always quick to forgive, said, "It's okay." She looked at Nora. "Can I tell Jack?"

"Tell him what?" Nora had picked up her pizza and was about to take a bite. *Please, can we let it go for now,* she thought.

She pointed at Lily. "Daddy will be like her daddy. Just like he is with us."

Jack said, "Okay, Clare," under his breath, and grabbed another slice of pizza.

To Brad, Clare said, "Mom said maybe she can call you Daddy."

Nora gave Jack a warning glance, and before Brad could say anything, she put her hand on Clare's. "We'll talk about this at home. Not another word about it."

They got through the meal. Clare quieted down, and they finished what they could of the pizza, not the amount they usually would have eaten, and got a box to take the rest home. Jack and

Clare wanted dessert but Nora, not able to bear another conversation with Christie and Clare, promised them ice cream at home. On the way home, Lily babbled, and Jack and Clare were quiet. Nora opened her window partway to let the cool air blow over her. Being caught by surprise at the restaurant was like a wake-up call and she knew what she had to do.

When they got home, after the ice cream, after she put Lily to bed, she came down to where Brad was setting out cereal and bowls for breakfast, already planning for the morning and the return to school and work. She was startled for a minute, having almost forgotten that he would be here in the morning, helping to get the kids ready for school. That it wouldn't be the frantic morning she was used to.

He turned to her. "Well, that was something. Are you okay?"

"Exhausted." She put her arms around him and leaned against him. "You really got caught in the middle."

"It had to happen sometime. Too bad it was there. We got through it." He laughed. "Poor Christie."

She stepped back and looked up at him. "Were you embarrassed? Was it awful?"

"A little. I was annoyed with Jack. And sad for Clare wanting everything to be perfect. And for you…"

"I sure made their lives difficult." She stopped herself. "We both did."

"We did." He put his arms around her and drew her close. "By the way, I'd be honored for Lily to call me Daddy."

"I love you," she said. At that moment she loved everything about him. Loved that he was so kind, loved that he didn't throw in her face judgment about her pregnancy and what it had done to Jack, loved that he admitted his part in the messy situation. She stepped back and smiled at him. "I'm glad you're here."

"Me too." He smiled at her and then his expression got serious. "I'd like to talk to them. About me and Lily and the Daddy thing. That I will be like her father even if I don't formally adopt her."

"I'll talk to Clare for a minute and tell her we'll sit down tomorrow together. Jack's the one I need to talk to tonight. Clare did me a favor bringing it out in the open." She moved to the sink to get a glass of water.

"Do you want me to come with you?"

"No. I need to do it by myself."

After Clare brushed her teeth and got under the covers, Nora sat on the side of the bed. "How are you doing, sweetie?"

"I was thinking," Clare said. "It was like a pause."

"What was like a pause?" Nora asked.

"Daddy leaving. We learned about pauses in school. A time between things, a break. But it doesn't last." She looked at Nora as if to see if she understood. "It's like an interruption…" She looked at the ceiling, her mouth partly opened as it was when she was doing her math homework and trying to solve a difficult problem.

Nora smiled and nodded. She watched Clare's face, wanting to hear more about the pause.

"Daddy didn't really leave…" Clare sat up. And like trying to explain something deep, she drew a circle with her hands. "It's like he was here," she pointed to the top of the circle, "went around and came right back to the beginning. Like a pause." She smiled at Nora proudly. "And now he's back home and can be Lily's father. Jack's wrong isn't he, Mommy?"

Nora, with tears in her eyes, gathered her into her arms. Poor Clare, trying to make sense of it all, Brad's leaving and coming back mixed in with the birth of Lily, trying to fit it all together and give it a happy ending. "We'll talk about it tomorrow."

"We all have the same last name," Clare said, sounding excited, as if she had just thought of it.

"Yes, your sister is Lily Stanton." She kissed her. "I love you, Clare. Sometimes, you are way too smart."

Before she went into Jack's room, she splashed cold water on her face and waited until her tears stopped. Jack was at his desk doing homework and didn't turn to look at her when she knocked and came in. "I need to talk to you," she said.

He didn't answer or look at her. Ignoring the clothes on the floor and the dirty dishes on his dresser, she sat on the side of his bed. She would not get into an argument with him tonight.

"Your father is living in this house. He *will* be like a father to Lily; he'll be a stepfather, like Noah has." Noah was a friend of Jack's whose parents had divorced, and the mother remarried. Jack still didn't respond. "Life gets messy, Jack. And confusing. For adults too."

Finally, he turned around. She couldn't read his expression. Not exactly angry. Curious, perhaps. With a hint of suspicion, he asked, "Will you lie to her? About her real father?"

"No, Jack. When she's old enough, we'll tell her. It won't be a secret."

He looked at her carefully, his eyes latched onto hers. "Tell her what?"

"About her biological father. His name is Jim."

He shifted his gaze to his desk and grabbed a piece of

loose-leaf paper and tore it into pieces and let them fall to the floor. "Does he know about her?"

"Yes, he knows," she said.

Eyes back on her, he asked, "Why didn't you get married?"

Nora felt an ache of sorrow that she hadn't tried harder to talk to Jack about his feelings, letting them fester, assuming when he grew to accept and love Lily, that everything was fine. She said, "He didn't want children. I still loved your father." She didn't tell him that it was a physical attraction more than anything else.

"I still don't get why Dad left," Jack said, even though they had talked about it in their sessions with Dr. Friedman.

She used Clare's description. "Think of it as a pause. A break. Something he needed to do." When he turned and stared out the window, she continued. "Twenty years is a long time to be together. I think we both learned a lot about ourselves during our time apart."

A gust of wind blew papers across his desk and he stood to close the window and then turned and said, "Noah calls his step-father Robert."

Nora nodded. "Noah has another father who he calls Dad. Lily won't have that. But we'll talk about it." He had grown tall— five-eight, as tall as she was—but his body hadn't filled out yet; he looked thin and vulnerable. She ached for him as she thought of how complicated it had been for him, and all that he had kept inside. She went over to him and put an arm around his shoulder. "What would you think of another meeting with Dr. Friedman?" she asked. "There's all this stuff still hanging there. Not only for you. It would help me too. And your father."

"I don't know. Maybe."

Maybe to her was a victory.

CHAPTER 71

By the end of October, Brad had emptied his apartment and moved Jack's desk and Clare's bunk beds into their rooms. His clothes were back in his dresser drawers. Nora had moved her things from his side of the closet and Brad returned his suits, shirts, and ties in the same order as before. After a few weeks, he inhabited the house like he'd never left. It had taken her several days to adapt to his presence in the bedroom; she remembered how long it took for her to become accustomed to the gaping hole after he left when at night in bed, she'd reach for him and find the empty space. After he returned, she would wake during the night, surprised to find him next to her.

Soon they had developed routines. Every morning Brad woke at six and went downstairs to make coffee and read the paper. If Lily stayed asleep, Nora had time for yoga before waking Jack and Clare. On weekends, Brad cooked big breakfasts for the kids, giving her time alone. At night, they worked together through the dinners and the evening rituals with the children and often collapsed into bed. Nora's day-to-day life was far easier with him back, and he seemed to thrive on their hectic schedules. They returned to Dr. Friedman and scheduled monthly meetings for Jack who slowly grew to accept Brad's role with Lily and even laughed when she called him a combination of *ba* and *da-da*.

It wasn't all tidy and serene. At first, they were careful with each other, but not for long. They worked to carve out their needs. She didn't want to fool herself—to disguise her feelings or her wishes in the dailiness of life. She caught herself when the familiar guilty feelings crept up, and mostly, was able to tamp them down. When they differed on certain things with the children, they talked about it, and they agreed sometimes and sometimes they didn't.

In fact, when they had their first disagreement, Nora welcomed it. It was a test for future hurdles and bigger quarrels. And when he questioned her logic, explaining why his way made more sense, she said things like, "No, Brad. That's not how I do it." When he made a comment about how she still mangled the tube of toothpaste, she bought him his own. That's not to say she didn't make concessions; she tried to remember to return the CDs to their cases and to load the dishwasher without stuffing it haphazardly.

Once the decision had been made for Brad to move back, Nora decided to invite her family for a visit. Brad had disappeared from their lives without a goodbye. During the summer, Nora had mentioned casually that Brad had been coming to the house for dinner, but nothing about them reuniting. Nora wanted to integrate Brad back into the family. They planned the visit for a Saturday in early November.

Brad was fine with it, but nervous about facing her family.

"It'll feel like when I first met them. Being submitted for their approval."

"We'll invite Ann and Nick," Nora said. "More people. That'll help."

He said with a forced smile, "I don't think I'll be welcomed with open arms like I was then."

Although she had her own worries, she hadn't shared them with Brad. "I talked to them," she said. "They're fine and looking forward to seeing you. My mother's thrilled." That part was true. But she didn't mention Becky's response when she had called to say Brad had moved back. Becky sounded doubtful. "Are you sure it's a good idea? Won't it be weird for him with Lily?" Thankfully, her mother's only question had been, "Are you happy?" When Nora told her she was, she said, "Then I'm happy too."

Nora hoped it wouldn't be too cold so Brad could cook on the grill. It turned out that the sky that day was cloudless with the temperature close to seventy with a light breeze. They would even be able to eat outside.

Her family planned to arrive about two o'clock. They had decided on an afternoon party, so her family could drive the two hours from Pennsylvania and return home in the evening. In the morning she and Brad kept busy. While he set out card tables in the yard and went to the store to refill the propane tank for the grill, Nora marinated the chicken and cut up vegetables for the dip and the salad. Her mother was bringing her potato salad, and Ann, her baked beans that everyone loved. Nora helped Clare put the chocolate frosting and sprinkles on the cupcakes they'd made. During the morning, she stole glances at Brad, at his pale face. At one point, she stopped and asked, "Are you okay?"

"I'll be glad when it's over."

"It'll be fine. I promise," she said, though she wasn't that sure. Not wanting to increase his nervousness, she tried to mask hers. "And it's only for a few hours. They're coming at two, I figure we'll eat by four. They'll be gone by six."

"That's four hours," Brad said with an amused smile. "Not a few."

When she saw the van pull into the driveway, Nora carried Lily out to meet them. Brad stood on the porch and waited. After greetings and hugs with Nora and Lily, they walked to the porch where Brad stood. *Like a receiving line,* she thought as she followed them. Rebecca and Will, in a hurry to find Jack and Clare, were first. Nora smiled as they did a high-five with Brad, and said, "Hi, Uncle Brad," as if he had never left. Her mother was next. Nora watched her face, her eyes, her smile. She had always thought her mother beautiful, and even as she aged and lines covered her face and her hair turned to silver, her warm brown eyes remained luminous and radiated kindness. She smiled at Brad. "I'm so glad to see you, Brad. I've missed you."

Brad smiled. "I've missed you too," he said and bent down and hugged her.

Becky gave him a half hug and Bill smiled and patted him on the shoulder. "Good to see you, Brad."

In the house, they all clustered around Lily in the family room. She had learned to pull herself up, and she held on to the coffee table and took hesitant steps around it. Soon Ann and Nick arrived with Eddie and Maddie and everyone went to the back-yard. Her mother carried Lily outside while Nora and Brad brought out pitchers of iced tea and lemonade and bowls of pretzels and popcorn. The children played badminton on one side of the yard and the adults clustered on the deck. When Brad joined them, she headed back into the house and listened to snippets of conversation: Jobs, how the kids had grown, mundane catching up of lives.

In the kitchen, Nora stood at the window and gazed at the scene in the yard, struck by how vivid the colors were. The sun slanted across the orange pumpkins and yellow mums lining the steps from the deck to the yard and mimicking the leaves in their autumn colors. For a few minutes, Nora studied expressions and interactions. Becky watched Brad as he set up folding chairs next to the tables. Nora figured Becky was checking to see what his role was, how connected he was; she wondered if he knew he was being scrutinized. When Brad finished, he pulled a chair over to her mother who was holding Lily. When Lily held her arms out to him, he lifted her, and she put her head on his shoulder. Becky stared at him with a curious expression.

Nora went outside to take Lily from Brad so he could grill the chicken and she carried her to where her mother sat. Her mother waved her arms to encompass the scene—Clare, Maddie, and Rebecca in a huddle, whispering about something, and Jack, Eddie, and Will at the basketball net—and she smiled at Nora. "It doesn't get any better than this."

"No, Mom, it doesn't." Nora hugged her. "I'm so happy you're here."

"I'm glad Brad's back." Her mother looked at Nora. "You look happy and so does he."

They turned and watched Brad as he placed the chicken on the grill. Ann and Nick and Becky and Bill gathered around him, all of them talking and laughing. "He was nervous," Nora said.

"We both were. I think he's relaxing now." He looked toward her and smiled with a pleased expression.

She sat Lily on her mother's lap, so she could finish getting the dinner ready. As she headed to the kitchen, Becky walked toward her. "I'll help you," she said. "It'll give us time to catch up."

Once Becky had gotten over the shock of her pregnancy, the tension between them had eased, but Nora still kept the familiar feeling of being on guard with her sister. She remembered her mother telling her when she was a teenager that she was too sensitive when Becky made barbed comments, that she needed a thicker skin. Over the years—especially the past three—Nora had developed the self-confidence she lacked as a teenager, but still was never sure if there was a hidden agenda lurking below the surface.

For a few minutes, they talked about inconsequential things, until Becky said, "I've been watching Brad."

Nora nodded. *I was watching you too*, she wanted to say. As she put cucumbers, tomatoes, and romaine lettuce into a salad bowl she waited for what would come next.

"And you. The two of you. He acts like a teenager around you. He keeps looking at you."

Not sure if she meant it as a compliment, Nora said, "It's working out. I'm happy." She arranged carrots and celery on a platter around a spinach and artichoke dip and didn't look at Becky who was quiet for a minute as she spooned their mother's potato salad into a serving bowl.

Then she looked at Nora. "How did he get over it?"

"Get over what?" Nora stopped and looked at Becky.

"Lily. Doesn't he resent her?"

"Resent her?" Pretending not to know what Becky referred to, she asked, "Why should he?"

"Well, you know..."

Nora felt a flush of irritation rise. "No, I don't. He's been great with her. They adore each other." She turned to see Ann standing at the edge of the kitchen.

"Can I help?"

Becky smiled at Ann. "What do you think about Nora and Brad? The in-love teenagers?"

"I think it's neat." Ann put an arm around Nora. "I'm thrilled Nora's happy."

"I don't mean I'm not happy about it," Becky said. "I'm just surprised."

Ann said, "I'm a little jealous. It's like the two of them are reignited, and we're just the same old, boring married couples."

They all laughed, and the tension ebbed.

Nora smiled gratefully at Ann just as Brad stuck his head in. "Do you need help?"

Becky said, "We were just talking about you." She looked at him with an amused grin. "It was all good."

Later that night Nora lay in bed in the dark after Brad had fallen asleep, too keyed up to sleep, thinking how pleased she was with the day. Yet it still seemed surreal, like they had arrived at a destination they'd nearly missed.

If Brad hadn't had his crisis, if he'd learned to live with his angst, she imagined a continuation of their marriage with them living on the surface and her going on as she had—drawing her identity from the illusion of her happy marriage—not voicing or even being fully aware of her wants and needs in the day-to-day containment of their marriage. Nora thought of Clare's words of the *pause,* the interruption, which, as grueling as it was, she had come to think of as a gift. Not just the gift of Lily, but the gift of herself that arose from the weight of the struggle.

Two weeks earlier Nora had turned forty-four. Brad and the children brought her breakfast in bed just as he used to. She came downstairs to find the house decorated with balloons and crepe paper. Yellow roses filled the pottery vase Brad had given her on their first anniversary. That evening, Brad gave her a framed calligraphy print with words from Robert Browning. *Grow old with me. The best is yet to come.* It made Nora think of their marriage vows: *For better or for worse. In good times and bad.* They'd been through the worst and emerged, a bit damaged, but sturdier and more resilient, readier for what would come. Reignited, as Ann had said, not with the intensity of when they first fell in love at age twenty, but with a freshness and a more attentive quality than what their marriage had faded to. Comfort mingling with desire and love.

As she listened to Brad's slow and even breathing, she inched herself next to him and the warmth of his body. With him back, the house was full and lively with his presence. She was filled with a sense that it had returned to its original function. Everything that mattered most was restored. The anniversary pictures of her and Brad—all twenty of them were back in their original place next to new pictures of their family, five of them now with Lily. The puzzle table, back where it belonged, held a new puzzle waiting to be assembled.

ACKNOWLEDGMENTS

I am indebted to Maribeth Fischer, Executive Director of the Rehoboth Beach Writers' Guild, for her insightful critiques as she supported and mentored me through countless revisions of *Becoming Nora*.

I am grateful to the following people who were with me along the way:

My children and grandchildren for cheering me on and to my husband Michael for his patience, encouragement, and inspiration.

My daughter Katy Friedman who read the novel and its revisions and offered critical suggestions and support throughout.

Jen Epler who was there from the beginning as a cheerleader of the novel.

Ceci Wraase who took the time to read the novel and offer comments.

Mary Ann Sack, an early reader, for her ongoing support.

The women in my novel classes who offered friendship and insightful critiques.

Emily Hitchcock, Doug Davis, and Shannon Page from Columbus Publishing Lab for their support and expertise.

Thanks also to Nancy Sakaduski. *Becoming Nora* grew out of a short story that appeared as "Untethered" in *The Boardwalk*, an anthology of short stories published by Cat and Mouse Press in 2014.

ABOUT THE AUTHOR

Margaret Kirby retired in 2012 after a career working with homeless individuals in Washington, DC. Following her retirement, she enrolled in writing classes and invested time in pursuing creative writing.

She is a member of the Rehoboth Beach Writers' Guild, the Eastern Shore Writers Association, and the Writer's Center in Bethesda, MD.

Margaret has stories, poems, and memoir pieces published in the following anthologies:

"Rehoboth Beach Reads": *The Beach House* (2013); *The Boardwalk* (2014); *Beach Days* (2015)

The Divine Feminine: An Anthology of Seaside Scribes (2017)

Visions and Voices of Seaside Scribes (2018)

Eastern Shore Writer's Anthology (2018)

Margaret is currently working on a novel entitled *The Music Room*.

She divides her time between Silver Spring, Maryland, and Rehoboth Beach, Delaware.